Extraordinary Praise for

CLINTON McKINZIE's
novels

TRIAL BY ICE AND FIRE

"*Trial by Ice and Fire* sizzles...suspenseful."
—*The Herald-Sun* (Durham, N.C.)

"McKinzie's forte: action, adventure, and a multilay-
ered chase and rescue...fires on all cylinders...."
—*Publishers Weekly*

"The rock-climbing scenes...are gripping and
suspenseful....But the real strength of this book is the
complexity of the characters, starting with Antonio....
This book is a worthwhile addition to a series that is
deservedly becoming more popular."
—*The Daily Camera* (Boulder, Colo.)

"McKinzie writes with verve and pizzazz."
—*Rocky Mountain News*

"Would make a great movie...With heart-stopping
suspense, breathtaking climbing scenes, vulnerable yet
untamed characters, and just a tad of romance, this one
has it all... captivating...highly recommended."
—*NewMysteryReader.com*

"Enticing...the writing whips along...Within two
weeks of reading one book [*Trial by Ice and Fire*], I'd
finished the other two [in the series]." —*Rock & Ice*

"McKinzie is carving out a nice little niche for himself: the rock-climbing suspense genre...the action is heightened—literally—by the tremendous descriptions of climbing the spectacular peaks of the Wyoming mountains, and the climactic rescue...is chilling and expertly drawn out for maximum suspense." —*Pages*

POINT OF LAW

"Its fast-paced plot is rife with legal references, law-enforcement lingo, smart dialogue, and vivid characters....This highly readable thriller is guaranteed to set readers' hearts racing and establish McKinzie as a rising voice in the genre." —*Publishers Weekly*

"Plenty of page-turning excitement."
—*Winnipeg Free Press*

THE EDGE OF JUSTICE

"One of the strongest debuts of the year."
—*Chicago Tribune*

"This book signals the start of a great new career. Clinton McKinzie delivers a story pulsing with intrigue and character that is as poetic as it is harrowing. This one's a true winner." —Michael Connelly

"A fast-paced and promising debut."
—*The Washington Post*

"Action-packed...[a] page-turner."
—*USA Today*

TRIAL BY ICE AND FIRE

Clinton McKinzie

A DELL BOOK

TRIAL BY ICE AND FIRE
A Dell Book

PUBLISHING HISTORY
Delacorte hardcover edition published July 2003
Dell mass market edition / March 2004

Published by
Bantam Dell
A Division of Random House, Inc.
New York, New York

Library of Congress Catalog Card Number: 2002041285

ISBN 0-440-23727-0

Manufactured in the United States of America
Published simultaneously in Canada

OPM 10 9 8 7 6 5 4 3 2 1

For Justine and Colin

ACKNOWLEDGMENTS

Danielle Perez, Nita Taublib, and Irwyn Applebaum at Bantam Dell continue to expertly guide me ever higher in this new career. One couldn't hope for a stronger team when it comes to undertaking this kind of expedition. Deborah Dwyer and Robin Foster painstakingly correct and tame my unschooled form. John Talbot, my agent, is always there for me, keeping me firmly on route with sound advice. Dempsey, my canine companion on many adventures over the last twelve years, gives me inspiration when it comes to the subjects of loyalty, friendship, and courage. Kara Kaufman, my sister-in-law, makes me look good in cyberspace. Mom and Dad and my brother Wayne catch my many falls, dust me off, and send me clawing for greater heights. And my brother Morgan is always around somewhere, just out of sight, brimming with enthusiasm and laughter.

SATURDAY

ONE

FROM THE TRAILHEAD parking lot the couloir had looked like a narrow, radiant column rising out of a snowfield near the center of the dark mountain. Now that I'm on it, attached by the spike of my ax and the sharp points of my crampons, it appears more like a wide strip of caulking in a deep cut running down the mountain's face. Gray-black walls—invisible from the trailhead—line the nearly vertical wound. They're broken and serrated, as if the long gash had been made by a God-sized shank instead of a scalpel.

The snow in the couloir is wind blasted and sun baked, but so far this morning there is no wind and there is no sun. At this hour the night sky is just starting its fade into indigo. Soon pink and orange rays will spill down from Teewinot's summit spire and the wind will begin to moan through toothy gaps in the ridge above us.

I had almost forgotten how much I love these early-morning ascents. How much I *need* this sense of exhilaration that comes enhanced by an inherent dread of heights and the dark.

Over the last six months I've allowed my passion for climbing mountains to be smothered by my work and an infatuation of a totally different, totally unexpected sort: for a pretty Denver newspaper reporter named Rebecca Hersh. As I plant my ax and kick my boots into the steep snow, I concentrate on the night's stillness and the dawn's coming colors. I ignore all thoughts of the recent trial, the failing romance, the weight of the pack on my back, and the burn of lactic acid in my butt and thighs.

The snow crunches with each high step, creating a syncopated rhythm that regulates my breathing. Over two steps I exhale, then I pause for a moment to suck in the cold, thin air.

As I inhale, I glance down at the young woman following me. She is cautiously placing her boots in the holds I've made. A purple fleece headband warms the tops of her ears and keeps the sweaty tendrils of blonde hair from her face. Above her head the pointed shapes of ski tips wave like antennae from where they're strapped to her pack. Although I'm a little wary of her, I'm also impressed that she hasn't once called for a rest. Not bad for a lawyer.

"How's it going, Cali?" I ask, trying not to pant too loud. The last six months have taken more than just a psychological toll.

"Fine." Her breath is as labored as mine but her teeth flash a smile in the darkness. "How much farther?"

Above me the couloir stretches upward for another two hundred yards before it fades into the vanishing stars. "Not much. Twenty minutes, I guess."

I kick another step into the snow with a plastic boot and think about where my wariness toward her comes from.

There is a slight twinge of guilt, as if I'm somehow betraying Rebecca by being alone with another woman in a place like this. A place where I feel so pumped up and alive. But this is, after all, just another job. Nothing to feel guilty about. I've baby-sat for lots of victims and witnesses before. Of course, none of them had asked me to take them into the mountains. But then I'd spent my college and grad-school summers dragging plenty of doctors and lawyers up Alaskan peaks.

This woman is different in other ways, too. It isn't just that she's good-looking or that she's semifamous. My wariness comes from the simple fact that she's strange. I can't figure her out. How many children of movie stars run from big-city glamour and move to a place like Wyoming? How many of them attend law school and then become small-town prosecutors when they're only twenty-six years old? How many of them like to spend their weekends jumping down dangerously steep snow with skinny boards locked to their feet?

The wariness, I decide, also comes from the way my boss at Wyoming's Division of Criminal Investigation told me to be careful with this one.

"For God's sake, don't screw it up!" Ross McGee had growled at me over the phone yesterday. "You're on thin ice as it is."

I could picture him hunched at his desk in Cheyenne, looking like some demented Santa Claus in a pin-striped suit, and issuing a stern warning to his most troublesome elf.

"You know that's not my fault, boss."

He responded with one of his signature phrases: "If you're looking for sympathy, QuickDraw, look it up in the dictionary. It's between *shit* and *syphilis*."

I smile to myself as I stomp a boot through the snow's crust, thinking of the obscenities he'd bellow if he could see us right now.

The snow above has slid away in a few places and exposed sheets of iron-hard ice. When I'm unable to stab my ax's spike in at least a few inches, I traverse to the north side of the chute, hoping to find deeper stuff and safer footing. I don't want to waste time tying into a rope. Before long the sun will start heating the dark granite walls that flank the snow. Frozen water shoaling narrow cracks will melt and send rocks whistling down toward us. I unconsciously touch the scar on my left cheek with a gloved fingertip. I hate rock-fall. It had branded me nearly a decade ago with a wound I took as a stern warning. My luck was used up a long time ago. I guess we have about an hour before the couloir becomes a shooting gallery.

Turning again to study the way she is steadily clumping up beneath me, I decide she's stable enough not to need a belay. But it would be more than embarrassing if she were to slip. Killing my ward would be a very bad way to mark my return to active duty.

"Watch out for the ice, Cali."

She responds with a feminine grunt: "Yeah."

The snow-filled chute extends down more than a thousand feet before it opens up into wider, more moderately angled slopes that continue another thousand feet to treeline. Below me it glows in the half-light like a long, gray ribbon. The steep ribs of rock confine it on both sides. The angle averages a little more than fifty degrees, although looking down it appears nearly vertical. This optical illusion is accentuated by the fact that if you fall, you're going all the way. Well over a mile below us I can see the lights of the small marina on Jenny Lake.

I kick two more steps and pause again to breathe.

Yesterday, after Ross McGee had told me the nature of the new assignment and warned me in his polite way not to screw it up, I entered Cali's name on Westlaw's news archive. Cali Morrow was the only child of Alana Reese, who was often still referred to as the Reigning Queen of Hollywood and also the owner of an enormous ranch in Jackson Hole. Her birth was celebrated in the numerous articles I found not just because of her mother's fame but also because of the oddity and tragedy of her paternity.

Her father had been a Forest Service smoke jumper who

died in a fire two months before Cali's birth. He'd been sort of famous himself at the time, having been pictured on a *Life* magazine cover with a burning forest behind him. Apparently Alana had met him while vacationing at her ranch—he was a bit of local color for the actress. He soon became even more famous when an award-winning book called *Smoke Jump* was written about the fire that had taken his life.

Cali's childhood was detailed in numerous tabloid-type articles. Reading them, I'd been appalled that her youth was so invaded by the public's obsession with celebrity. Even her pre-teen birthday parties made the news. And her mother didn't help things by making the occasions lavish, star-studded affairs.

I'd skimmed the articles, gleaning the essential facts.

Cali Morrow grew up in Santa Monica, California, attended a private school in Bel Air, spent her summers on her mom's ranch in Jackson Hole, and was the occasional child star of several TV movies. The critics called her teenage performances wooden and hoped she would improve with the years. But it seemed that upon her eighteenth birthday she made a determined effort to leave the spotlight her mother kept focused on her. Cali attended college at Brown University, where she was the captain of the women's ski team. She continued to return to Wyoming each summer, following in her father's footsteps by fighting fires on an elite Hot Shot ground crew, which was second in prestige and danger only to the parachuting smoke jumpers. Upon graduation she enrolled in law school at Michigan. Following that, just one year ago, she tried again to jump from the face of the earth by permanently moving to Wyoming and taking a job as a prosecutor with the Teton County Attorney's Office.

"Some deranged piece of shit . . . has been sending her letters . . . then he tried to crawl through her window last night," McGee had told me over the phone, pausing in his peculiar manner to suck air into his emphysemic lungs. "A family friend walking by scared him off . . . but he left behind a stun gun and some duct tape. . . . You get the idea, lad? This asshole's serious."

"Any suspects?"

"No, not a sure thing, not yet . . . all I've heard about so far is a local cop . . . some guy she was dating but dumped recently. . . . That's the reason why . . . the County Attorney up there laid it at our feet . . . that and the fact that she's a prosecutor."

Although my office, Wyoming's Division of Criminal Investigation, is a statewide law-enforcement agency primarily concerned with stopping the distribution of illegal drugs, we are often brought in when a case is particularly important or complex or when there is a conflict of interest within a local police department. A conflict usually means you've got a cop or a prosecutor for a victim or a suspect. Here there's both. You don't want a department investigating one of their own in a case like this. Especially if the victim is a celebrity's daughter.

"The ex's name is Charles Wokowski . . . and the County Attorney admits it's unlikely he's our boy," McGee continued. "But so far he's all we've got. . . . They call him Wook or Wookie, after some beast in a movie. . . . Not quite as flattering a nickname as yours, eh, QuickDraw?"

"Don't call me that, fat man," I told him for the thousandth time. He responded only with a chuckle—half cough and half choke—before hanging up the phone.

After talking with McGee and conducting my quick Internet search, I'd looked up Cali's number at the Teton County Attorney's Office. When I told the spirited and unlawyerlike voice on the other end of the line my name, she said, "Wow! Antonio Burns, huh? I can't believe they assigned *you* to watch my butt! Everybody's been talking about you, you know. You go by Anton, right? Or do you like—"

"Anton's fine," I'd interrupted.

I'm not famous. Not like her or her parents, anyway. For an uncomfortable amount of time, though, I've been notorious. And it has grown worse over the last six months, culminating in the media frenzy a few weeks ago when I was cross-examined for five of the longest days of my life. Any dirty laundry the defense attorneys could find or make up about me was fully aired after being carefully spun to put me in the worst possible light. And the jackals in the press (my Rebecca abstaining) ate up every scrap of it. *Three Cheyenne gang members shot in suspicious circumstances. Another man dead on a mountain. An Air Force colonel for a father who'd been court-martialed and was now living in South American exile. A drug-addicted brother, a killer, too, recently escaped from prison.* I must have earned some truly shitty karma in a previous life.

When I didn't say anything else, Cali asked, "So when do you start looking for this creep?"

"Tomorrow. My boss is coming up, too. With the help of another guy from DCI, I'm supposed to keep an eye on you when you're not in your office or in court."

"Great! You used to be a big mountain guide before you became a cop, right? How about skiing the East Face of Teewinot in the morning? I've been trying to get someone to go with me all spring. Pick me up at three? Okay? In the morning?"

Maybe baby-sitting her wouldn't be so bad, I thought as I hung up the phone. God knows I've needed this kind of release for a while. It was high time I fed the creature my brother calls the Rat. He'd been gnawing away in my chest for far too long, begging for the adrenaline rush that nourishes his furry little body.

I reach the top of the couloir with Cali panting hard at my heels and leaning heavily on her ax. Once again, I'm impressed that she's made it without a single complaint. Whining had been one of the things that had ended my guiding career. The "office" in Alaska was unbelievably gorgeous, but the beauty of the place couldn't make up for the clients.

Carrying their gear. Cooking their meals. Short-roping them up to grand summits that were defiled by their moans. Chasing after drug dealers with a badge in my wallet and a gun in my hand was a lot more fun, at least when it didn't involve lawsuits, cross-examination, and my picture in the paper.

The chute tops out at a break in the peak's southeastern ridge a few hundred feet short of the summit. A cornice has formed here, a twenty-foot cresting wave of snow. I move onto the broken field of talus to the left and pick my way above it, stepping carefully so as not to send rocks rolling down on Cali's head.

I dump my pack on a flat, rocky shelf that the previous afternoon's wind has swept free of snow. I turn and stare out at the brightening pastel sky to the east. In another few minutes the yellow orb of the sun will emerge over the low mountains on the other side of the valley. The daylight is already beginning to reveal the forests, meadows, and lakes in between. Although it's only late May, the land below us is already dry and brown—an omen of what everyone says will be another hot, fire-swept summer.

"It's all going to burn," Cali confirms as she comes up out of the chute and drops her own pack onto the rocks. The skis clatter against the aluminum avalanche shovel also strapped to the pack. With her hands resting on her knees and her breath coming fast, she adds, "This is wild. I can't believe you used to do this for a living."

"I can't believe you used to fight forest fires."

She grins. "You've been checking up on me, huh? I guess it's mutual, then."

Despite the early-morning cold, she's wearing only a pair of black polypropylene leggings and a gray zip-neck shirt. Both are skintight and dark with sweat. Straightening up, she pulls a Gore-Tex shell from her pack and puts it on.

Her face is almost a perfect oval, rising from a pointed chin, and curving around prominent cheekbones. Her eyes are emerald green. Short blonde hair lifts from beneath the headband in a single curl.

On flat earth she might be considered a little plain because of a broad nose and too pointy a chin. But up on a mountain like this, with her eyes bright in the dawn and the smile on her lips, she could be modeling for a brand of expensive vodka. She'd sell a lot of it. I have to admit that my wariness toward her is thawing.

"Do you want to go all the way?" I point at the granite spire above us and to the right. It makes me feel a little strange, stopping short of the actual summit. My brother likes to say that the best place to be is *where the only way to get higher is to fall.*

"Hell no, Anton. Not unless we can ski down it. I'm a skier, remember, not a rock jock like you."

To follow the spiny ridge up to the apex would take a lot more time and the use of the rope and other gear. I have all that in my pack but I'm relieved she doesn't want to continue. The rising sun is already starting to heat the couloir. Soon rocks will start screaming down and ripping through the snow.

I take out a bottle of sugary tea, drink some, then offer it to her.

"How are we going to do this?" she asks. At first I think she means the descent, but she continues, "How are you going to look after me and find this guy at the same time?"

"My partner and I will work the case when you're in your office or in court. You should be safe enough in both places. After work, I'll follow you around. Basically, I'll stalk you myself."

She makes a wry face. "Great."

"Don't worry about your privacy. I'll keep my distance as best I can."

She drinks half my tea. "No, that's all right. I don't have much to keep private these days. No boyfriend or anything.

Not anymore. Besides, I want to hear firsthand about that wild shoot-out in Cheyenne."

I smile back but without any pleasure and don't respond.

After a minute she asks, "Do you have any idea who's doing this?"

"I heard there's a possible suspect. Your ex-boyfriend. Wokowski or Wookie or something like that."

She shrugs. "Wook. Sergeant Charles Wokowski. I don't know if it's him or not. I probably shouldn't have mentioned his name to my boss—I only did because everyone knows we haven't been getting along. A month ago, before we broke up, I would have said there's no way it could be him. Now, I don't know . . . Wook's been acting pretty weird around me lately. And the County Attorney's pissed off at him because of an excessive-force case."

Most stalkers I've dealt with were ex-boyfriends or exhusbands, so it makes sense to give him a very hard look. Although with her being a celebrity, some random freak who would be tougher to find could have easily fixated on her. I hope that isn't the case because it will require a lot more work. But I don't want it to be a cop either. Arresting fellow officers is dangerous—I should know. At DCI we frequently have to investigate cops for a variety of allegations. They are always armed and know the rules of the game too well. And arresting a cop never fails to stir up a political maelstrom. But I also know that cops all too often become infatuated with their former lovers. Cops are so accustomed to being dominant and in control that sometimes they can't take it when they're rejected.

I push away a thought about Rebecca and ask, "Tell me a little more about him."

She shrugs again. "He's with the Teton County Sheriff's Office. He's a big deal in the department. A leader, kind of. Maybe the next sheriff. Everybody looks up to him. They would protect him. But I just can't believe it's him. It's not his style. He's an in-your-face guy, not some sicko who'd write sick letters or try to crawl in my window with a stun gun." As she says this she shivers.

Then she drinks some more from my bottle, fixing me with those green eyes. "He can be a mean bastard, though. He never touched me in anger or anything, but he looked like he wanted to a couple of times. When we broke up last month he said he wished we were both dead. Is that a threat or what? A guy I dated in law school said the same thing once. What do you think?"

I hesitate for a moment. Despite her saying it isn't his style, this Wokowski is already looking pretty good for it. "It sounds like you have lousy taste in men."

She hands me back the now-empty bottle and laughs. "I'm sorry to hear you say that, Anton. I was beginning to like you."

I smile, too. "I guess that proves it."

I'm not sure if she's flirting or just screwing around. Either way, it makes me think of Rebecca again. We've been living together in Denver for the last six months, the first three of which I was on mandatory leave and the second three when I was the primary witness in the high-profile trial of the state's governor-elect.

Like the trial, our time in her downtown loft started out great. We visited my parents in Argentina for Christmas. Back in Denver I climbed and skied the Front Range while she worked at the paper. Every night we slept naked, limbs entangled, beneath her down comforter. Then, just a few weeks ago, everything began to come apart. The manslaughter charge against the governor-elect was summarily dismissed for lack of evidence, leaving only an accusation of obstruction of justice to go to the jury, and thereby causing me to doubt the last flimsy strands of faith I had in the law as an instrument of justice. Day after day I came home—angry and getting angrier—to find Rebecca growing more distant. She no longer slept with her head on my chest and with one hand cupping the back of my neck. She began turning away from me, curling into a tight ball, not touching me at all. There were sudden and uncharacteristic crying jags as well as questions of my long-term intentions, asked with searching eyes. And I was too mad and too preoccupied to launch an investigation into the cause of the change.

I feel like I don't know her anymore. She'd once been the most stable woman I'd ever known. So poised and confident. She'd been my life preserver when I was tumbling down rapids. Now we've become cautiously formal with each other, where a few months earlier we were as happy and exuberant together as a couple of puppies.

I tried to call her late last night only to discover that she wasn't answering the phone. And reporters always answer the phone, no matter what the hour. It wasn't until after I'd left a message—probably not concealing my irritation very well—that I realized my name had been taken off her answering machine.

Screw it. Focus on where you are now, Ant. Look around. There's no better place than this.

"Are you going to confront Wook?" Cali asks, bringing me back.

"Maybe. First I want to talk to some people, see the report on the attempted break-in, and find out more about what's going on. Then I'll see about talking to him."

She puts on a pair of amber-tinted glasses that only half hide her eyes. "I know everyone says you're a badass, Anton. But take my word for it—you'll want some backup around if you get in his face."

I don't bother trying to refute the undeserved reputation. I'd done enough of that on the witness stand. Instead I just nod and say, "Okay."

After a few minutes' rest we unstrap the skis from our

packs. I walk out onto the rocks to one side of the cornice and study the chute below, trying to fix the dangerous gray patches of ice in my mind. I don't want to make a mistake today. It isn't just because of McGee's warning about not screwing it up, but also because it's been a long time since I've skied anything this steep. The first few hundred feet of the couloir are about ten degrees steeper than anything I've done in years. A fall here could easily be fatal. I would slide faster and faster, bouncing off the couloir's stony walls that stand like the brown-stained teeth lining some great beast's mouth. There would be no way to self-arrest on something this steep. The rock and ice and snow would chew me up until it vomited out what was left in the forest twenty-five hundred feet below.

Fear wraps its arms around me, embracing me with a cold but familiar hug.

As I stare down I hear a faint whispering. It doesn't come from the rising wind beginning to rush over this high notch in the ridge but from somewhere deep inside my chest. The Rat is calling. He's hungry for a meal, that surge of adrenaline required to calm and sate him. He's starting to feed.

"How are we going to do this?" This time Cali means the descent. Her voice is sharper, her face a little paler with excitement. "I haven't done much off-piste, you know. Nothing like *this*."

"Jump turns. Don't even think about pointing your skis downhill." I say this more to myself than to her. She'd been the captain of her college ski team so she's probably a far better skier than I. But because I'm supposed to be the former big mountain guide as well as the state cop who's protecting her, I add, "I'll go first." It seems like the gentlemanly thing to do. Maybe I'll somehow be able to stop her if she falls.

My heart rate is starting to accelerate. The thought of flying from the cornice's lip, of my stomach floating up into my throat, of the thirty-foot free fall through space and then leaping down the steep chute below, makes the Rat begin to sing with something approaching delirium.

"I hope your edges are sharp," I tell her as I finger my own.

Looking me in the eye, she picks up one of her skis and holds it before her face. She grins then sticks out her tongue.

"Don't—" I start to say, realizing what she's about to do.

But she ignores me. Her pink tongue touches the ski's metal edge and she licks a short distance along it. Then she spits in the snow at her feet. A red stain appears. "Okay?" she says. "They're sharp."

I shake my head. This girl is full of surprises. She's going to be a lot of trouble. But she's not at all reserved, not at all like Rebecca in recent weeks. The Rat is delighted—he thinks he's found a new friend.

I check my bindings to be sure the pressure indicators are maxed out. A prerelease here would be fatal. Then we both click in and slide out, snowplowing, onto the wave of wind-packed snow. Leaning over our quivering poles, we try one more time to examine the couloir below. But it's hard to see from this angle on top of the cornice. There's just the sloping forest far below. And beyond that, more than a vertical mile down, is the blue water of Jenny Lake. It feels like with a powerful enough leap I might be able to splash into it. Cannonball among the white shapes of the small fishing boats that are already starting to dot the lake.

I look over at Cali and she's staring back at me. Still grinning with a bit of blood rouging her lower lip. Despite her sunglasses, I see white all the way around the jade irises. I can almost hear her heart beating over the pounding bass drum of my own. The adrenal glands are squeezing out their sweet juice. The sky has turned Wyoming blue—the kind of blue that's neon through my own colored lenses.

"Still want to do this?" I ask, smiling back now.

"Hell yes!" she shouts.

The Rat is howling some frantic, mad chant. Enticing me to *Jump! Jump! Jump!* And I do it, too scared to scream, too ecstatic to whoop, trying to just focus on leaning forward and fighting the instinctive reaction to slump back. If I hit the snow with anything but my skis springing beneath my hips, I will bounce out into space. Into the forest. Into the lake. I stretch out my arms and the poles that are clenched in my fists like frail wings.

Suddenly, in midflight and with the wind tearing at my clothes, the fear blows away. It's replaced by absolute rapture. The adrenaline shoots through my veins as if it's being plunged there by an enormous syringe. I'm truly flying, like an eagle in the heavens, soaring far out above the dry earth.

But somewhere buried deep beneath the thrill and the rush is a sense of foreboding. If I could see just a week into the future, I might imagine my wings being plucked clean off. I might imagine falling hard and fast then crashing— breaking right through the planet's crust. Right into the fire that some people say burns below.

TWO

SEVERAL HUNDRED FEET down, the angle eases off and makes it safe to finally stop. I wait for Cali in a dripping, icicle-fanged alcove alongside one bronze wall. God, she's good. She skis with the sort of grace I wish I had. My twisting leaps felt jerky and panicked but hers are smooth, polished, and graceful. She's having way too much fun to stop beside me. I hear her scream something before she pelts me with a shower of hard crystals and then she's past. I watch her all the way down.

The angle continues to relax as the slope broadens and she soon changes her jump turns into quick, carving arcs. Her skis remain perfectly parallel as she shifts her weight from one foot to the other without apparent effort, picking up speed, until it appears she will shoot over the bare talus below and crash into the trees. I take a short breath, readying to shout some useless warning.

But before I can she arcs a final time and a great wave of spray rises up from her skis. Even though I'm almost a thousand feet above her, a wide grin is plainly visible when she looks up at me and waves a pole.

"You're insane," I say when I catch up.

"You aren't so normal yourself," she laughs. "I've heard about some of the crazy climbs you used to do."

With her cheeks still flushed from the rush of adrenaline, Cali chatters at me all the way down the trail. "That was unbelievable, Anton! It reminds me of—" She talks about other steep runs she'd skied on holidays in Austria, France, and Switzerland. It sounds like she has done just about everything there is to do on skis. All that's left are the big mountain chutes like this one. She talks about some others here in the Tetons she has her eye on. The Skillet Glacier on Moran. The Middle Teton Glacier. Even, more ambitiously, the Ford Couloir on the Grand.

"I've got plans for you, my friend," she says, whacking my stomach with the side of her pole.

I'm too amped myself to really listen. The thrill of making those flying turns on the steep snow lingers like helium in my heart and brain. It has lifted me above the fatigue of an almost sleepless night and the general weariness with which I've lately been regarding my life. I feel truly alive for the first time in a long while.

With nylon skins stuck to the bottom of our skis and the heels of our bindings released, Cali and I pole over shaded white drifts in the dense forest until the trees begin to widen and the snow becomes patchy. The sun beats down through the spruce branches with an intense heat. It's far warmer than it should be at this time of the year. Ahead are some brown meadows where weeks ago the bright spring sunlight already has melted off the winter's accumulation. Although the leaves on the cottonwoods near the road are new and green, the young grass beneath them is dry in the morning heat. We pause where the snow turns to dirt and unclip from our skis.

I'm peeling off the skins and slotting the skis through the

straps on my pack when I realize she's asked me a question. She's watching me, her eyes still lit with a little fever, but there's something else in them, too. Maybe a bit of fear.

"Sorry. What were you saying?"

"You aren't even listening to me, are you? Kind of spacey for a bodyguard, Anton. I was just asking if you think the creep will try again."

"There's no way to know. Not for sure." I don't want her overly scared, but remembering what McGee had said about the duct tape and the stun gun, maybe she should be scared. "But yeah, we need to be watching our backs."

She looks at the trees around us then, catching herself, lets out a nervous laugh.

"Who's with me tonight? You or your partner?"

"Tonight I'm on."

"Good. My mother's coming into town today and there's a party at Molly's Steakhouse. She's rented out the whole place for her *entourage*." She says the last word with an exaggerated French accent.

I feel my mouth drop into an involuntary grimace. I'd been expecting that watching out for her in the evenings would be easy, like sitting in front of her house in my truck and listening to a book on tape, while during the day I could work on finding her stalker as well as my original assignment—the reason I'd been sent up here in the first place—of hunting meth labs in the woods for the local SWAT team to dismantle. I never thought that there would be parties, especially not Hollywood-type parties. Jackson is full of celebrities and it's a crowd I have no desire to play with.

It's too bad Rebecca's not here, though. She would deny it, but I suspect she might like the idea of being close to a little *Vanity Fair*–type glamour. In Denver there aren't too many opportunities for her to hang out with and maybe even interview real West Coast movie stars.

Cali looks hurt. That frown I'd made has cooled the light

in her eyes and has apparently brought her high crashing down. I'm beginning to realize that despite her background, she's surprisingly insecure.

"You don't have to. I'll be safe enough there. My mother has her own bodyguards. Real ones."

"Sorry, Cali. I didn't mean—"

But she interrupts me. "A lot of guys would be happy to be my date, you know. You could have just said no—you don't need to make that agonized face. You don't need to be a jerk about it."

Sighing, I let my pack and skis tip over in the dirt. I stand upright and look at her. "Listen, Cali, it's not you. So far you're the best victim I've ever baby-sat. No one else has taken me to do something like that," I say, nodding up at the couloir. "I'm just not real big on parties and crowds. I've been a sort of hermit lately."

She pulls off her jacket while looking back at me. "Is it because of all that 'QuickDraw' stuff that's been in the news?"

"Pretty much. Yeah."

Cali nods, looking somewhat mollified as she stoops to pick up her pack.

The hated nickname refers to a shooting that occurred more than two years ago. I was working undercover at the time, infiltrating a small Hispanic gang in Cheyenne called Sureno 13. One night when the wind was blasting snow down from the Medicine Bow, I found myself standing outside a decrepit ranch house at three in the morning. I'd refused to admit it when being cross-examined a few weeks later, but as I shivered in the storm I had death on my mind. The men inside, the men I'd spent months monitoring and befriending, had hours earlier abused a child in front of her tied-up parents during a home invasion. If I'd built my case faster it wouldn't have happened. I walked into a darkness far blacker than the snowy night to find the three young gangbangers pointing guns at me. I'd been burned, but I knew that before I stepped through the door. What happened next I can barely remember much less explain, but I walked out and somehow, through the last bit of luck I could expect in this life, the three bangers didn't.

A skeptical media accused me of killing the three men in cold blood. The epithets QuickDraw and the Butcher of Cheyenne were the creation of a local columnist whose son I'd once arrested for selling ecstasy. At the columnist's prompting, the dead men's families sued both the state and me. They claimed I acted outrageously and with excessive force, and that I caused their loved ones' wrongful deaths. Rather than try the case and have a jury exonerate me, my cowardly superiors at the Attorney General's Office preferred to pay out a hefty settlement. And the nickname QuickDraw stuck.

I'd thought all that was finally behind me when the civil case settled the previous fall. But then this spring it all came up again. Bigger than ever, and for the sole purpose of impeaching my credibility in the unrelated trial of the state's governor-elect. It was the defense attorney's way of casting a reasonable doubt onto everything I said.

"You shouldn't let it bother you," Cali is saying, her pack balanced on her back now and the belt buckled around her slim waist. "You know you did the right thing. That's all that matters. Besides, no one tonight will know anything about it. Or care. These people think Wyoming's just a big cowboy-movie set. They're all flying in from California today, to start preproduction on Mom's next project. The only local who's going to be there is my uncle Bill—I call him uncle, anyway. Bill Laughlin. He used to be a hotshot climber, too. You guys can talk ropes and routes."

I recognize the name. "How do you know him?"

"He was my dad's best friend. He took care of me when I was a kid, when I used to spend my summers out here."

The party suddenly sounds less painful. At least there

will be someone there I can relate to. "Okay, Cali. I'm your date. What does one wear to a Hollywood party?"

"It's a Western theme. Get some sleep today, because it could be a late night."

That isn't likely to happen. I'm due to lecture the SWAT team on raiding meth labs in a half hour, and after that I have to go over the threatening letters and other evidence with my boss. God only knows how long it will take.

We finish strapping the skis to our packs and continue clumping down the trail on the rockered soles of our boots. She walks ahead of me, seeming happy once again. Her arms swing high and she moves with an athlete's loose-jointed saunter.

I'm your date—that was a stupid thing to say, Ant.

But I can't help admiring the way her thighs and calves look so strong beneath the backpack. Catching myself, I think of my girlfriend instead. Rebecca's legs are even more spectacular, although ballerina-thin and not as suited for strenuous mountain life. But then she won't ski and climb with me anyway—I'd tried to infect her with my addiction during our winter vacation to see my family in Argentina and I'd failed miserably. Maybe it was that, what was supposed to be a beginning, that had been the start of the end.

The trip started out fine. Rebecca practiced her high-school Spanish with my mother and the vaqueros on the *estancia* while I hiked and climbed the nearby crags with Dad. My brother, Roberto, was away in the Torres del Paine, whose peaks were as dangerous a lure to him as the needle. After three days I loaded packs onto a mule and led Rebecca on horseback to the base of a small unnamed spire across the Chilean border.

I thought its south ridge would be the perfect way to introduce her to my world. The hardest moves weren't much tougher than climbing a ladder but the exposure—nearly two thousand feet of it near the summit—would give her a good pump. Rebecca was wide-eyed and grinning as I belayed her up pitch after pitch. It was the first time I'd ever seen her truly spontaneous—she was talking and laughing without her usual contemplative pause and dark-eyed stare. Her curly brown hair swirled around her head in an enormous, tangled halo after she lost the rubber band that held it back. When she laughed at something I said she blew strands of it from her mouth. She was learning to trust me and the rope. To like being tied to me and anchored to the mountains I loved.

It went well until we were within two pitches of the top. That was when Roberto showed up, climbing after us.

The sudden appearance of my fugitive brother—ropeless and with eighteen hundred feet of empty space beneath him—nearly made Rebecca sick. The slightest mistake, or even a rotten hand- or foothold, and Death would grab him by the ankle and yank him off the rock.

"Do you do that?" she'd demanded, her mouth twisting into an expression I'd never seen on her face before.

"Not often. Not like him," I'd answered admiringly, awed as usual by my brother's audacity. Watching him recklessly rushing to greet me.

"Take me down, Anton." It was the last time Rebecca tried climbing.

Rebecca is a city girl. And that fact, as well as the five hundred miles between Denver and Jackson and whatever else it is that's going on in her head, is pulling us apart.

THREE

THE TOWN OF Jackson is nestled at the extreme southern end of the wide valley known as Jackson Hole. To the west the brown grass wall of Gros Ventre Butte—a mere twelve-hundred-foot-high foothill to the peaks behind it—looms up and over the town, and to the east is a ski mountain called Snow King. The valley extends all the way north to Yellowstone, broadening as it goes and bristling on the left with the sharp spires of the Teton summits. Although the official start of summer is still a few weeks away, the highway in the valley and the streets in town are already coursing with motor homes and Harleys.

Because of all the tourists, I can't find any parking on the street outside the Teton County Sheriff's Office. So I pull into a space in the fenced lot that says "Official Vehicles Only." And because my old rust-stained Land Cruiser—Rebecca calls it the Iron Pig—probably doesn't appear very official, I put a business card on the dashboard.

Before getting out I take a minute to compose myself. I spit in my hands then smooth down the spikes of short brown hair my ski hat had raised. There's one persistent tuft that always stands up like a single devil's horn. With a fingertip I touch the line of slick tissue on my left cheek. Thin and white and shaped like a lightning bolt, it cuts from just below my left eye almost to my lips. The several-year-old scar has given my once honest and vaguely Hispanic features, I've been told, a sinister twist. Dark eyes, dark hair, and sun-bronzed skin turning too early to leather seem to emphasize the jagged white line's menace. I smile disarmingly out at the street, practicing, then climb out and slam the door.

The morning's climb has taken longer than expected. After dropping Cali off with my new partner to watch over her, there was no time to shower, change clothes, or even let the wolf-dog Rebecca had recently given me out from my rented cabin for a bathroom break.

So I walk into the building looking like a vagrant, or the living-out-of-my-truck climbing bum I used to be. I'm wearing muddy fleece sweats, sandals, and an old black poly-propylene shirt full of holes. A female duty officer at the front desk looks me over for a long moment before asking if she can be of any help.

"I'm here to meet with the SWAT team," I explain, getting no immediate reply but a suspicious look from the heavyset woman. "I'm with DCI. My name's Antonio Burns." I reach into my back pocket and show her the badge in my wallet.

The deputy's eyes widen a little when I say my name. Then they fix on the scar. But she doesn't smile or say a word. Instead she studies the gold shield skeptically, as if it's something I don't deserve to be holding. She hands it back with another lift of her brows and a slight wrinkling of her nose. She points a finger at a hallway. With her other hand she presses a buzzer under the counter that makes the electric lock on the swinging gate click and hum.

It isn't a surprising welcome. But the irony of it still distresses me. Good cops all too often shun me, believing the worst, while the bad ones treat me like a hero. They sometimes ask in low, admiring voices, *How the hell did you get away with that?* Judging by her obvious disdain, she's probably one of the good ones.

I follow the extended finger and the sound of voices down the hall to the conference room. It's a large space containing several scarred wooden tables and a podium at the far end. A couple of greaseboards hang amid all the flyers on the walls. Donuts, bagels, and an urn of coffee have been set out on one of the tables. Six big cops—both in and out of uniform—look up at me when I walk in. All male. All white. The laughter and talk I'd heard coming down the hall is abruptly cut off.

I try my disarming smile but no one smiles back.

"QuickDraw!" a familiar voice roars from somewhere among them. "Gentlemen . . . meet the state's greatest liability. . . . This man's cost us more in lawsuits than the coal industry!"

A squat, bald man built like a fireplug appears from amid the throng of younger and taller deputies. He's wearing a rumpled suit and jerking his way forward on an aluminum walker. A white beard that's littered with donut crumbs extends halfway down his chest, and his freckled, bald pate gleams under the fluorescent lights. His small blue eyes shine wickedly from beneath bristling brows. In another life he might have been a depraved Viking warlord. In this one he is my boss, the Deputy Assistant Attorney General in charge of the Criminal Division, Ross McGee.

In his time he'd been responsible for putting several worthy candidates on death row. But age, various diseases, and an ever-increasing vulgarity have made him no longer presentable in front of a jury. Seven years ago, about the time I became a cop, the higher-ups assigned him to ride herd on me and the twenty-six other special agents. It was a saddle they hoped he would soon die in. So far he's proved too ornery.

Despite his constant abuse, the other agents and I are intensely loyal to him. He insists on following the law, on not simply using it as a tool to pry himself up into higher office. And he backs us up with the ferocity of a wounded grizzly bear even when we, in his words, "screw the pooch."

With effort, I maintain my smile despite his very public use of the hated nickname. There's no doubt he's done it to annoy me. It's one of his favorite pastimes.

"You're early, Ross." He must have left Cheyenne in the predawn hours in order to have made it across the entire state by 11:00 A.M.

"It doesn't take long when you've got a heavy foot . . . state plates . . . and a shiny tin badge."

Several officers chuckle politely at this. But their eyes don't seem to be laughing—instead they watch me with blatant interest.

"I thought having a fat ass might slow you down some." Then, to the men behind him, I introduce myself. "My name's Antonio Burns. Call me Anton. I'm going to be working with you for the next couple of months."

McGee continues lurching toward me on his walker. "And God help you all. . . . Special Agent Burns is thoroughly filthy, in body and soul. . . . I should know . . . I trained the bastard myself." He makes a show of sniffing at my shirt. "What's this? Are you modeling the latest . . . in undercover apparel?"

Then he growls softly, just to me, "You're late, lad. Where the hell have you been?" His breath is appalling, flavored with sour coffee, tobacco, and bourbon.

"Climbing," I say shortly. I'm not eager to explain more.

But he forces the issue in a not-too-gentle whisper. "You were supposed to be watching the girl."

"I was," I admit.

McGee squints at me and shakes his head. "What? You trying to kill her yourself? . . . Before this guy has the chance?" He turns to the assembled deputies and bellows, "Let's get this goat fuck started!"

I walk to the front of the room and start talking as I unpack my briefcase. "Over the next few months—after I clear my current caseload—I'm going to be your spotter, identifying meth labs for you and showing you how to go in without getting yourselves shot up or blown up. You'll get to know me, and you'll also have the great misfortune of getting to know Ross McGee."

I go on to talk about the state's growing methamphetamine problem and the federal grant that will be paying my salary while I'm here.

In Wyoming, a state with a population of less than 500,000 people spread over 97,000 square miles, we have five times the national average use of meth. Maybe it's because there's not enough for kids to do if they don't discover rodeo or rock climbing early on. Maybe it's something in the ever-present wind. In any event, one in twenty teenagers admits to having tried it. A lot of them get hooked. It's so prevalent because it's so easy to make. Any high-school dropout with a bathtub, a stove, paint thinner, a carton of Sudafed, and some ammonia product—even stale urine—can stir up a batch. The resulting high makes you feel pumped up and powerful before the quick downside leaves you jittery, pissed off, and rattlesnake-mean. *Tweaking*, it's called. Meth is highly addictive and gives those who snort, inject, or smoke it the urge to do something really violent. Even Roberto, my smackhead brother, won't touch the stuff anymore. He claims his preferred speedball blend of heroin and cocaine is much more "*sofisticado.*"

I take a clear plastic bag with black writing on it from my briefcase. It had been evidence in another case and is now slated to be destroyed. Although I make an effort to handle the half-pound of dirty gray crystals inside casually as I talk, I can't help but feel their evil power. They're heavy in my hands and feel as dangerous as split-nosed bullets. I don't agree with my brother—to me this is indistinguishable from the shit that's ruined his life, put him in a cage, and now made him a wanted man. It's the shit that will kill him if gravity doesn't do the job first.

I hold up the bag. "This is what we're after."

The deputies stare at it. They've all seen it before but probably never this much. I'm glad that at least their attention has been distracted from me. Before I could feel them weighing each word I said. *Did he or didn't he do it? Is he a killer or just a very lucky bastard?*

I demonstrate how to work the notebook-sized quick-test kits we'll use to perform on-the-scene tests of minute amounts. Thorough analysis will be done later at a lab, but some needs to be tested immediately to determine if there's probable cause to make an arrest.

The officers handle the crystals gingerly when I pass them around. Like me, they give the stuff an amount of respect it doesn't deserve. As if it's the root of all evil, or at least a lot of evils. But as I watch them, I wonder if I'm losing my repugnance toward the stuff. Going after it and destroying it had once seemed like a calling, my way of avenging my brother. Now I realize that Roberto and the other junkies will do what they want. This drug or another. And that prison only makes their cravings more urgent, and at the same time makes the addicts meaner and tougher and more resourceful.

McGee is watching my performance from the back of the room. Every now and then I catch him lifting a silver flask from inside his coat and taking a sip. I wonder if I'm being spied upon, if the high-level bureaucrats have sent McGee up to this part of the state to determine if I'm still capable of functioning after all the trauma I've been through lately. But I'm probably being paranoid—it's more likely they just wanted to get McGee out of their hair for a while. Besides, they trust him even less than they trust me.

The men joke and laugh as they perform their own tests on the drugs at the tables. They feel it, sniff it, plop tiny drops of chemicals on it, and then I get them to taste it. They grin at one another's bitter-beer faces. Crank tastes about like you'd expect—kitchen Drāno cut with piss.

I notice that the officers seem to gravitate around one clean-shaven deputy sheriff with a thick, weight-lifter's build. They appear to look to him for approval in almost everything they do. Every joke, every comment, is addressed more to him than to the group.

Once the kits have been packed away, I talk about spotting methamphetamine labs.

"They're pretty easy to find because you can smell the chemical stink of the ammonia sometimes for miles. Another dead giveaway is a trash pile full of empty packages of Sudafed and other cold remedies. Once we get running in a couple of weeks, I'll be patrolling the forests five days a week, looking for trailers or shacks on National Forest land where you won't even need warrants—you'll be able to go in as soon as you can get your respirators on and the fire department on standby. You'll want to watch out when you go in because the cooking process is highly explosive."

McGee calls from the back of the room, "Just throw a lit match in the door. . . . You'll know soon enough if it's a lab or not."

Several good questions are asked. What are the likely dangers inside a so-called clan lab, or clandestine laboratory? Are they often booby-trapped? What kind of weapons do these amateur chemists tend to carry? As I answer them I start to feel a growing sense of camaraderie with these officers. They're starting to trust me.

But then, abruptly, it all goes south.

When I ask for more questions, one thick arm is raised

by the weight lifter in the sheriff's uniform—the one who seems like the leader of this group. His crew-cut blond head is the size of a cinder block and his jaw muscles bulge as if full of gum. He has dark brown eyes that are set far apart, like a pit bull's. And they look about as predictable. I also notice that he's the only one wearing a sergeant's three stripes. His plastic nametag says "Wokowski."

"So when we go in," he asks in a quiet, measured voice, "do we wait for them to draw on us before we shoot 'em?"

The room grows very quiet. Then someone snickers. A challenge is clear in the air from all the way across the long conference room. I feel a scarlet flush creeping into my cheeks. And I can't help but remember that night—the blood rushing in my ears, the explosions of gunfire, something wet slapping my face, the Glock banging away in my hand—

I stifle the memories and focus. Every police agency has a few alpha types who resent the attention I'd received as much as I do. They're actually jealous, the dumb fucks. They'll go out of their way to make it as hard for me as possible to accomplish anything, and would like nothing better than to see me embarrassed. Wokowski might as well have said what the defense attorney and press strongly implied just two weeks before—*QuickDraw my ass. You murdered those boys.*

I keep my voice slow and flat, and even manage to smile. "Well, Sergeant Wokowski, when your presence and identity have been exposed, or are even suspected, then obviously the best thing to do is withdraw and wait for a better opportunity. If you can't do that, then you do whatever you have to. But you'll have to live with the consequences—the official inquiries, the lawsuits, and having to answer stupid questions from idiots who've never been in a similar situation."

God, I hope it's you, I'm thinking. *I hope you're the one. It will be a pleasure to ratchet the hooks over your beefy wrists.*

One of the other five officers lets out a low groan. "Oooh." It's the sound you heard in high school when someone made the final, fatal insult about another's mother and a fight was imminent. It has come to this so fast—just minutes ago I'd begun to believe that everything was going so well.

Wokowski's still watching me without any discernible expression. His wide-set eyes don't even seem to blink. It's hard to see what Cali could ever have seen in him, but then he does have a powerful, almost animalistic aura. He opens his mouth to respond.

A crack sounds like a gunshot, cutting him off before he has the chance to speak. McGee has shoved his walker into a table leg.

"All right, gentlemen, that's enough for today," he says.

I have no doubt that there will be a tomorrow for Sergeant Wokowski and me.

FOUR

I WAIT FOR McGEE on the parking lot's asphalt under a hot sun while he takes his time hobbling outside. I focus on my breathing, attempting with deep breaths to center myself the way Rebecca had tried to teach me. *Close your eyes and think good thoughts,* she'd said while she showed me how to pretzel my legs before her. Then she'd laughed. *Not those kinds of thoughts, you pervert. Calm thoughts. Pure thoughts.*

As I inhale all the way down to my belly and let it out slowly, I picture her in what had once been our bedroom. Facing me, just two feet away, her legs are folded and her spine is straight. Pale eyelids sealing off the windows to her soul. This is the way we'd started the day for almost one hundred mornings as the sunlight lit up the snowy peaks of the Front Range beyond on the loft's big windows. With her naked except for a pair of my oversized boxers. Her breasts firm and high, the nipples very pink against white skin. The pine floor very cold beneath our bottoms.

The meditation never worked for me—I never quite felt its soothing effect—but then the attempt never failed to make me feel good. Cheating, my eyes open and staring, I would wait for her lids to slowly rise, the brown orbs descend, before I would gently pull her onto me, laughing and struggling.

But now the memory doesn't work. My hands are still trembling with the aftereffects of the confrontation.

I was once so amiable, so cool—it's what made me successful when I was working undercover. Even my high-school class at Lackland Air Force Base had voted me Most Likable. But now I am someone else. Or at least I'm perceived as someone else. A cold-blooded killer. And a voice in my head worries that it's what I will become. From the simple and overwhelming force of public opinion.

"That went well," McGee says when he clanks up, huffing over his walker. "We're going to have a fun time here in Jackson. . . . You've got a way with people, QuickDraw."

This time I don't bother asking him to stop calling me that. By protecting me from the criminal investigation the office administration had been pressured to mount, he'd earned the right.

"Assholes," I say instead. "You'd think cops would be smarter. Those yahoos in there actually believe Mo Cash and that fucking columnist in Cheyenne."

Morris Cash was the lead defense attorney who had cross-examined me during the governor-elect's trial. He did everything he could to ridicule the idea that I survived a shoot-out with three armed men. The purpose of the unrelated incident was to impeach my credibility with the jury. The result, I hate to admit to myself, is that I'm no longer effective as a peace officer—at least not on the witness stand. McGee and I are going to have to work at plea-bargaining my old cases. Using Mo Cash's transcript as a road map, any half-assed defense attorney can tear me apart. And none of it can be brought out on direct examination so that I will at least have a chance to explain. Criminal law is funny that way. It's considered bolstering, and it's therefore inadmissible on direct. But the defense is free to go into it on cross, make my past look like some horrible secret the prosecution has been trying to hide. They can force me to answer with only a "Yes" or "No." Questions like "Isn't it true, Agent Burns, that you shot to death three men, who you claim were armed, during this so-called ambush?" "And you walked away without so much as a scratch?" A disbelieving chuckle. "Don't you agree that such an outcome is highly unlikely, to say the least? Implausible, even?" "Isn't it true that you killed another man, your fourth, I believe, during *this* so-called investigation?" "Isn't it true that you've been investigated by your own office for the crime of murder?" "Isn't it true that you've been suspended from duty on three separate occasions?" I have to wait for redirect in order to try and explain about self-defense, unlikely outcomes often being true, standard officer-involved-shooting investigations, and mandatory suspensions following the use of a firearm. In the last trial I'd been red-faced with fury by that time and the jury looked away from me while the reporters in the gallery smacked their lips, mistaking outrage and righteous indignation for a guilty conscience.

This is why now all I'm suited for is ferreting out clan labs and this new assignment of basic bodyguarding. My face is too well-known for undercover work and my background is too dubious for serious investigations requiring lengthy testimony. The only reason I hadn't quit months ago is that I don't want to go out as a loser, a chump. Too many people would be happy to see me go.

McGee starts to growl, "If you're looking for sympathy—"

But I interrupt. "Screw you, Ross. I'm not in the mood."

He gives me a glare that feels like the burn of twin laser beams and the snarled white hair of his beard seems to bristle. Then he whacks me on the back with his hoary hand.

"Suck it up, lad. You know the truth. That's all that matters."

It's the same thing Cali said just two hours ago. The same thing Rebecca said when I'd come home that day with clenched fists and a mouth raw from spitting obscenities. And it's bullshit.

But even so, the words are pretty surprising, coming from McGee's lips. It's even more surprising when he adds, "Come on. I'm going to buy you lunch."

He leads me two blocks west to the town square, his wheels rattling on the wooden sidewalks, to where a hot-dog vendor is taking advantage of the unseasonably warm spring air. He's set up his umbrella and metal cart beneath one of the arches of piled elk antlers that frame the four entrances into the small park. There isn't much business for him to-day—Jackson's rich and healthy residents probably don't eat many hot dogs, and the full-blown tourist season is still a few weeks away.

A menu is bolted to the side of the greasy cart. I look at it skeptically.

"Know what's in 'em?" McGee asks, reading my mind.

"What, Ross?"

"Cow lips and butt holes." He turns to the vendor. "Give me three with everything . . . jalapenos, too."

Although I know I need nourishment, I'm not going to touch one of those things. My stomach already burbles with enough acid, and it's been years since I've even touched a good steak. The sight of too many bodies torn by bullets or ruined by needles can do that to you. I order a pretzel and lemonade instead. McGee grunts disapprovingly as he bares yellowed teeth and rips out a bite. We eat a silent meal— silent but for McGee's gnashing and satisfied groans—on a park bench while watching a group of youths in a circle kick a Hacky Sack on the grass.

Although they're only a few years younger than me, it seems like they live in a different world. The men are bare chested in the sun, and the women wear little more than thin cloth above their baggy shorts and sandals. Tattoos, bracelets, anklets, and facial piercings flash in the light along with quick, bronzed limbs and the sound of laughter. When they shout at one another, their accents range from West Coast surfer to Appalachian hick. I hear them talking about "heinous rapids" and "sick rock pitches" and "steep-ass chutes."

They are the mountain freaks. The happy, obscenely healthy fringe dwellers. They'd once been my people. My tribe. But my job and my badge have long since made me an outcast.

"Look at those bouncers," McGee says. "Haven't those girls heard of brassieres? . . . Ahh, it does an old man's heart good."

"Let's get on with it, Ross."

We walk back toward the Sheriff's Office where his sedan—he ranks a new Chrysler New Yorker—is parked in a tow-away zone. A business card similar to mine is prominently displayed on his dashboard.

The car is hot inside. It reeks from the odor of his foul cigars. We sit with the engine idling and the air conditioner turned on high, which I hope will remove the stench of tobacco and hot-dog breath as well as my own dried sweat. McGee's leaning over me, his mustard-stained beard almost in my face, as he struggles for a minute or so trying to get his briefcase out from behind my seat.

His problem is that there isn't enough room between his big belly and the steering wheel for him to turn. He grunts and wheezes, too proud to ask for help, until I begin to fear that I'll either asphyxiate on the fumes coming from his mouth or that he'll have a heart attack and I'll have to give him mouth-to-mouth. I twist around and yank the big leather case onto my lap.

"Open it," he orders, annoyed that I've helped him.

Inside are twenty pounds of statute books, his old service automatic from his Korean War days, and a single slender folder. The folder contains the photocopied pages of an incident report completed by the Jackson Police Department.

"Read it."

The first two pages are an officer's report handwritten in capital letters. Two nights ago, at 11:36 P.M., Jackson officers responded to a 911 call at 452 Colter Street within the Jackson city limits. According to the dispatcher, the caller was an assistant county attorney named Cali Morrow who claimed that someone was coming through her kitchen window. The officers wheeled up to the address five minutes later with lights blazing but no siren. They found an elderly man sitting on the front steps with his arm around a young woman. Both were recognized by the responding officers, and later formally identified as Cali Morrow and William "Bill" Laughlin.

After speaking to the witnesses, the officers observed a broken window on the first floor/southeast side of the house, a half-empty roll of duct tape on the ground beneath a bush, a stun gun beside it, and boot prints around them in earth that was wet from being freshly watered.

The house was searched but no suspect was found. The garages and exteriors of the homes around Ms. Morrow's were also searched by additional officers with flashlights. Again, no one was found.

The next two pages are the witness statements. Cali's is brief, no more than two paragraphs. It states that she had walked home late from the courthouse and entered her kitchen in order to feed her cat. The window over the sink had broken inward as she was standing before it, showering her with glass. She grabbed the cordless phone and ran to an upstairs bathroom that had a lock on the door. There she called 911. She could not identify the perpetrator—it appeared that he was wearing a dark-colored jacket and hood.

An afterword adds that she has been receiving odd letters over the last few months. She thinks she still has two of them, which she will turn over to the investigating officer. The writer of these letters is unknown to her.

Despite the straightforward language of the statement,

through the neat but shaky handwriting I can sense a little of the terror she must have been feeling that night.

The second witness statement is even briefer. Bill Laughlin writes that he was taking a late-night walk through the neighborhood when he heard the sound of glass breaking from the side of Cali Morrow's house. A dark-clad figure was trying to crawl through the kitchen window. He shouted, and the man dropped from the window and ran west toward Main Street. No, he cannot identify the man.

The final page in the file is from a crime-scene technician. What he reports is a big zero. No fingerprints on the sill, the shards of glass, or on the side of the house around the window. No prints on the stun gun or the tape—they'd recently been wiped by a cotton cloth. The ground below the window was too soft and spongy with wood chips to hold a usable shoe tread or outline.

"Jesus, Ross. There's nothing here. We're going to need a friggin' confession to get this guy."

"Then we'll get it. We can't write this one off as a bungled burglary attempt . . . by a tweaked-out meth-head. . . . Not with a stun gun and restraining tape lying in the dirt. . . . Not with *these* letters."

He reaches across my lap and slaps the folder shut. Stapled to the back are three photocopied pages.

The first is a letter that's unsigned and undated. It's handwritten in block letters on a regular-sized piece of paper. The writing shows an element of cunning—squared-off capital letters such as these are hard to match to any one person's handwriting. It's the sort of thing a cop would know. All capital letters is also the way cops write their reports.

"CALI, CALI, CALI," it begins. "GODDESS OF ALL DESTRUCTION. YOU ARE MEANT TO BE MINE, YOU CRUEL BITCH. YOU ARE MY BRIDE, MY PRETTY HIDE, MY CUNT TO OPEN WIDE." Other than some crude pornographic drawings, there's nothing more but the closing. It reads "CALIFORNIA DREAMING," but those two words have been crossed out with an X. Underneath it says "CALI-FORNICATING DREAMING."

"Is this the first?"

"No, she'd gotten some earlier over a period of months . . . threw them away without even reading most of 'em. . . . It was only when our boy tried to come through the window . . . that she got concerned enough to tell someone. . . . She was able to save these two and the envelopes out of the trash."

I read it again. "This is sick stuff. There's definitely an imminent threat here. Especially when you combine it with the attempted break-in and the dropped stun gun and tape."

"No shit, QuickDraw."

"Where were these sent to?"

"Her home in town. . . . She bought the place two months ago. . . . Before that she was staying at her mama's. . . . Most of the ones she threw away were mailed there."

That means the letter writer knows her pretty well. He knows where she's been living. Cali had said she and Wook were dating until about a month ago, so he certainly knew where to find her. But it doesn't make sense that he would be sending her obscene, threatening letters while they were dating. Unless maybe he hoped it was a way to cause her to cling to him—the physically powerful cop—when he felt her drifting, sort of scare her into staying with him.

The second letter is a bad attempt at poetry. It says:

YOU ARE GOING TO LOVE ME, BITCH
YOU'RE GOING TO PAY FOR MY FEVER AND
   ITCH
YOUR DEVIL EYES WON'T BE ABLE TO HIDE
WHAT'S ALWAYS BEEN BURIED DEEP INSIDE.

At the bottom he'd written, "I'M COMING. I'M CUM-MING. SPREAD YOUR LEGS AND PREPARE TO MEET ME." This one, too, is signed "CALI-FORNI-CATING DREAMING."

The third stapled page shows photocopies of the envelopes the two letters had come in. A handwritten note from a lab tech indicates that it's unknown which letter belongs to which envelope. The envelopes appear to be ordinary, the kind that can be bought in any grocery store or 7-Eleven. They are both postmarked in Jackson. The first was mailed four days ago—two days before the break-in. The second was mailed ten days ago.

Even with my limited experience in these kinds of cases, I know that there are generally two kinds of serious stalkers. The first type are those who want to get revenge on someone who they believe has done them wrong. An ex-boyfriend, for instance. The second type are the wackos trying to get close to someone they don't have a chance in hell of actually knowing. Like the guys who follow movie stars around and break into their homes. And sometimes, I remember, recalling a famous Los Angeles case, even manage to kill their victim. The motives are the same for both types of stalkers—control, vengeance, and/or delusion.

McGee doesn't try to guess when I mention this. Instead he says, "Just don't screw this up, QuickDraw. . . . It's too high profile. . . . You let her get killed, we're both out on our asses."

McGee has been a thorn in the office's side for more years than I've been around. It isn't really the justifiable concern that someday a secretary or female agent will take his lewd comments and playful gropes seriously and sue for sexual harassment, it's more the fact that he forces the suits in admin to walk the straight and narrow instead of taking political advantage of the cases the Criminal Division prosecutes. Or should prosecute. I recall that he'd once been ordered to prosecute several gay men who had been rounded up in a nighttime raid on a public park. They were initially charged with Indecent Exposure, a crime that would require them to register as sex offenders for the rest of their lives. Nothing but a conviction at trial or a guilty plea would do, the Assistant Attorney General told McGee. So McGee allowed the men to plead guilty to Following Too Close, a two-point traffic infraction.

Ornery or not, the day he's fired is the day I hand over my badge and go back to guiding.

"Prints on the letters? Saliva on the envelope?" I ask.

"Nada. Our boy is too clever . . . despite his abysmal rhymes."

"What about the stun gun and duct tape?" I ask him. "Where are they?"

"They're at our crime lab in Cheyenne. . . . The sheriff here arranged for them to be couriered down by the Highway Patrol. . . . The prod is a common brand. . . . Three stores here in Jackson sell 'em. . . . We'll have Jim check out the stores . . . get a list of buyers."

I don't know my new partner on this, Jim Guinness, very well. All I know is that he's also a pilot, that he lives out of his old plane to save on rent, and that he uses the pilots' facilities at airports as his personal washroom. The plane might be useful when we get down to the business of looking for clan labs in the woods. That was why McGee had assigned us to work together; I'm to be the ground-pounder and he's to be the eye-in-the-sky.

"What kind of stun gun is it?"

"Something called a Stun Master, 625,000 volts. . . . It's supposed to be the most powerful one commercially available. . . . Nasty thing, they advertise that it'll drop a bull moose. . . . If you can sneak up close enough to zap one."

I flip through the file one more time. "There's nothing here. All we've got is an ex-boyfriend."

"Have you talked to her about her former amour?"

"No, not really. I brought up his name with her this morning, but she doesn't think it's his style. You realize, of course, that he was the guy busting my ass in there?"

McGee just chuckles.

"Thanks for warning me, Ross."

I realize now that it's quite possible Wokowski's animosity toward me might be based on something other than the question of who's going to be the alpha male in local law enforcement. I begin to feel a little paranoid. "Does he know we're on this? Who else in Jackson knows about this?"

McGee shrugs his shoulders. He has no neck, so the pads of his suit bulge up to his ears.

"Everybody, probably. . . . The town police who showed up and investigated . . . her boss, the County Attorney. . . . Everyone knew the locals would be taken off it . . . because of the vic's status."

"There won't be any doubt as to who's been assigned when they see Jim and me escorting her around."

"If it *is* him, it might draw him out." McGee grins at me with his large, crooked teeth. "Might focus his attention on you instead."

I have the feeling it's already focused in my direction.

"This is your priority for now, lad," McGee continues. "Forget about clan labs and drugs until we get this asshole rounded up."

"I'm watching her tonight—going with her to a party her mother's throwing. I'll find out more about Wokowski then. I'll ask about other boyfriends, too, or weird guys she might know. She mentioned that Bill Laughlin's going to be at this party, too, and I'll see if he remembers anything else about the guy he saw at the window. Tomorrow we should go through all the cases she's prosecuted and make sure there are no other possibles there." I say this last part reluctantly, wanting the sergeant known as Wook to be my man. But long ago McGee had taught me about following evidence rather than picking a perp and trying to build a case to fit him. "Hopefully Jim will find that Wokowski made a recent stun-gun purchase. Or maybe the Sheriff's Office issues them to SWAT team members."

McGee lights a cigar while I roll down a window. The cigar is one of those cheap ones with a plastic nipple that tastes like honey. Its stench and the hot air that wafts in the open window make me feel light-headed. The morning climb and the surge of anger I'd felt at the meeting have left me exhausted.

He chuckles to himself. "So you're watching her tonight, eh, QuickDraw? . . . Tell me . . . she look anything like her mama-san?"

"I'm meeting her mom tonight, so I'll let you know."

His satyr's grin grows broader. His eyes are unpleasantly bright with mischief.

"Should I call my goddaughter . . . let her know you may be out late this evening . . . with a movie star's daughter? . . . I'd come along to chaperone if I weren't having dinner with the County Attorney."

I've had a lot of bad luck in the last two years, but some-times I think the very worst of it is that McGee served in the Army with Rebecca's father. He is her godfather, God help me. And he'd even been inadvertently responsible for us first meet-ing. At the time he'd said, "You don't have a Popsicle's chance in hell, QuickDraw." Until recently I thought I'd proved him wrong. But then maybe I've been reaching too high. Hubris.

"What does the young lady think about you coming back to work? . . . She glad to be rid of you?"

"Ask her."

"Don't worry, I'll do that. . . . I'll let her know she's a hell of a lot better off . . . without you mooning around. . . . With any luck she'll meet a real man."

Then his face grows serious. His eyes are even brighter

but they lose their mischievous gleam. "Now I've got to ask you something, Burns ... and I don't want you getting all pissy and silent on me, okay?"

I nod, wondering what he's up to and half expecting a joke. But he looks like he did two years ago when he took a statement from me about what had happened that night in Cheyenne. It's a lie-detector look, and for no particular reason I can think of, right now I feel a drop of sweat roll down one side of my ribs.

"Where's your brother?"

I look out the window and let out a breath. An obscenity, too. "Why do you want to know? He's not wanted in this state."

"He's wanted in every state. You know that. . . . It's a nationwide warrant. . . . The Feds have been calling. . . . They thought they had a deal with him and then he goes and disappears. . . . They want to know what's going on . . . and they want to interrogate you, see if you know anything about it . . . but I held 'em off. For now."

Still looking out the window, watching a man and a woman walking by holding hands, I say, "Tell them I don't know where he is. As far as I know he's still going to turn himself over in Salt Lake next week. He's probably in the mountains somewhere, getting in some last climbs. My parents said he took off almost two weeks ago without a word."

FIVE

WHAT DOES ONE *wear to a movie star's party?*
In an exhausted daze I stare around the cabin's downstairs bedroom. Until I have time to get settled, I'm using it as a closet. My two court suits hang from a clothesline on one wall next to Gore-Tex bibs, rain shells, fleece underclothes, and an assortment of ice axes. Skis are propped nearby, with plastic boots, rock shoes, crampons, sleeping bags, and ropes spilling across the pine floor. The room's log walls are covered with nails supporting more climbing gear.

Mungo, my wolf-dog, stands beside me and also stares at the mess. Even though she always holds her head low in a submissive shrug, she is tall enough that her snout is high against my thigh. With one hand I absentmindedly knuckle her bony skull. She seems to wince at my touch and slinks a few feet away. It makes me sigh.

"You don't have to be afraid of me," I tell her. "You know I won't hurt you."

Rebecca had thought this pathetic creature with gray fur hanging over a gaunt frame like oversized clothes could replace Oso, the loyal beast I'd lost last fall. The dog who'd once hamstrung a fleeing suspect, who'd frightened and awed the drug dealers and cops I worked with, before being shot by a man who was coming to kill me.

Mungo is no replacement, though. Not even close. She's such a wimp that she'll wet the floor if I speak much louder than a whisper or utter the word "No." So when she gnaws the oak table's stout legs or the leather arm of the couch, I'm forced to discourage her by softly saying things like "Um, you know, Mungo, maybe that's not such a good idea. You might get a splinter or something."

Now the wolf watches me with averted eyes, her black lips pulled up slightly to expose her long canines. Nervousness makes her look a little devious. Rebecca calls it her "sly smile."

I take a suit off the clothesline, hesitate, and then hang it back up. Cali said it's to be a Western-themed party. I have no idea what Hollywood people wear to such things, but I expect it will be something that no Wyoming native would be caught dead in. I smile as I picture blow-dried actors, producers, agents, and flunkies awkwardly dressed in expensive cowboy boots, ten-gallon hats, and leather chaps. Feeling sanctimonious, I put on my usual khaki painter's jeans, worn-out running shoes, and a loose brown corduroy shirt that I leave untucked to hide the .40 H&K I'll clip to the side of my pants before I leave. In case the party turns out to be more formal than I anticipate, I also pick up a ridiculous cashmere coat—an expensive gift from Rebecca, an attempt to dress me up a little—to throw in the car.

The main room of the funky old A-frame is furnished with a heavy leather-and-wood couch and matching chair. A solid oak table supports last night's pizza box and two empty bottles of Snake River Pale Ale. I clean up and then go about preparing dinner. Mungo becomes a little less cringing when I offer her the crusts of the two peanut-butter-and-jelly sandwiches that make up the meal. She snatches them from my fingers with a delicate nip then stands back, her long tongue snaking in and out as she attempts to clear the sticky stuff from the roof of her mouth.

I should be accustomed to this kind of food, to this kind of home, and to this kind of living. Except for the times when my mother, Roberto, and I lived on Grandfather's ranch—when Dad was on leave or off on assignment somewhere too dangerous for dependents—and my few happy months in Rebecca's apartment, this is the only kind of home I've ever known. Rented walls, appliances, and a roof. Pizza, oatmeal, granola, rice, beans, and peanut-butter sandwiches. I feel more comfortable in a tent in the wilderness, dozing on the ground beneath alpine walls, than I've ever felt in town. The realization isn't a particularly happy one. *Maybe we are too different.* But I'm getting too old for living like a college student or a climbing bum. And it's getting lonely.

This place is somewhere in between real grown-up life and my old life. It's a solid structure at least, with semimodern appliances, but it sits well out of town on a wooded hillside above Cache Creek. Guiltily, I recall how claustrophobic I'd felt at times in Rebecca's downtown Denver loft. It disturbed me to hear all the street noise rising up. The voices, breaking bottles on weekend nights, and sirens.

Mungo watches me get ready to leave from her cut-down sleeping bag in the corner of the cabin's main room. Although her tongue is still snaking in and out, her yellow eyes are narrow with reproof. She can't believe I'm leaving her again after being gone half the night and most of the day.

"I'm sorry, Mungo. It's my job. You'll have to amuse yourself. Do something useful while I'm gone. Guard the cabin, okay?" I try to give her a rawhide chew stick but she turns her head away from it.

I avoid looking in the mirror when I go into the bathroom to brush my teeth. I had a bad experience with it my first night in this place that I still haven't recovered from. I woke up in the early-morning hours when, fuzzy from tequila drunk alone, I stumbled down the steep steps from the loft and cracked my shin on the toilet bowl. I turned on the light and was unpleasantly surprised by what I saw. It seemed that when I turned my head the reflected image moved a fraction of an inch too slow. And there was something in the image's coffee-dark eyes I didn't like. A sort of smirk fighting to emerge. It reminded me of when, as a child, I'd made a practice of avoiding mirrors. I was afraid I might see a doppelganger staring back at me—with my features but wild-eyed and bloody-fanged. Reaching out to pull me in.

I know that it's stupid now that I'm a grown man, but I check my reflection in the window instead of the mirror to be sure I've washed away all the toothpaste.

And all the breath leaves my lungs in a rush.

What I see there is far worse than anything I'd ever imagined in the mirror. I leap backward and fall, rolling through the bathroom's open door. My butt smacks the pine floor an instant before my elbows and then the back of my head. The fingers of my right hand automatically claw at the side of my pants—where my gun would be if it weren't on the oak table. My eyes remain fixed on the window but in the periphery of my vision I see Mungo springing out of her bed and scurrying away from me. Her claws scratch at the floor as if she were trying to burrow into it.

The window is empty now, revealing only aspens and spruce. But a moment before, a dark face had been pressed against the glass. The lips were sealed on the pane, the cheeks puffed up like a blowfish's, exposing white molars and a red tongue. The eyes were squinted almost shut.

I roll to my feet and lunge to the table for my gun. But as I wrap my palm around the beveled grip, I realize I know that face. Not the contorted features, exactly, but I know those eyes. Even narrowed to mere slits they're unmistakable. They'd been a pale glacier blue with almost no pupils evident in the irises. I'd seen those eyes ten thousand times.

" 'Berto! You maniac!" I yell at the window, striding back into the bathroom with the gun tight in my hand.

The face is gone. But there are still lip prints and a circle of vaporizing breath on the glass. When I look out I see him on the carpet of pine needles with his hands on his knees as he laughs. His tangled black hair covers his face. I can hear him through the thin pane. He's saying, "Should've seen your eyes, *che!* Thought they were gonna pop out of your head!"

I call for Mungo to come. She obeys reluctantly. With her ears forward and her chin almost scraping the ground, she follows me out the back door and around to the stand of trees on one side of the cabin. Scenting then spotting my brother, she begins to growl uncertainly—something for which I'm proud of her.

"Good girl," I tell her. "Now sic him."

She continues staring at Roberto and steps behind me. She watches him from around my hip.

"What the hell are you doing here?" I yell at my brother. "The Feds are looking for you. My boss asked me if I knew where you were just an hour ago."

Roberto finally stands up straight to grin at me. His face is a lot like mine, but it shows more of Mom's Indio ancestry in its high cheekbones and broad nose. His eyes are all Dad's, though. They are extremely disconcerting when they peer at you from amid the dark skin and black hair. So much so that he usually wears sunglasses to hide them. Otherwise the madness is too obvious. Prison muscles are still evident beneath his faded black T-shirt. The thin fabric is stretched taut over his chest, shoulders, and arms but is loose around the waist. His forearms look as big and as hard as fenceposts. Dirty jeans and motorcycle boots hide the leaner, long-distance muscles of his legs.

"Sorry, Ant. But I had to make sure you were alone, you

know. I came to get you to go climbing with me. One last time. I've got a week before I got to turn myself in. Time enough to do the Teton Traverse. Not just the south summits, but starting all the way up at Moran."

Mungo surprises me by inching forward around my side. She's no longer growling. Roberto holds out his heavily calloused hand to her. She sniffs it, and, to my amazement, lets him caress her cheek with his fingertips. She lifts her lips an inch and gives my brother her snaggle-toothed grin while her tail comes out from between her legs and starts to swing. It's like she recognizes him as a fellow wild thing.

"Look at that," Roberto says, chuckling, before I can respond to his absurd invitation. "A dog that smiles." Then looking back at me, "You with me, bro?"

"Jesus, 'Berto. I can't. No friggin' way. I'm on a case and besides, you're still a wanted man until you turn yourself in. If you get caught here I'll be an accessory. And the Feds will burn their deal with you. We'll both go to jail."

Roberto escaped from a Colorado prison six months ago while I was in the midst of the investigation involving the state's governor-elect. He'd been serving an eight-year sentence there for manslaughter—for killing a man who crudely groped Roberto's girlfriend in a Durango bar. Beating him, then stabbing him with a broken beer mug. According to the many witnesses, he was laughing as he did it.

My brother did the first two years of his sentence the hard way. Very hard. I'd always thought he had too much energy to be confined by the earth and now he was shoved down into a little cell. When I visited him I could see he was on the verge of being burned up by his own volatile energy. It was either get out or die—I knew it even then. A week after the one and only visit he'd permitted me, he scaled a sheer thirty-foot wall at night, climbed some fences wrapped in razor wire, and took off. Within another week he was back in

Argentina, where our maternal grandfather's old friends from the Dirty War could protect him from extradition.

What I'd learned of the deal had come through my parents, who had learned it from the Buenos Aires lawyers they paid to negotiate on Roberto's behalf. The U.S. Attorneys were offering a reduced sentence in a federal rehabilitation facility and dropping the Colorado escape charges if Roberto would cooperate with them. They wanted him to work as an informant against one of his old buddies from his muling days across the Mexican border. The target, Jesus Hidalgo, had recently carved up a DEA agent in Tijuana and the Feds were desperate to bag him. Desperate enough to cut a deal with my brother. I don't know why Roberto would even consider cooperating—he's always been intensely loyal to his drug-dealing friends—but now's not the time to ask.

"I don't trust those fuckers anyway," he's saying. "What I'm going to do, see, is have a friend fly in to the rendezvous at Salt Lake on my passport. You know Miguel? At the ranch? Dude who looks a lot like me? Anyway, I'll be skulking around somewhere to check out what kind of reception he gets. Check out the vibe, you know. Then I'll either walk up and introduce myself or walk away."

Mungo is groaning and twisting up her head as he rubs her rear end.

"So I've got one week," he continues, giving me the full effect of his blue-eyed gaze, "to feed the Rat with my little bro. We need to do this, *che*. It's been too long. And it could be a lot longer before I get the chance again."

I can feel my face growing hot. The way he's endangering my job and my freedom makes me angry. The guilt trip he's putting on me makes me even angrier.

I struggle to keep my voice even. " 'Berto, I'm a cop! I should arrest you right now and call the FBI."

He chuckles at that but there's something I've never

before heard in his voice when he speaks again. He's staring right into my head.

"C'mon, bro. Pretty please."

I take then let out a long breath. Then another. "I can't. I'm sorry, 'Berto, but I can't. I can't have anything to do with you until you do the deal. You need to get the hell away from me. From here."

He finally looks away from me and down at Mungo. But before his eyes leave mine I can see a wounded look in them. They're tight and hard, the pupils contracted as if in a defensive posture.

"All right, *che*. It's cool. You change your mind, you can call." He stoops and brushes away some pine needles then writes a number in the dirt with the tip of his finger.

"I can't even call you, 'Berto. I'm going to have to pretend this was just a bad dream."

"Whatever, Ant. Call, you change your mind." Still without looking at me he walks up the hill into the forest.

Back in the living room I pick up my keys, put them down, and rub my face with my hands. Mungo settles back onto her sleeping pad and watches me as I pace. Her look seems to say *I can't believe that you'd do that to him. Your only brother.*

I pick up the phone and punch the buttons.

Rebecca's answering machine comes on and I listen to the outgoing message that no longer includes my name. It's Saturday, but next I call her desk at the newspaper anyway. She answers on the first ring.

"The *Post*. Rebecca Hersh."

"It's me."

There's a pause at the other end of the line. My heart sinks from what had been a desperate, hopeful height at the sound of her voice. Like hitting the bottom of a big roller-coaster drop. It's amazing the way such a short moment of silence can do that.

"How are you, Anton?"

"I'm missing you." I want to blurt out that I'd just seen my brother but I know I can't. Not right now. Not just because of the legal implications, but because that one time she'd met him—on the ridge in Chile—he'd really freaked her out.

There is another pause and then a sigh. I picture Rebecca leaning back in her chair and tucking her hair behind her ears.

"It's only been four days, but it seems like forever, doesn't it?" Her voice sounds detached, and the words are guarded.

For the past six months, throughout the trial that has taken up so much of my time and energy, I'd been commuting to the Federal District Courthouse in Cheyenne from Rebecca's apartment in Denver. During that time I'd gotten to know her better than I have ever known any woman. And it was fantastic. Unbelievable. Even though my career had gone to hell, the relationship was better than anything I could imagine. I would return each night to find her making me a simple dinner at home because the publicity was so bad we didn't like to go out. We would drink wine or sangria or beer. After eating we'd put on music and then make love. Each time it was memorable. Slow on the floor in front of the fire. Laughing as we braced ourselves at the kitchen counter. Growling as we tore up the bed. With wet bodies smacking and slinging water in the shower. I can still hear her growling and shouting as she'd bitten my neck.

The change was abrupt. It had been about a month ago. I came home from a particularly grueling day, when I'd had to swallow insult after insult on the witness stand, my face growing bright red with shame and caged fury, to find Rebecca with an almost fearful look in her eyes. I didn't know if she was starting to believe the things that were being said about me or if she'd found another lover or if it was something else entirely. She wouldn't say. And I was too afraid of pushing her to ask.

Over the next few weeks, until I left for Jackson four days ago, we still sometimes half-dreamily talked about our future together. But she did it with a measuring look in her eyes, as if I were being given an exam. My responses never appeared to be quite correct. I could feel her growing away from me. It was like a diaphanous curtain had dropped between us. I couldn't quite touch her—feel her naked skin— the way I had before.

"Yeah, it seems like more than forever, 'Becca. I tried to call you late last night but you didn't answer."

Another pause. "I was staying at my dad's place in Boulder."

I realize I could call him and check in some casual way. Use my investigative skills. But I won't do that. Love is supposed to be about trust. And anyway, I won't demean myself in that way. I won't become some jealous boyfriend watching from the shadows. A stalker. I won't start down that dark path—who knows where it might lead?

"I tried to call you, too," she says. "Early this morning."

"I was climbing. Skiing, actually."

"Where?"

"The East Face of Teewinot. Why do you want to know?" She'd never before asked about the details. They wouldn't mean anything to her.

"Alone?"

"No, I had a partner. A prosecutor here who's being stalked." It seems like a bad time to mention any more of the details, like the fact that it's a young woman, a movie star's daughter, and someone who loves doing that sort of thing.

Rebecca sighs audibly. "Were you safe?"

I know what this sigh means. Ever since Patagonia at

Christmas, when the sight of my brother soloing up toward us had caused such an intense reaction, she has disapproved of my need for getting lethal amounts of air beneath my heels. The sigh shows that at least she still cares if I kill myself or not.

"Of course. It was easy. Just a hill, really."

"How do you spell Teewinot?"

"Why?"

"Because I'm looking it up on the Internet to see if it's really a hill or not."

Damn. Unlike me, she has no qualms about using her investigative skills.

I spell it for her and recall the post-Patagonia climbing I had done over the last few months when I was living with her. The times I set the alarm for the 2:00 A.M. drive to Rocky Mountain National Park—where there are thousand-foot walls smeared with winter ice—she clung to me in our bed and asked me not to go. And when I went anyway she would be pissed about it for days. I had reveled in her resentment, thinking it came from love.

She tried to explain her aversion to my climbing forays during one of our recent but less passionate arguments: "I can't understand it, Anton, why you love going to those places, risking your life like that. It's all so macho and superficial. Monochromatic, too. Devoid of life. Rocks. Ice. Snow. You only see blue sky occasionally, between storms. People aren't supposed to be there. What are you chasing? Or running from? There's nothing up there."

But if I'm superficial and bent, then that's what I am. You can't change something that elemental. I was good enough for her before—what's changed? But as I think about her words, I realize what I love about her other than her sleek, pale body and the occasionally sharp tongue. It's her ability to put things into words, to take things I never even consider and put them before me in a neat package. It's what makes her a very good journalist. She's my guide to my own world.

"You lied, Anton. That's not a hill. Christ. I can't believe you skied that." There is no admiration in her voice. Instead it's accusation. There is something brittle, breaking, like she might be about to cry. It's so uncharacteristic it makes me grip the phone until my knuckles turn white.

What the hell is going on?

"Can you come up here next week?" I ask. "I really want—I really *need* to see you. We need to talk, 'Becca."

"Yeah. I guess we do."

There's another long pause. Do we approach it now, five hundred miles apart, or do we put it off until we can look into each other's face when we say and hear whatever it is that needs to be said? By putting it off at least I'll be able to hold on to hope awhile longer. I close my eyes and hear the blood starting to pound in my ears. I'm getting angry as well as scared.

"Call me tonight and I'll let you know if I can make it," she says before laying down the phone.

SIX

IT'S ALREADY DARK when I pull up in front of Cali's house. The two-story Victorian stands near the center of town. It has a six-foot hedge surrounding the front yard and obscuring most of the lower level. The house must have been purchased with Hollywood money, as no assistant county attorney can afford this kind of real estate. I know from looking for my rental that property like this sells for almost a million dollars in glamorous Jackson. But the house is small and simple compared to the magazine pictures I've seen of her mother's fifteen-thousand-square-foot ranch house up in the valley.

A man looks asleep behind the wheel of a small sedan parked across the street. A Hertz sticker on the back bumper indicates that the car is a rental. The man inside is illuminated by a streetlight a little ways down the block. A goatee attempts to hide a recessed chin and his red hair is pulled back in a ponytail. He doesn't move at all when I walk up alongside his car.

I stand there for a minute, watching through the open driver's-side window as the man's chest rises and falls with the slow rhythm of unconsciousness. His mouth is hanging open and he snores lightly through it. His head is tilted back, the prominent Adam's apple bobbing. Looking at him, I feel the anger building once again. And I realize that tonight I'm slightly unhinged. Seeing my brother and then talking with Rebecca has shaken me; I feel like a steep slope precariously packed with wind-loaded snow. There's a lot of energy on the verge of being released.

Next to him, on the front seat, a handgun is half-hidden under a newspaper. A cheap baby monitor rests on the seat, too. Quiet static issues from the tinny speaker. Through the hiss I can hear a distant clunking sound, probably a drawer being slammed shut.

Leaning into the driver's-side window, I reach over the man and slide the gun from under the paper. Incredibly, he doesn't wake up. I hold the 9-mm Glock pistol at an angle in front of his face then slam back the chamber so the bullet inside leaps into the man's gaping mouth.

He comes awake with a loud squawk—"Aack!"—and throws himself away from me, across the seat. Then he recognizes me through blurry eyes. "God!" He spits the bullet onto the dashboard.

"I'm not, Jim, but McGee and I will make sure you burn in hell if anything's happened to the girl."

He rubs his face. "Hey, I'm sorry, Anton. It got hot in the sun and she wasn't doing anything anyway—said she was going to take a nap, and I guess I just—"

We both look at the speaker as the sound of a woman's humming grows louder for a moment before it fades away.

"Where did you put the transceiver?"

"In her living room. Look, man, I told her all she had to do was scream and I'd come running."

"If we were in the Army, Ross McGee would shoot you for falling asleep at your post. This guy came after her with duct tape and a stun gun. It's serious, so stay awake when you're watching her. Understand?"

"Yeah, man. Look, I'm sorry—" Jim says, staring down at his lap as I treat him like a misbehaving child.

"Shut up, Jim."

Then I get a little more control over myself. "Listen, this guy's for real. And it's possible he's a cop." I tell him about how Cali had broken up with a sergeant in the Sheriff's Office only a month ago, and that he hadn't taken it well. I describe Wokowski, too, saying he's a big, blond guy with an attitude and a face like a pit bull's. Jim will know what I mean if he sees him.

"Go back to your plane or wherever you're staying and get some sleep. I might need you to take over again later tonight. Leave your cell phone on."

Even though Jim is ten years older than me, I've been senior to him since my second year as a DCI agent. People I've talked to say he's a good guy but suspect he's spent too much time under cover, hanging around with low-life producers of methamphetamine. Their lifestyle has infected him, reducing his ambitions and eliminating his cop's zeal. They say he's perpetually trying to get the men he informs on—his friends, as he's come to see it—special deals with the state's prosecutors. And he's often too chickenshit to take part in the arrests. McGee should have fired him years ago but McGee is as loyal to his agents as they are to him. At least until there is evidence that they've committed a crime.

Jim pulls himself together and drives away without looking back at me.

Watching his taillights turn the corner, I feel a little less angry but diminished in some way. I'm not cut out for bullying. I stand in the street for a minute, breathing deep, willing myself to lighten up.

The upper windows of Cali's house are all bright. Lace curtains prevent me from seeing much inside, but I'm reassured by the ornate iron bars that have been bolted to the downstairs windows and the outdoor floodlight that clicks on crisply as I push through the wooden gate between the tall hedges.

I walk up onto the porch. An illuminated alarm keypad has been installed to the right of the door. I notice that it's turned on—the red light is lit, indicating it's armed. While Jim might not be very good security, the alarm system is. Before I have a chance to knock the door swings open.

Cali stands just inside, wearing a sleeveless black sheath dress that reaches almost to her knees. Black cowboy boots cover her feet and ankles. Her short blonde hair is curlier than it had been earlier. There are diamonds in her ears and, in concession to the party's Western theme, a red bandanna folded and tied around her neck. It appears she's even wearing makeup. She couldn't look more different from our ski trip in the morning. This is almost like another woman.

"Excuse me, ma'am," I say, pretending to peer beyond her. "I'm here to pick up Cali Morrow."

She grins before stepping forward to punch me hard in the chest.

"Don't give me a hard time, Anton." She glances at my untucked shirt, tan jeans, and worn-out running shoes with their mismatched laces and duct-taped toes. "You look, uh, fine, too."

"I've got a coat in the car. Real cashmere. From Italy, I think."

"Don't worry about it. There's no one you need to impress unless you're thinking about taking up acting."

I laugh and touch the scar on my cheek. "Not with a face like this."

She looks at me speculatively. "You're not giving yourself enough credit. It gives you character."

A chubby orange cat slinks onto the porch between her boots. It starts to entwine itself between my legs. Even though I've never felt much of an affinity for cats, I politely bend to stroke it.

"Who's this?"

Before Cali can answer, the cat hisses then spits. The hair spikes all the way down its back. It leaps away from me as if I'd touched it with a hot wire and disappears into some bushes.

"What happened? What did you do to him?" She looks as alarmed as the cat. She scans the yard and the bushes that wrap around it.

I hold out my hands innocently. "I just petted him. He must have smelled my dog."

"But Lester *likes* dogs."

"Mine's sort of an unusual dog. She's actually a wolf." Then I address the bushes. "Sorry, Lester."

Cali finally smiles again, unsure if I'm kidding and then seeing from my expression that I'm not. "A wolf? Wow. I want to meet her."

"I'll bring her around sometime," I say without enthusiasm. Mungo is not the sort of pet I'm proud to own. Aside from smiling, wetting herself and cowering are not great dog tricks I'm anxious to show off. "Is it okay for Lester to be running around loose? With all the coyotes and big cats around town?"

"Oh yeah. Lester can take care of himself. I've had him forever. He's been doing his own thing for nine years."

She closes and locks her door behind her. I note the gleaming dead bolt with professional approval. Like the bars, security lights, and alarm, it appears brand-new. "I hope you got some sleep today, Anton. This could go late."

I receive another punch when I grimace the way I had on the trail.

"You're going to have fun, jerk."

SEVEN

THE PARKING LOT at Molly's Steakhouse is overflowing with rented SUVs and Hummers, and even the street in front is loaded to capacity. We end up parking the Pig on a residential street almost two blocks away from the barn-shaped restaurant. Cali laughs when I press a button on my key chain to trigger the truck's alarm.

"Who's going to steal that pile of rust?"

"It's not as crappy as it looks. It's got a new engine and a CD player," I tell her, not mentioning that there is also a small .22 Beretta hidden under the dashboard, and red and blue flashing lights concealed behind the front grille. "And I know you'll find this hard to believe, but there are a few people in this state who don't like me very much."

"I've heard that about you," she teases.

I try to enjoy the walk in the night air, which has finally begun to cool. The hours ahead, I expect, will be filled with too much noise and too many people. My vision scans the sidewalk ahead for any sign of a lurking psychopath. The eye in my head, though, is watching me. That trouble-waiting-to-happen feeling is still there. I could easily do something really dumb tonight.

A warning flares in my mind when Cali's fingers brush against my wrist. The fluttering touch is repeated several times as we walk side by side on the narrow wooden sidewalk. Then her fingers lock around my wrist and slide down to my own fingers, where they entwine themselves. I don't have time to think about what to do or say—we're already there.

People are standing in line to enter the restaurant. They're dressed as I feared, wearing what real Westerners would only wear to a rodeo or as costumes on Halloween. Nearly everyone sports cowboy hats and boots. Embroidered denim and leather make up the rest of their clothes. At the door a young man with a ponytail and a discreet earphone checks names off on a list. A smile-faced sign is tacked on the wall behind him, reading, "No Media, Please," as if Wyoming is full of hungry tabloid reporters. Two crew-cut security guards, probably local off-duty cops, stand behind him ready to enforce the edict.

Cali doesn't speak to anyone as we wait our turn to enter. I assume she has been out of the Hollywood limelight too long to be easily recognized. And I'm relieved to realize that none of these out-of-towners appears to recognize me. The only good thing about my notoriety is that it's local. Even the security guards are too busy ogling the women and the movie people to pay any attention to me.

Cali gives her name and the kid with the ponytail shows us a too-perfect set of small, feral teeth. "Of course!" he says happily. "It's good to finally meet you, dear." He kisses her cheek. Then he beams at me as he crosses off Cali's name and writes *with date*. When I answer his query about my name, I'm happy to see that he scribbles *Antonio Burns* as if it were *John Doe*.

We follow the line of partygoers into the restaurant's single, wide room. It's about the size of a basketball court. The peanut shells that cover the floor crunch under our feet.

There are already fifty or sixty people inside, and there is room for about a hundred more. They are packed ten-deep around the long bar at the far end of the room. Banquet tables with red-and-white-checked tablecloths stand in perfectly aligned rows down the restaurant's center. These are empty except for flowers, discarded purses and coats, and tin buckets of peanuts. Bluegrass music plays over the speakers.

We start to move past three men with drinks in their hands. They're slouching against a wall just inside the entrance. About my age or younger, all three are dressed as foolishly as the rest of the crowd in embroidered pearl-button shirts, fringed vests, and big hats. One of them wears all black like a television gunfighter. He has an ornate holster of Mexican silver slung low around his waist. There are a pair of toy pistols with long barrels on his hips.

Ignoring my attempt at a polite smile, the three "cowboys" all stare intently at Cali. Their eyes linger on her legs and butt as she passes ahead of me.

One of them says loudly in a fake-Western accent, "Fine-looking heifer you got there, pardner. I bet she could take my bull by the horns."

I slow and pause, trying to take in the extent of the comment. His friends snicker and leer some more, glancing at me then away again at Cali. One of them even bends forward and cocks his head for a better view of her ass. Cali keeps moving but I see the muscles tighten in her shoulders and back.

"I might have to put my brand on her," the wanna-be gunfighter in black says in the same mocking accent. "Then we could take turns milking each other." His two friends bray with laughter.

I come to a complete stop and stare at the men who've dared to say these things loud enough for Cali to hear. Who have said them to me, as if I'm expected to just take it, blush, and keep on moving.

Their eyes are already red and watery from too many

drinks. The one who spoke first looks away from me then down at the floor. The gunfighter meets my stare, still smirking. I can no longer hear the music. In the periphery of my vision I note Cali turning around and coming back toward us. Her hand touches my arm but it feels as if she's touching someone else.

"Let's go, Anton," she says.

"What did you say?" I ask the gunfighter.

He speaks with deliberate slowness, as if he's talking to an idiot. "I said I'd like to fuck your girlfriend. Up the ass, maybe." His eyes finally leave mine and leer again toward Cali. His tongue parts his lips, flickering.

"Don't say anything, Anton. Let's go," Cali says from far, far away.

"Come outside. We need to have a talk," I say to the man.

He puffs up his chest and sticks out his jaw. "Do you know who I am, scar face?"

I feel a broad smile tightening my cheeks. I can't hold back a short laugh. "Do you know who *I* am?"

One of the other three men steps between us. "Don't mess with him, dude," he tells me. "You know who he is? He's Danny Gorgon."

The name is a little bit familiar. Some action-movie hero, I think. Shoot-'em-ups with lots of gunfire, broken glass, and blood. All of it fake. I push away the man who'd reverently spoken his friend's name without taking my eyes off Gorgon.

"Come outside," I say again.

"Get out of my sight, cocksucker." He pulls one of the toy guns from his holster and touches the barrel between my eyes.

Moving my right hand across my body then up and out again, I catch the wrist of the hand holding the gun and jerk it around. The pain of the twisting joints in his elbow and shoulder spins Gorgon until he's facing the wall. The toy gun drops softly into the broken peanut shells at my feet. His hat is knocked off his head when his forehead touches the plaster.

In profile, as Gorgon turns, I see his mouth drop open in anger and shock. When he tries to shake free from my grasp, I bounce him hard off the wall then lift his turned wrist high up between his shoulder blades.

"You're under arrest," I say softly in his ear. "For . . . Disorderly Conduct." I try to remember from my police-academy days seven years ago if the elements of that crime include offensive language or fighting words. I think so. I hope so.

Someone's fingers pull at my shirtsleeve but I knock them away with my free hand. I reach up under my shirt for the handcuffs clipped next to the H&K on my belt. People are gaping from the entryway. Others are hurrying toward us from the bar. At the forefront is a woman dressed normally in a navy blue suit. Like me, she is Hispanic—another exotic at this party. Also like me, she's armed. Her jacket flutters open as she trots and I see an old-fashioned shoulder harness and the butt of a surprisingly large automatic. A real one.

I've gotten the handcuffs around only one of Gorgon's wrists when he tries to shake loose again. I bounce his face off the wall a second time.

"Let go of him!" the woman wearing the big gun says as she comes up to us. She has a hand up under her jacket now, touching her gun. The two friends of Gorgon's, who have been crowding in behind me and yelling, quiet down and make way for her.

"Miss, you're interfering with a lawful arrest. Back off."

She looks puzzled and stops, but she doesn't step back.

"Who the hell are you?"

"Wyoming Division of Criminal Investigation." I snatch Gorgon's other wrist and ratchet the remaining cuff tight around it. Tight enough that it should hurt. "You better explain to me why you're carrying that cannon," I add over my shoulder.

Another woman is now pushing through the gathering crowd. She's asking, "What's happening? What's happening?" I glance in her direction and immediately see why the crowd is parting so eagerly for her.

She could be Cali's older, prettier sister. The features of her face are the same—the color of her eyes, the oval shape, the small, pointed chin—but on this woman the overall effect is much leaner. Sexier. Like Cali she's blonde and tan, only her hair is far longer and her tan has an orange sheen to it that you don't get from the sun. A pair of low-cut blue jeans so tight there must be Lycra in the denim that encases her legs and, just barely, her hips. Her upper torso is covered by a short leather vest studded with rhinestones. She appears to be unusually delicate and tiny because I expect her to be much bigger. Screen-sized. She moves with an easy grace and assuredness that her daughter does not possess.

"What's happening?" Alana Reese asks again, this time to the woman with the gun.

"Apparently this guy's a Wyoming cop. He's arresting Danny for something."

"Why is there a policeman at my party?"

"I invited him, Mom," Cali says, stepping forward.

"Oh Cali! What have you done now?" Alana Reese says it with a despairing chuckle then opens her bare arms to embrace her daughter. "You're always causing trouble," she chides. "Now, please, ask him to stop whatever he's doing, dear. Have him let Danny go."

"Anton," Cali says, "please let him go."

The reality of the situation is beginning to dawn on me. Arresting a celebrity on a petty charge like Disorderly Conduct will probably only get me in more trouble with the office. My employment there is tenuous enough. And I'm embarrassed to once again be the center of attention. I don't need to make it worse just because of a juvenile sense of chivalry or machismo. So like a well-trained guard dog I fish in my pocket for the handcuff keys and release Gorgon.

He rubs his wrists and then his forehead. There's a red

spot that will turn black-and-blue from where I'd twice bounced him off the wall. He fixes me with an action hero's deadly glare before allowing his friends to pull him toward the bar.

"You'll pay for that, asshole," he says to me before moving into the crowd.

I kick his hat through the peanut shells after him. "You forgot something."

EIGHT

"PLEASE, EVERYONE, GO AWAY." Alana Reese makes shooing motions at the mob that's pressing in around us.

Like good flunkies they wander off while talking excitedly to one another and stealing glances back at us. The bluegrass music continues to play on the restaurant's sound system. The sound is slowly coming back to me as my narrow focus recedes.

"Mom, meet Antonio Burns. He's going to find the guy who tried to get in my window."

Looking at Cali's mother, I feel the full force of her beauty and poise. She holds out her hand and I shake it gently. The hand is cold but electric. While I've always been smug and unimpressed with the occasional Hollywood people I've seen vacationing in Wyoming, I can't help but feel as if I'm in the presence of a superstar. There is definitely something otherworldly—a bit of magic—in a woman like this. A woman so sure of herself.

"You appear to know how to make an entrance, young man," Alana Reese says with a smile. "Let me introduce you to another police officer. This is Angela Hernandez. She's with the FBI, and she's hoping to arrest someone who's been bothering *me*."

The federal agent doesn't smile when she grasps my hand. "Where have I heard your name before, Antonio Burns?" she asks.

I shrug. "I have no idea." Then to Cali's mother I say, "I'm sorry about the commotion. But that man said something unbelievably crude about your daughter—"

Alana Reese laughs and interrupts me. "Please, Mr. Burns. Don't be ridiculous. Being in the spotlight makes our skins thick. I'm sure my daughter took no offense."

I look at Cali, sure she had been offended to the core, but she just shakes her curls at me.

"Danny can be quite ungovernable. And passionate, too. But I assure you that whatever he said, he was just having a little fun. Now if you'll excuse me, I have some guests to calm."

My eyes can't help but linger on her as she turns away. She glances over her shoulder and catches me with another knowing smile. "Cali, would you mind coming with me?"

I'm left alone with Angela Hernandez, although I keep a close eye on my ward as she moves around the room with her mother. We both stand with our backs to the wall, right about where I'd pushed Danny Gorgon's face against it. I sense the FBI agent studying me carefully, maybe disdainfully, taking in my shoes, my painter's jeans, the heavy brown shirt with its fraying collar, and then scrutinizing the scar on my face. A bit of arrogance is a given with FBI agents; like us at DCI, they call themselves special agents. Unlike us, they seem to take the "special" part seriously. Being a minority woman in a traditionally white man's job, a certain defensiveness and aggressive response is understandable.

"Are you Latino? *Habla español?*" she asks.

"*En el lado de mi madre.*" On my mother's side.

"*Me pienso recuerdo donde oí hablar usted.*" I think I

remember where I heard about you, she says, turning fully to face me.

I cut her off. "Ms. Reese's being threatened, too?"

Hernandez rolls her eyes. "She's been getting threats for more than twenty-five years, and she's got private bodyguards three times my size. I think she just likes having a pet agent with a badge as a part of her traveling show."

"Why is the FBI involved?" I would have expected that the Los Angeles Police Department would handle any threats against the Hollywood elite. And the town police or Teton County sheriff's when she's at her vacation home in Jackson.

The agent answers my question with a question. "How come you're involved in Cali's case?"

"She and her boss, the County Attorney, called the State Attorney General and asked that our office be assigned. There's a potential conflict of interest, with Cali being a prosecutor here, so they wanted us to handle it."

"These kind of women usually get what they want. You wouldn't believe it if I told you who Alana called to have the FBI assigned to watch out for her."

Money and fame have their privileges. I remember hearing that Alana Reese is one of the few Republicans in the movie world, and that she actively campaigns for that party's candidates. A Republican administration would owe her a lot of favors. I guess that Agent Hernandez was selected to be the movie star's personal guard dog because she's attractive in a full-figured way. Or could be if she smiled. She has glossy black hair pulled back in a ponytail and a face like a Mayan princess— broad cheekbones, a pinched, curving nose, and very little chin. The man's white shirt she wears beneath the navy coat is unbuttoned to the top of a lacy bra. A good portion of her prominent breasts are lifted into view. Despite the conservative blue suit, that unbuttoned shirt looks pretty Hollywood for an FBI agent.

"I'm still hoping this will be temporary, but unfortunately the lady likes me," Agent Hernandez tells me.

"Well, that's easy to fix."

"You could probably give lessons, judging by your performance here already." For a moment I think she might smile. Her lips, though, remain horizontal. Only the skin around her eyes crinkles. "It wouldn't be good for my career, though. And anyway, just between us, I've been trying to write a screenplay. So all this may work out to my benefit someday."

I like her candor. Most FBI agents that I've known would be furious at being assigned to what amounts to guard duty—although some of the men might be pleased by the potential fringe benefits. Instead, Angela Hernandez accepts it cheerfully and intends to use it to her advantage.

"How serious is the threat to Cali? You think this guy will come after her again? Alana's worried about it."

"She doesn't look too worried." I nod to where the star is standing with a man wearing a cowboy hat, laughing close to his face and massaging his upper arm with one hand while holding a martini glass with the other.

"Yeah, I know how it looks," Hernandez says. "She's like this all the time in public. She could have two broken legs and she'd still be smiling like that. Tell me about what happened— I just heard the secondhand version from Alana."

"I just saw the report for the first time today. I'd say it's pretty serious. And weird. The guy broke her kitchen window and tried to crawl through with a stun gun and a roll of tape. He didn't seem too concerned with stealth, although he did run away when an old family friend came along."

"Any idea who he is?"

"Nothing definite. No prints or anything—he was wearing gloves. Anyway, I'm just getting started. How about the threats against Mom?"

She holds one hand in the air, palm to the ground, and lets it waver back and forth. "Like I said, I think she just likes bragging that she has a personal FBI agent. She gets boxes of the stuff. Threats, love letters, pictures, and all that. A few months ago some *demente* cut off his penis and mailed it. So now all mail coming into all her houses goes through an X-ray machine and then is opened by her private security staff. The only thing that's happened up here, though, is that some crazy fan broke into her ranch a couple of weeks ago and stole her old wedding dress and some other personal things. We should compare notes sometime. In the last few months I've become an expert on stalkers. Plus I have a master's in psychology."

We exchange cards and arrange to have coffee on Monday morning.

"If you are who I think you are, it might be interesting to get to know you better," she says, finally giving me a slight smile.

I look back blankly, pretending I have no idea what she's talking about. "I look forward to it. See you Monday."

When she leaves, I'm left standing alone against the wall near the entrance. Cali is still with her mother at the bar, smiling as they talk with a circle of her mother's admirers. Aside from that group, everyone else in the place seems to be gawking in my direction. Their stares don't look friendly. Either they have figured out who I am or I've offended them all by accosting one of their stars.

A waiter comes by and I order a beer.

A half hour later I'm finishing my third Snake River Ale and still standing alone. Even though I'm not thirsty, the beers have been necessary because I have nothing else to do. Cali finally returns to end my awkward vigil. The times she had been in view between bodies and big hats I watched her put away at least three martinis. Now she looks a little unsteady on her high-riding heels as she comes toward me.

With her is a tall, older man, who I'd noticed earlier also alone on the fringe of the crowd. He is dressed in boots, jeans, and a Western shirt, but they look authentic on him. The clothes are well used and not ironed or starched.

"Anton, I want you to meet my uncle Bill." Then to

Laughlin, "This is Antonio Burns. He's the cop who's investigating what happened the other night."

He looks older than I'd expected, this legendary hardman. But then he must be in his mid-sixties by now. He'd been putting up hard routes in the Canadian Rockies long before I was born. Wrinkles pattern every inch of his tan face. But he still looks very fit, strong, and spare, with stooped shoulders from decades of carrying a pack in the backcountry. His white hair lies in wisps on a freckled skull.

"It's a pleasure to meet you," I say, shaking his hand. It is calloused and I can feel the power radiating down through the sinews of his forearm. There's a tremble to it, too, that surprises me. I notice that the tremble runs through his entire body. "I've been up some of your routes in the Bugaboos. About five years ago my brother and I did Black Lightning on the North Face of Snowpatch Spire. If you don't mind my saying so, 5.9 A2 my ass."

That makes him smile in a lopsided way. His eyes are wet and rheumy but sharp beneath the fluid when he looks at me.

"You didn't like my grades."

"We felt sandbagged, my brother and me. And that must have been twenty years after you did the first ascent." I recall reading in a guidebook that all Laughlin's early routes had asterisks beside them because, the editors believed, it was commonly known that they were often dangerously underrated so that a second ascensionist would have no idea what he was getting into.

He asks what other routes I'd done and I tell him. The memories are plainly visible on his face as I mention their names. He smiles at his drink and nods his head.

"Are you still climbing?" I ask him.

"Nope. Last time I tied into a rope was a long time ago. I lost the desire when I lost too many friends."

The mortality rate was high for climbers of his generation, before there were modern means of placing protection.

In his den my dad has a collection of photographs of friends and partners he'd lost in the early days. And he'd been nowhere as prolific a climber as Bill Laughlin.

" 'Course," he continues, glancing at Cali and nodding slightly as if in apology, "some of my best friends I lost in other ways." Then he turns back to me. "You're looking after my girl, Officer Burns?"

"Yes, sir." The *sir* is strange coming out of my mouth. I don't use the word lightly. But it feels natural when addressing this man. "I understand that you may have saved her life the other night."

"Nah, it wasn't like that. I was just walking down the street. Can't sleep much these days—you think too much when you're old, so I do a lot of walking at night. Anyway, I heard glass break and saw a fellow trying to crawl in Cali's window. I yelled at him and he ran off. That's all."

"Did you get a good look at him?"

"Nope. My vision's not what it used to be. And I think he was wearing something that covered his face."

"Any idea of his size or shape?"

He shakes his head. "He was just a shadow. But he was no climber—could see that," he adds with a smile. "That fellow was having a hard time with the window. Now excuse me, I think I'd better be getting home. I'm tired and I'm afraid I've worn out my welcome in these parts."

Cali starts to protest but he holds up his hand. Instead of speaking she cuts a glare to where her mother is standing close to two men and smiling coquettishly as she sips from her glass, then Cali stands on tiptoe in her cowboy boots and kisses Bill Laughlin on the corner of his lips. I like watching her do it—I like watching the way the old man's eyes seem to light up and get even wetter.

When he's gone Cali says to me, "We need to go." Her face is suddenly tight and there is a teaspoon-sized bulge of clenched muscle by each jaw.

"What's the matter?"

"Mom wants you—us—out of here, too. Danny and his pals are looking to make some more trouble."

I know she added the "us" part to soften the blow of my being ejected from the party. Voluntarily or not, I'm happy to leave.

At the bar I see Danny Gorgon and his friends looking our way. It pains me not to gaze back, but then I could be stuck standing here for minutes in a childish stare fight. Instead I do something equally juvenile—I touch my forehead with the heel of my hand and give him a smiling wince— ouch!—to remind him of the way I'd bounced his head off the wall a half hour earlier. He doesn't smile back.

I remember a lesson my father taught my brother and me. *When you hurt a man, hurt him bad. You don't want him waking up in the morning thinking maybe next time he can take you. Thinking about revenge. You want him waking up scared, not mad.* From the look in Danny Gorgon's eyes I suspect I've violated Dad's rule.

It's full night when we get outside. The air is chillier now and Cali stays close by my side as we walk the two blocks back to the truck. I hear boot heels thunking on the plank sidewalk behind us. When I turn around there are three silhouettes about a half block away.

"How long are they going to be in town?" I ask, staring at the dark shapes.

"Two weeks. Ugh. They're doing readings for my mom's next movie. Development, it's called. Danny is going to play her love interest. He must be more than twenty years younger than her. By the way, that was really gross, what he said before you handcuffed him. So, even though Mom doesn't agree, I want to say thanks. But she's right, too, you know. You should just ignore them. They're bored and looking for some excitement. And guys like Danny, they don't have any limits."

NINE

"I DON'T WANT TO GO HOME YET. God, after all that, I really need a drink."

We are back in the Iron Pig, pulling away from the curb. I spin the wheel hard to U-turn on the narrow street and feel the oversized tires rub against the fenders. The headlights play over the sidewalk we'd come down but the three shadows are gone.

"I saw you put down a few already. Martinis, it looked like. That's not enough?"

She laughs. "Not nearly. I'm just getting started. It's Saturday night, Anton."

We drive to a small bar she suggests. I'm not particularly surprised by her choice—it's a bar where I've heard the local cops hang out—but I am surprised by the reception she receives. When we walk into a murky, smoke-filled room that's lit only by neon beer signs and a few very dim overheads behind the bar, the welcome is in the form of averted eyes and a few sullen stares.

Cali appears oblivious to the hostility. Smiling and waving

to people who don't smile or wave back, she leads me through a moderate crowd to a high-backed booth against one wall. As we slide in I recognize one of the men standing near our table from the afternoon's meeting. He ignores me as well as Cali despite having seen us. I check for Sergeant Wokowski's broad pit bull's face and am relieved to not see him. After the exchange of barbs at the SWAT team briefing and the roughhousing at the party, I've already had two confrontations too many today. The jukebox starts playing a Lenny Kravitz song—"American Woman"—so loud that everyone in the bar has to shout. A waitress appears and before I can stop her, Cali orders us each a shot of tequila and a beer.

"I'm sort of on duty," I tell her. "Those drinks are all yours."

"Please don't be a wimp, Anton. I need a drink and I need someone to drink it with."

"If your pen pal makes a move tonight, I don't want to be stumbling around and trying to find my gun." I'm also afraid that, as tired as I am, any more alcohol will increase the likelihood of further stupidity on my part. If I were really smart, I would call Jim right now, tell him to take over, and go home. But I still haven't talked to her about Wokowski. And I'm curious about the way she'd held my hand in hers earlier.

The waitress, who is tan and strong and either a climber or a kayaker judging by the size of her forearms and the rippling muscles in her shoulders, returns with the four glasses—two big and two small—on a platter. She puts one mismatched set in front of each of us. I push my pair across the table, then hesitate and end up pulling back the beer. Looking at me, Cali lifts a shot of tequila and tosses it down. No lime, no salt. The agaves twist her face until she composes it again with a long pull on her beer.

"I can't believe the old dragon kicked us out," she says,

breathing hard from the shot and the fire that must be spreading through her belly.

"She didn't want you to leave. Just me. And I probably deserved it."

"She knew you were with me, and I'm her damn daughter! She totally snubbed Uncle Bill, too, and she has to know how sick he is."

"I noticed that he didn't look too good. And I saw how much you like him."

Cali toys with the second shot, tilting it back and forth so that the gold liquid threatens to spill from first one side and then the other.

"He's been like a father to me. He was my dad's best friend, you know. Uncle Bill was with him when he died in a forest fire. They were both smoke jumpers. My dad did it so he could ski all winter without having to work. Bill did it so he could climb."

I'm reminded again of my old life, living out of the back of my truck and thinking of nothing but mountains. Right now I'm missing it more and more despite the longing for a home I'd felt before calling Rebecca.

"What's wrong with him? He was shaking like he had MS or Parkinson's."

"An aneurysm, in his brain. It bled once already, then stopped on its own. An MRI showed that it's inoperable. It's in a place where it would be too dangerous to cut. And they say it's going to bleed again. Probably soon."

"Are they treating it?"

"He's taking some pills that are supposed to help, but the doctors say another bleed is inevitable. He doesn't have long to live."

I'm sorry to hear it. I'd enjoyed getting to meet the legendary hardman. And I see clearly by the expression on her face just how much Cali adores him. But I'm glad that he still seemed strong and proud. He'd flirted with death for years—it wouldn't be hard to fall into its dark embrace.

"What did he mean when he said he'd worn out his welcome at the party?"

Cali sets down the shot glass and sips from her beer instead. "He probably meant Mom was ignoring him again. See, I'm pretty sure he's in love with her, and always has been. Ever since I can remember he's always done anything she's asked him to, from looking out for me in the summertime to taking care of her house and horses. But she's never liked having him around when she's in town. She acts like he's some pain in the butt that she only puts up with for my sake. I had to beg her to invite him tonight—and I think from the way she was avoiding him, he figured it out."

"That sounds pretty sad." I have an ever-greater feeling of sympathy for the hardman. I wonder if I'm going to spend the next forty years pining after Rebecca. Could he be a future reflection of me?

"Life's a bitch," Cali says. "And sometimes so is my mom."

"Why doesn't she like him?"

Cali shrugs. "Maybe she blames him in some way for what happened to my dad—for being with him when he died and then surviving. It's probably that he brings back bad memories for her. And Mom doesn't like anyone who makes her feel down."

"It can't be easy, having a mother as famous as that."

Now Cali picks up the shot again, salutes me with it, and pours half of it down her throat. After she washes away the taste with more beer she says, "You don't know the half of it, Anton. Most people think I'm so lucky—money, fame, and all that for the asking. But I didn't ask for any of it. And I sure as hell didn't earn any of it. It was just an accident of birth. Mom, on the other hand, has worked all her life for it. It's all that's important to her. It's like when she's not in the spotlight, being beautiful and sexy and glamorous, then she doesn't exist at all. And I don't exist for her either."

She tells me a story about when she'd been competing for a spot on the national ski team. Her mom was supposed to fly in for the competition but her private jet was delayed by a storm. When Alana found out via the telephone that her daughter hadn't won, had in fact come in near last, she'd turned her plane south and gone to the Bahamas instead of attending the dinner and award ceremony with her daughter.

Cali continues smiling faintly as she talks but it's just the alcohol lifting the corners of her lips. There is nothing happy about the way her eyes are growing watery. Bloodshot, too. Then she laughs self-consciously.

"Sorry, Anton. This isn't like me, getting trashed like this. Talking like this. I want to know something about you. Where did you grow up and all that?"

Lately I haven't enjoyed talking about my family, but it would be cruel to put her off after the way she's been opening up.

"My dad was in the Air Force, commanding a unit that performs rescues all over the world," I tell her. "He met my mom when he was training a similar unit in Argentina. After that, my brother and I grew up on military bases from Okinawa to Alaska to Saudi Arabia. It was a weird way to grow up, a shitty way, actually, but not nearly as weird as yours."

She hesitates while asking, "Is, uh, the stuff I've heard about your brother true?"

I sip at my beer. This is exactly the reason I don't like to talk about my family. Suddenly Roberto's standing in front of me again, his ever-present smile fading when I refuse to climb one last time with him. When I more or less told him to get out of my life.

"The general facts probably are," I admit. "He's a junkie and a felon. And he's killed two men that I know of. But he's not evil or vicious. Or some cold-blooded murderer. He's a good man who can't follow rules. He does what he feels is right without considering the aftereffects. My mom says he's *destraillado*. It means unrestrained. Unleashed. He has no sense of consequences. I became a cop because I thought it was the drugs that did it to him. But I'm starting to think I was wrong. It's just the way he is."

"Where is he now? I read about how he escaped from Canon City in Colorado last fall."

"I saw him last Christmas," I say carefully. "He was at my grandfather's *estancia*—ranch. In Argentina."

She looks surprised that I would tell her this. "How come he's not being extradited?"

"My mother's father was a bigwig in the government before he died a couple of years ago. In the bad old days, the Dirty War. My mom's family still has a lot of friends in high places. So Roberto's safe down there. Or as safe as he'll let himself be." I think of Rebecca and my Christmas visit and the solos Roberto has been doing. "He's supposed to come back to the U.S. I've heard he's worked something out with the U.S. Attorney's Office, exchanging information for the dismissal of the escape charge."

"Why would he come back?"

It's something I've been wondering about, too. "I don't know. I guess maybe because he can't. So of course he wants to. And maybe he's trying to atone for some of his past sins. It's hard to say with him."

The two beer mugs on the table are empty. So are the shots in front of Cali. The sight of all the dry glasses reminds me that I'm talking too much. Thinking too much. Cali catches the waitress as she passes and asks her to bring us two more beers.

More people come into the bar. They're mostly men, the blue-collar types you would expect in a bar like this. Boots and belt buckles. Cowboy hats—real ones, sweat-stained and creased. There are a few big women with big hair. A popular fashion in the state is for women of a certain economic background to iron their bangs straight up, often six inches or more. I marvel at the heights.

Someone turns up the jukebox and the bartender dims the lights even more. I notice that the cops and their friends at the bar are still pretending to ignore us.

Needing to change the subject, I lean closer across the table and ask, "What's with the cops in this place? Why aren't they over here saying hi?"

She looks over her shoulder at the bar and smiles crookedly. " 'Cause I dumped their superstar. And because I got him in some hot water."

"Tell me about it." It's time to stop screwing around and get to work.

The waitress sets two full mugs on the table and leaves them with the other empty glasses. Cali waits for her to walk out of earshot before she speaks.

"When I started going out with Wook, it was cool. I had fun with these guys. We'd mess around with each other at the courthouse and all that. I even jumped with them a couple of times."

"Jumped?"

"You know, skydiving. Wook learned it as a smoke jumper, and despite his bum knee, he keeps on doing it."

Maybe the fact that Wokowski was a smoke jumper, just like her father and Bill Laughlin, her adopted uncle, explains some of her attraction to him.

"Then one night about a month ago, I was out to dinner with Wook and a couple of his buddies. We'd just come from a motions hearing on a DUI case where the defendant had also supposedly resisted arrest, but the case was pretty strong and no big deal. At dinner somebody made a joke about how the old man had already paid for his crime, and we should mail him a copy of the videotape after the trial to remind him. I didn't know about any tape—there wasn't one in any of the discovery I'd handed over to the defendant's attorney.

"So I started looking into it, and the next day found it *accidentally* mislabeled in the evidence locker. It turned out that one of the patrol cars had a dashboard-mounted camera running. It showed Wook slamming the guy on the hood, then punching him in the stomach. Like he'd lost it or something. I guess the guy was too drunk or too embarrassed to tell his lawyer about how he got beat up. Maybe he thought no one would believe him. Or maybe they were just waiting to spring it on us at trial. You know, like a discovery violation. Anyway, that day I turned over the tape to the defense attorney, Suzy Casey. She was as pissed about it as I was. She wants Wook charged for assault and misconduct and everything else. It's being investigated internally right now by the Sheriff's Office—I don't know why they didn't bring you guys in on it. Probably they don't want to make too much of a stink. I wanted to dump the DUI, but because the old man has a prior for Careless Driving Causing Injury, my boss is making me go ahead with it. The trial starts Monday. Boy, is that going to be fun." She shakes her head and looks over her shoulder again at the bar. "Ever since then, I've been persona non grata around here. Those guys have even been resisting my subpoenas, failing to appear for hearings, and stuff like that."

"I want to hear more about Wokowski."

Cali drinks some more of her fresh beer. I don't touch mine.

"Wook's smart and handsome. And until that thing with the tape I thought he was the most honest man I've ever met. I've known him my whole life, practically. I spent the summers here, living on Mom's ranch with her caretaker or at Uncle Bill's. Wook grew up here, too. When we were old enough, we both volunteered on Forest Service fire crews. We both became Hot Shots—those are the ground guys that get 'coptered in—at about the same time, then when I went to college he went on to become a smoke jumper until he blew out his knee on a jump in Oregon. He became a cop after that. Anyway, he was always really nice to me when we were on the crew together, but I pretty much ignored him. When I started working for the office we became pals. He came on real strong, and, after a while, I kind of liked that. He'd known me all my life so he wasn't nervous or weird around me. And I didn't get the impression he was trying to make himself into a celebrity or anything. So we dated pretty seriously for a couple of months."

"When did it end?"

"When that thing happened with the videotape. He was upset, said he wanted to explain, but I told him that he was a big fake. That he could go to hell."

I take my first sip of the new beer. "I met him this afternoon," I tell her. "While you were napping, I briefed the SWAT team about identifying clan labs. He seemed like a really nice guy. I liked him a lot."

She cocks her head quizzically for a moment then sees I'm only joking. "He's a jerk. To do that to an old man."

I nod in agreement. But from the look on her face I'm not sure she's entirely over the big, rugged-looking cop.

"Is he a climber? Bill said the guy he'd seen trying to get in your window didn't look like much of a climber."

"No," she answers, with a slight wrinkling of her nose. "His thing is *hunting*. He shoots elk and deer then eats them. If you ask him why, he gives you this spiritual back-to-nature speech that he has down pat."

In Wyoming almost everybody hunts. All the men, at least. Most do it badly, for the simple thrill of killing. But some, unfortunately only a few, do it well and cleanly and without much emotion. Which kind of hunter is Wokowski, and does it matter? I wonder what Angela Hernandez with her master's in psychology would think about a stalking suspect who hunts. Someone who is capable of killing an animal bigger than a man. Then butchering it. I make a mental note to ask her about it when I meet her on Monday.

Cali is looking down at her beer. In a quiet voice, like she's making a confession, she adds, "I don't think he broke the window, Anton. Or wrote the letters. Until the other night, I thought they were just someone's sick joke. I wish my boss hadn't mentioned his name."

I weigh this in my head, taking into account what I suspect about her feelings toward him and the number of drinks she's had. It doesn't add up to a lot, evidence-wise. Wokowski's still at the top of the list. The only guy on the list, as a matter of fact.

"Tomorrow my partner, Jim, is going to try to find out who's been buying stun guns around here. I'm going to go through your old cases and look for any other potential subjects. Right now the playing field is wide open. But, Cali, you've got to admit that Wokowski looks pretty good. You need to watch out for him."

We sit in silence for a while. The jukebox is playing some old Led Zeppelin now. People are yelling at one another and crowding the floor. I finish my beer without thinking and regret it immediately.

"I'm going to the bathroom," she tells me, sliding out of the booth.

I stand up, too, and Cali laughs quickly. "I'm a big girl, Anton. You don't need to hold my hand in the toilet. No one's going to mess with me in a bar full of cops and witnesses."

I look around the bar one more time, searching faces and the breadth of turned backs for something resembling Wokowski's, then let her go. She slips between a shouting couple and disappears into a narrow hallway at the back of the bar.

Alone, I'm more aware of the scrutiny I'm receiving from the bar's mirror and the busy floor. The music is so loud it's giving me a headache. Robert Plant is screaming from the jukebox about a wicked woman standing on street corners. The song ends abruptly just as I'm glancing at my watch to calculate how long it's been since I've slept.

Even over the usual bar noise of laughter and yells, the sound of a distant scream knifes through the smoky air. It's more of an angry shout, really, than a fearful shriek. But it's the same voice I'd heard shouting something far happier this morning. A banging sound accompanies it: *thump-thump-crack!* The jukebox abruptly smothers the noise by launching into something else with lots of guitars and heavy drums.

TEN

NO ONE SEEMS to pay any attention to the shout and bangs that could be heard during the music's interlude. Even the cops I'd noticed earlier only glance toward the rear of the bar—a little puzzled, maybe—before they go back to drinking and yelling over the music. Catfights and domestic spats would be common in a place like this. But hadn't they seen that it was the assistant county attorney they'd been so deliberately ignoring heading back there only minutes earlier? The one they all *knew* had been the victim of an attempted kidnapping?

I stand and begin to shove through the big men and big-haired women. I push at a broad back that blocks my path, knocking a man and the mug of beer in his hand into the little group gathered around him. Someone pushes me back and curses, spraying the back of my neck with spit. As I half run past the jukebox, I punch the glass over the display hard with the heel of my fist in an attempt to shut it off. The CD bounces and begins to repeat. A new chorus of obscenities rises up from all around me. I don't bother stopping to try to turn it off more permanently. I don't bother trying to explain.

Paneled with fake wood and down two short steps, the hallway leading to the bathroom is even darker than the bar. But three doors are evident in the gloom; two small doors on the right and a bigger steel door at the far end. That last one is swinging shut as I leap down the steps. It has an aluminum bar running across its middle and is marked with an "Emergency Exit Only—Alarm Will Sound" sign. I don't hear any alarm.

The first door on my right opens, spilling light into the hallway. A man in a cowboy hat steps out with his hands at his crotch where he's working the buttons on his fly. He looks at me as I approach then steps back. "What?" he says. Behind him is a toilet stall missing a door, a stained urinal, and a sink. Other than that it's empty. "What?" he asks again, looking at me then looking away. He looks nervous and scared as he gently closes the door in my face.

I push open the second door with my left hand so as to keep my right hand free.

This time no light pours out to fill the hallway—it's pitch-black inside. But from the minute amount of ambient light coming from the neon lights in the bar I can make out the gleam of a porcelain toilet bowl and a pair of pale, booted legs kicking on the floor. Over the raucous beat of the now-revived jukebox, I hear angry grunts coming from the writhing shape.

"Cali!" I say as my eyes adjust to the darkness. Four pale limbs are now visible, skittering toward my feet on the floor. My gun is in my hand, pointing at the flailing arms and legs.

The limbs all seem to belong to one person. The torso is cloaked by the black dress that has been pushed up above the triangle of dark-colored underwear. I feel the inside wall for the light switch, find it, and flick it on.

The sudden light reveals Cali swimming out from beneath the scarred wooden walls of an open toilet stall, her shoulders half pinned beneath it as she scoots backward and feetfirst. When her head appears I notice that her hair has become a Medusa tangle. Her eyes are so wide they're almost bulging. A peeling gray strip of duct tape is plastered unevenly across one side of her face. Even when she sees me and the gun pointing at her, she continues making the strange sounds, half outraged grunts of exertion and half sobs of fear.

"Are you hurt?" I yell at her, already turning toward the fire door.

She doesn't answer the question but she doesn't look hurt. Not seriously, at least. There's only a little blood on her forehead from a cut at her hairline.

Holding the H&K in the guard position, two-handed and pointed in front of my feet, I step back into the hall and shove open the emergency door with my hip and shoulder. It swings out into an empty alley full of trash cans and cars. It reeks with the scent of rotting food and stale urine. There's no one in sight, and not even the sound of footsteps fleeing into the night.

The alley is searched by me, uniformed members of the Jackson Police Department and the Teton County Sheriff's Office, several off-duty cops who'd been in the bar, and a couple of drunken "volunteers." After the alley we search the block and then the surrounding blocks but find nothing. It isn't surprising, as none of us are sure exactly what—or who—we're supposed to be looking for. I'd love to find Wokowski crouching behind a trash can, but I don't share this with his brother officers.

Paramedics stay with Cali in the bar, which is now more or less quiet and brightly lit. When I return from my laps around the neighboring blocks they tell me that she's uninjured and alert-and-oriented times four, meaning that there's no indication of impairment to her level of consciousness. Obviously they haven't given her a breath test. Her forehead is a little swollen around where the cut has been cleaned and covered with a Band-Aid.

There's a brief tug-of-war between me and the responding officers. The locals, both town police and county sheriffs, want to be in charge. Only with a lot of badge-waving and declarations of "This is *my* case"—which one of the off-duty cops snickers at because it appears I haven't been managing it too well—am I able to get Cali alone. We sit at a booth in the far rear corner where I face the room and use my best glare to keep the onlookers at bay.

"The lights went out and I said 'Hey!' or something," Cali tells me, her voice unnaturally calm and her eyes still wide and slightly unfocused. "I stood there in the dark for a minute, thinking one of those bastards at the bar was playing a prank or something—you know, turning off the light and leaving. Then the stall door blew open and banged into me. Someone grabbed me and started pulling me out by the neck and hair. He tried to slap something across my face."

I have the strip of duct tape, which the paramedics sealed in a bag for me, in my pocket. But I already know it will be clear of prints, just like the stun gun and the tape that had been left behind during the previous attempt at kidnapping her.

"I fought him as I hard as I could. I yelled and thrashed around, hoping I could get him to let go. Our legs got tangled together. We both fell down and I tried to crawl back to the toilet while I kicked at him. I must have got him good, because he let go. It wasn't like he was trying to rape me—he wasn't grabbing those places—just like he was trying to control me. Subdue me or something."

"Did you get a look at him?"

"No. I told you—he'd turned out the lights."

"What did he say?" One or two of the sheriff's deputies are staring back at me as they talk to each other. I think I see a derisive smile on both their faces. *Those DCI "special agents" can't even guard a victim properly,* is what I imagine them saying.

"He didn't say a word. He just grabbed me and started pulling, trying to get a hold on my wrists—"

"C'mon, Cali," I say, "try to remember. There must be *something* you can tell me about him."

"Don't get mad at me! It was pitch-black in there, and I didn't know what the hell was going on! It was only when I started yelling and pulled myself back under the stall that he took off."

"How did his hands feel? Big or small?"

"I don't know, Anton!"

"Could you get a feel for how tall he was? When he held you from behind?"

"I don't know!" She starts to tremble. An emotional response is overdue. Her eyes begin to fill with water and her lips quiver before she puts her face in her hands. "Maybe he's tall. He felt tall to me. But I don't know." Her whole body starts to shake.

I lean back in the booth and grit my teeth. Then, after a minute, I say in a softer voice, "Hey, Cali, you did great. You fought the bastard off. But I should have been there for you. I really should have been there." I get out of my side of the booth and slip in next to her. I put one arm around her, pulling her to me and holding her while her overdue tears and running nose soak my shoulder and neck.

It's painfully true. I should have followed her to the bathroom, checked it out to make sure it was empty, then stood with my arms folded outside the door. But I hadn't imagined someone who'd tried to creep in her window late at night would also be so bold as to make a move in a bar full of cops. I had underestimated both his audacity and his drive.

Over the next half hour I interview the bar's patrons— off-duty cops and civilians alike—but no one had noticed anyone or anything unusual. No one had seen a man lurking in that unlit hallway. The entire bar had been crowded and dark. And it turns out that the back door was unlocked during operating hours, so that anyone could enter from the alley or vice versa. The bartender tells me that the fire-exit alarm connected to the door was disengaged years ago because people kept tripping it by going out to use the alley as a bathroom when the regular toilets were occupied.

At one point I close my eyes and try to recall the men and women I'd seen around the bar before Cali got up. I try to recall if anyone had headed toward the hallway before or after she had. But every time I think of a particular face, I look around the well-lit room and spot them talking to uniformed officers. Anyone who left could have simply walked back in the front door. I finally suck up my courage and approach the SWAT team officer I'd noticed at the meeting.

"Where's Sergeant Wokowski? Is he on duty tonight?"

The man, a short, tough-looking guy, eyeballs me for a long moment before saying, "You're out of your fucking mind if you think Wook had anything to do with this."

"Just tell me if he's on duty or not, Deputy."

"If he was on, he'd be here right now, doing your job for you. But he doesn't clock in 'til midnight." Although it feels far later, midnight is still forty-five minutes away.

"You're going to stay at my place tonight. Okay?" I say to Cali.

She'll be safer there than she would be at her own house. And I'm not really up to dealing with the stalker if he decides to put in a further appearance tonight. I ignore the part of my brain that suggests that the two of us alone in my cabin might not be such a hot idea. Especially not with my brother prowling around.

Cali's still in the corner booth, slouched beneath the high-backed wall, with her back to the room. She has my jacket covering her like a blanket. It's pulled up so that the upturned collar hides the lower part of her face.

She nods without opening her eyes. Her eyes and nose have long since gone dry. When she stands up and takes my arm, I notice that her face is locked into what seems an almost comical scowl. It doesn't fit her pretty features. The fingers on my arm are tight enough to leave a mark. She's no longer scared, I realize. That emotion's fled. Now she's mad. And I know how she feels.

As we walk out I see elbows being nudged into ribs by the bar. The entire place watches us leave.

ELEVEN

MY RENTED CABIN, nestled on a hillside above Cache Creek, is only about fifteen minutes from the center of Jackson. Cali talks most of the way out there, her voice getting more and more slurred, saying repeatedly, "I want you to get him, Anton. I want this to stop."

I reassure her the best I can. I want to get him, too—not only for her, but also because whoever he is, he's made a complete fool of me tonight. It could have been far worse, though. He could have taken her out of there and carried her off into a waiting car in the alley. The thought of what might have happened then makes my empty stomach clench and my head ache.

We walk up the three steps to the porch with me holding her elbow, steadying her. The alcohol and the attack seem to have taken away her center of balance. Over the sound of young aspen leaves rattling in the wind, I hear the cabin's rear door being shut softly.

I freeze, thinking, *Roberto, you maniac.*

"Stay here for a sec," I tell Cali. "Don't move."

I unlock the front door with the keys in my left hand. My right is up under my shirt and resting against my lower ribs, touching the gun again. Just in case. There's no sound of anyone walking up the hillside behind the cabin, no sound of crunching leaves and snapping twigs. But then Roberto has always moved like a panther—he wouldn't make a sound.

When I push the front door open the main room is brightly lit and empty except for Mungo, whose body faces the rear door although her head is craned back to look at me. With a glance I see several bottles of beer are on the kitchen table and that the labels have been peeled off. Roberto does that when he drinks. He shreds the labels down to the glue and the glass. I hear myself blow out a short, exasperated breath.

Cali steps past me through the open door. Suddenly, at the sight of the animal, she is fully animated again, saying, "A real wolf! I can't believe it!" She rushes the poor creature.

With her yellow eyes wide, Mungo tries to slink away but Cali soon has her cornered. Mungo lowers her head and stands shakily with her legs spread wide in abject submission as Cali reaches out to scratch her ears. "Who's afraid of the big bad wolf?" she coos, bending over to hug Mungo around the neck. Mungo's lips are pulled all the way back and she's shaking. I'm impressed by the speed with which Cali has recovered her spirits. Or maybe this, too, is a reaction. I've seen assault victims seesaw wildly between euphoria at their survival and abject terror at what could have happened.

"She's probably not full-blooded. I think she's got something else in her—some husky or German shepherd, maybe." I say this as I go to the back door and raise the lace curtain to peer out the window. There's nothing out there but night. I push the button to lock the door and make a mental note to install a dead bolt.

"Look at that shit-eating grin! You sure look like a real wolf, like you've been up to something. I've never seen a dog do that!" Cali is saying, addressing first Mungo then me. "How long have you had her?"

"Only a few weeks. She was at a private reserve in Ft. Collins. The reserve was going to be shut down if they didn't get rid of some of the animals. Timorous neighbors didn't like wolves being kept near their pets and kids. They were going to put Mungo to sleep."

"You poor thing. What the hell kind of name for a girl is Mungo, anyway?" Cali asks, trying to peer into her scared eyes. "No wonder you look so unhappy."

I open the front door again so Mungo can escape. She slides around Cali and darts for the door. I hope she won't try to follow my brother to wherever he's headed. Her tail rises from between her legs as she scurries past me.

"This place looks like a hotel room," Cali informs me, looking around. "I know this isn't very PC, but seriously, Anton—you could use a woman." Her eyes—the whites now very red and watery—are crinkled with amusement for the first time in hours. She peeks into the second bedroom with all the gear strewn around and laughs. "So the famous Antonio 'QuickDraw' Burns is a slob."

I wince at the nickname but say nothing. I look around me at the main room and realize again how stark and barren it is. How empty. There are no pictures on the walls but the standard Ansel Adams prints that came with the place, no personal effects of any kind. Not even a photo of Rebecca to remind me of what I'm in the process of losing.

"Give me a break. I just moved in."

She studies a cardboard box full of books that's shoved against one wall. They are mostly outdoor adventure books with titles like *Touching the Void, Kon-Tiki, Endurance, The Worst Journey in the World,* and *The White Spider.* There is also a compilation of old magazine articles called *The Sharp End* that includes a chapter on my brother and me and a climb we did on Foraker. I notice her pause when she sees to one side the book I'd bought the day before, *Smoke Jump,* after I'd done my Internet search on her. She looks like she might say something about it but then decides to hold her comment in.

After a while she says, "So, where am I going to sleep?"

"Either the couch or I can dig out the bed in the back room." Cali makes a face at both options. "I sleep upstairs," I add, pointing up at the open loft, "and I don't have any clean sheets."

She takes a second look at the piles of ropes, skis, and boots in the back room and decides on the couch.

"Mind if I take a shower? I'm feeling pretty grungy after crawling around on the bathroom floor."

"Go ahead."

She disappears into the bathroom and I hear the shower start up. A little later I hear her use my toothbrush, then gargle and spit. I try to quiet down my stomach with a banana and a glass of milk.

When Cali comes out she has a towel wrapped tightly around her body. Her short hair is still wet and pasted to her skull. If it weren't for her bloodshot eyes, she would look far younger than her twenty-six years. I go to the front door, open it, and whistle for Mungo. She glides in like a gray ghost. Her eyes slip past Cali and me almost guiltily, and then she looks back out into the night before I shut the door. She pads across the room on her oversized feet and collapses onto her sleeping bag.

"Do you have anything I can wear?"

The towel isn't particularly large—it barely covers her thighs—and Cali's hands twitch over her stomach and hips as if she's aware of it.

I fetch her a scratchy wool blanket for the couch and a random, oversized T-shirt from the stack in the gear room. She looks at the shirt, frowning, as she unfolds it. Too late I realize it's a T-shirt my brother gave me years ago. Paper-thin and black, it has worn letters in red that read, "The Dead Kennedys." And underneath, "Too Drunk to Fuck."

Cali lets out a whoop then covers her mouth with her hand. "Oh my God! That's the truth! If only Mom could see me in this!"

"You want some water? Some aspirin?" I wonder what my brother will do if he looks in a window and sees this pretty young woman in the T-shirt. I bet I'll be able to hear him laughing out in the night. It's better than the other image I have of him, alone and rejected, curled in a sleeping bag in the woods.

Cali agrees to both. I fill a glass from the sink and find some ibuprofen—climber's candy—in my toilet kit. She washes four tablets down while giving me her steady pink-and-green-eyed gaze over the rim of the raised glass. I turn away from it to busy myself checking that the windows are locked and turning off all the lights but the bathroom's. She might need it unexpectedly.

"Good night," I tell her as I climb up the ladderlike stairs that lead to the loft. I take the copy of *Smoke Jump* with me but discreetly place its cover against my hip and hide the back of the jacket with my hand.

Upstairs I turn on the little light by the bed. Before settling in, I lean out over the railing and glance down at the main room. Cali remains standing below, still in her towel, and looking down at the T-shirt in her hands. It looks like she might be smiling. I remember what I'd thought of her this morning: that she looked like trouble. But once again I can't help but be impressed. It's hard to believe she's a lawyer.

TWELVE

I WAKE UP to hear the electronic chime of the "Mexican Hat Dance." The sound is coming from below, in the cabin's main room. It takes me a moment to realize it's the new cell phone I'd been issued, the one that some wag at the main office—certainly McGee—had programmed to play that tune. It takes me another groggy moment to remember that I'd promised to call Rebecca tonight, to make arrangements for her to come up so that we can have our "talk." How could I have forgotten? I sit up in bed and rub my face. I'll have to go down and get the phone then call her right back.

I hear the rustle of blankets below. Too much rustling for Mungo. There is a quiet feminine curse. With a jolt, I remember that Cali is sleeping on the couch down there. *Don't answer it.*

"Hello?"

Shit. I scramble up, smack my head on a solid rafter, and look for my pants.

"Yeah, he's here. Hang on a sec. Anton?"

Where are my pants? The steep stairs to the loft creak as

Cali starts coming up them. I can't find my pants so I flop rigidly back in the bed like a condemned man and pull a sheet up to my chest.

Cali climbs up into the loft with the cell phone in her hand. Near the top of the steps she loses her balance but manages to catch the rail with her free hand. She laughs at herself. In the bright moonlight coming in through the sky-light I see she's wearing my old T-shirt. Her strong legs are pale and bare. The blonde hair, still wet and shaped by a pillow, stands out from her head in a lopsided tangle. After handing me the phone she sits Indian-style on the far corner of the bed.

"Hello?" I ask into the phone.

Rebecca's voice sounds hesitant, as if it's wavering between feeling hurt and angry. "What's going on, Anton? Who is that?"

"That's Cali, the assistant county attorney I'm looking after. She's the one who's being stalked by a guy who tried to break into her house two nights ago. And tried to attack her again tonight." Even to me, my voice sounds guilty although I haven't done anything wrong. I tell myself this again and again. But it's the appearance of impropriety that has me feeling almost as guilty as if I have done something.

Cali's smiling at me apologetically. In the moonlight I can see that her eyes, though, are sparkling with mirth. She mouths the word *Sorry* and covers her lips with a hand.

"She's sleeping here on the couch, 'Becca. She was afraid to go home. So how are you?"

There's a long silence on the other end of the line. These silences and the sinking feeling in my chest that accompanies them are becoming too familiar. Then Rebecca says in a weary voice, "I'm not sure."

I sigh, struggling to sound normal. "If you're not sure because another woman answered my phone, then put your mind at rest. I was tired and forgot to bring the phone upstairs with me, that's all." It's not like Rebecca to be jealous. To not trust me. We've drifted so far apart in such a short time. Doesn't she know me anymore?

Cali nods, moves her hand down from her mouth until she's holding it out to me, and mouths with another bleary smile, *Let me talk to her.* I shake my head vigorously and try to wave her off my bed.

Again Rebecca doesn't respond right away. When Cali doesn't budge, I pivot to face the skylight so that I can at least pretend that she's not sitting half-naked a few feet away.

"Okay, Anton. I'm just calling because I thought you were going to call me tonight. And I wanted to tell you that I'm coming up there in a couple of days. You were right about what you said this afternoon. We need to talk. In person."

"I'm glad you're coming, 'Becca. Really glad." I try to make my voice enthusiastic, but I feel nothing but dread. I figure this "talk" will be the end. "When will you get here?"

"I don't know. Maybe Monday night—I've got a story to knock out before then. I think I'm going to drive."

"Why don't you fly? It would be safer and faster."

"I've got some thinking to do," she answers tiredly before hanging up.

I wait a few seconds before hitting the END button. Then I turn to the girl on my bed and say, "Goddamn it, Cali!" There is the strong urge to punch out a window, to overturn the bed, to throw everything including the girl down the stairs. "What the fuck were you thinking!" My voice is low and hard and the words wipe the smile off Cali's mouth.

Wide-eyed now, she pulls her knees to her chest and peers out at me from between them. She looks like Mungo. Craven. "I'm sorry, Anton. I . . . I don't know. The phone rang next to my head and I picked it up. I didn't know . . ."

"Fuck!"

This time I'm berating myself instead of her. She didn't intend for this to happen. I can't blame her for my own stupidity. I lift up a pillow and shove it down over my face. "Forget it," I say, my voice muffled by the down. "It's not your fault."

Whatever grasp I'd once had on Rebecca has slipped. I'm holding nothing but air. For the first time I'm pretty certain that I've lost her.

I feel Cali's fingers touch my ankle through the sheet. "I'm sorry, Anton. For whatever's going on with her. And for making it worse. I should have thought of that."

I don't move. Her hand doesn't move either. She no longer sounds the slightest bit drunk. "But I have to say something. . . . I think you're a pretty cool guy, Antonio Burns. If she doesn't see that, well, then it's her loss."

She unfolds her legs and turns away, spinning around slowly so that she ends up lying down next to me. Not touching, but only a few inches away with her back to me. I can feel the heat coming off her skin. We both lie very still for a few minutes.

Then, almost feeling like it's someone else doing it, I put a hand on Cali's shoulder and roll her gently onto her back. She obliges, raising her hands over her head either in surrender or preparation to embrace me. I rise up over her on an elbow and stroke her hair and face with one hand as I bring my mouth down to hers. With my other hand I pin both her wrists above her head. Her slack mouth tastes of tequila and mint. Her tongue traces my teeth and I remember the way she'd licked her ski's edge before leaping off the cornice, the way she'd shouted with delight as she carved her way down Teewinot's East Face. Her breasts are soft and hot against my chest through the thin cotton of the T-shirt.

Maybe this is what I need, I tell myself. To just fall into space. Like letting go when a climb gets too hard.

But I'm fooling myself. I think of Rebecca and my ribs constrict around my heart with a white-knuckled grip.

Without a word I let go of her hands, get out of the bed, pad down the stairs, and stretch out on the couch. Mungo's claws click-clack across the floor. I can sense her looming over me, studying me. She sniffs the air inches from my face. "It's me," I tell her. "It's okay." She thumps down on her elbows and chest beneath me.

SUNDAY

THIRTEEN

SHE WAKES ME with her bad breath and rough tongue. Sleepy eyed, I get up and open the front door to let the wolf out. I don't notice the white scrap of paper that's been slipped halfway under the welcome mat.

Cali comes down from the loft once I have coffee brewing and a bowl full of Cheerios on the table in front of me. She has pulled the sheet off the bed and wrapped it around her shoulders. The trailing ends nearly cause her to once again fall down the steep stairs. I get a shy, uncertain smile from amid the wild blonde curls and below puffy eyes before she disappears into the bathroom.

"How are you feeling?" I ask when she comes out.

"Fine," she answers shortly. She doesn't look at me or speak as she eats her own bowl of cereal. We both stare at yesterday's newspaper spread out on the table.

A little later I shower, shave, and get dressed. When I come out of the gear room/closet Cali is back in last night's dress with the bandanna now holding back her short mane of hair.

"What are your plans for the day?" I ask. "Jim's going to be staying with you."

Cali is crouched by Mungo's prostrate form, stroking her fur while the wolf's legs jerk and tremble and her lips pull up.

"Good," she says quietly and with a short nod. "It's Sunday, but I need to spend the day at the office. I've got that trial tomorrow I want to prepare for."

Mungo leaps to her feet when I pick up my keys and then stares at me with pathetic hopefulness on her long, hatchet-shaped face. It reminds me of the way I feel on the phone with Rebecca. Pathetic. I decide to let her spend the day with me. "Okay" is all I have to say and she races happily out the front door and stands alertly by the truck.

"What's that?"

Cali's pointing at a scrap of paper on the porch. I crouch to pick it up, and my heart rate picks up, too. It's a small piece torn from the corner of a topographical map. On the back, in pencil, is written: *You rat me out to the cops, bro? This road was like a pigpen at feeding time last night.* Below that is a signature that's indecipherable. Farther down is: *P.S. Who's the girl? She's got the look, you know? And definitely NOT too drunk!*

Cali is reading over my shoulder. "What is this? Who's this from?" Her voice sounds a little breathless. A little high.

I fold the note in half and stick it in my jeans pocket. When I look at her, her expression shows alarm and concern.

"A friend of mine. Someone who's been watching the place, I guess."

For the first time this morning she's giving me a direct look. "Oh God, when I saw it there, I thought it might be a letter from the guy who's after me. That maybe he followed us out here last night. But it's your brother, isn't it? He calls you *bro*."

I don't answer right away. I unlock the truck so that Mungo can leap inside as I think about what I should say.

Cali's a prosecutor, a sworn peace officer as well. With a phone call she could have Wokowski and the SWAT team out here combing the hills, and me arrested as an accessory. But it would be foolish for me to try a lie.

"Look, my brother showed up yesterday. Unexpectedly. He's working a deal with the Feds, and he's supposed to turn himself in later this week. I'm pretty sure he's going to do it. I don't want to screw things up for him. I don't really have any right to ask this, but—"

She smiles, breathing better now, and puts her hands on her hips. Then she cocks her head to one side, saying as she looks back up at me, "Okay. Don't worry, I won't say anything. I never saw the note. Besides, he's not wanted in Wyoming for anything, right?"

"Right. Well, not on a Wyoming-based warrant, anyway."

"Okay, so you owe me now. That means you can't mess with my head, Anton."

Suddenly the taste of tequila and toothpaste is back in my mouth. The kiss. Now that was stupid.

"Cali—"

She brings up her hand and touches my lips with her fingertips to shut me up.

"Don't say anything. I don't want to talk about it right now. I know you're dealing with something with that girl who called last night, and I shouldn't have gotten in your bed. Just don't mess with me, okay? That's all I want to say."

Her fingers are still on my lips so I just nod. They're cool in the morning air, the kind of cool that's not really cold but still makes you want to warm them. We stand this way, looking at each other, for several seconds. Then she takes her hand away.

"Now tell me, what does he mean about cops being around here last night?"

"I don't know, but I'm going to find out."

I walk around to the side of the house. The hillside is

thick with aspens and green spruce but that doesn't stop me from squinting into the morning light and looking for a bit of cloth or skin that might betray my brother's presence. Even a bright glint of his mad eyes. But I see nothing but a pair of squirrels cavorting high in some branches.

There are still faint numbers scratched into the dirt beneath the bathroom window. Surprisingly, the sequence is only ten numbers long. An Idaho area code, not an Argentinean one. He must have gotten a new phone when he arrived. I copy it down onto the piece of paper before scuffing it out with the heel of my shoe. I'll try to call him later, when I'm alone.

Mungo hangs her head out the truck's window when we turn onto the pavement at Cache Creek Road. As we pick up speed her ears and lips flap in the wind, her tongue lolling far out of her mouth. We haven't driven more than a half-mile when I see a County Sheriff's black-and-white Chevy Tahoe coming toward us from the other direction. Like the time I'd once seen a killer whale cruising the Inland Passage during a kayaking trip, I feel a sense of menace pushing ahead of the actual object.

"Uh-oh," Cali says. "That's Wook's car. He supervises the midnight-to-ten shift, so he must be about to get off."

The windows of the police vehicle are darkly tinted, but the shape of Wokowski's square head and protruding jaw muscles are discernible through the glass as we pass. For a fraction of a second he and I stare at each other from just a few feet away as our trucks intersect. Even through the obscuring tint I think I can sense animosity radiating toward me. Maybe even something stronger than that. A moment later in my rearview mirror I see his taillights flash on then off before he vanishes around a corner.

Cali turns around in her seat to look out the rear window. She doesn't say anything.

"You still think he's not the guy?"

She shakes her head, still twisted back in her seat and looking out the window. "I don't know anymore. It's spooky, though, him coming out here. Are you going to talk to him?"

"Soon. When I have some evidence linking him to the letters or the break-in. Right now all I've got is that he's your ex and that he's following you around."

Cali puts her hand on my shoulder as she settles back into her seat. "Remember what I said before, Anton. You'll want to have some backup around when you talk to him."

I drive on, slowly now, but the big truck with the gumball lights on top doesn't reappear in the rearview mirror.

FOURTEEN

EVEN THOUGH IT'S SUNDAY MORNING, Lydia Grayson, the manager of the County Attorney's Office, consents to meet McGee and me in front of the courthouse. She is a stern little woman who greets us with a small nod and a disapproving gaze. Around her neck is a heavy wooden cross on a chain. We have probably interrupted her weekly worship and she doesn't look too happy about it.

I'm taken aback when my boss mentions to her that he had known her late husband, a state Fish and Wildlife officer, who was, in McGee's words, a "feisty son of a bitch." I wince, unable to imagine this woman not being horribly offended at having her dead spouse described in such terms.

But McGee somehow gets away with such things. The hard, wrinkled face softens a little as she says, "Let me assure you, Mr. McGee, that he often described you in similar terms."

My boss gives her his depraved grin. "You're just being kind, Mrs. Grayson."

She promptly replies, "No, but I'm sure he was."

McGee's bark of laughter turns into a rough, hacking cough that causes him to double over on his walker.

I look back at the street behind us while McGee recovers and Mrs. Grayson unlocks the glass doors. Above us, to the west, the massive wall of West Gros Ventre Butte looms over the town like a cresting tsunami. The steep hillside is thick with dry, brown grass. It wouldn't take much to ignite it—just a careless smoker tossing a butt or a kid with a bottle rocket.

From across the street Jim gives me an earnest wave. *I'm awake. See?* He has parked his rental car so that he can watch the entire front of the glass-and-sandstone building. I'd told him again to keep an eye out for the big cop with the big jaw and to call me on my cell phone if he so much as drives by and gives the courthouse a long look. And, of course, to make sure he comes nowhere near Cali Morrow.

Parked in front of Jim is Cali's black Volkswagen Jetta. She is already somewhere inside, preparing for her trial tomorrow. I figure that the courthouse is a good, safe place for her to be. Until I can nail down enough probable cause for a warrant with Charles Wokowski's name on it anyway. The only place safer would be somewhere far out of town—a subject I need to raise with her.

After leaving her in Jim's care at her house on Colter Street, I'd driven back out to the cabin to see if either my suspect or my brother was lurking around. No one had been there. I'd called the number Roberto had scratched in the dirt but there'd been no answer. No greeting either. Just the sound of a beep, after which I'd left a terse message—"Call me"—and my own cell-phone number. Then I'd met with McGee and told him almost everything about last night.

Mrs. Grayson, now happily trading barbs with my boss, leads us to a room stuffed with files on floor-to-ceiling shelves. I set my father's cast-off briefcase on the room's only table and take out a legal pad. McGee rolls up on his walker, huffing over it, while Mrs. Grayson begins pulling manila folders from the shelves. When she's done she places a six-inch-high stack of these on the table in front of me.

"These, Mr. Burns, are all the criminal cases our Miss Morrow has prosecuted since starting work with us. I assume you aren't interested in traffic violations. Now, would you gentlemen like coffee? Milk or sugar?"

When she leaves us alone and closes the door behind her, I say, "I don't know how you do it, Ross."

"I'm so goddamn irresistible . . . it gives me goose bumps sometimes," he growls as he collapses into a chair on the far side of the table. "Now tell me why we're here on a sacred Sunday morning. . . . I should be drinking whiskey in a grog-shop somewhere . . . not violating the Sabbath with a degenerate such as yourself."

I examine the stack of slender folders. "It's probably a waste of time, but I want to see if anybody Cali's prosecuted could have fixated on her."

"Why's it a waste of time? I thought finding the guy was your job."

"Because I'm pretty sure Wokowski's the guy. He was cruising by my place this morning when I left to take Cali home."

McGee's grizzled eyebrows leap up high on his forehead. "Oh ho!" he barks. "So the lass spent the night with you!"

I'm not sure if McGee is shocked or amused. With him it's hard to tell. Despite all his swaggering lechery, I've never known him to follow through on it. I suspect he'd been entirely faithful to his wife of forty years before she'd died the previous winter.

"I slept on the couch," I add too quickly. I'm glad Cali's somewhere out of sight and hearing in the building, where McGee's bright eyes and hairy ears will be unable to pick up any vibe or tension flowing between us. I don't want him thinking I'm screwing around on his beloved goddaughter.

"Sure you did . . . and I'm the Queen of Siam."

The sarcasm is a good sign. If he didn't believe me it wouldn't be there.

"Like I said, I'm pretty sure Wook's the guy. But I want to check out other possibilities, too, so that a defense lawyer can't say we didn't look at all the angles and pop us in front of the jury with an alternative suspect." It's a common defense strategy. All they need is the tiniest bit of doubt to get a jury to kick their client loose, and an alternative suspect, no matter how unlikely, can often do the trick. Juries, at a defense attorney's prompting, too often mistake beyond a reasonable doubt for beyond a shadow of a doubt.

McGee grunts and nods his approval, still showing me a lot of teeth. In other circumstances I would take it as high praise. "Besides, until I can talk to the local pawn and gun shops, I won't know if he's bought a stun gun in town lately. And the stores don't open until noon."

McGee now lowers his eyebrows to give me a suspicious look. "I thought Guinness was going to do that."

I look down at the files. "I'm going to do it while he watches her." McGee is regarding me closely now but he doesn't comment on why I, the agent in charge of the investigation, would pick up on the boring scut work.

The stack in front of me is arranged in chronological order with the oldest cases on top. On the cover of each is colored tape spelling out the name of the defendant. Below that are the charges alleged and their statutory codes. On the backs of the files are handwritten notes regarding the disposition of each case.

Flipping through them, I see that most of the cases are simple drunk-driving charges. A couple of bar fights, a few charges of Narcotics Possession, three cases of Misdemeanor Domestic Violence, and one case alleging five counts of "Abuse of a Corpse," a crime I've never heard of, to add some spice. There have not yet been any serious felonies in the young prosecutor's caseload. I read Cali's handwritten notes on the backs of the folders and see that most of the defendants chose to accept a plea to a lesser charge rather than face the uncertainties of a trial. In one year as an assistant county attorney she'd only gone to trial four times.

The suspect in the Abuse of a Corpse case seems to have the most potential for a wacko stalker, so I read that file first. A booking photo clipped to the inside cover shows a young man with messy brown hair almost as long as my brother's. Other than that he is very normal-looking for someone charged with such a ghoulish-sounding crime.

The defendant, a twenty-one-year-old seasonal ski patrolman named Myron Armalli, had worked summers as a driver for the local coroner's office. One of his duties was to transport corpses from accident scenes to the morgue, and then from there to local mortuaries. His address was a number on the highway running over the mountains between Jackson Hole and Lander. Next to it is a handwritten comment about the property, "Condemned."

According to the file, someone had sent an anonymous note to the Sheriff's Office, advising them to check out Armalli's website, where he sold a personalized line of greeting cards. It turned out that the cards were grotesque photographs—like of naked corpses seated before birthday cakes. Apparently Armalli had been hijacking the bodies and taking them home, where he posed them for pictures and did God knows what else. It was never discovered for sure if he was abusing them sexually, because the County Attorney's Office was unwilling to disinter the dead victims. But the photographs were enough. Cali had taken the case to trial three months ago—just about the time when the letters began coming, I realize—after a final plea bargain was refused.

McGee pulls the state's copies of the evidence from the folder—five sample greeting cards—and studies them carefully.

"The AG's birthday is next week. . . . You think he'd like one of these?"

"Only if it were a picture of you, Ross. Or me."

McGee chuckles, the scowl momentarily fading, and slips a card into his coat pocket. I do nothing but shake my head at him. My boss's boss is in for a surprise.

I decipher some of what Cali has written on the file's backside. It reads: *D takes stand despite atty's reluctance. D argues frame, claims personal vendetta by P. Claims 1st Am. rights. Jury out less than five minutes. Guilty x 5. Sentenced to two years probation with a mental-health eval and treatment. Add'l condition: No use of Internet.*

D is shorthand for *defendant* and *P* is for the state, or the *prosecutor*. I wonder if Armalli's belief of a "personal vendetta by P" refers to Cali or to the County Attorney's Office as a whole. This is exactly what I was hoping I wouldn't find—an alternative suspect to keep me from focusing all the way on Wokowski. Just the kind of guy who would write filthy letters, too.

Inside the folder is a pretrial competency evaluation that had been stipulated to by both parties and ordered by the judge. It is a five-page single-spaced document written by a local psychiatrist after several interviews with Myron Armalli. It finds him competent to stand trial—he can understand what is taking place around him and is capable of assisting in his own defense—yet the shrink also felt compelled to add that Mr. Armalli exhibits all the signs and symptoms of someone suffering from schizophrenia. He cites but doesn't describe episodes of bizarre behavior, irrational statements, the admitted hearing of voices, inappropriate laughter, "unusual" sensitivity to stimuli, and staring without blinking as evidence of the disease.

I also learn from this report that schizophrenia most often develops in young people between the ages of sixteen and twenty-five, and that it's a common disease, affecting one in a hundred youths. The sickness generally doesn't involve violent behavior but it's hinted that Armalli might be an exception, as phrases like *antisocial behavior* and *potentially violent psychosis* pepper the report. The doctor recommends various antipsychotic medications, including Thorazine and Haldol. With counseling and these drugs, the shrink believes, there is a good chance Armalli will be able to function positively in society.

With some alarm I also realize that Armalli's address, at the time of the trial and marked "Condemned," is not far from Alana Reese's ranch in Jackson Hole.

"We've got a monkey in the works," McGee says after reading the file.

"This guy looks pretty good," I admit, feeling the weight of disappointment settle on my shoulders. "I'll talk to Cali about him, see if he seemed to be fixated on her during his trial."

I look at the photo again. He looks perfectly normal except for the messy long hair, but even that is the fashion on young men in Jackson. His face is plain and ordinary, maybe a little anemic. His eyes look right at the camera and there is the barest hint of a smile on his thin lips.

All the other cases are more or less innocuous, standard fare for a small-town prosecutor. The three domestic-violence cases are of the usual drunken spouse-beating variety. The DUIs are ordinary, too, as are the bar fights and the drug arrests. There are no more indications on the file notes of anyone else taking a dislike to or a particular interest in the young woman who had prosecuted them. At least there are no more monkeys.

"What's the plan now, QuickDraw?"

"Wokowski's still the focus. We check out his internal file with the sheriff, find out if the SWAT team members have access to stun guns and whether or not one might be missing, and get customers' names from the stores around here that might sell them. But we'll still have to check this wacko out."

I get up and study the jackets on the walls, trying to figure out how they've been filed. With relief I discover it's alphabetically. I'm able to search for other cases in which Armalli had been a defendant in the past without calling Mrs. Grayson back into the room and risking Cali wandering in to see what's going on. I don't want to talk to her in front of McGee.

There are no more jackets with Armalli typed on them. Apparently the corpse-abuse had been his one and only adult offense in Teton County. But I realize I'll need to run his name on NCIC, the FBI's database, and make sure there aren't other offenses in other jurisdictions. Then some shelves off by themselves catch my eye—the manila file jackets stored there are all marked in pink. They're the juvenile files, which technically should be sealed after the subject's eighteenth birthday, and only opened with a court order.

Checking to see that the door's still shut, I scan the files for Armalli's name. Three are together on the highest shelf and are bound together with a rubber band. I pull them down.

"I'm not seeing this," McGee says. He's a stickler when it comes to the law and following it to the letter. I'm a little surprised when he doesn't indignantly order me to put them back.

One of the cases is for cruelty to animals. Apparently Armalli had been charged with setting a horse on fire when he was fifteen years old. He was given a deferred judgment—meaning eventual dismissal—provided he seek and receive psychological counseling and pay restitution to the damaged horse's owner. The statutory violation on the cover of the second jacket is for the crime of harassment, and this time he had been adjudicated a delinquent. A quick read of the statement of probable cause tells me that seventeen-year-old Myron had groped and fondled a high-school classmate during gym class. His sentence was a term of probation and more counseling. The third folder makes me groan out load. On the cover it says, "Wy. Statute 16-2-506—STALKING."

The victim had been the same girl as in the harassment

case. Armalli was charged with a pattern of conduct that amounted to the crime of stalking: leaving her letters, following her around, and telephoning constantly. But then the charge had been dismissed when the girl moved out of state with her parents and was unavailable to testify.

All the files give the same address for Armalli: the highway address I recognize as being not far from Alana Reese's property in the valley. A brief psychologist's report states that Myron appears "very disturbed," that he was abandoned by his mother at the age of five, and that his father was going bankrupt and had recently sold the family's home to the government.

"This guy isn't a monkey. He's a gorilla," I say, slipping the files into my briefcase. Motive, means, and opportunity, even a prior. It's all there.

My hopes for arresting Wokowski on charges of stalking, burglary, assault, and attempted kidnapping are drifting away.

Something buzzes in the pocket of my painter's jeans like an angry wasp. Then the "Mexican Hat Dance" begins playing from the vicinity of my crotch. McGee shows me his big yellow teeth as I dig the phone out, his grin leaving me with no doubt as to who had programmed the irritating jingle. I'm not going to answer it in front of him if it's either Rebecca or my brother. But the urgently flashing text on the screen says JIM GUINNESS, so I press the TALK button.

The voice on the other end sounds near panic.

"You better get out here, man."

FIFTEEN

HOT SUNLIGHT is pouring in the windows at the front of the courthouse from high above Gros Ventre Butte. Squinting against the light as I come into the lobby, I can see Jim's back through the glass doors. He's standing in front of them with his skinny arms outspread. It looks as if his hands might be shaking. Beyond him, facing in, is Sergeant Charles Wokowski.

He's out of uniform now, dressed in a pair of crisp khaki pants and a white polo shirt that's all-the-way unbuttoned to make room for his tree trunk of a neck. The shirt is a little too small, tight over the swollen muscles of his chest and showing off the bare skin of his arms. Mirrored sunglasses hide his eyes, which surely must be bloodshot after a long night on duty. His tan face is freshly shaven. In his left hand he holds a black nylon gym bag.

I slow down and push open the door gently, using it to move Jim out of the way and to one side.

Wokowski's jaw flexes as he catches sight of me.

"What's going on?" I ask Jim but keep my eyes on my

own twin reflections in the big cop's lenses. Maybe it's him after all.

"He wants—" Jim starts to say.

Wokowski's deep voice is calm but anger vibrates through it when he says, "What I want is none of your business. Get out of my way. Both of you."

Jim steps back against the railing that stands to one side of the door at my back. I don't have to look at him to sense his enormous relief that I'm here to take over. But I'm proud of him—he'd stood his ground as long as he needed to. And while I'm as scared as he surely is, the thrill of fear is as welcome as Rebecca's touch. For some reason I feel more like my brother at these times than like myself.

"The courthouse is closed. It's Sunday," I tell Wokowski.

He doesn't reply. His sunglasses remain unwaveringly directed at me.

"Shouldn't you be sleeping, Sergeant? You must have had a long night, and I thought your shift ended about the time you were cruising by my cabin this morning."

The staring continues. The sun is so bright in my eyes that I can't keep it up any longer. Glancing down, I look at the small gym bag in his hand and see that the knuckles gripping the strap are white. *What the hell's in it?* I wonder. Another stun gun? More duct tape? Would he be reckless enough—sick enough—to go after Cali in broad daylight, here in the center of town? Would he make it that easy?

When he still doesn't say anything I decide to prod him some more. "Cali doesn't want to see you."

Red splotches materialize on his cheeks. The jaw bulges even bigger, the muscles there and in his neck flaring like a cobra's. Without consciously being commanded, my right hand brushes my pants and slips toward the gun holstered beneath my shirt high on my hip.

"Then let her tell me that," he says.

I shake my head, not letting my eyes leave his glasses

now no matter how bright the sun burns. If I even blink it might be too late. It's like I'm on top of that cornice again, the fear curdling in my stomach while the Rat happily laps it up.

"No. *I'm* telling *you*."

"This is my town, QuickDraw. My courthouse. Get the fuck out of my way." He's starting to swing the gym bag now. Back and forth at his side. We're at the very edge now—I can feel it. Both of us teetering there. Wondering if we're going to grab each other and throw ourselves off.

"You make a move in any direction but toward the street and you're going to be arrested right here, where everyone can see," I tell him.

A smile twitches at the corner of his lips. It alarms me more than anything else. My hand literally aches with the need to touch my gun's beveled grip. My fingers are curled just above the butt.

"You've got a restraining order?"

"Not yet, partner, but it's in the works. Along with a warrant for stalking, burglary, assault, and attempted kidnapping."

It's out in the open now—and I hope it will spur him into doing something rash, going over. It's a gamble—I could go with him—but I think it's worth it. Wokowski keeps swinging the bag with his smile taking shape now, growing broader. The lips are pale and the red splotches are draining from his face.

"You really think I—"

"I *know*," I interrupt. "I *know* you're the guy. You tried to break into her house two days ago. You tried to grab her last night. You've been writing her nasty letters. Cali dumped you and now you want her no matter what it takes. Even if it's against her will. And that's sick, man. Really sick. You got a problem and you need to get it straightened out."

He makes what I suspect is meant to be a disbelieving chuckle but it comes out as almost a snarl. Then he moves.

He takes a step forward and with his right hand pushes Jim back against the railing beside the door. The bag pendulums forward then cocks back, and I realize that with another step he can swing it into my crotch. Suddenly my gun is in my hand. It's pointing at the ground between us but I know that with a flick of my wrist I can point it at his belly.

Wokowski's mirrored lenses flinch down toward the gun. The bag freezes in its backswing then slowly comes to rest at his side. Time freezes, too, and I'm not aware of anything but the two us standing here, three feet apart, with a .40-caliber H&K between us. Heavy in my hand. I feel loose and fluid and fast, as if all the joints in my body have been freshly oiled then scrunched down like loaded springs.

It is a long time before he speaks. Or at least it seems that way.

"You're a fucking maniac, QuickDraw Burns. A dangerous fucking maniac." He says it directly into my face from just two feet away. His toothpaste breath reminds me of Cali's.

"Look who's talking, Wokowski."

Very slowly and carefully, he steps back and down the single step that leads onto the sidewalk. He stares at me for a while longer before he turns and walks back to the black-and-white SUV parked down the street.

Inside the lobby, Jim hunches over with his hands on his knees. He's breathing hard and fast. I'm feeling a little light-headed myself. Wasted, too, as if the confrontation with the sergeant had sucked out all my strength. Even though we'd never touched, it feels like we'd gone fifteen rounds.

McGee, who has parked his walker by the glass and is staring out at the street, says, "Thought I was going to have to go out there . . . save both your candy asses."

"How—come—you—didn't—arrest—him?" Jim pants at me.

McGee answers for me. "Because we don't have a goddamn thing on him. . . . Five minutes ago . . . we were thinking he was out of it altogether."

"It's got to be him. He's back in the number one spot," I say.

"No shit," Jim agrees, standing upright now and looking pale. "That guy is a hand grenade, man. I thought he was going to lose it out there. Blow his shit up. Whew, that was close. When we take him down, we'd better have some more guys around."

I nod in agreement. I'd noticed when Wokowski finally walked away that his pant cuff had bulged on the inside of his left ankle. He was carrying. That's not a surprising fact, since he is a cop, but it makes me realize again how hazardous it can be to go hunting your own kind.

"What did you learn?" McGee asks.

"I took a chance. I let him know he was our chief suspect, hoping he'd say or do something to seal it."

"Well? Did he make any statements? An admission?"

I shake my head. "No. Nothing we can use. But it was real close out there, Ross."

"What'll he do now?" Jim asks.

"I don't know. Probably go home and steam. Maybe get some sleep. Wait for a better day."

"He might see the error of his ways," McGee says. "Become more crafty. Maybe even give it up."

"Or it might stoke him up all the more. We've got to be careful now, watching Cali," I say to Jim. I remember what McGee had said yesterday, about getting the stalker to focus on me. My boss's plan might be working, although I'm not sure if it's my favorite course of action. I'd returned Wokowski's insult at the meeting yesterday, spent the night with the object of his obsession, and I'd just bested him in a face-to-face confrontation. I'll be watching my own back a lot more carefully now.

"Anton? What's going on?" Cali asks, coming into the lobby from the County Attorney's door and looking puzzled.

All three of us turn to her. It seems amazing that someone could be in the building, just a hundred feet away, and not be aware of what had just taken place outside the courthouse door. It had felt like the tension should have bowed the tree limbs outside her window, forced her to pop her ears. After I'd left her in Jim's care at her house she'd changed into a green silk T-shirt and well-worn jeans.

"Your boyfriend Wokowski just stopped by to say hi. I talked to him and he changed his mind."

She looks at me, eyebrows raised, figuring out why we all look so tense and drained. Although I don't further explain the encounter, she reads it in our faces. I see goose bumps on her arms.

"Cali, you know Jim already, but I don't think you've been introduced to my boss, Deputy Assistant Attorney General Ross McGee. Boss, this is Cali Morrow."

The old man's eyes light up. He rolls toward her on his walker and holds out his meaty hand. When she reaches out her own to shake it, he pulls it up to his beard and kisses it loudly.

"You're a ripe little thing, aren't you?" he says before releasing her hand. He's looking at her chest.

The tiny bumps on her arms disappear as her face flushes red. Her expression is uncertain, vacillating between offended and amused. The amusement wins out and she grins crookedly at him. I roll my eyes at Jim.

"It's nice to meet you, Mr. McGee."

"Ross, my dear, call me Ross . . . or anything else you like. . . . I can see your mother's features in your face . . . and, uh, elsewhere," he says.

"You know Mom?"

McGee nods his square head enthusiastically. "I knew her well . . . she and I spent a lot of nights together . . . when I was a young grunt serving in Southeast Asia."

She frowns for a second in confusion, saying, "Mom's never been to . . ." then catches his meaning. She laughs and finally manages to withdraw her hand from his grasp. "You'll have to meet her while she's here and see if she remembers your adventures together."

I'm impressed, watching her manage his lechery so well.

McGee smacks his lips. "I'd like nothing better, young lady."

Without thinking I joke, "Alana Reese might find you a little rough around the edges, boss. She didn't like me when I met her last night, and you know how smooth and charming I can be." Immediately I put my foot in my mouth. I hadn't told McGee about my encounter with Danny Gorgon and don't intend to. That sort of thing was too close to the excessive-force accusations that had caused my semi-disgrace and nearly resulted in my being criminally charged. I don't ever want to do anything to make McGee doubt his decision to protect me.

McGee is turning to look at me inquisitively when Cali says, "She liked you fine, Anton. She even told me that you were a 'pretty Mexican boy with obviously hot, Latin blood,' and that your scar looked sexy."

This makes McGee laugh and cough. He repeats "pretty Mexican boy" twice before saying, "This pretty Mexican boy . . . with his delusions of charm. . . . I can assure you that he's the devil. . . . He's gotten my otherwise intelligent god-daughter . . . to think she's halfway in love with him." He looks at me as he finishes speaking with what I take as a warning. Instead of feeling any guilt, all I can do is wonder when he last spoke to Rebecca.

The cell phone in my pocket starts to play its stupid song again. This time, though, it earns me no smug grin from

McGee. He's still busy with carving his unspoken warning on my flesh with his watery laser-beam eyes. No name appears on the phone's screen, but the number preceded by an Idaho area code tells me who it is. Excusing myself, I walk back out through the front door and onto the street.

"So, you rat me out or what?" my brother asks in his soft, amused voice.

"You know I didn't, 'Berto. Where are you?"

"Should I be telling you that?" He laughs. "Who's with you right now? A bunch of cops?"

"Actually, yeah. Two DCI guys and a county prosecutor. But they're ten feet away, on the other side of a window. So where are you?"

"Coming down. Did a couple of routes in Death Canyon."

"What'd you do?"

"The Snaz and Cottonmouth."

"Solo?" I already know the answer, but I have to ask in a kind of horrified and awed wonder. The routes he'd mentioned are both long and hard, each topping out at close to a thousand feet off the deck.

"Until you stop avoiding me, *che*, and tie yourself in."

"That girl you saw last night at my place? She's the case I'm on. Somebody's after her in a serious way and I can't bail out on her right now. Tell me, what did you see last night?"

He laughs again, a slurry sound like slow water running over rocks. "You acting all sanctimonious, going up the stairs alone. Then you coming down after she went up. You're getting soft, bro."

"Rebecca's coming up this week," I say by way of explanation.

"Soft and whipped," he sighs. "*That* girl doesn't like me much."

"What were you doing anyway? Peeping in my windows all night?"

"As a matter of fact, yeah." He'd probably been too high

to sleep, too pumped up from an injected speedball and cooling his heels until the sun would invite him onto the rock. "If you were any kind of family, Ant, you'd buy a TV and stick it in the window. Or at least get the girl naked."

"What about the cop car last night?"

"Big sucker, one of those Expeditions or something. Must have come by six or seven times after you came home. It was really bringing me down, thinking that maybe my own bro had called him in. Couple of times I almost put a rock through the windshield."

"Did you get a look at the driver?"

"Nah. The windows were tinted and I was kinda trying to stay out of sight, you know? Dude just cruised by and then would come back an hour or so later. Had his lights off, too."

"I think he's the guy, 'Berto. The guy who's after her. Tell me if you see him around the cabin again."

"Want me to grab him for you?"

Now it's my turn to laugh. Roberto is perfectly serious. Despite everything, the warrants out for his arrest and the possibility of blowing his deal with the Feds if he gets picked up early, he's perfectly willing to grab a cop to help out his little brother. Even as I laugh I feel my throat grow tight.

"No. Just give me a call. And be careful, 'Berto. Don't screw things up for yourself. Be careful."

"Sure, *che*. You know me. So when are you going to climb with me? I've only got five more days."

I surprise myself by answering, "Soon."

Cali comes swinging through the big glass doors before I have a chance to recompose myself. She stands in front of me, a few inches closer than she would have before last night, and asks, "You look a little pale, Anton. Who were you talking to?"

"My brother." My voice is a little bit hoarse and I clear my throat.

"Oh."

Apparently my expression keeps her from asking more. The sun's in her face, revealing the tiny sun-etched lines at the corners of her eyes as she squints up at me. There is something needy about her posture and the way she shifts from foot to foot, a little like Mungo. I note that she looks very nice. A touch of peach-colored lipstick brightens her mouth. Somehow I know without a doubt that she has dressed for me. I move back a step.

"Cali, how about taking a vacation? Getting out of town would make you a lot safer."

She chews her lower lip like she is giving it some serious thought. It will be safer for her—and for me—to have her somewhere far away. Like Bali.

But then she says, "I can't. The trial of the guy Wook beat up starts tomorrow. I started it, so I need to finish it. I can't run away from that. After that, we'll see." A smile lifts her lips and her eyes sparkle. "Maybe you could use a vacation, too?"

"I just got back from leave," I say, looking through the window into the lobby where I can see through the dark glass that McGee and Jim are still talking. I recall the promise I'd made her this morning. Not to mess around with her. "Look, I've got a girlfriend. For the time being, anyway. And as much as I like you, Cali—" I leave it there. It hangs awkwardly.

Her eyes lose their light a full second before the smile fades from her face. I might as well have slapped her.

SIXTEEN

I GO ALONE to what I can't help but consider enemy territory: Wokowski's province and fiefdom. It's only around the corner and down the street to the Teton County Sheriff's Office, but the walk feels much longer. Then, at the doors, it suddenly feels way too short. I had called ahead and found out that the sheriff was in her office, working on Sunday to catch up on paperwork.

McGee, Jim, and Cali have gone together to a restaurant in the other direction called Thai Me Up. I don't envy them eating a meal with McGee, especially not a spicy one. Even with mild food it's not a pretty sight.

"Special Agent Burns," Sheriff J. J. Buchanan acknowledges me coolly when I knock on the sill of her office's open door. "I don't have much time, but I understand we need to talk."

She is a large woman but not particularly fat. Just strong and sturdy, like so many Wyoming natives. The Anglos here tend to be big people—I think it must come from a ranch diet of steak, potatoes, and corn. The sheriff's plain face is kindly even though it's wearing a frown. The desk beneath her elbows is littered with papers and forms, which are the bane of modern law enforcement even in a town like this.

"It's nice to meet you," I say, hoping the frown is nothing more than the result of having to work on a warm Sunday afternoon.

She studies me for a long moment before dispelling my hope. She says, "I wish I could say the same."

I let out a sigh. "Why is that, Sheriff?"

She leans back in her swivel chair and continues examining me. "You have a reputation for using excessive force, Agent Burns. I'm told you've only been in town a few days, and already I've had a complaint about you."

Unasked, I close the door and sit down in one of the hard chairs opposite her desk. "Sergeant Wokowski, right?"

She tilts her head at me, the way Mungo does when she doesn't understand one of my rare commands. "Actually, the complaint came from Alana Reese, who I consider a friend to both myself and this county. She said you assaulted Mr. Gorgon, who was a guest at her party last night."

I'm surprised Cali's mother had been the one to complain on Gorgon's behalf. She knew I was protecting her daughter at the party, even if she believed what I did in response to the insults was unnecessary. But then she is the one who owns property here, and is therefore more likely to have attention paid to her. I have no doubt, though, that Gorgon put her up to it. I'm glad McGee isn't here. I hadn't told him about the incident.

"She doesn't want any charges pressed against you—she said she doesn't want that kind of publicity for Mr. Gorgon—but she made it clear that she would like you to be kept away from him."

I hold her eyes and speak quietly and forcefully. "He directed some extremely foul language at her daughter—one of your assistant county attorneys. Then he pointed a plastic gun at my forehead when I spoke to him about it. I responded with reasonable force to keep him from resisting arrest for Disorderly Conduct. I released him at Ms. Reese's request. There was nothing more to it. As for my reputation in general, all I can tell you is that you've heard only one side of the story. I'd appreciate it if you would give a fellow peace officer the benefit of the doubt."

The sheriff is still studying me. Despite the politics and the paperwork, which is probably about as close to real police work as she comes these days, she still has a cop's assessing eyes.

After a minute she nods. "All right. I'll take your word for it. Just do me a favor and stay away from Mr. Gorgon. Understand? I know you're going to be with us for a while, hunting down clandestine labs for the SWAT team after you finish with the Morrow investigation, but please, I don't want any more complaints."

I nod. "I'll try to avoid it."

"Please do. Ms. Reese was also quite distraught when she learned that her daughter was again assaulted later last night in the bar. She claimed that you weren't doing your job, that you allowed it to happen."

I feel heat coming to my face. This meeting is going even worse than I had anticipated. I'm not appearing here as a skilled state investigator but as a fuckup, someone who can't help but harass innocent civilians and can't manage to protect a woman in a crowded bar. Someone who might have been the perpetrator of a triple homicide. *The bar was full of cops,* I want to say. *I couldn't have foreseen . . .* But I could have. And I should have. I resist the urge to look down at the floor and instead hold her gaze. "That won't happen again. I blew it."

It's her turn to nod. "Now what did you want to see me about? And why do you think Charles Wokowski would make a complaint about you?"

"Because a half hour ago I let him know that he's my prime suspect."

The sheriff smiles uncertainly and bends forward in her chair. "You're kidding me, aren't you?" Before I can answer she adds, "He's one of my most reliable men. In fact, I've all but chosen him to be my successor when I leave office in two years. When the County Attorney suggested we bring your office in, it was to avoid even the appearance of impropriety—we certainly didn't think you'd begin by focusing on one of our own."

"You know about the break-in? The stun gun and tape?"

"Of course. This is my county, Agent Burns. I was at the scene five minutes after the call came in. I was the one who interviewed Bill Laughlin, the man who ran the attacker off. I was the one who took possession of the tape and the stun gun and arranged for them to be sent to your crime lab."

"Until recently he and Cali Morrow were dating. I understand their parting was strained."

"I know ex-lovers are always considered suspects. But he's a cop, and a darn good one. He would never—"

I interrupt her. "When they broke up he said something to her about wishing they were both dead—"

"Lots of men say stupid things—"

"Cali stayed at my cabin up on Cache Creek last night because she was afraid to stay in her house. Wokowski drove by several times during the night and then again this morning."

"He's a patrol supervisor—it's his job to patrol," she says, but now her voice is a little less adamant and her face a little less certain.

"Just a half hour ago he tried to go into the courthouse to see her. When I wouldn't let him in, things were very close to getting out of hand."

"At least *that* doesn't surprise me. He wouldn't like you

telling him what to do, keeping him out of a building within his area of supervision—"

"In his off-duty hours?"

"But that doesn't add up to a lot of evidence, Agent Burns."

She's right, of course. There's no real evidence. This is why I've come to see her in the first place.

But before I can start asking my questions, she leans back again in her chair and continues in a less-defensive tone, "He and I talked about you some when you were in the news. He felt that you should have been prosecuted after you shot those drug dealers who raped that little girl, that there might have been something to the ambush theory."

Now I sit forward on the edge of my chair and put my hands on my knees, squeezing them. The heat I'd felt coming into my face earlier cranks up by several degrees. It takes effort to keep my voice low and reasonable, even amused.

"He said as much when I addressed the SWAT team yesterday. As I told you before, it's bullshit. The only ambush was them waiting for me. But we're getting off the subject, Sheriff. I've heard Wokowski's being investigated for using excessive force himself."

"That's true," she acknowledges. "*I'm* investigating him. And except for this one isolated incident, Charles's record has been exemplary."

Even though I like this sheriff—I can't help believing that she does her best to be fair as well as loyal to the officers she commands—I like her even better when she's the one being defensive instead of me. "He slammed a handcuffed suspect—an elderly man—on the hood of a patrol car and punched him in the stomach. It's on video, isn't it?"

"There are some extenuating circumstances with that."

"What are they?" I expect that she's waiting to see how things will shake out at Cali's trial tomorrow. If the jury regards Wokowski's transgression as no big deal, and if the local press ignores the videotape the defense attorney is bound to show if Cali doesn't show it first, then she'll probably want to handle it very quietly so as not to make any unnecessary waves and possibly ruin her sergeant's career.

"The man Charles *allegedly* roughed up, Dale Watson, has been arrested for drunk driving on *six* prior occasions. On only one of those occasions was he convicted. Two years ago he ran over a little boy on a bicycle and fled the scene. That boy was—is—paralyzed. A quadriplegic, Agent, who will never walk or move his arms or legs again. When Watson was finally arrested for *that* incident, we could no longer prove the intoxication element necessary to make the crime a felony. So all he could be charged with was Leaving the Scene of an Accident. A misdemeanor punishable by only up to a year in the county jail. Charles's family is friendly with the boy's family. I'm told that ever since the accident, Charles has visited the boy at least once a week and reads to him. Takes him to ball games, too. So you see, he was understandably upset when he found the same man who crippled the boy driving drunk once again."

I don't want it to, but the level of my dislike for Wokowski drops a few notches. Would I have done the same thing? I might have done a lot worse.

"What about stun guns? Does your department use them?"

"Only in the jail. And only in the event of trouble. We have five of them. They're kept with the SWAT team's arsenal and have to be signed out."

"Wokowski heads the SWAT team, doesn't he?"

She doesn't answer.

"Let's take a look at the arsenal."

Still without speaking, she lifts a ring of keys from a drawer. I follow her out into the hallway and then past several more offices—one empty but with Wokowski's name on a placard on the desk—to a locked metal door. As she turns the key in the lock I feel excitement welling in me.

The arsenal is nothing more than a large closet. Stuffed full of gear, it resembles a neater, much smaller version of the guest bedroom in my cabin. Only much of this gear is lethal. Flash-bang grenades, bullet-proof vests, shotguns, battering rams, automatic weapons. On one shelf are the stun guns resting in their green-lit chargers. There are five chargers and five stun guns. I try not to show the disappointment I feel, but the sheriff doesn't attempt to conceal her smile of relief. Still I make a show of checking the brands and voltages, which only increases my disappointment. These are a different model, and only 500,000 volts, where the one dropped outside Cali's window was 625,000.

SEVENTEEN

I LEAVE THE Sheriff's Office intending to hit the pawn-shops then drive out to the ranchette where Armalli grew up and, according to the files I'd borrowed, still resides as a squatter. I'd looked up the address on a county map at the Sheriff's Office and seen that I was correct in supposing what I had when I first saw the address—the place is disturbingly close to the remote east end of Alana Reese's far-larger property. This Myron Armalli—horse burner, schizophrenic, and convicted stalker—is looking better and better all the time.

My cell phone starts chiming before I even crank the Pig's engine. The digital screen shows a 213 area code. Los Angeles? It puzzles me for a moment until I hear the voice on the other end.

"Burns? It's Angela Hernandez. We met last night, after you put on that wonderful performance at the party."

There's the sound of throbbing music in the background, as if she's really in Los Angeles, in a nightclub perhaps, at two on a Sunday afternoon. Her voice sounds less formal than it had at the party. Almost playful.

"Have you caught your stalker yet?" she asks.

"No, but I have some leads. And some questions for someone with experience in this kind of stuff and a psych degree. Can we get together anytime earlier than tomorrow morning?"

"Actually, Burns, that's why I'm calling. I may not be able to make it tomorrow—I have to take a little hike for Alana. Could we do it this afternoon? I'm in town right now with Alana. I might be able to shake free in a few minutes when she heads back to the ranch with her driver. Maybe we can get a beer or something?"

"Where are you now?"

Angela names a clothing store that she describes as being about two blocks away, just off the square. The background noise doesn't sound like any store I'm familiar with but I get out of the car and start walking down the planks in that direction.

The store isn't hard to find. From more than a block away I observe a pack of men and women standing in front of two big plate-glass windows facing the street. Bright, artsy graffiti is painted on the brick above and between the windows. The spectators are lined three-deep against the glass, staring in. All of them appear to be tourists, and a couple of them are aiming handheld video cameras inside. Some others snap away with conventional cameras. I excuse myself as I shoulder through the crowd and try the door. It's locked.

"They're not letting anyone in," a fat, balding man in a golf shirt says to me. He winks and rubs his sweaty palms together. "But boy oh boy, I wish they would."

A woman next to him, probably his wife, backhands his arm and laughs loudly.

Through the glass I see Angela Hernandez glaring at the sightseers outside. She is wearing tight jeans over her sturdy legs, a white T-shirt, and, despite the heat, a hip-length leather jacket to hide her old-fashioned shoulder harness. She appears to be taking this Hollywood/FBI thing to heart. Her arms are folded across her chest. Behind her Alana Reese parades around the racks of snowboard-and-skateboard-chic merchandise.

It's immediately obvious why the tourists are gaping. The movie star has shed her clothes—right down to her black bra and underwear—as she tries on a close-fitting orange shirt and a pair of very baggy parachute pants. A salesgirl trails behind her, picking up the items Alana discards on the floor. Cali's mother has to be aware of the slavering crowd outside but she never looks our way.

Although she must be in her early fifties, she really does remain worthy of the attention. From a physical standpoint, anyway—morally I'm not too fond of her right now. Her skin glows with a pale coppery color, and, despite the lithe muscles moving beneath it, it looks as soft and smooth as butter. Each move she makes is languidly graceful. But to me it all seems a little too practiced, a little overdone. I remember what Cali had said about her mother only feeling alive when she is the center of attention.

I knock on the glass door. Angela looks my way with an annoyed frown. She recognizes me, shakes her thick hair, and then walks over to turn the lock. As I slip through the door, one of the men says to me, "You *lucky* bastard!" I'm not so sure. White hip-hop music is banging over the store's speakers. The singer is probably one of those middle-class white kids striving to sound dangerous and persecuted.

Before I can say hello and see her reaction, Alana dances off toward the back of the store with the clerk in tow. I turn around to greet Angela and instead my eyes are drawn past her to all the hungry, leering faces pressed against the glass. I can fully understand Cali's aversion to this sort of life. But at least for once it's not me who is the subject of all the attention.

"Quite a show," I shout to the FBI agent as she relocks the door.

She shakes her head again, glowers over her shoulder at the window, then checks to see that her ward is out of earshot. "How the hell am I supposed to protect her? She might as well put up a sign: 'Stalkers Apply Here.' "

"Last night she told me that it came with the territory, or something like that."

Turning away from the window, Angela switches off the glower and smiles at me for the first time. "Like living in any territory, you must want to be there." She blows a small pink bubble then sucks it back in with a small pop. "So how come you haven't caught your stalker yet, QuickDraw? You aren't going to screw up your perfect record on this one, are you? I know all about you now—I know about the gangbangers and then the thing with the governor."

I study her grin for signs of sarcasm but see none. All the same, I can't quite keep contained the sudden flare of my blood. "Right, Angela. I lost my professional reputation and nearly my liberty because of the former, and the latter, the governor-elect, he only got probation—no jail—for helping get a couple of kids snuffed and knowingly almost giving two yokels the needle for something they didn't do. Does that sound like a perfect record?"

Her smile fades. "Are you serious? Hey, I'm sorry. I didn't mean anything."

"And don't call me 'QuickDraw,' either, okay? The guy who made it up didn't mean it in a nice way, as I'm sure you read."

"Yeah, I noticed. But you can't take that stuff seriously, Burns. If everything the media wrote was true, I'd be an anal-retentive man in a navy suit, with sunglasses and an earphone, cross-dressing in secret. That's about how they portray the Bureau. Anyway, reading about you was, uh, pretty colorful. I might be able to use some of it. For my screenplay, you know?"

The bile that had been bubbling up my throat sinks back

down to my stomach. "Oh God, please don't," I say, smiling a little myself now. "Just let me ask you some stuff about this guy and get out of here."

Angela scrunches up her face and points at the speakers mounted in the corners of the shop. "I can't think over this crap."

Alana Reese steps out from behind a rack of clothes. A short, tight shirt that is a wild pink covers only her arms, shoulders, and breasts. Other than that, all she is wearing is the black underwear. The matching bra has disappeared— it's quite obviously not under the pink shirt. The young salesgirl trails at her heels with a mound of clothes hugged to her chest.

"Angela, dear, could you take some of these from the poor girl?" Alana purrs over the music. "I'm afraid she's running out of arms. Oh, Mr. Burns—Special Agent Burns, that's what they call you people, isn't it? It's nice to see you again. But don't you think you ought to be looking after my daughter right now?"

Her tone is saccharine-sweet, but the intent of her words is emphasized by a spot of color on each high-boned cheek and the razor-sharp gleam in her green eyes.

"Nice to see you, too. Another state agent is with Cali right now."

"Well, I'm certainly glad to hear that!"

"It's really heartening to know you're so concerned," I tell her.

Her mouth twitches up in a smile that's not a smile as she pivots away from me and toward a rack of tie-dyes. Angela, a clandestine look on her face, reluctantly takes an armful of clothes from the salesgirl and dumps them on the counter.

Alana pulls a multicolored Lycra shirt off a rack, studies it for a minute, then hands it to Angela. "You would look wonderful in this, dear. You should try it on."

"Thanks," Angela tells the movie star. "I will. A little later.

Do you mind if we turn down the music? I'm trying to talk to Burns here about the guy that's bothering your daughter."

Alana appears not to hear her. Bobbing and snapping her fingers, gyrating a little with her perfect rear end twitching to the music, she disappears once again into the racks. The salesgirl dumps her remaining armful on the counter and turns down the music a couple of clicks. The volume now is less painful, but the music still hurts. Then she vanishes after the actress.

"She's quite concerned about Cali, you know," Angela says with a straight face.

"Yeah, she looks it."

Angela allows another smile. "Actually, she really is. This is what she does when she's upset—makes a spectacle and buys things. Alana doesn't talk a lot about anything except herself, but when she does, she talks about her daughter. Last night she was up half the night, drinking Stoli, and asking me again and again if she should call in the FBI to take care of Cali. I told her no, that you could handle it."

"Thanks for the vote of confidence. I don't think she likes me very much. The Teton County Sheriff had a talk with me earlier."

"Oh shit. She did it, didn't she? Called 'her dearest friend' the sheriff? I told her not to do that. Sorry, Burns. Everyone else kind of enjoyed seeing Danny made to look like an ass. Just not her. She's sleeping with him, you know. And he's sleeping with absolutely *everyone*. And I think she's beginning to realize it and it's making her insecure—that's why I've got to take a hike tomorrow, to follow Danny. She suspects he's been taking local girls up to this hot spring near her property." She laughs. "No, you're not too popular with that crowd, Burns. Danny Gorgon wants to, as he says in his movie-macho talk, rip off your head and shit down your neck."

I shake my head. "Don't you mind following her around and carrying her clothes? Dealing with these people?"

"No, not really. I want into the business, so I'll pay my dues. When I started at the Bureau I dreamed of being a profiler, but ever since they made that movie, it's like the most competitive posting there is."

"*The Silence of the Lambs*, right?"

She rolls her eyes. "Saw it when I was fifteen and right then I decided to get a master's in psych and a federal badge."

"My brother felt the same way about *Top Gun*," I say without thinking. But then he found other ways of getting high, ways where he wouldn't have to answer to anyone or follow orders.

At the mention of my brother, Angela's smile grows wider, almost predatory. "I was hoping your brother would come up. Roberto Burns came close to making the Bureau's Top Ten for a while last year. But the Argentineans wouldn't extradite him—your family's got some kind of pull down there, apparently. I was in L.A., you know, when he caught that flight to Buenos Aires. We missed him by this much." She holds up a thumb and finger that are a half-inch apart. "Saw his picture in the file, too. If he ever gets clean and does his time, he could be a movie star himself. Maybe there's a place for him in my screenplay, too."

"I'll pass that along the next time I hear from him. In fact, he might be meeting some of your colleagues soon."

"Really? He's gonna do a deal? From what I read in his file, he's got the contacts to make it happen if he's willing to switch teams."

"That's what I hear," I say, shrugging and wanting to change the subject. "Can I get you to pretend you're Jodie Foster in that movie for a minute and help me do some profiling?" Striving to talk quietly over the still-too-loud music, I give her a strictly factual summary of the letters, the attempted break-in, and last night's attack at the bar. "Tell me what you know about the guys who do this kind of stuff."

She wrinkles her nose with an expression of disgust.

"Okay, Burns, there are generally two types of serious stalkers. There are the Spurned Suitors, the guys who've been rejected. Those losers either want to reestablish the relationship or get revenge for having been dumped. They can be dangerous and often lethal. Then, especially with celebrities, there are the Predators and the Insane—subsets of the same general category but alike. Sometimes they can be pretty dangerous, too. Because of the letters, it sounds possible that whoever's doing this is at least mentally ill, if not schizophrenic."

"As Alana may have told you, Cali was dating a sergeant in the Sheriff's Office until about a month ago, when she dumped him." I tell her about how he'd driven by my place all night and then about our brief confrontation outside the courthouse.

Angela rubs her chin with her knuckles and considers. "Jealousy, following, lurking, all that fits a Spurned Suitor type. But it doesn't match up with the rambling letters."

"Maybe they were a ploy. You know, scare her so she'll feel like she needs him. Needs his protection."

I'm pleased when Angela purses her lips and nods thoughtfully. "If he were pretty smart and cunning, yeah, that's possible. If he's the guy, you'd better be watching your back. He could just as easily focus on you when you're getting in his face and she's spending nights in your house."

"For her protection," I point out, feeling the need to.

Angela smiles. "Sure."

Less enthusiastically, I tell her, "I've got another suspect, too. A local kid who sometimes works on Ski Patrol at the resort. He was diagnosed as schizophrenic two years ago, and before that he was charged with stalking a high-school girl. Letters and all, although I haven't seen them. His mother abandoned him at an early age and his father disappeared after going bankrupt and selling the family's home. Cali prosecuted him for hijacking stiffs from the coroner's office and trying to sell photographs of them. His defense, in part, was that the cops had a vendetta against him. That he was being framed."

"Why are you bothering with the cop, then? A schizo with a history of stalking sounds right on target. Particularly when Cali was the one who stood up in court, in public, and pointed her finger at him. He might view her as his persecutor, a symbol of all that he imagines is wrong with the world."

I want it to be Wokowski, not Armalli. I don't like the way everything seems to point away from Wook except his constant menacing presence. But I resolve to do my job and follow the evidence instead of my machismo. "Why would he want to kidnap her, though? Why not just take a shot at her, or run her down in the street or something?"

"He probably wants to scare her as well as do something symbolic, make her suffer in some way. More than anything, he might want to get her alone so that he's the dominant one, in control, and where she has to listen and do whatever he says. A role reversal from the jail and courtroom, you know?"

That makes a lot of sense. Armalli has once again overtaken Wokowski and eased back into the top position.

"This is all just speculation, but it sounds like you're playing a dangerous game. You should get Cali out of town until you find this guy and get him under control."

I explain that I'd tried to do exactly that, but that Cali is determined to go through with tomorrow's trial—the case where Wokowski's beating of the old man will be revealed to the public.

Angela looks out at the faces pressed in on the glass and keeps talking.

"When I was in grad school I did an internship for a professor who worked at the forensic unit of the state mental hospital in Virginia. She took me to this conference with her where they had these virtual-reality goggles and earphones. It was some drug company thing, trying to show you what an unmedicated schizophrenic's world was like. You'd look through them and see the world the way a schizophrenic does." She shivers and crosses her arms. "It was unbelievably freaky, Burns. Through the earphones you heard all these voices—some of them commanding you to do things, others just shrieking or totally incomprehensible. It was chaos. What you saw through the goggles was even worse. Every time you looked at someone's face it was a different face. Sometimes it was an old man's or a baby's and sometimes it was a monster's. Spiders would crawl by like they were crawling over your eyes. It was un-fucking-real."

I remember something I'd noticed in Armalli's most recent file. "He's supposed to be taking a drug called Haldol to control his symptoms. Is that kind of thing effective?"

"Antipsychotics like that can be. They're commonly used to treat diseases like schizophrenia and dementia. But they call these guys paranoid for a reason. They often won't take them unless it's monitored."

"How well would Armalli be able to function without the drugs?"

"It depends on his level of psychosis. Timing, too. Some people are so inundated with voices and mania that they can't function at all. They just sit in a corner and sort of get comatose. Others can be quite resourceful. Look at John Hinckley. He had enough intelligence to get past Reagan's Secret Service with a gun. Or Ted Kaczynski, who hid for years in Montana despite the Bureau's best efforts, wrote very lucidly, and built some pretty impressive explosives from scratch. They can be very cunning."

I thank her for her help and turn to shoulder my way back through the crowd outside the door. Angela touches my arm to stop me and says, "You'd better get this guy locked up quick."

EIGHTEEN

"YOU GOT A WARRANT?"

How many times have I heard this? When you're a cop, it seems almost like an automatic greeting—*How's it going?*—anytime you show your badge.

The man in the gun shop is tall and big bellied. His gut swells out over the counter far enough to almost hide the cheap handguns that are displayed below with paper price tags tied with string around the trigger guards. He wears an army-surplus tank top to show off his fading tattoos. His breath smells of hot dogs and beer. Around his waist is a holster that holds a ridiculously large revolver. Behind him, mounted on the wall, is an assortment of pepper sprays and stun guns.

"No, sir. I'm simply asking for your help with a case I'm working on."

"I'm not gonna tell you nothing 'less you gotta warrant," he says with a barely concealed belch. "Don't have to."

"Why not help me out, save us both the trouble? It's better to be asked than told, isn't it?" I try out that smile I've been practicing.

"You guys think you can take away our God-given right to bear arms. You should read the Constitution, pal. It's right there in the Second 'mendment—"

"Mr. Richter, I'm not trying to take away your guns. All I'm trying to do is find out if—"

"You look kinda familiar. Lemme see your badge again."

I sigh and flip it open again. Badge envy, I'm thinking. More than guns, these yahoos want badges. As if carrying a gun isn't enough power. If they were to get a badge, too, they'd just learn that they're still powerless. Wives and girlfriends will continue to ridicule them, and their parents will still tell them they're wasting their lives. Respect has to be earned. And sometimes even then you don't get it.

But I'm wrong when it comes to Leon Richter, owner of Leon's Pawn and Guns. It's my name he wants another look at.

"Holy shit, you're that guy—"

"Look, I'm kind of in a hurry, Mr. Richter. Could you—"

But he's not listening. He slaps the worn leather holster with a practiced move and mimics pulling the gun off his hip. He points his index finger at my chest. *"Bang bang bang,"* he says. "Planted those three spics in the ground." He looks suddenly worried and lets his hand drop back to the holster. "No offense, man. There's spics and then there's Mexicans, just like there's niggers and then there's blacks."

"Kind of like how there's trash and then there's whites, right?"

He nods and smiles at me. "Yeah, that's right. We got our trash just like everybody else."

"Can you tell me who's bought a Stun Master 625 from you lately?"

He considers this as he continues stroking his holster's cover. "Law doesn't require me to keep any records of that. Normally, I'd tell you to go to hell. Just on principle, you know, not 'cause I got anything to hide. See, I don't like cops. But seeing as how you're sort of a celebrity, and 'cause far as

I know none of those fucking liberals in Washington is trying to take the zappers away, I guess I can help you out."

"I'd appreciate it."

"But first you got to do something for me."

"What?"

"I want you to sign something."

While he rummages under the counter, I wonder if he means a receipt or something. Or some sort of waiver stating that I promise to never try and take away his guns. Or even a petition saying that I believe every insecure asshole in the great state of Wyoming deserves a concealed weapon on his eighth birthday.

He pulls out a paper target from behind the counter. It shows the silhouette of a man. Three bullet holes make eyes and a mouth, and there are several more through the chest. One humorously intended hole has been punched through the groin.

"You want me to sign this?"

"That would be great, Mr. Burns."

Feeling stupider than I've ever felt in my life, and with my face turning red, I sign the damn thing. It's easier than getting a judge to sign a warrant. But after doing it I actually look over my shoulder to make sure McGee isn't about to walk into the store.

Then Leon Richter tells me he can't really say who's bought the ten or so stun guns he remembers selling in the last year. "Don't take names, man. No registration required." Now that he's gotten what he wants—my signature on the target lying on the greasy glass counter before us, he's turned churlish again.

"If they pay cash, like most of the geezers who buy these things, I don't got even a credit card receipt."

"Do you recall if anyone young has bought one lately? Someone about my age or even younger?"

"Nah, like I said, it's the geezers that want 'em. Afraid of muggers or something. Sorry, dude. That's all I know."

After enduring the shame of signing his target, the only thing I learn from Leon is that Stun Masters can be ordered through the mail and over the Internet. And I remember that Myron Armalli is web-savvy, that he sold his charming birthday cards over the Internet. I can call the company, but there's no doubt that they'll demand a warrant before turning over records of sales to Wyoming. While it will be useful when it comes time to prosecute the stalker, it's going to take too long. Weeks, maybe months, to get it signed and served to their corporate headquarters.

This thought, as well as Leon's lack of information, allows me to get a little churlish in return.

"How much you sell these targets for?"

"A quarter. That one, with your name on it, I bet I can get a hundred bucks."

I put a quarter on the counter.

"Hey! What are you doing?" he yells at me as I walk out the door tearing up his target. As he'd told me, he doesn't like cops anyway.

The grass in the meadow is so dry that it crackles beneath my shoes. Flying insects dart and drone in the heat above the parched stalks. Thorny seeds stick to my pants and shoelaces as if autumn is already here, and the plants are clawing at me with the desperate need to breed. Encircling the small clearing are woods so dense that it looks like it would be impossible to move through them. At some time over the past few years a storm had knocked down half the trees in the forest and created an enormous blowdown—a labyrinth of tangled branches and splintered pine trunks.

Despite the buzzing insects and clinging seeds, this place feels very dead. But underneath that cemetery sensation there is a strange sort of volatile energy, and I realize that this entire valley could explode with the drop of a match.

Mungo seems to sense some danger, too, because for once she doesn't sprint for the trees. Instead, uncharacteristically, she stays close by my side.

As I'd seen on the big county map in the Sheriff's Office, the old Armalli homestead almost borders the large ranch Alana Reese has owned for twenty-eight years. They are separated only by a narrow strip of public land, two miles wide, that is a part of the Elk Refuge. According to the case files I'd borrowed, Myron Armalli was born and raised on this same piece of land. It's easy to imagine young Myron creeping through this oppressive forest, binoculars or perhaps a camera swinging from his neck, to spy on the celebrity's daughter growing up almost next door. Or heading off on a dark hike to set horses afire when he wasn't photographing hijacked corpses.

The Armalli land was a small twenty-acre parcel, dwarfed by Alana's two thousand and some. This clearing is where the house stood until it was condemned and knocked down by the Forest Service, after Myron's mother abandoned him and his father went bankrupt. Then Dad abandoned him, too. It lies in a small valley bordered by high ridges on two sides. The weedy double-track road I'd come in on is the only open end. The valley dead-ends a few hundred yards to the east in a third ridge bordering the Elk Refuge.

"Stay close, Mungo," I say as she snuffs her way toward the pile of broken concrete that was once the Armalli residence. My words must have been sharper than I intended, because she flinches and looks at me with a guilty expression.

"You don't want to get a rusty nail in your paw," I explain in a softer voice.

Sheriff Buchanan had told me that Myron was believed to still be living somewhere on his parents' old property. Squatting there. She also told me that Myron was currently under investigation by Game and Fish for hunting violations—it was suspected that he'd been shooting deer and elk out of season and without a permit.

Circling the ruin, which is little more than a pile of rubble squared off by four corner pillars and a stone chimney, I can't shake the feeling that I'm being watched. The sensation is all the more disturbing because it's still daylight—you should only feel something like this at night. A Wyoming boy and a hunter, Armalli is sure to have a rifle. The .40 H&K clipped to my sweating side would be about as useful as a squirt gun against a rifle in the woods.

And I can't shake the recollection of Angela Hernandez telling me what it had been like to see the world through a schizophrenic's eyes.

I hadn't seen any other cars on the long, bumpy drive in, but the road branched off everywhere into little trails that were probably made by logging survey crews. A thousand cars could be parked unseen in woods this thick. There were fresh tire tracks in the dirt closer to the highway. When I got out and studied them, it appeared that several different cars had left them. There was no way to tell if one of them was the '88 Ford F-150 pickup that, according to Motor Vehicle Services, Armalli drove.

Mungo is sniffing at something and looking off into the trees in the direction of the northern ridge. She scratches one paw in the dirt and sniffs again. Looking at the ground where she's focused, I see freshly cracked stalks of grass and some seeds scattered in the dirt. I look around again and now see trampled plants ringing all the way around the ruined house. The clearing is littered with them. A faint, fresh trail leads off in the direction the wolf is staring. It looks as if heavy things have been dragged in that direction, scarring the dry earth.

It would be easy to follow even without Mungo pointing her nose toward the dense forest below the ridge. But I don't. The sun has sunk behind the distant hills that obscure the Tetons, and I know it will be night in less than an hour.

And I don't like being out here by myself, with only Mungo the cringing wolf to watch my back. All the bravado I'd felt in the gun shop has fled. Time for me to be fleeing, too.

Calling for Mungo to follow, I start crunching back through the meadow to where the Pig hulks at the end of the Forest Service road. A cold spot the size of a silver dollar suddenly slides across one shoulder and settles just above the small of my back. It's got to be my imagination, but the impulse to dive into the weeds is almost overwhelming. I stay on my feet, though, as pores all over my body release a clammy film of sweat.

Pride is the only thing that keeps me upright. If he is out there watching me, I'm not going to crawl on my belly all the way to the truck. Crawling wouldn't keep me from getting shot anyway. Instead I walk faster, and Mungo senses my urgency and leaps into the backseat without being ordered. I press hard on the gas pedal, spin all four wheels in the dirt, and get the hell out of there.

NINETEEN

THE PLAN FOR THE NIGHT is that Cali will stay with me again at my place while Jim attempts to discreetly trail Charles Wokowski. The Teton County Sheriff's and the Jackson Police Department have BOLO instructions—Be On the Lookout—regarding Myron Armalli and his Ford truck, as do the Highway Patrol and the park rangers. They'll hold him for questioning if they come across him. Tomorrow I'll go exploring around Armalli's place with someone to watch my back other than my cowering wolf. With luck I'll find both him and enough evidence to arrest him. For the time being, I think, I have all the bases covered.

At seven o'clock Cali answers the door with an overnight bag in her hand. She doesn't look particularly happy to see me. When I'd called ahead I initially told her she should go to her mother's, where there was an FBI agent in addition to her mother's regular bodyguards. Cali refused, which really wasn't such a bad idea because that would have just put her that much closer to where I suspect Armalli is hanging out. She counter-proposed spending the night at her uncle Bill's in town, but I couldn't trust a dying old man—even one who is a legendary hardman—to protect her. So we settled on the unhappy compromise of her staying another night in my rented cabin.

Initially there's not a lot for us to say to each other. She no longer looks hurt like she had in the afternoon. Instead she looks a little angry. And I'm still carrying the guilt from kissing her last night. *God, what a stupid thing to do. What the hell had possessed me?* But thinking about that quickly leads down a black path to even gloomier thoughts about Rebecca.

Cali gets in the Pig and slams the door shut behind her, shaking the truck's rusty frame. I wince. I'm in for a fun night. Mungo grins painfully as she gets a quick, unwanted pat when Cali twists around in her seat to greet her. "I'm glad to see *you*, at least," she tells the wolf.

We stop by a health-food store and pick up pasta and jarred sauce for dinner. Some fresh vegetables, too. Cali speaks to me for the first time, saying she's hungry, that she should carbo-load before her trial in the morning anyway. "I get so nervous during those things that I burn calories like a blowtorch," she adds, momentarily, it appears, forgetting to be angry. Remembering then, she looks at me with suspicion. "I just hope you don't expect *me* to do the cooking."

I only shake my head.

By the time we get inside the cabin, Cali is addressing me through Mungo again.

"How can you live with this guy?" Cali murmurs loud enough so that I can hear. "He doesn't know how to treat a girl, does he? I don't think he knows what he wants. What do you think, wolfy?" Mungo lets out a low groan of assent before slumping down on her sleeping bag.

They're both wrong. I know what I want—I'm just afraid that I can't have it.

To keep from thinking I try to keep busy. I go into the second bedroom to drag the pile of cams, ropes, and carabiners off the bed. I throw it all into a corner, making a jangling racket.

I'd picked up a set of twin sheets in town earlier and I toss them on the bed for Cali to use. I don't intend to make it up. Out in the main room my portable stereo/CD player comes to life. She's selected Train's first album from the small stack of CDs. Maybe the music will mellow us both. Assuage my guilt and lessen her anger. After a moment of further straightening— kicking at the gear to get it out of the way—I find myself ripping open the plastic-wrapped packages and stretching the sheets over the bed. I should listen to music more often.

When I go back out, Cali is already in the kitchen. The sounds from the CD player appear to be having an effect on her, too—her prior irritability appears to have dissipated somewhat. She helps me with dinner. My elbows occasionally touch her upper arms as I chop broccoli and once she bumps me away from the sink with her hip. The intimacy is disconcerting, but pleasant. As we work together without speaking I think of good times with Rebecca. How cooking in the kitchen would often lead to us lying naked on the cold tile floor. A little voice in my head disrupts my reverie by wondering if we'll ever do that again.

Sitting at the big table, we slurp our pasta. The only other noise is the music. Mungo watches us eat with wet eyes and drool spilling from her mouth but is too shy to beg. I try to avoid looking at Cali but she still manages to catch my eye.

"Tell me something, Anton. Are you stringing me along?" Her green eyes bore into mine like she's trying to look past them. Through them, into my brain.

I put down my fork and spoon. "No," I say flatly. Then with less certainty but more honesty, "Yes. Shit, maybe."

Cali looks amused at my equivocation. I find it hard to hold her gaze but I force myself to do it.

"What's going on with the girlfriend?"

"She's coming up tomorrow. To dump me, I'm pretty sure. Things have been kind of rough lately. I don't know."

"If she's going to dump you, why doesn't she just call then? Or write a letter?"

"That's not her style."

"So I'm the bench warmer, huh?" she asks with a small smile. "Second string?" And it hits me that I *am* stringing her along, keeping her ready and willing so that if Rebecca does finally cut our ties then I'll have somewhere to go for comfort. The realization makes me feel like an ass. I resolve to keep things more professional from now on.

So instead of answering her question, I ask, "Tell me about Myron Armalli."

The smile fades away. "*That* guy," she says with distaste. "He's a freak, a real loony. I prosecuted him about three months ago for dressing up corpses he was transporting for the coroner's office and taking pictures of them. Maybe doing more. Why do you ask?"

"I was reading about him today. His files. Did you know Armalli had a prior for stalking a girl in high school? Right here in Teton County?"

"No. It must have been a juvie case—this is the first I've heard of it. Where did you learn about that?"

I don't mention taking the sealed files. Having already told her about my brother, she has more than enough information to get me in trouble if she wants to. Instead I ask, "Did he give you any weird vibes during the trial?"

"Sure. But he gave everybody weird vibes. The guy's weird, really weird. He yelled in court—in front of the judge—about how I would regret taking away his liberties or something like that. A lot of other strange stuff, too. Are you thinking that he might be the guy? Not Wook?"

"I'm starting to think there's a pretty good chance," I admit.

I'm still having a hard time with the fact that it's not Wook. Nothing would make me happier than to have him be the stalker, to link his wrists behind his back and put him in a cage. After all, I know he's following her around. I know he hates my guts. And what did he have in that gym bag this morning? But I resolve again to follow the evidence, not my impulses. I'm still carrying a cold spot in the center of my back from my afternoon visit to the old homestead.

Cali tells me more about Armalli, and on my mental notepad I can see the evidence mounting. When he'd taken the witness stand he'd blabbed on and on about his "art" and his First Amendment right to make it. About how Hollywood and the modern art establishment were trying to stop him. Oppressing him. He apparently believed his greeting cards were revolutionary, that they would remove the boundaries between life and death, break down the barriers, or some bullshit like that. I think I can begin to see a little into the head of this young madman I've never met but whose presence I'd felt earlier in the afternoon. Does he think of his prosecutor—his persecutor—as a future piece of performance art? Hadn't Angela Hernandez with her master's in psych talked of the stalker maybe wanting to do something symbolic?

"Did you ever talk to him alone?"

"Just once. When we were in the courtroom before his attorney and the judge and jury came in. He said in a real quiet voice, not looking at me, that he'd known me when I was a kid. That was it. I ignored him when he said it, his attorney not being there and all."

"Did you know him?"

She looks a little bit uneasy. "In the file I saw his address. He grew up practically next door to Mom's ranch. I remember sometimes seeing a kid in the woods by the meadow where I rode horses. A shy kid who never came out and said hello or anything. Now I think it might have been him. And it makes me feel bad, because I never made any effort to talk to him. I was a pretty self-involved little girl. Mom's influence, you know."

"Then, when he was on the witness stand, he said you were going to regret charging him?"

"Yeah. That's what he said. I didn't think anything of it. I thought he meant because he was such a great artist or something like that."

I don't say anything.

"You know what?" Cali asks, looking down at her hands. "I do regret it. Not talking to him when he was a kid. Ignoring him when he spoke to me in the courtroom. I should have reached out to him. He's a messed-up kid, that's all."

"One who's trying to kidnap you. And do who knows what after that."

There's nothing more to say about it. Wook's name is off my suspect list for the stalker. At least off the list for the guy who's trying to kidnap her. But I can't help feeling that although I've erased his name, I can still see it lingering faintly on the page in my head. I still believe that he's a danger. To both of us. *What the hell did he have in that gym bag?*

After a few minutes' silence I ask her, "Are you going to put Wook on the witness stand tomorrow?"

Cali sounds eager to talk about something else. "He'll be my second witness. First I want to put on the good cop, the guy who initially made the stop. I know everyone thinks I'm just taking this thing to trial to punish Wook—embarrass him for what he did—but I really want to win. I want to get this old guy off the streets for a while. But the defense will argue—or imply—that the jury should walk him because of the police misconduct."

I know that this bit of misdirection will probably be effective. The jury won't be told about the defendant's prior history of drunk driving and running over small children. Wook won't even be able to explain *why* he did *what* he did on the witness stand because it would be prejudicial to the defense. All the jury will know about is that he punched an

TRIAL BY ICE AND FIRE   163

old man for a relatively minor offense. Justice and criminal law are incidental, I remember McGee once telling me.

"Are you going to play the tape?"

"I've got to," she says, as if there weren't any choice. And it's true that now that she's shown it to the defense attorney there is no other choice, but she never had to give it to the defense attorney in the first place. That was an uncommon act of bravery and integrity for a new prosecutor who will have to work with the local police. Especially when she was implicating her boyfriend in a crime that could cost him his career.

After we eat, Cali puts Counting Crows on the stereo. This, too, is a good choice. I busy myself doing the dishes after she helps me carry them to the sink. The chair creaks when she sits back down at the table and begins flipping through the pages of her case file, reviewing witness statements and the law regarding the admissibility of Intoxilyzer results. I wash out the pot and scrub the dishes. Then I go upstairs and bring down from the loft the copy of *Smoke Jump*. This time Cali sees it in my hand.

"Do you mind me reading this here?" I ask her. "I can go back upstairs."

She looks down at her legal pad and blows air out of her cheeks. "No. I have a copy of it, too, but I've never been able to read it. It's supposed to be a good book, all about Dad and Bill and Mom and what happened on Elation Peak before I was born."

"From what I've read so far, they were pretty ballsy guys. Parachuting into forest fires and all that. Getting their kicks, but doing something with a real purpose, too. Your dad sounds like someone I would have liked to have known."

Cali nods a couple of times. She starts to say something then clears her throat. I wait, but she doesn't try to speak again. Instead she goes back to work. I lie on the couch and read.

It's a good book. Like Norman MacLean's *Young Men*

and Fire, which is referred to many times, the author gives more than technical information about fire fighting and what went wrong on Elation Peak. He provides details about the men who do this for a poorly paid career, talking about their backgrounds, training, and the off-season hobbies that the job supports. Much of it centers on Bill Laughlin and Patrick Morrow, Cali's father, and much is made about their friendship. They'd known each other since childhood. Patrick had been handsome and sensitive, a terrific skier but not good enough to win races; Bill, a kind of good-natured bully and sometimes a practical joker who was addicted to putting up hard routes on alpine walls. Together they made an unlikely but extremely close pair.

Salacious details and a complication in the friendship are added when young actress Alana Reese buys a ranch in the valley and meets Patrick and Bill one night in the Million Dollar Cowboy Bar. Both men pursued her keenly, but after a time her affections were won by the skier rather than the climber. The author, citing Bill as his source, speculates that perhaps this was because Patrick's passion was more accessible to the actress. She could fly him off to a luxurious chalet in St. Moritz, but she couldn't sleep on an icy ledge with Bill. I remember Cali telling me in the bar about how Bill's always been in love with her mother. Again I have to push away thoughts about Rebecca.

I'm just getting to the part where a fire is building outside Lander, Wyoming, when my phone rings. Jim's name is flashing on the screen.

"What's up?" I ask.

"Sorry, man. He got away from me."

"What happened?"

Jim explains that he'd followed Wokowski to a house south of town earlier in the evening. The sergeant was inside for about fifteen minutes, then came out carrying a little boy in his arms. He put the boy in the front seat of the department SUV, then he and a woman—the boy's mother, probably—loaded a wheelchair in the back. They drove to a baseball field in town where a Little League game was being played and parked next to the field. The only time Wokowski got out of the car was to go and buy hot dogs and Cokes. "I thought they were there for the duration, man. So in the third inning I went to get myself something to eat. When I came back, they were gone."

"Did you go back to the boy's house?"

"Yeah. Even peeked in the window—he'd brought the boy back then taken off. So I drove back over to Wook's place but his truck wasn't there either. So now I'm just cruising around, looking. According to the desk, he's supposed to go on duty at midnight. I'm sorry, man."

I can't really reprimand him, although I'm tempted to. I'd done something far worse by leaving Cali unprotected when she went to the bathroom in the bar last night. Besides, Wook is no longer a suspect for the attempted kidnappings so it really doesn't matter. But I do want to know what he's up to. What his intentions are.

"Okay. Keep looking. Come by out here and see if he's lurking around again tonight. Don't worry about it, though. He's not looking as good as he did this morning."

Jim promises to do just that. Right after I hit the END button another phone starts ringing. Cali, who's been watching me talk, gets up and takes her phone out of her bag.

"Is it Wook?" I ask as she studies the screen.

"No. It's Suzy Casey, the lawyer in the trial tomorrow." Then she answers the phone by saying with a smile, "You aren't going to ask for a continuance *now*, are you, Suzy?"

Her smile fades as she listens to the answer.

"When did it happen?" A moment later, "Is he going to be all right?" Then finally, "Okay, of course I'll have no objection. You can tell the judge for me in the morning."

After she hangs up she smiles again, but there's a wrinkle

running across her forehead. She closes the case file with finality and puts her legal pad on top of it. "Her client was drinking and fell down some stairs about a half hour ago. Broke his collarbone and his nose. A concussion, too, the doctor said. The trial's off for another week or two."

"Was anyone with him?"

"No. He was at home, alone." The wrinkle grows more pronounced. "But he managed to crawl to a phone before he passed out."

I go to the window and look out at the night. All I can see is my own distorted reflection in the glass. "Jim lost Wook about an hour ago."

Behind me Cali doesn't say anything. But I know that both of us are wondering just what the hell is going on.

TWENTY

A LITTLE LATER she goes into the bathroom and comes out wearing an unlikely pair of pajamas. They have cartoon cats all over them. I can't help but smile at her. She grins back and says, "I'm not the 'Too Drunk to Fuck' girl tonight." Then she heads for the bed in the gear room. "I'm going to try and forget about this thing with Wook and Armalli and my defendant and get some sleep. Let's go into the mountains in the morning, okay? I can take a day off since the trial's postponed, and I've got to get away from this shit. We can stop by my house and pick up my skis."

"That's more than fine with me." I can wait until the afternoon to go looking for Armalli. And the desire to get a little air beneath my heels is almost a craving. *Feed the Rat.*

She takes one last long look at me before she closes the door between the bedroom and the main room. There's no smile on her face now. Just a serious expression that's hard for me to read. It might be something close to pity. She shakes her head ever so slightly as she softly shuts the door.

I pick up my cell phone again and call for Mungo to

come with me out onto the porch. As soon as we step out into the night the wolf heads for the trees. The light from the front window casts a glow out over the hood of my truck and into the lane. In that light I can see Mungo's tail lift high before she disappears. For a minute I listen and watch intently, half afraid of and half wanting to hear the rumble of a Sheriff's Office SUV and see a sweep of lights coming up the lane. If I knew anything for sure I would feel a lot better.

But the night is still.

I do the deep-breathing thing Rebecca had taught me, filling my belly with air then expelling the carbon dioxide in a steady puff along with the bad thoughts in my head. The first thing that goes out is any thought of Cali, the sight of her in her cat pajamas and last night's taste of her lips and tongue. Then goes Armalli and what I suspect is intended to be a horror show of performance art, and then Wokowski and his unknown intentions. After that I exhale my brother and my worries about what's going to happen to him. Finally, the thought of a life without Rebecca goes out, too, but then I somehow manage to suck it back in. Like it's some sticky phlegm putting up a fight. A cough that just won't clear. After a few more deep blows I feel its grip lessening. Ten or twenty more and I'm dizzy, seeing stars that aren't there, but the notion is finally no more than the leftovers of a mild cold.

"Hi," I say when she picks up the phone. It's eleven at night, the time when Rebecca smokes the first of her three daily cigarettes before starting her best writing hours.

"Hi, Ant." She sounds almost normal. It makes my heart involuntarily swell with hope. From those two words I can tell that the distance between us has fallen away temporarily. Maybe, just maybe, this is all going to work out.

"Are you coming up, 'Becca?"

"I'm coming." I pump a fist into the night sky and grit my teeth with determination. If I can just see her then I'll win her back. Woo her, beg her, whatever it takes. "For just a couple of days. I'm taking some sick time. I'll be in Jackson tomorrow night. Dad and I will leave Denver at about ten, and according to MapQuest, we'll be in town by eight."

"Your dad's coming?"

"It was his idea to come along. He wants to get out of town, too. He's been pretty stressed out lately."

Her father is a law professor at the University of Colorado in Boulder. I like and respect him but we've not been close. I can't figure out what it means, her wanting to bring him up when we have such a personal discussion planned. I know I'm not his idea of the perfect companion for his daughter. Afraid of hearing something I don't want to hear, something that will undermine my newfound confidence and determination, I restrain myself from asking more.

"Will you stay with me? He can stay here, too."

"With you and your stalking victim, you mean? That place you rented doesn't sound all that big." Her voice isn't mistrustful, the way it had been last night. There's a lightness in it now. The hard edge that started appearing about a month ago is apparently in remission tonight.

"No, 'Becca. Just you and me. I'll put my vic somewhere else for the night if I need to. But I'm hoping to wrap this up anyway tomorrow afternoon. I'm pretty sure I know who he is and where he's hiding out." This is more than optimistic, considering the new wrinkle with Wook and Cali's injured defendant. But still, I'm *determined*.

"You'll be safe, won't you? None of that soloing BS, not in the mountains or when it comes to arresting bad guys, okay?"

I want to laugh, it's so good to hear her talking this way. "Promise."

"Good. My dad's gotten us a condo at a place called Spring Creek Ranch. He's feeling pretty down—this week is the fifth anniversary of my stepmom's death, you know. I really feel like I ought to stay with him."

"You can both stay here. There's the spare bedroom

downstairs. I'll clean the place up," I tell her quickly, wanting to press my advantage while it lasts. "I'll make you both dinner. I'll serve you breakfast in bed. And I'll throw in some serious lovemaking. *Quiet* lovemaking for once, so he won't hear. I'll even throw in some earplugs, just in case. And maybe a muzzle for you."

Rebecca laughs.

More seriously, letting out everything I feel for her and trying to put it in my voice, I say, "Stay with me, 'Becca."

She manages to ignore whatever she hears in my tone. "He's already made the condo reservations, but we'll see. We'll be getting in late. Meet us at a restaurant called the Granary at nine o'clock. We'll see where we go from there."

MONDAY

TWENTY-ONE

THE DAWN IS UNUSUALLY DARK, with low clouds blocking out the stars. According to the weather-forecast recording at the park headquarters, these clouds, which could hang around all day, offer little hope of rain for the parched valley. When the sun starts to brighten the eastern horizon it looks like a gauzy curtain has been draped over the Teton Range.

Where we're headed isn't one of the big mountain chutes Cali has on her tick list. There's not enough time for that today. I want to find Myron Armalli before the sun goes down—before Rebecca arrives—and I can't risk the uncertain schedules caused by the higher peaks. I need to be back on the hunt by noon. The northeast face of Mt. Wister initially sounded dull to Cali, but when I explained that we just might find two thousand vertical feet of late-season powder stashed between the peaks there she agreed to give it a try.

At seven o'clock we're two hours up the trail and sharing an orange at the start of the North Fork of Avalanche Canyon. Mungo, on a long leash tied around my waist, sniffs at every plant or mineral protruding from the ground. Below us is the steep wall of Shoshoko Falls, which we'd just ascended by switchbacking up through mud and snow and downed trees. The number of splintered trunks lying shattered near the wall's base gives literal meaning to the canyon's name.

Mt. Wister's steep north face is hidden by the clouds even though it can't be more than a few hundred yards to our left. The entire cirque, formed on the north by South Teton, Cloudveil Dome, Shadow Peak, and on the south by Wister's three summits, is completely shrouded. All that's visible ahead is the still-frozen surface of tiny Lake Taminah.

Sucking down the orange slices Cali insists on feeding me, I feel a breeze rise up behind and below us. The mist, mingled with the waterfall's spray, is wet on the back of my neck. I turn to look back down the canyon, hoping the wind will lift the fog enough so that I can spot the mother moose and the calf we'd passed near the base of the headwall. We'd had to hurry past because Mungo was doing her best to pull me off my feet and send me mud-skiing behind her in pursuit of moose burgers.

There is something moving down there, but it's not a moose's gangly shape. It's upright and walking very slowly. The parka is indistinct at this distance—it could be blue, black, or green. The hump of a dark pack is also evident. I watch it as it drops into a crouch, maybe studying our tracks.

"Looks like we're not alone," I say.

Cali looks down and spots him, too. "Should we check him out?"

Then the breeze dies and, like a sheet being spread over a bed, the mist drops again. There's nothing to see now but particles of moisture suspended in the gray air.

"It's probably just a hiker," I say. But I think it's probably Roberto, being a pain in the ass. I'd checked for headlights following us to the trailhead but hadn't noticed any. I realize now that I should have employed a simple counter-surveillance technique and pulled over at some point.

He'd shown up again last night just as I was getting off the phone with Rebecca. I smelled him before I saw him. And Mungo, who'd joined me on the porch, had smelled him long before me. She'd been lifting her head in the direction of the forest on the other side of the lane, snuffing at the air, and wagging her tail for several minutes. The scent of sweat, sunburnt skin, and wood smoke reached me as I pushed the button to end the conversation.

Across the road a match flared and my brother's lean features were revealed in its orange light. He was lighting a joint that he'd rolled as tight and as expertly as a commercial cigarette. Illuminated by the match, I could see that the backs of his hands and his fingers were wrapped with dirty athletic tape. The tape was dark with blood.

I'd followed Mungo as she danced up to him.

"What's shaking, *che*?" he asked.

I fanned the marijuana smoke away into the night. "How was the climbing?"

"Fantastic. You should've been there. The Rat ate his fill and then some. I'm just mellowing out now." He took a long drag on the joint and held in the smoke. "So, you hook your boy yet?"

I shook my head. "Not yet. It could be the cop you saw around here last night, but it's looking more and more like it might be another guy, a twenty-one-year-old psychopath who knew her when she was a kid. The cop, Wokowski, he might be lovesick and bent, but this other guy's a certifiable wacko." Then, with a smile, I added, "No offense, 'Berto."

After listening to him chuckle out the smoke, I described Armalli, adding, "*He's* a guy you can grab if you see him skulking around here." I thought it would be nice to wake up in the morning and find Armalli bound and gagged on the porch. It would save me the trouble of going looking for him myself in that combustible hollow.

"Be a lot more fun to bag the cop."

"Only if you want to get yourself shot, 'Berto. Or end up back in prison."

"When are you going to get this wrapped up? Time's running short, bro. I'm turning myself in on Thursday, you know. That's in four days."

Buoyed by my talk with Rebecca, I made a decision that I *will* climb with him one more time. Blood is more important than the risk to my deteriorating career. I couldn't let myself forget that.

"Day after tomorrow, I hope. I'm going to ski in the morning with the girl in there then try to find the *demente* in the afternoon. After that, I'm having dinner with Rebecca. Give me a call or something the next morning."

Roberto's ever-present smile grew broader. "How 'bout I come along in the morning? You got some extra boards, don't you, *che*? Keep you on the straight and narrow, pure for your little reporter."

I'd like nothing better than to see my brother ski again. He might even be a match for Cali—whatever skill he lacks he more than makes up for in gusto.

But I had to look my brother—who's risking his deal with the Feds and his freedom to get into the mountains with me—in the eye and say, "You can't come. She's a prosecutor, 'Berto. And I'm a cop. I can't even have you hanging around like this."

Who could say whether Wokowski would barge in right then to profess his love, or whether Myron Armalli might decide to pay a visit with a new stun gun and another roll of tape. In either case it would be hard to explain an escaped fugitive's presence in my cabin. Or his accompanying us on a skiing jaunt.

The grin fell away from my brother's face. Most people would have flinched at what replaced it, but I knew him too well. It was hurt he was feeling. Rejection, not anger.

"I thought you said you told her, and that she was cool with it."

My voice was almost pleading as I said, "Yeah, but being *seen* with you is something else. I'm willing to take the chance, but I can't put her out on the edge like that. I'm supposed to be protecting her, not getting her into more hot water."

Without another word Roberto faded back into the dark forest.

"Ready?" I ask.

Cali smiles at me, her green eyes bright behind the yellow lenses of her sunglasses. "Ready."

We climb through snow interspersed with patches of talus up the south side of the cirque. Although Cali and I find ourselves struggling to posthole through the deep snow, Mungo dances on the surface with her big snowshoe-like paws. The prints she leaves are as big as my hand when I spread my fingers. Soon the rock wall of Wister's north face is visible through the mist, as is the steep snowfield to the left. We seem to be reaching the top layer of clouds. Although the saddle between the summits remains murky, the slope itself looks even better than I'd hoped.

It is wide, several hundred feet across, and not quite as steep as what we'd skied two days ago on Teewinot's East Face. The angle appears to be no more than forty-five or fifty degrees but because of the mist it's a little hard to tell. White and untracked, the snow is bright even beneath the gray sky and it looks like soft powder. There's far more of the stuff than I'd expected. Because of the northeast aspect of the face and the cirque's high, shielding peaks, hardly any sunlight would reach it. Here it might as well be midwinter still.

I plow on up through deepening snow and angle for the right side of the snowfield, where it meets the steeper rock. I'm moving faster now, resolving to ignore the fact that my brother may be trailing us and getting more and more excited by the thought of making turns. We're only at the base of the snowfield and already I'm sinking up past my thighs. As difficult as it is to wade up through the stuff, Cali is close at my heels and is clearly getting excited, too.

We pause to leave Mungo at the last semiflat spot. Unable to find a horn of rock to loop her leash around, I slot a wired nut into a crack in the granite and clip the leash to it with a carabiner. Mungo looks unhappy at the prospect of being tied up and left behind. Her long face grows longer.

"Stay, Mungo. We'll be right back, girl." The wolf faces away from me and stares mournfully down into the cirque. "Think about how lucky you are that I brought you this far."

The logic of it seems to have no effect on her mood—she won't look at me. Cali and I keep churning our way uphill through the soft, white powder.

"We should have brought beacons," Cali says when we're halfway up, referring to the radio devices that allow a skier to be located after being buried under an avalanche. I'd been beginning to feel the same apprehension.

"I didn't think we'd need them this late in the season. I didn't think there'd be this much snow."

In Alaska, avalanches occurred year-round. But I hadn't seriously considered the danger here, not in late May in the lower 48, especially not after a weeklong heat wave.

"We're still going to do it, aren't we?" she asks.

To the left the snow looks so perfect. Like a brilliant white canvas, just begging to be painted with a half-helix down its center. The only marks that mar its surface are three vertical columns of rocks that define the entry chutes at the top. But there's also an ominous bulge beneath the small cornice on the opposite side of the slope. It's a two-story-house–sized mass of snow stuck to the side of the incline, the kind of convex hair trigger that a skier's weight could easily pull.

"Let's dig a pit." I stamp out a platform to hold my pack then shrug it off. I assemble the shovel that's strapped to the pack and start cutting into the mountainside, throwing snow. The first few scoops are easy—the snow is almost without mass. Deeper down the blade starts to crunch a little and the snow gets heavier. Ten minutes later we have a pit almost six feet deep with a vertical wall on the uphill side. Finally the blade scrapes on stone.

What I see at the bottom of the pit isn't encouraging. Instead of broken talus to anchor the snow, it appears that the slope sits on a smooth slab of rock. I hope it's just in this one place where I happened to dig, but I know it's dangerous to make assumptions like that. Worse still, the bottom layer of snow has been crystallized by the unseasonably warm weather into little ice pellets the size and shape of ball bearings. I scoop out a gloveful and make a fist, compressing it. When I open my palm the snow remains uncompacted and sifts through my fingers. It wouldn't take much additional weight to cause the snow to collapse down onto those pellets and get the whole thing rolling on the granite slab.

It had been sensible to dig this pit. Not so sensibly, I decide to ignore the implications.

"It's sketchy," I admit, "but I've never heard of a big avalanche this late in the season. We should be all right. But we'll have to watch each other, go down one at a time and avoid that bulge over there."

Above us at the top of the snowfield are the three chutes leading down from the right-hand edge of the ridge. I head for the one closest to the rock wall because it looks less steep and the cornice at its crest appears smaller.

Thirty minutes later I'm using my ax to knock off the cornice's whipped-cream swirl, carving a path to the ridge top. I swim more than climb up it and find myself on a knife-edge spine between Wister's easternmost summits. On the other side is a vertical drop that disappears into the cloud. While Cali swims up after me, I set about stomping out a new platform and cutting away at the cornice with my ax. Unlike the cornice atop Teewinot, which was so hard as to be almost ice, this one is like a pile of fluffy cotton.

"Have you seen the hiker?" Cali asks.

The cirque is so hazy with mist that I can barely make out Mungo, wagging her tail anxiously twelve hundred feet below us.

"No, but I can't see much. Don't worry about it. It was just a hiker."

Cali throws her pack down in the snow and begins unstrapping her skis. "I can't get it out of my mind that it could be the guy, you know?"

"If you want to know the truth, it was probably my brother, okay?"

She stops what she's doing and stares up at me with a questioning look. "Why didn't you tell him to join us?"

"Do you want to go to jail as an accessory?"

"No, but I'd like to meet him. No one would see us together up here."

The truth is that I don't want to be in her debt more than I already am. I already owe her for keeping his presence around my cabin a secret. Having her actually meet him would just be like doubling or tripling the outstanding sum.

When I don't say anything she goes back to readying her skis. "What if it's not him?" she asks.

"I'm going to go down first, so if whoever it was *did* follow us up the canyon, I'll be able to check him out. Don't worry about it. Just spot me, okay? If it slides, keep an eye on where I am."

Despite the familiar adrenaline beginning to leak into my bloodstream, I can't entirely dismiss a rising anxiety about the stability of the slope. But I snap into my bindings anyway, and set my poles under my armpits and lean out to pick my line.

"Make it a good one," Cali says, reading my thoughts and following my gaze. "I'll eight you if you don't make a mess out of it."

I plan my route. I'll make the elevator-shaft drop dead ahead—jump turns at first until the angle eases—then cut right. Start making real turns, staying to the left side of the face until beneath that fat house-size bulge. Then carve it up right down the middle.

"Watch me," I tell Cali again.

"Go go go!" she says.

I shove off and hit the snow fifteen feet below, sinking in nearly up to my waist. The snow explodes silently under my weight and starts spilling downhill. My next twisting leap lands me in the middle of the mini-avalanche of fluff I've set off. My heart rises into my throat and I hear myself shout something delirious and ecstatic.

Just as they had been on Teewinot, my first turns in the chute are a little bit jerky, a bit unbalanced. I lean back too far and start to lose control. I barely manage to keep from blasting into the rock rib flanking the chute. With a conscious effort I throw my body forward, downhill, and the skis follow. Big bursts of loose snow slide with me on each turn, but as I pick up speed I start to outrun them. The snow is so light it feels like nothing more than tiny clouds are wrapped around my legs. The wind begins to roar in my ears and I can feel the Rat snarling with delight in my chest as he presses down on the accelerator.

I wonder if my brother's watching from somewhere in the shrouded cirque. He'll be grinning, too.

A few more 180-degree leaps and I'm out of the chute and onto the snowfield proper. It's less steep here and the snow is deeper still. I begin to carve instead of leap. Forgetting the line I'd picked from above, the Rat spins the steering wheel to the right where the snow looks so light and deep I might need a snorkel. I don't pay any attention to the threatening bulge as I drive into the fluff beneath it. All I can hear is Cali hooting from above.

The three sharp cracks sound like blasts of lightning.

They echo off the ridge, the peaks, and the canyon walls. Someone's shooting—but with the echoes it's impossible to tell from where or at whom. I almost go down as I whip my head back and forth and try to slow.

I manage to come to a stop in the waist-deep powder. I look up, taking a big breath to shout a warning to Cali.

That's when I feel more than hear a groaning sound coming out of the snowfield itself. From directly beneath my skis. Like a bomb going off. The mountain bucks beneath my boots.

TWENTY-TWO

THE EARTH IMPLODES. The Tetons are collapsing. The ground gives way so quickly, so suddenly, that it heaves me onto my uphill shoulder. I try to stop the fall by reaching out with my arm but it sinks all the way into the hissing snow a fraction of a second before my head does. I'm sucked in. The mountain rears up and swallows me whole. *Avalanche!* My soundless scream echoes around the inside of my skull as the light goes out and the cold, stinging snow washes over my face and shoves down the neck of my jacket.

I come up only to immediately go under again. The snow around me presses in with greater and greater force as it compacts with the thrashing velocity of a steep downhill slide. It spits me out a second time, blinding me with white light. My skis jerk upward and my face pops out and then my legs are yanked over my head. In a single, snapping gulp the mass of snow swallows me again. It's seizing and tearing at my limbs with incredible force, releasing momentarily before grabbing somewhere new. It punches and kicks me and stomps on my flesh. I'm being savaged. Ravaged. Torn apart. The noise that fills the air is like a freight train rolling over me.

At one point I somehow manage to get my skis pointed downhill so that I'm riding with the rush of frozen water. It's gripping me up to my chest, whipsawing my torso and legs at different speeds, but at least I'm able to breathe. I try to angle to one side as my legs are sucked back and forth, up and down, and in opposite directions. The pressure on my knees is almost unbearable. *Cut your way out! Lean back! You can make it if you can keep your feet!* Then an enormous slab strikes me in the upper back—like a major-league slugger swinging a bat— and it sends me diving head over heels into what's become a gushing torrent of semisolid cement. I start to scream—out loud this time—but the sound is chopped off as my face goes in once again.

Tumbling and twisting, my head comes up one last time. This time instead of screaming I have the presence of mind to inhale as deeply as I can. What I draw in is mostly cold spray. *Snow is porous,* I'd once learned in an avalanche-safety class during my guiding days. *You can breathe for a few minutes at least. If you don't get it packed down your gorge.* I manage to put one glove over my mouth as I'm again yanked down deep for the finale.

Abruptly everything stops. The blows stop coming. The noise is gone. So is the light. The only thing that doesn't stop is my panic. It's increasing in speed with every beat of my heart. Someone's lit the Rat on fire; he's shrieking and clawing and biting in my chest. And the pressure is immense— thousands, maybe millions, of pounds of force-compacted water-weight is pressing in on me.

I sense that I'm upside down. My left hand is still over my mouth, wedged there now like a gag, but my right arm has been torn away somewhere to the side. Neither will move even an inch. The pain coming from the compressed disks in my back and the screaming tension in the muscles of my quadriceps and stomach alert me to the fact that my feet have been pulled around behind my head, bending me into an inverted U. I make a conscious effort to open my eyes. I see nothing but black. I know I'm in deep.

But there's no telling how deep. With the amount of snow that had come down and the length of the ride, it could be ten feet or more. Twenty. Even thirty or forty. Another recollection comes back from avalanche-safety classes—how often victims are buried so deep that it isn't until late in the summer before bodies can be retrieved. Sometimes it takes a couple of warm summers to melt their graves away and pry their frozen carcasses from the snow.

My first instinct is to howl in fear. To rant and babble. To pray. Worse than the pain is the pressure, the unbelievable weight of all the snow. And worse still is the way it's squeezing my ribs. I can't breathe. I try to move my glove away from my mouth but the snow holding it there won't budge. Not even a millimeter. Cement.

A fresh spasm of terror writhes through me. What breath I can draw is in tiny, shallow pants that become shallower still with each weak exhalation. I can feel the snow around my face turning to ice from the heat and moisture. Forming itself into what's known as an alpine death mask. *God God God God* runs through my brain like a high-speed chant.

A scream builds in my chest even though I don't have the breath to let it out. My mouth opens wide involuntarily, in a jaw-tearing rictus, but no sound emerges. I can taste the leather palm of my glove. Tears begin to melt through the snow that's pressing against my eye sockets. The drops of salt water crawl up and over my forehead, proof that I'm upside down. *God God God God* is now going ten times faster than the raging beat of my pulse.

*   *   *

It's still repeating, but growing fainter, when I think I hear a soft *crunch*. It's hard to tell what's real and what's not. The mantra has been blessedly slowing, growing quieter in my head and becoming almost soothing. The wetness that's been running from my eyes up to my forehead and under my ski cap is so warm that it burns. For some reason I welcome the sensation. The pain of my hot tears is so gentle compared to everything else I'm experiencing.

Crunch.

The awful ache that's been racking through my spine and limbs is going, too. I'm not as much trapped by the weight of the snow anymore so much as I'm embraced by it. It's becoming womblike, a swaddling hug.

Crunch! The sound is a little closer now.

It's *so* easy to let go. So much easier than holding on. So much easier than staying and fighting. It's a little sad, giving up like this, but not too bad. More wistful. Sort of like when I left home at sixteen—against my parents' strident wishes—and took off on a climbing tour of Patagonia. "Let him go," Dad said. Mom just cried. It feels like I'm pulling away from the curb in a slow wreck of a car that's overloaded with packs and gear and old, long-dead friends. Even my old beast Oso is in the car, hanging his massive black head out a backseat window and letting the sticky ropes of his drool start to swing onto the rear fender. My hand is raised out a front window but I'm not really looking back. Not wanting to see any sad faces getting smaller behind us. Just moving my hand in the air. There's excitement ahead. Mountains to climb. *Later, Rebecca. 'Berto. Mom and Dad. Ross. I'll catch you later. I know I will.*

CRUNCH!

Something hard and sharp bites my knee, which is stretched over my head and feels about a million miles away. The pain jerks me half the distance back. Then there's a strange scrabbling on my thighs, moving down toward my groin. Like claws tearing at numb flesh. Ripping at what's now nothing more than refrigerated meat. The scrabbling stops as I hear a high-pitched yelp and a heavily muffled voice yell, "Mungo! Get back!"

Crunch! Crunch! Crunch!

The shovel blade starts biting around my legs. Then I feel hands tug hard at my knee. More bites. I can picture a blonde girl in a deep hole in the snow digging frantically. All around her is a broken moonscape of crushed white debris. A wolf is pacing the hole's edge, trying to jump in with the girl but being pushed back with elbows, the shovel's handle, and curses. The girl's crying and swearing and scraping at the bottom of the pit. And I'm being pulled back against my will, drawn in, but the snow holds me with a very determined grip. More warm water is rolling from eyes to forehead and up onto my scalp. *Let go. Let go. C'mon. That's enough.*

More bites. One hard between the legs but I'm beyond caring, beyond feeling it hurt. I sense the blade chopping at my stomach and, a moment later, my chest. It seems to be going on for hours. *Enough, Cali. Don't bother. Let go.* I will be gone anyway by the time she gets down to my head. *Too deep. Too far.* But I find myself almost caring, almost wanting her to reach me, if for nothing else than because she's working so hard. There's a spark of hope, a brief desire to stop the rattletrap car, but it would take too much effort to blow it into a flame. Once again I'm struck by how much easier it is to let go than to hang on.

But the best things are hard. That's what climbing is all about. Kicking Death in the face when he grabs at your ankles, bony fingers clutching from billowing sleeves. The best things are worth fighting for.

The realization makes my teeth grind together before a new attempt at a scream opens my jaw. And I wish I hadn't come back. All the panic returns. *Fight, Ant! Fight, you weak-willed son of a bitch!* With an effort greater than anything I've ever exerted on a cliff face, I struggle to control my breathing. Try to stop the rapid, useless pants and the racing of my heart.

The blade chops at my exposed throat. Then somewhere just underneath my chin. So close, but I can't move a muscle. My forehead and cheeks are gripped by the mask of ice caused by my exhalations. Suddenly the chopping stops and gloved fingers are tearing away the ice from my face.

The light sears my eyes. I'm not sure if this is the proverbial light at the end of the tunnel, but it seems too bright to be the cloud-wrapped daylight I'd left so long ago. I blink but nothing will clear the liquid of mingled tears and melted slush that films my face. My lungs, though, fill with sweet, dry air.

It takes a long, long time for Cali to clear enough snow so that I can move even my head. My right arm is buried deeper, outstretched beneath me, and my legs are still locked almost behind me and uphill in the frozen cement. But finally I can see and hear and breathe.

The pit is a jagged hole more than six feet deep with more snow sloughing down from above. My wolf's face peers down at me as she circles the rim. Her ears are all the way forward and her tongue droops halfway out of her mouth.

Cali is sobbing as she digs, with sweat running down her cheeks and dripping from her hair. Mungo's whining is a constant hum and she keeps jumping into the pit to lick at my face and throat. Cali has to force her back several times with gloved cuffs to the wolf's shoulders and head.

"Thank you," I say, spitting snow and lifting my head. "Thank you. Thank you. Thank you." I can't seem to stop. I'm ashamed of the tears that now roll to make stinging tracks over my temples and toward my ears but I'm as helpless to control them as I am to control my gratitude.

"Shh," Cali whispers as she works, the sound coming out as almost a grunt. "Shh, Anton. Be quiet."

A little later she tries to lift me up. My arms are both free now, back-paddling against the pit's walls, and she's standing astride my arched chest and lifting at my shoulders. She manages to raise me to a sitting position. I'm clawing weakly at the snow above my still-encased legs for some sort of purchase when she lets go. My torso flops back down, sending a new shriek of pain running up my spine—my vertebrae clacking like a dropped stack of dominos—and ripping through the muscles of my stomach. For the first time I wonder if I'm paralyzed.

Cali apologizes and climbs back over me to dig around my legs. When she frees them I slide headfirst into an upside-down heap in the bottom of the pit. My toes and fingers are tingling as if a thousand fire ants are sinking in their teeth.

It takes a long time, but she manages to right me. Slowly my limbs begin to work. I'm not paralyzed, I realize. My back's not broken. But something else seems to be. Not any bones or tendons but something in my head. Something in my soul. I can't believe I'd almost given up. I can't believe I'd been so weak.

"You nearly chopped my head off," I tell her after she helps boost me out of the pit.

"Let me see."

I tilt back my head and she studies the wound on my throat. Her fingertips come away a little bloody but not streaked with too much red.

"It's just a scratch," she says, and begins laughing.

We're sitting in the snow next to the pit that had been my prison and torture chamber. And very nearly my grave. It's almost at the bottom of the snowfield, meaning that the avalanche had run more than a thousand feet as it picked up speed and material. I can see the fracture point far above us.

The slab that cut loose beneath my feet must have been fifteen feet thick. Cali is sitting so close to me that she's almost astride my ankles. Her green eyes are enormously wide and the smile on her red-streaked face is crooked.

"Jesus, Anton. I didn't think I'd ever find you. You popped up a couple of times in the middle of the slide but I couldn't keep track, it was moving so fast. If it hadn't been for Mungo . . ."

She'd already told me that it had been Mungo who started digging before Cali was even able to pick her way down the slope. Mungo was actually moving toward the slide before it even came to a complete stop. The rope leash I'd anchored her with had been bitten in half—not gnawed, but sheared with a single bite. She'd sniffed around for only ten or so seconds in the still-settling debris before she began pawing madly at the snow.

I seize the ruff of the wolf's neck and gently shake her. "Thank you, girl. Good girl."

She lets out a low moan and sweeps the air with her tail.

Without thinking I grab the back of Cali's neck, too, and pull her face into my chest. I almost pull her to my mouth. She leans forward willingly, turning her cheek to press it against me. "Thanks, Cali."

She'd come down the slope knowing someone was shooting. Knowing the shots had started a massive avalanche, and knowing she, too, could be caught in the slide, or trigger another. She'd risked her life for nothing but a meager hope of saving mine. But strangely no more shots had come her way. Whoever had been firing the gun had been swallowed by the mist as I'd been swallowed by the snow. He hadn't stuck around to finish the job. And that wasn't smart, because now that my strength's coming back, I know without a doubt that I'm going to finish him. Bury him. The humiliation I feel for having given up only pumps up the volume of my building rage.

I'd been the target this time, not Cali. McGee's prophecy has come true. I don't know for sure who'd drawn the bead on me—at least I don't have any proof yet—but Myron Armalli, with his abortive experience as a ski patrolman, would sure as hell know a lot about triggering avalanches.

TWENTY-THREE

THE LITTLE VICTORIAN HOUSE feels way too small inside. Like the walls are slowly moving in, the ceiling dropping down an inch each time I blink my eyes. I want to be outdoors, where I can sense the upward pull of the sky and gulp lungfuls of fresh air. But I endure it so that they'll think I'm all right. That everything's just fine.

An entry hall the size of a walk-in closet leads either into a living room, into a cramped kitchen, or up a narrow flight of stairs to a second floor. The tiny living room is furnished with a pair of oversized slipcovered chairs and a matching couch. The three pieces are crowded with chunky pillows. McGee has sunk so deep into one of the chairs that I'll probably have to use my truck's winch to get him out. The other chair embraces Sheriff Buchanan's large backside. Cali and I sit side by side on the couch, with Lester getting stroked on Cali's lap. The cat glares up at me while wrinkling his nose disgustedly at the lupine scent on my clothes.

"You should get checked out at the hospital," the sheriff tells me.

"I'm fine."

McGee is watching me with his wet, assessing eyes. In his gaze I sense something beyond the normal measuring of what's going on in his protégé's head and heart. Concern, I think. I'm not sure if it's for my well-being or for the office's.

On the wall facing me is the framed cover from an old issue of *Life* magazine. The ash-streaked face of a man is shown with a burning forest behind him. "The West on Fire!" the caption reads. The date of the issue is August 1974. I recognize the man pictured there from the cover photo of *Smoke Jump*. The father Cali never knew.

Above the fireplace's mantel is a battered Pulaski—a sort of combination shovel and ax, used by smoke jumpers and Hot Shot crews for cutting fire lines—that could have belonged to either Cali or her dad. Law-school casebooks and novels teem on the full-length shelves running over two entire walls, along with trophies and plaques honoring Cali's achievements on slalom runs. There are candid pictures of her and her mother, photos her mother must hate. In each of them the actress is caught in a rare awkward moment. In one her mouth is open as if she's speaking to someone out of sight. In another her eyes are closed. In a third she's caught at an unflattering angle that shows lines of flesh beneath her chin.

"I've talked to the rangers and they've come up with nothing," the sheriff is saying. "It was probably too late by the time they got word. The tourists that go to the Taggert Lake parking lot usually just drive in, snap a few pictures, and leave. They couldn't find anyone who even remembered seeing *your* truck, Agent Burns. They say they'll keep asking around, though."

It had taken us a long time to stagger back to the Pig. Without skis—mine were buried somewhere beneath a thousand tons of snow and Cali had abandoned hers up on the ridge—we postholed through knee-deep snow like drunken cowboys for much of the way. When we finally made it down, the empty lot in which we'd left the truck in the predawn hours was half-full of cars and RVs. I used the cell phone to call the rangers and the sheriff and then started canvasing the crowd myself. People had shied away from me, not liking something they saw in my manner or in my eyes. In any event, I'd met with no better results. No one had noticed Armalli's Ford F-150 pickup. No one had seen a big Teton County Sheriff's SUV.

Before I can formulate a civil way to put it, McGee bluntly asks for me, "Was Charles Wokowski on duty this morning?"

Buchanan stiffens in her chair, a scowl sharpening her matronly features and tone. "He supervised the swing shift, Mr. McGee. Midnight to ten A.M. I saw him myself when I came in this morning at nine."

McGee looks at me with his shaggy eyebrows raised high as he rolls his cane back and forth between his spread legs. Wondering if I'm disappointed, I guess. And I am. Wokowski is undoubtedly in the clear now. For this, at least. The faint etch of his name on my suspect list has faded completely. There's no way he could have hiked two hours, fired either at me or the slope, and gotten down and back to town by nine o'clock without anyone taking note of his absence.

"And I think you owe him an apology, Agent Burns," the sheriff adds. Her voice is stiff with straightforward Western reprove.

After meeting her gaze for a moment I nod slowly in agreement.

I still don't like him. I'm still feeling the sting of his insults. And I still think he's pursuing Cali too hard even if it's not with criminal intent. What about the old man, Cali's defendant, falling down some stairs shortly after Jim lost track of Wook? But I don't allow myself to dwell on it. Now, more than anything, I want to find Armalli and make him pay for burying me beneath that slope.

There's a tentative knock at the door. Cali starts to get up to answer it but both the sheriff and I simultaneously shake our heads at her. Being smaller and quicker, even when this stiff and sore, I beat the sheriff into the entry hall.

Standing on the porch is Bill Laughlin, Cali's self-appointed uncle, dressed in jeans, boots, and a short-sleeved Western shirt. I open the door.

"Heard about the avalanche," he tells me in his laconic manner, staring down at me without smiling. "Came over here straightaway."

"Cali's fine. Me, too. But thanks for coming."

With more than expected gruffness he says, "You should've known better than to take her up to that aspect. Even in weather like this, it could slide till July. You should've known that."

Rebuffed, I back away from the door and motion him in. He's right. I should have known better. Especially after I dug that pit and saw the signs. And I sure as hell shouldn't have assumed it was only Roberto following us.

Once I get out of the way, the sheriff greets the mountain legend formally but with obvious respect. Cali, having heard his voice, comes into the entry hall behind her to embrace him. He stoops down to return her hug with his long, corded arms wrapping around her waist. While doing so he gives me another gray-eyed look. I notice that one of his pupils looks enlarged, and I wonder if his aneurysm is bleeding.

The cramped living room is packed to capacity with the five of us in it. The sheriff had given up her chair for Laughlin and squeezed in with Cali and me on the couch. McGee managed to lean forward from his deep chair to shake the hardman's hand when Cali introduced them. Lester is nowhere to be seen. He'd left with a hiss when we returned to the room. Like me, especially after this morning, he's probably not a fan of crowded spaces.

Cali tells the story of what had happened on Mt. Wister

again for Laughlin's benefit. He listens without expression
on his sun- and age-etched face. During her recital he looks
toward me a couple of times, frowning. I find myself looking
away each time—especially when she mentions the pit and
the sugary pellets of snow we'd found and ignored. As before, when reporting to McGee and the sheriff, Cali makes
no mention of the fact that I'd assumed it was my fugitive
brother trailing behind us.

"You got any idea who it was?" Laughlin asks me when
she finishes.

"Yeah. There's some crazy kid—a schizophrenic—named
Myron Armalli with a history of stalking. Do you know him?"

Laughlin shakes his head.

"He grew up near Mom's ranch," Cali says, "but I didn't
really know him. Then he said some things to me in court not
long ago, when I was prosecuting him for a misdemeanor. He
said I would regret oppressing him or something like that."

The sheriff adds, "He was trouble as a kid. Burned some
horses, we think, and bothered a girl in his school. He
worked ski patrol on the mountain for a while but was fired
for being unreliable. Since then he's been in and out of our
jail, for causing public disturbances and things like that. We
think he's squatting up on some land his family used to own
near Ms. Reese's property."

"He's probably had some avalanche training," I say.
"Working with the ski patrol."

Both the sheriff and Laughlin nod thoughtfully. "Tell us
again what you saw," the sheriff says.

I close my eyes for a second and try to picture the distant
figure I'd seen. "He was maybe a half-mile behind us, crouching down near where our tracks would have been," I explain.
"All I could see was a dark-colored parka and a backpack. I
think the backpack was darker, but the light was bad and it
could have been green, dark blue, or even red. Then the clouds
came down again and we couldn't see him anymore. The next

indication I had that someone else was out there was when we heard the shots, which sounded like they were coming from below. Maybe a little ways up on the mountain opposite us."

I can hear the three shots cracking again in my ears. And then the explosion before the mountainside gave way beneath my skis. Twin droplets of cold sweat run down my flanks and I rub my forehead with my sleeve.

"Do you have any idea what caliber?" the sheriff asks.

"No. Not really. It was echoing all over the place. And I was more worried about one of us getting hit, or . . ."

We're all silent for a moment. I imagine them imagining *me* buried beneath all that snow. No one's looking my way now but Laughlin.

The hardman, in his slow, gruff voice, fills the silence by telling some avalanche stories of his own. He recounts the time his tent and partner had been swept off Mt. Robson in the middle of a storm, just seconds after he stepped outside to answer a midnight call of nature. Another concise story begins on Mt. Logan in the Yukon but shifts without warning to another place and year. He seems to be getting confused, starting to ramble. His words pick up a slight slur at their tail ends.

The second story dies away without ever ending. Another awkward pause follows. Cali is staring at him, her green eyes damp and shiny.

The sheriff says to McGee, "Bill Laughlin is a town treasure. Literally. He used to give a slide show every winter, and I swear, half the town would turn up. Climbers and sane people alike, just to hear him talk." Smiling, she says to Laughlin, "You should do that again this year."

But that's not an inspired idea. As fit as he looks, with his corded arms showing beneath his shirt's short sleeves, and the way his lean waist doesn't really need the piece of old rope he uses for a belt, it's pretty clear that his mind is being affected by the ballooning vein within. It's invading his thought processes and his memories. I feel bad for him. It would be better for a legend like him to go out in a blaze of glory on a high peak.

I've been unconsciously massaging my own neck and upper back, leaning forward with my elbows on my knees. I notice I'm doing it only when Cali tries to take over. Her hands knead at the twin triangles of sore muscle between my shoulders and neck. With a jolt of apprehension I feel McGee's eyes on me. And Laughlin's. And the sheriff's. All of them speculating.

I shrug off Cali's hands, saying, "I'm all right. Really."

Laughlin stands up and slaps his lean thighs, like he's somehow aware that his speech had become rambling. He makes for the door without much of a good-bye. I follow him out, taking with me the folder that has Armalli's booking photo in it. Cali doesn't come after us.

"I appreciate you coming by," I tell him. "I know Cali does, too."

"No worries," he replies distractedly as we cross the lawn toward the gate between the tall hedges.

"Can you hold up just a second? I've got something I want to show you."

Bill Laughlin stops with one hand on the gate. When he turns to me his lips are locked tight into a thin white line, and there's a faint flush coloring the leathery skin on his face. He looks back at the house instead of at me.

Not wanting to delay him or cause him any further embarrassment, I hurriedly open the folder and pull out the photo of Myron Armalli. I hand it to him. "Have you seen this guy before?"

Laughlin does little more than glance at it. "This the guy who's been after Cali?"

"Yeah, I'm pretty sure—almost positive. Do you recognize him?"

Laughlin glances down at it again and pushes it back at me. "Don't think so. Looks like a hundred kids around here."

"Think back to the night you chased off the guy who was trying to get in Cali's window. Could this be him?"

He takes another look down at the photo in my hands and starts to shake his head. But then he stops. His calloused fingertips rub against the back of my hand as he takes back the photo. "Wait a minute. Maybe I have seen him before. A couple of times when I've been walking around the neighborhood, this guy's been sitting in an old pickup. Just sitting."

"Are you sure?" I ask, feeling myself getting excited. Feeling, in a way, as if I'm putting on my armor, getting girded for battle. Weak as it is, this is the first bit of solid evidence that will stand up in court. If Laughlin lives that long. And if this ends up in court—if *Armalli* lives that long. "When have you seen him? And how many times?"

But now Laughlin goes back to shaking his head. He hands me the picture for the second time. "Couldn't say. I've seen him around, is all. I live only a couple of streets back, so I'm walking around here a lot. Always assumed this guy just lived on the street."

I give him a card with my cell-phone number written on it. "I'd appreciate it if you'd keep an eye out for him and call me if you see him."

Laughlin nods. "I'll do that." He turns to go.

I hesitate, feeling bad for him and feeling embarrassed for greedily having put Cali in danger this morning, then add, "If you ever want to do any climbing, let me know. I'd love to tie into a rope with you sometime. It'd give me something to brag about."

He laughs shortly and looks at the ground. "I'm not much good on the rock anymore. Too damned old. But I still can hike. Maybe I'll belay you sometime. I'll let you know."

He opens the gate then turns to latch it between us. He looks steadier now, out on the street. I flatter myself by thinking that maybe my words have reminded him of his former strength. After taking two steps, he turns back to me.

"You look out for her, you hear? She's a lot like her mother. Gives off a scent or something, you know? Makes guys go crazy. Do the damnedest things."

I walk back in just in time to hear the sheriff asking Cali, "Do you know what's the matter with him?"

"An aneurysm. It's in his brain."

"Oh God. I'm sorry, Cali. Is it bad?"

Cali nods. "The worst."

"Is he getting treated? I don't imagine a man like that carries insurance." Even in his youth, with parachuting into forest fires as a profession and an avocation of putting up risky new routes on lonely alpine peaks, Bill Laughlin would have found it hard to get insurance.

"No," Cali says quietly. "It's not because of money, but because of the aneurysm's location in his head. They can't operate on it. Once it starts bleeding then it's not likely to stop."

"Let me know if there's anything I can do," the sheriff says, looking genuinely sorrowful. She looks like she really would do something if she could.

"The only thing anyone can do is get my mom to be a little nicer to him," Cali says. "That's really about all he wants." On the hike in this morning Cali had talked about him. About how when she was cleaning his house once she'd found a scrapbook secreted under the kitchen sink. It had been articles about and pictures of Alana. Pictures of her and Bill and Patrick in those early days. The three of them smiling with their arms around one another.

A weird thought strikes me. Am I going to keep a scrapbook about Rebecca Hersh and the six months she loved me? Am I going to spend the next forty years clipping and concealing the articles she's written?

I take the seat Laughlin had deserted. It's across the cof-

fee table from Cali. McGee is still slouched in the other chair
and his eyes are closed. Although he and Laughlin are probably close to the same age, it's hard to believe that McGee—
emphysemic, diabetic, obese, and alcoholic—will outlive the
still-muscular and tough-looking hardman. My boss's ragged
breath is deep and sonorous, and I wonder if he might be
asleep.

I tell them about Laughlin's tentative identification of
Armalli. McGee's eyes remain shut.

Making an effort to lift the mood, Cali asks in a bright
voice, "So, it looks like ol' Myron is my anonymous suitor.
And Anton's avalanche-safety instructor. What are we going
to do about it?"

"I'm going to go get him."

Something in my words or tone has everyone looking at
me sharply.

I explain how I'd gone to his parents' old property yesterday, and that I, too, believe he's camping out somewhere
around there. The sheriff confirms that she's heard the same,
and that he's wanted for various hunting violations. I don't
mention the way I'd sensed his presence, and how I'd nearly
belly-crawled back to my truck through the dry meadow
grass. I'm not afraid of him now—the only thing I'm afraid of
is what I'm going to do to him.

Then I'm reminded of the one thing I'm still very much
afraid of. McGee brings it up, opening his eyes. "Just make
sure, lad . . . you're back in time for dinner. . . . It's at nine
o'clock, I understand."

Rebecca and her father must have called him and told
him that they are coming to town. I just hope like hell they
didn't go so far as to invite him to join us. Having her father
there will be surreal enough.

The sheriff, too, is studying me. From the worried expression on her face it appears that she's not all that confident in what she sees. "Why don't I have some of my officers

go out there and search for him? It might take a day or two, but we could set up a full-blown search of the area. Now that you're apparently the victim of an attempted murder, Agent Burns, perhaps you might not be the best man for the job."

Before I can protest, McGee says, "Don't worry, Sheriff. He's not going to go cowboying . . . out there by himself."

"I'm not sure what choice I have," I add. "We need to pick him up now, and Jim has to stay here and watch Cali, in case Armalli's still on the move." Besides, I really want to go after Armalli by myself. I don't know if I'm really capable of hurting him, but it will be interesting to find out. If he resists arrest, hey, shit happens. Everyone thinks I crossed the line long ago anyway.

"You're not going out there alone," McGee repeats.

"Then how about you, fat man? Want to go sneaking through the woods tonight?"

An evil grin parts his beard. "No, not me, lad. I've got a better idea."

TWENTY-FOUR

TO GET TO the former Armalli property, we have to drive north through the broad valley of Jackson Hole and then keep going all the way past the hamlet of Moran Junction before we're even halfway there. On the left the sun is descending onto its Wyoming bed of nails, those sharp snow-covered spires. The sight of them makes the Rat stir in his cage—the avalanche had knocked the little guy down but apparently it hadn't knocked him out. He still wants to get high. On the right we pass the entrance to Alana Reese's ranch, which is unmarked but for two enormous log posts supporting an ornate metal gate in between.

At the junction, where to the left the Skillet Glacier beckons to me with its vertical handle running all the way up the summit of Mt. Moran, we turn right onto Highway 287. A sign beyond the town reads, "Fire Danger," and beneath it is a half-circle chart. The needle points all the way over to the right, indicating the word "Extreme."

"No shit," Charles Wokowski comments as he looks out

the passenger's-side window. "I've never seen it so dry this early in the season."

Passing the sign, we begin the long circle around the backside of Alana Reese's property and the Elk Refuge.

The drive seems to take a lot longer than it did yesterday afternoon, when I was alone but for Mungo. Except for his one comment, Wokowski and I don't speak at all until I turn off the paved highway and onto the dirt Forest Service road.

"I can't believe you called me for this," he says, shaking his big head in wonder.

I don't say anything.

"Called *me!*" He sort of half laughs, still turning his head back and forth and watching me. "You got balls, QuickDraw. I'll give you that much, man."

I grip the wheel as the Pig rattles over some washboard ruts, the rusty iron squealing in protest. "Don't call me that."

We bounce along, passing numerous offshoots, some of which have been blocked with big boulders to keep redneck four-wheelers from tearing up the meadows. It isn't easy to spot the little numbered plaque that marks the main track in the thickening twilight. This place is a living maze. In the dusk it appears completely different from what I remember of yesterday's aborted search. I slow almost to a stop a couple of times to study the topographical map spread on my lap before creeping on.

Wokowski decides to provoke me some more. "It's a pretty nice, accurate name for a guy who's inclined to use his gun. I'm surprised you don't like it."

We aren't going all that fast, maybe ten miles an hour, but he's cut in half by his lap belt—all the old truck has—when I stomp on the brake and we skid in the dirt. It causes him to slap his meaty palms on the dashboard and nearly smash his face on the cracked vinyl.

"Let's get something straight, asshole," I say, twisting in

my seat to face him directly. "What you've read or heard is bullshit. That was no execution. I was jumped."

Staring back at me, his eyes as unreadable as ever, Wokowski asks, "You sure 'bout that?"

I want to snarl, or, better yet, butt him on the bridge of his nose with my forehead. But my voice stays low and even. "Yeah. I'm sure. I got very, very lucky."

"Three guys. All armed and waiting." He purses his lips and lets out a low, derisive whistle. The air moves over my face, carrying the fruity scent of his gum.

I could explain that there was no aiming involved in that abandoned ranch house in Cheyenne. No thinking even— just sheer terror and fury and my gun banging in my hand, the Rat shrieking away like it was the biggest thrill the little beast had ever had. But I don't waste my breath.

"Like I said, I was very lucky. Especially since none of them were elderly, handcuffed, or spread on the hood of my patrol car."

Now—for the first time—there *is* something readable in his eyes. The dark pupils within the brown irises seem to contract until they are fine, sharp points. Like daggers dipped in poison. His breath comes faster, too. It blows on my face in short, fruity blasts. The windows of the truck must be close to exploding from the pressure inside.

This could be it, I think. What we've been working toward for the past two days.

Wokowski exhales a hard breath that almost causes me to leap at him. Then he leans back in the seat, tilts back his head, and looks through the windshield out at the sky. It's cobalt between the trees. Almost night. He sighs a second time.

"Okay. I fucked up," he says.

After a minute he adds, "And I deserved that, because the truth is, I lost it. Not as bad as I could have"—here he glances at me significantly, not sure whether he should believe my denials regarding the shooting of the gangbangers—

"but I fucking lost it. And I'm going to pay for it, too. Maybe get suspended. Maybe get charged, too, when the sheriff finishes her investigation and after this whole thing gets exposed at trial."

"*If* it goes to trial. I hear the victim, I mean the defendant, is having a hard time walking down stairs these days."

Wokowski looks over at me again, slower this time. But he still doesn't explode. Instead he grins at me. A sick, lopsided sort of grin. "You think I did that? You're wrong, Burns. The guy's a fucking drunk. I was nowhere near him last night. I messed up enough once—I'm not going to do it again."

I stare back at him, scrutinizing his broad face and eyes for any sign of deception. But his gaze is steady and his expression neutral. The words sound genuine. For some reason I find myself close to believing him, against my will, or at least willing to give him the benefit of the doubt. The way I wish everyone would do for me. The way he seems to be doing for me now.

"I know about the kid," I say. "That's why you roughed him up in the first place, wasn't it?"

He nods and goes back to staring out the windshield. His voice is heavy and sad. "It wasn't that way for you?"

I also look out at the coming night.

"I don't know. I think I pretty much knew it was a setup, but I went in anyway. I don't know what I was thinking."

From outside the pulse of the crickets is starting to make itself heard even over the engine's idle. A ragged, discordant rhythm, not yet mature this early in the year. The first stars are becoming apparent, with the Big Dipper ladling at the horizon. It's a long while before Wokowski speaks again.

"Are you sleeping with Cali?" He's still looking through the windshield, pointedly not looking at me.

"No."

His expression is doubtful when he turns to me. "She's been going out with you, staying at your place . . ."

"I'm supposed to be protecting her."

"So, you guys are friends or what?"

"Yeah. We're friends."

We sit quietly for a while longer. I wonder where this is leading now. This big man is full of surprises, too.

"I want to show you something," he finally says.

He reaches up and turns on the overhead light, illuminating the truck's interior. Then he unbuttons his shirt's chest pocket and pulls out a ring. He pinches it carefully between his thick index finger and thumb. The gold band is not much wider than a piece of wire, and the tiny stone embedded in it glitters when he moves it.

"I was going to ask her a month ago, but then everything went to hell. I'm still going to ask her. Sometime. If I can ever get her to hear me out."

"That's a nice ring, man." A lot of the animosity I've felt for him over the last few days is beginning to bleed away. The pressure that had felt so close to blowing out the Pig's windows is deflated like a slashed tire.

He rolls the ring in the light for a moment, making it sparkle. "Think I've got a chance?" His tone is flat and casual, sort of self-mocking, but underneath it I can hear what sounds like genuine anxiety.

I can't get a grasp on what's happening here—I begin to feel a little paranoid. Could he be playing me for a sucker? Was the sheriff covering for him when she'd said she saw him this morning? No, it can't be true. She might try to protect one of her officers, but she wouldn't cover for him in the attempted murder of a state agent. That's too vast a conspiracy to have any credence. And stalking is a solo game. But still, I can't help but wonder. I play along anyway.

"I don't know. Maybe. If you can make her understand what happened with the old guy."

"That's what I was trying to do, when you and me had that standoff outside the courthouse. I was bringing her the tapes of Toby—that's the boy—and the accident. You know, the tape of the accident scene and then some video of him talking to me in his chair."

So that's what was in the gym bag. If he's telling the truth.

The engine kicks up to a higher idle, as if to suggest movement and a way of getting me out of this bizarre situation.

"Okay," Wokowski says, nodding slightly. He tucks the ring back in his shirt pocket and buttons it up. "Okay. Let's go say hi to Myron."

I take my foot off the brake and the Pig starts rolling forward.

"Do you know him?" I ask.

"Oh yeah. I've locked him up a couple of times. Drugged and disorderly, mostly. You know, standing around yelling, holding up traffic, that sort of thing. I never filed any charges on him. Never bothered. I'd kick him loose once he got back to normal again."

It's dark enough that I should be using the headlights but I don't turn them on. I don't really need them anyway— everything seems unnaturally bright and intense, the way it always does after strong emotions have shot through you. The adrenaline provides light enough.

"If you guys know he's out here, how come you haven't picked him up on the hunting violations?"

"A guy's got to eat. And he's got no money, so it's either poaching or a soup kitchen. Jackson doesn't have many soup kitchens. If I were him, I'd be poaching, too."

This is yet another side to this new Charles Wokowski, and it's disconcerting, the way he's blowing away all my preconceptions. The man who deeply regrets his mistakes, and who remains true to his love, is also the man who takes care of his own. Surreal. That's how it seems to me. But I don't allow myself to worry about it. I let it go for now.

"You know him a lot better than me," I say. "I've only

seen his picture and read about the charge Cali prosecuted him for. How do you think we should do this?"

"We'll talk to him. He'll come easy. He always does. He'll remember me. I always treated him right."

We finally come to the weedy double-track that branches off from the main Forest Service road. There is nothing to mark it other than a warm and fuzzy welcome sign that reads: "No Trespassing. Trespassers Will Be Shot on Sight." The lettering is faint with rust and there are numerous bullet holes adding emphasis to the boldly printed words. Even though the double-track goes for a couple of hundred yards before it reaches the clearing with the ruined house, I kill the engine here.

"Shit," Wokowski says as he squints to read the sign in the dark. "Maybe we should've suited up. Worn vests. Myron can get a little squirrelly sometimes."

He takes off his seat belt and unsnaps the cover of the old-fashioned leather holster he wears belted around the waist of his jeans. I get my gun out from the storage box between the seats and slip it into the nylon holster in the small of my back.

"There's a small clearing a couple of hundred yards up the road. That's where the house used to be. I checked it out yesterday. He's got to have a tent or a shack nearby. We'll stay in the trees at the edge, sneak up on him. Okay?"

Wokowski nods. "Sure."

We get out of the truck and bump the doors shut with our hips.

Outside in the night the season's first mosquitoes are already buzzing in the air, zeroing in on the warmth of our breath. The stars overhead are dazzling. Miles from any town, there are no ground lights at all to dilute their brilliance. There must be millions visible up there. They're bright enough that Wokowski and I cast faint shadows when we start to walk even though there is no moon.

About a quarter mile up the track we come to where it

opens up into the clearing. The ruined house, with its chimney and four stone corners the only things left standing upright amid the rubble, looks like some pagan place of worship. Like a funeral pyre waiting to be lit. The stars twinkling beyond it dance and flare like an omen of the sparks to come.

The menace of this place is as strong as it had been yesterday afternoon. Stronger even. But the anger that had been born beneath a mountain of snow pushes it off. And even though the day's heat still lingers in the air, the darkness is a comfortable cloak. At night the odds are well in our favor. The rifle isn't much of an advantage when there's a lot less to see.

I stay to one edge of the meadow with Wokowski walking a little ways behind me. The grass whispers beneath our boots. I come to the place where yesterday I'd seen the little path leading into the trees. Standing still for a minute, then turning and studying the thick, dark forest, I think I see a faint light through the trees beneath the hillside's steep, timber-choked slope. It looks like one of the tiny stars has descended to Earth.

I point it out to Wokowski and he nods. "Lantern," he says.

"Keep following me, but hang back a little more," I tell him.

With every step I wonder if I'm tripping an alarm. A little fishing line is all it would take, strung through the trees to a rock in a tin can. Meth labs I've hunted out in the past have had far more sophisticated and effective countersurveillance. But is Armalli that smart? That secretive? There's simply no way to know if he's expecting us.

The path winds through the trees up toward the ridge for several hundred feet. Although dead wood and rotting trunks lie across it, we're able to see well enough in the starlight to not make much noise. Ahead I can see the yellow light again, bigger now.

Near the ridgetop, the forest opens up into a small clearing of pine needles and dirt. The light is coming from cracks around a boarded-over window of a ramshackle hut. It's a sort of lean-to that's been built against the ridge crest, where the upturned edge of a granite plate has punched out of the earth at a sharp angle to form a fifteen-foot overhang.

Over the night noise of crickets and other insects I can hear the distinctive hiss of a Coleman lantern. Then, after a moment of listening, I distinguish the buzz of many flies. The additional sound comes from where a large shape is hanging from a stout branch. Too big to be a person. An elk, probably, poached from the preserve.

The shack becomes clearer the longer we stand in the protective embrace of the night and the forest. It has been hammered together out of rusty sheets of corrugated iron, rotting boards, and what looks like the hood of a car. The structure is tiny—it can't be more than five feet high, eight feet across, and six feet deep. I guess that it's been partially dug out and into the ridge because of the low roof. An old Ford pickup hulks to one side of the hut. God only knows how he gets it in and out of here.

There is no good way to approach such a place. I want to surprise him, but knocking on the door made of split boards seems like a good way to take a bullet right through it. Waiting for him to come out—maybe until morning and thereby missing my dinner with Rebecca—is out of the question. I remember the feeling I'd had yesterday of being scoped, feeling crosshairs tattooing the small of my back.

"You want me to yell?" Wokowski asks from behind me.

"Yeah, I guess so."

He calls in a loud voice, so loud it causes me to jump, "Hey, Myron. It's Charlie Wokowski. Teton County Sheriff's. You home, man?"

Immediately the light goes out in the cracks around the covered window. Then there is the distinct sound of a rifle's bolt sliding a shell into the chamber. *Chick-chick.*

"Shit," Wokowski says quietly as he slips off the trail

with his gun in his hand. He stands, crouching slightly, behind some thick pine trunks. I do the same on the opposite side. None of the trees here are broad enough to provide total cover. But in the darkness it's safe enough.

"What do you want?" a voice shouts from the hut. It's a high voice, almost cracking. Like an awkward teenager.

"You remember me, don't you, Myron? I've had to lock you up a few times in town but I always fed you and let you go. Remember?"

I note that Wokowski is smart—he doesn't look out from behind his tree and he doesn't speak toward the hut, where the sound of his voice would be easy to trace to the source. Instead he throws his voice by yelling in another direction. I just wish that it weren't *my* direction.

"What do you want?" the high voice demands again.

"We just want to talk to you."

"Who else is out there?"

Before Wokowski can do his ventriloquist's trick again, I call out, "I'm Special Agent Antonio Burns of the Wyoming Division of Criminal Investigation. We just want to talk to you. Put your weapon outside the door right now."

There's a long pause. Then the voice from the hut says, "I don't know you. Didn't you see the 'No Trespassing' sign? No one's supposed to be out here. This is my land."

At least he doesn't ask if we have a warrant. "This is government land, Myron," I yell back. "Either you come out right this minute or we're going to fill your shack with holes and drag your corpse out." Wokowski looks at me sharply, and I guess that my bluff sounds convincing. My tone comes with the weight and pressure of a hundred thousand pounds of snow.

When he doesn't respond, Wokowski whispers from across the trail, "What do you want to do?"

I'm thinking about how this has to be the guy who took a stun gun with him when he tried to go through Cali's window. Who attacked her a second time in the dark of a bar-room bathroom and made a fool of me. Who buried me in that avalanche. What I'd like to do is find a shovel and dig a pit here in the dirt, put him in it, fill it up, and never come back. I'd like to walk away hearing him scream from under the ground the way I'd been screaming beneath the snow.

I'm still savoring this thought—it's far better than pondering the frustration of our apparent standoff—when Myron calls, "What do you want to talk to me about?"

"Either put your weapon outside and turn your lantern back on or I'm going to start shooting," I yell back.

I sense Wokowski looking in my direction. Wondering if I'm really serious and maybe having a moment's doubt about the denial I'd made earlier in the truck.

Some scurrying noises come from inside the hut. A match scratches and a minute later there's the hiss and the leaking yellow light of a propane lantern coming from the cracks in the plank walls. Finally a door stutters open on the earth before it. More light spills out, becoming a flood.

"Throw out the rifle, too."

A man's silhouette appears in the small doorway—just a head and torso, as if he doesn't have any legs. It looks remarkably like the targets we use on the range. He's leaning forward a little, peering out into the night.

"I don't have a gun," he says in the same high voice but softer now.

"Yeah, sure he don't," Wokowski whispers to me.

I'm not going to stand in the trees all night arguing with the psycho in the hut. I make a decision. "Just cover me," I whisper back.

I step out from behind my screen of spruce trunks and walk toward the legless figure. I have my H&K tight in my hand. The short barrel is pointed at the doorway, my index finger caressing the trigger guard. It would be a simple thing for the shadowy figure to reach to either side and grab the hidden and far more accurate rifle. But I know I can at least get off a couple of shots before he'll be able to bring the longer weapon around. And, while my aim's always sucked at a distance, I'm confident I can at least dive for the shrubbery and wriggle into the darkness out of a rifle's sight.

It feels funny, having Wokowski behind me, pointing his pistol in the general direction of my back, and Armalli, a certified psychopath who's already almost succeeded in killing me once, in front of me with a rifle probably within reach. It gets my blood pumping. I step carefully. It would be a bad time to trip.

And an unsettling thought overtakes me. I wonder if Wokowski could have been screwing with me in the truck, acting like everything was cool. Putting on a show to get me in a position just like this. I hadn't thought so at the time, but now, with his gun pointed in the general bearing of my back and a psycho in front of me, I'm not so sure.

The shadow in the doorway comes into focus as I crunch closer on the litter of small stones and pine needles. He's still standing in the doorway but within the hut, no longer leaning forward. Myron Armalli is wearing a too-small sweater that's tight on his torso. His face looks a satanic red from the way the propane lantern's light behind him is reflecting off the interior walls on either side of him; the interior walls have been painted a vivid crimson. Like blood. You'd have to be crazy to paint walls that color. You'd definitely be crazier after spending a night between them.

Aside from the red glow, his face is thinner than in the picture but normal-looking. The only other difference is that bags of skin hang from beneath his dark eyes. Young, little more than a kid.

"You know who I am?" I ask.

He looks at me in the starlight then looks down at my gun. With almost wonder in his voice he says, "You're the man in the mirror."

I hear a strange-sounding chuckle come out of my own

throat. And I feel myself shiver. "I don't know what you're talking about," I say. "Now where's the rifle, Myron? I heard you pull the bolt." *Make a move,* I'm thinking. *Make a move.* The sound of the avalanche is in my head.

His face remains expressionless. I'm only ten feet away now with my pistol unsighted but plainly pointed at his chest. I stop. The feeling of being trapped beneath the snow swims up again as I look at him. My finger is not over the guard the way it should be—it's on the trigger. God, he looks young.

"I, uh, don't have a rifle. I don't know what you're talking about."

I'm tempted to question him, to bring up that I'd clearly heard a rifle and that he'd definitely used a gun that morning to bring down the avalanche on me. For evidentiary purposes, I'd like to have an admission. But the answers would be useless—there's no question that he's in custody here with my gun pointed at him and the admission would be worth nothing in court. Besides, the only court this guy's probably going to see is a competency hearing.

"Come out of there," I say instead. "Keep your hands where I can see them."

He reaches forward and grabs the door frame on each side to pull himself out. I notice the big hiking boots he wears. They're covered in dried mud, just as my randonee boots had been when Cali and I had finally managed to make it down to the trailhead.

Of course the mud could be explained a thousand other ways—he lives in the forest, after all, among streams and small lakes and marshy meadows—but it's all the confirmation I need.

Myron pulls himself all the way out to stand in front of me. At full height on level ground, he's not much taller than I am. He would be a lot taller if he stood at full height instead of cringing slightly. Like Mungo. He's thin to the point of emaciation. It's a wonder he'd been able to keep up with Cali and me on the trail.

"Turn around and put your hands on the wall."

I hesitate before stepping forward to pat him down. I remember something I'd once seen at the state prison when I was there to bust the guards for selling contraband. A bunch of convicts in the exercise yard were taking turns bracing themselves against a wall. One inmate, playing the role of cop, would come up from behind another to check for weapons. The one bracing the wall would reach between his own legs in a lightning-fast move and grab the "cop's" ankle then pull up hard. The "cop" would go down on his back between the prisoner's legs. The prisoner would pretend to stomp him. The sight of this practice session had given me nightmares. And now I think about how madness can make you very strong and very quick.

"Wokowski!" I shout into the night behind me. "Come up here."

I don't turn around but I can already hear him walking on the carpet of pine needles.

"I thought you said you just wanted to talk," Myron says to the wall.

"We've talked. Now you're under arrest."

"You sure you've got enough?" Wokowski says from behind me.

Reluctantly holstering my gun in the plastic clip on my belt, I run my hands around Myron's waistband and over his sides. Where the legs of his dirty jeans meet his boots, I point at the mud and look up over my shoulder at Wokowski. He's standing just behind me with his gun in his hand. I'm relieved to see that it's pointed down at his feet.

He furrows his brow then nods in comprehension. But he doesn't look so sure. I pull Armalli's thin wrists behind him one at a time and cuff them together.

"Let's take a look in there," I tell Wokowski.

"You c-c-can't," Armalli stammers. He's shaking now. "You gotta have a warrant."

"This is government land, Myron. We can look wherever we want." I check to see that the cuffs are ratcheted as tight as they'll go and jerk him around to face me. Instead of the bullet I'd like to give him, I shoot him through the head with the best glare I've got. But he won't meet it. He just stares at the ground.

Wokowski looks as though he thinks I'm being hard on this madman barely out of his teens. But Wokowski hadn't been buried ten feet deep under all that snow. And he doesn't know what I'd been thinking of doing.

"You remember me, don't you, Myron?" the sergeant says to him in a gentle voice. "We've got to take you to the police station for a little while. But I'll take care of you like I always do. Don't worry."

"Watch him," I say to Wokowski. Then I step down into the hovel.

In the harsh, hissing light of the propane lantern the red paint hurts my eyes. The first thing I see is a rifle propped just inside the door. It's a long-barreled 30.30 with a scope mounted on top. I sniff the muzzle and smell oil and old powder. There's no way to tell if it's been fired recently, this morning or a week ago. But I pick it up anyway and work the bolt. A single bullet pops out.

I scan the rest of the tiny interior. The entire place is not much bigger than a king-size bed. The floor has been dug down almost three feet into the sandy and thickly rooted earth. It's covered with planks and other debris. There's an old army cot alongside the far wall, which is made of the ridge's stone. A square-shaped rock holds a backpacking stove—the same kind of WhisperLite I have in my gear room. To one side is a shelf with a variety of canned food stacked on it.

What's even more arresting than the paint and the rifle are the pictures thumbtacked to the walls. All are of Cali.

Most of them have been roughly cut out of magazines and show her from childhood to her teens. But some are also yellowed photographs taken from a distance. They show a contemporary Cali. Coming out of the courthouse, coming out of the front door of her house in town, and several that show her outside an enormous log mansion that must be her mother's. In several she's lying in the sun wearing only a small bikini. Some of the photographs and old magazine clippings have been defaced in an obscene way. CALI CALI CALI is scrawled in black paint. All caps, just like in the letters.

I climb back out into the night. Wokowski is still talking gently to Myron but he looks at me. I wave my hand for him to take a look. He sticks his head in, the glow of the red paint making his face turn red. As he stands there looking without moving, his face grows redder still. He steps away from the doorway and slams shut the rickety door.

In the darkness Myron looks at the cop then drops his eyes. Then he looks at me.

"You've got quite a thing for Cali Morrow, don't you?" I ask him.

Something happens behind his eyes when I say her name. There is a sudden pop of energy like a flashbulb going off. It's there and then it's gone in an instant. But for that split second my hand jerks a little toward my gun and my heart pumps faster.

"I would never hurt her," he whispers, looking down again quickly.

"Sure. Just beat her up twice and avalanche me."

Myron remains motionless with his head hanging on his scrawny neck.

"C'mon, Myron," Wokowski says in a harder voice. "You're going to jail. You're either going to stay there for a while or you're going to the state hospital at Evanston."

It's done, I tell myself. *Cali's safe.* The thought that I could be terribly wrong never crosses my mind.

TWENTY-FIVE

I FEEL WEIGHTLESS as I approach the table. Airless, too, as if I've lost the ability to breathe. My lungs just won't fill.

The restaurant is called the Granary. It's attached to what is supposed to be the most expensive hotel in the western United States, the Amangani, which sits almost fifteen hundred feet directly above the town atop West Gros Ventre Butte. At $680 a night, I would feel out of place here even under normal circumstances—especially because of the bizarre "prosperous" native decor, something that hadn't become close to authentic until the advent of Indian casinos. With burrs clinging to my painter's jeans and duct tape wrapped around the toe of one shoe, what I feel now is beyond discomfort. It's more in the realm of nail-biting anxiety. But the alien economics of this place and its outlandish furnishings have nothing to do with it.

The cause of my apprehension is unaware of my approach. She sits with her left shoulder to me, nodding gravely at something her father is saying to her from across the table. The curtains of her auburn hair are pulled back to expose smooth, pale skin and the sharp contours of her face. Tonight Rebecca looks young and vulnerable as well as a little exotic. Almost Asian because of the collarless black tunic she's wearing. It has Tibetan designs scrolled across the shoulders and down the open neck.

Beyond her is an enormous plate-glass window. A ghostly image of this woman's profile is reflected in it. Through the image I can see a jagged tear of black on the northern horizon where the Teton masses blot out the stars. It looks as if half the night sky has been ripped away.

"Speak of the devil," McGee growls, the first to see me coming.

Rebecca's father turns to look but doesn't smile at me. He simply nods at a fourth chair beside his daughter.

Rebecca does smile, though. It's a small smile, strangely shy, but it still lights me up from the inside out. Suddenly I can draw a breath again. When I do, it pumps oxygen into my blood, plants my feet firmly on the ground, and brings her into brilliant focus. The rush I feel being on the receiving end of that smile is even better than adrenaline.

I gradually become aware of the noises and odors of a busy restaurant as well as the table and empty chair before me. The plates have already been cleared and the coffee served. It had taken longer than expected to book Armalli into the jail—the psychopath was sane enough to want to call an attorney—so I'd missed the meal. It's no loss. I couldn't have eaten anyway. Not before I know how things stand.

Rebecca pushes back her chair and steps toward me. I take her in my arms, my palms running over the bones in her back through her silk shirt as I pull her in. Her small breasts and narrow hips push against me with enough force that I want to groan her name out loud. I happily eat the pain that snarls up from my bruised ribs.

She allows me to kiss her lips once, lightly, before she slips out of my grasp. "Hi, Ant."

"Stop groping my goddaughter, you pervert," McGee orders. "You're going to make me vomit up . . . what was until now a fine meal."

"I'm really glad you invited my boss to join us," I tell Rebecca, earning me another small smile but not the laugh I'd hoped for.

It's only when the smile fades as she returns to her chair that I notice something different about her. A darkness beneath her eyes, and a single faint line on each side of her mouth. They're the first physical signs of her thirty years of age that I've ever noticed. Other than for those, she could still pass for under twenty. And for some reason these new features make my heart swell to a degree that's near bursting.

Rebecca's father stands and leans across the table, holding out a hand to me. I feel even more underdressed as I note his expensive-looking brown sport coat and his crisp white shirt, and I'm glad the tablecloth hides my duct-taped shoe from his view. At least I'd remembered to put on the cashmere coat that had graced my truck since Saturday night.

His face has a surprise in it, too: a coldness that I haven't seen there before. Even though he's never been exactly friendly—in many ways he was the typical overly protective father of an only daughter, one whose choice in lovers was something less than ideal—he'd always at least been gracious. I take the hand and receive a knuckle-grinding grip from this normally mild-mannered law professor.

"How are you, Mr. Hersh? You've been working out, I think." When he releases my fingers I shake them out in the air.

"Sorry, Antonio," he says with a quick, tight grin that looks a little bit embarrassed. "It's David. You've been calling me David since the day we met."

Before today he had appeared far more approachable.

More familiar. It's his somber bearing that tonight had made me use his surname.

I take the remaining chair beside Rebecca and facing my boss and her father. I wonder again why she'd brought him. She had never before seemed like the type who needed her father's support. In fact, she'd never even seemed all that close to him despite the fact that they live only a half hour apart. But then she'd never before acted so strangely.

A thought strikes me like a punch to the stomach—could she be afraid of me?

"Well? You get Armalli?" McGee asks.

"Hooked and booked. Some good stuff for the evidence room, too," I say, meaning the defaced photos and the rifle we'd dragged out of Myron's hut. I'm still looking at Rebecca's father, trying to find some hint to explain his presence and demeanor. I know McGee will provide no clues—he's ornery as ever.

"It's good to see you again, David," I tell Rebecca's father, cutting off McGee's interrogation. "Thanks for coming up with 'Becca." And then I turn to Rebecca. "And I can't tell you how good it is to see *you*."

She smiles back but not enough. And she doesn't reply.

McGee growls, "What about me?"

"Fuck you, boss," I say, stretching myself out all the way to try to lighten the mood.

But it doesn't work. Only McGee chuckles. Rebecca and her father might not have even heard me—they're both looking out at the black void. I've never known her to be this quiet. Especially not when there's so obviously something to say. It's like there are strong currents in the air above the table, swirling around and among us all, but I can't get a fix on them. I can't read them at all. It's a foreign language that I can't even hear, much less understand. All I can do is feel it and worry.

"How was the drive?" I ask, desperately hoping for even the tiniest bit of illumination.

The professor gives Rebecca a few beats to answer and then responds in her place. "It was very nice, Antonio. Rebecca gave me a running commentary of your old haunts along the way. Let's see, there was Vedauwoo, the Snowy Range, Split Rock, the Wind River Range, and finally the Tetons. I'm sorry we came over the pass too late to really see the Tetons. I hear you consider them your old stomping grounds. But what you do up there, I have to admit, I don't quite understand. Ross was just telling us about how you spent a good part of this morning lying upside down beneath an avalanche."

I shoot McGee a malevolent look and try to decide how to answer. I'm starting to feel defensive, like I'm back up on the witness stand with a slick lawyer pretending to be my pal while he sharpens his knives. But maybe that's not what's going on. Maybe he is really trying to understand.

"I went up there just to do a little skiing. The guy I arrested tonight caused the avalanche by shooting off a gun. It was, uh, unforeseeable." It sounds lame to my own ears.

"But why go up there in the first place? What's this fixation you have with doing dangerous sports in those mountains?"

An old saying about climbing pops into my head: If you have to ask the question, you won't understand the answer. Instead I say, "My father took my brother and me on our first big climbs here in the Tetons. The place was kind of a playground for us." In the days before Roberto got out of control and found both the needle and higher peaks, I don't add. And in the days before I killed three men in a blaze of not glory but suspicion and condemnation.

A waitress comes by filling cups and I request some coffee, too. McGee asks for amaretto in his.

"But it's really Vedauwoo that's my favorite place," I babble on, intentionally not answering his question. "It's where we learned to climb when Dad was stationed at Warren. I don't get back there much anymore." It's too close to Cheyenne and too full of recent bad memories. I quickly add, "It wasn't until we were a little older—in our teens—that he started bringing us up here."

"I should hope so. But tell me, Anton—I'm really trying to understand—what draws you up there? Why do you feel the need to climb mountains?"

McGee says something rude about limited intelligence but I ignore him.

There's no way I can explain it without putting Rebecca's father in a harness. It would be like a believer trying to explain to an atheist why there is a God. I find myself looking to Rebecca to answer for me. One layperson could probably better describe it to another, and Rebecca had at least tasted it even if she hadn't swallowed.

"It's like a drug. Cheating death," she says, speaking her first words since saying my name.

"It's more than that," I protest. "It's not dangerous at all if you're careful and you know what you're doing. But there's the illusion of danger even when you're roped and belayed. You still get the chemical rush that fear brings on. And that feels like when you have a close call in your car . . . when you nearly head-on a car going the other way on the highway or something like that. You pull over and you feel so totally focused, so alive." *Stop babbling, Ant.*

"I'm very frightened when that happens," her father says. "I don't find it exciting at all, and I don't ever want to feel that way again."

"Anton's not being entirely honest, Dad. A lot of the time he doesn't wear a rope. Both figuratively and literally." Rebecca doesn't look at me as she says it. And I can't help but be struck again by how much smarter she is than me, how much more insightful.

I feel as if I've walked into a trap and I frantically try to think of a way to extricate myself. Then I'm saved, but not in a way that brings any shelter. McGee, Rebecca, and her father are all looking up somewhere above my head.

"Anton?" a voice asks. It's Cali's.

My name hangs there in the air over our heads. Alarm bells clang inside my chest.

I stand up too fast and bump the table with my thighs, causing the coffee to slosh.

"Cali. What are you doing here?" I'd called her from the Sheriff's Office to tell her that she was safe, that we had Armalli in custody. I'd called Jim, too, to let him know he no longer needed to be looking out for her and could go back to his plane. "This is my girlfriend, Rebecca Hersh. And her father, David. You already know Ross McGee."

To Rebecca and her father I add, "Cali is a prosecutor here in Teton County. I've been working with her on the arrest I made tonight."

Both Rebecca and her father stand and shake Cali's hand. A look passes between Cali and Rebecca, their eyes connecting for a fraction of a second too long. It isn't anything threatening—it's more like they are asking each other telepathic questions. Questions that are far more dangerous than the ones I've already been wrestling with.

"I've heard a lot about you," Cali tells Rebecca. "Anton talks about you quite a bit."

To me she says, "Excuse me, but can I talk to you for just a minute?"

I excuse myself, trying to look at Rebecca as I do with something resembling calm and assuredness, and follow Cali to an alcove near the restaurant's front door.

"Jesus, Cali. You could have called me on my cell."

She gives me a small, pitying smile. "Yeah. But I wanted to see her for myself. You know, scope out the competition."

I shake my head at her then ask, "What's up?"

"Nothing. I only wanted to ask you if you're absolutely

sure this Armalli's the guy. See, Wook called a little while ago and asked if I'd have lunch with him tomorrow."

Wokowski's not wasting any time.

"He said he wanted to take me on a picnic tomorrow, and something about how he wants to explain to me what's been going on. You know, beating up my defendant and all. By the way, he denies throwing him down the stairs."

"I know."

"Well, now that you have Armalli in custody, do you think I should go?"

I think of the thin gold ring with the tiny diamond on it. "That's up to you. But Armalli's definitely the guy. He had pictures of you all over the inside of this hut he lives in. A gun, too. Wokowski's in the clear as far as that goes, and I think he might be in the clear about the beating. Morally, at least. Maybe not legally, but that's his problem. Anyway, yeah, I don't think there's anything wrong with you hearing him out."

Cali nods distractedly. She's looking past me at Rebecca again. I don't turn around to see if Rebecca is looking back.

"You okay?" I ask in a softer voice.

"Yeah. You sure you . . ."

"What?"

She looks up at me then away. "Never mind."

"I need to go back to the table now. I'm sorry. But this is important." But while I'm anxious to get back to Rebecca, I'm not eager to have the odd interrogation by her father resume.

Cali nods again and keeps staring past me. "She's beautiful, Anton. Really beautiful. And nice, too. I don't know that I'd be so polite. So don't be an idiot. Don't let her get away. I don't think you know what you've got there."

"I know. I know what I've got."

She looks up at me for a long time, and then once again toward the table. She smiles sadly. "No, Anton. I really don't think you do."

* * *

"I thought you'd wrapped that up," McGee says when I return to the table. His mouth is frowning hard beneath his beard but his eyes seem lit up with evil amusement.

"So did I. There was a loose end."

Shrugging it off, I try to conclude the previous examination by saying, "Mr. Hersh—David—you should let me take you climbing sometime. We could do it near your house in Boulder. Top-rope a low crag, which is incredibly safe. You might like it."

"No, Antonio. I don't think so. I have a daughter to think about. You—"

Rebecca interrupts, standing up and pushing back her chair. "Dad, Ross, do you mind if Anton and I take a walk?"

When I get up to follow her toward the door I have the feeling that someone else is watching us. I glance over my shoulder before going out into the night, expecting to see that Cali has stayed to see the rest of the show. But it's not Cali's eyes that I feel on me. Sitting at a corner table is a large party. And one of them is staring at me blatantly with a big, shit-eating grin on his face. It's the action-movie hero, Danny Gorgon. It's hard to see from this distance but I think he winks at me.

Outside it's cool, although not nearly as cool as it should be at this time of year. At this altitude and latitude there should still be night frosts. My hands are shoved deep in my pockets as if it were much colder. A muscular wind rustles through the grass alongside the resort's paths and makes the waxy new leaves on the aspen trees rattle together. There is a small pond with a wooden plank walkway around it. The water in it is being whipped up by the gusts, forming tiny whitecaps. We head in the other direction, side by side, on a trail that leads to the top of the butte.

She walks with her head down. I look for her hand but, like me, she's tucked them both away in the pockets of her leather jacket. I'm starting to feel angry. At myself, more than anything, for acting like a scared, love-struck kid. Like a fool. Overhead the stars are very bright. We walk among some noisy aspens with bone-white trunks.

Below us is the entire Teton Valley, Jackson Hole. The town is literally at our feet. It's all lit up by streetlights, head-lights, and neon signs, and a hazy glow rises above the whole place and forms a sort of bubble over the south end of the valley. We stop at the very edge of the steep, dry slope that leads down a thousand feet into the light.

"That's where my cabin is." I point across the valley. A few pinpricks of light are nestled in Cache Creek Canyon. "It's a little valley between the ski area and the Elk Refuge."

"It looks pretty remote."

"It's only about ten minutes from downtown. See the three farthest lights? I think mine is the one up on the left."

"You left a light on for Mungo? Are you taking good care of our baby?"

She must notice my hesitation in answering, because she turns to look up at me. I know I've been neglecting the wolf. I should have brought her, but I didn't want to take the time to drive by the cabin and pick her up. I had another motive for leaving her behind, too, one that I mention now.

"She misses you. Why don't we go see her?" I ask. "I can drive you there right now and back again in the morning. Your dad can keep your car."

"No, Anton. I'm going to stay here with him tonight." She says it firmly, so I don't try to argue.

My brother says the only way to face fear is to jump right into it. To crash through it as if it were one of those Japanese paper walls.

" 'Becca. What's going on?"

She turns to me, her hands still deep in her jacket's side pockets. The wind blows the loose tendrils of hair across her face. I ache with the need to hold her.

"What are you doing, Anton? Up here, I mean. In Wyoming. Six months ago you told me you were going to quit."

"It's my job."

"It's not a job," she says. "It's a vendetta."

I look away from her and back out into the darkness above the haze of artificial light.

Following the arrest of the state's governor-elect, and the four deaths he had indirectly caused by covering up a crime and trying to save his own skin, I'd had enough. I was done with law enforcement. All that remained was to figure out what to do from there. Rebecca had talked about law school, to which I'd said *No way—I've had enough of lawyers and the law.* I had thought about maybe going back to guiding. But I had to stay on for the would-be governor's trial, and as the trial progressed I had realized the inevitable result. That the governor wasn't going to prison where he belonged. That my reputation would suffer in a much greater way. And I just couldn't quit like that. I couldn't let the governor and the defense attorneys and the office win. I couldn't go out like a chump.

"I don't know, Rebecca. I can't quit now. I've got to finish."

"Finish what?"

I can't tell her that it's the game I need to finish. To see who wins. And that it's my ego calling the shots. And curiosity about who I am; the wonder of the fact that I hadn't put a bullet through young Myron Armalli even though I'd wanted to, the fact that I hadn't made love to Cali two nights ago even though I needed to. But thoughts aren't as bad as deeds, are they? In any case, I don't have the vocabulary to express such things. I'm not comfortable enough with these thoughts to even try.

"This case," I say lamely. "My reputation."

"Even if it means finishing us?"

My temperature rises a couple of degrees. What is this?

Blackmail? I almost died today and here she is, dumping on me.

I make an effort to keep my voice flat but emotion manages to creep into it. "What do we have? We had something spectacular early on. But lately, this last month, I don't know. You've been treating me like shit. What's going on, Rebecca? Is there someone else or what? What do *you* want?"

It's her turn to look away out into the darkness.

"I want you—us—to have a normal life." She speaks very slowly, as if choosing her words carefully. "I want safety. Security. No guns. No crusades. No hanging off cliffs for a thrill. I do *not* want someone who's addicted to living life on the very edge. I want a man I *know* will come home to his family every night."

And that's not me. Not me. Not me. The words echo in my head.

"Is there someone else?" I imagine that there has to be. Someone who has the vocabulary to discuss with her the issues of life and living. Someone with an interest other than climbing mountains and putting dope dealers in jail. Someone who doesn't desire anything so much as to be by her side. Always. I want that, too, but I need the mountains. Like a true addict, I can't imagine a life without them would be worth living.

"In a way, I guess you could say there is."

It doesn't register right away. Despite my suspicions, what I'd believed was paranoia, I can't believe it's true. Not Rebecca. I stare at her. She's still looking out over the valley, her hands out of her pockets now and clasped with intertwined fingers across her stomach.

"I'm pregnant, Anton."

She turns to me as she says it. Her eyes are black and indecipherable in the darkness, each one confined between two tiny slivers of shiny white.

At first I feel absolutely nothing. Through six months of

nearly daily lovemaking, I'd been so centered on myself and the governor-elect's trial that I'd somehow never got around to considering the possibility. And she'd never raised the subject, even when we'd talked dreamily in the early days about the possibilities of a life together. I'm as hollow as a gourd, and there's nothing in me but the dull moan of emptiness like when you put your ear to a hollow thing. What's happening? My first impulse is to grab hold of her. To kiss her face and neck and slide to my knees and press my face to her stomach. But the stiffness of her posture—she's almost leaning back, away from me—and her black eyes stop me cold.

"It's going to be all right," I tell her. "*Better* than all right." I try to work some surprised joy into my voice but it's so clearly out of place with her mood that it sounds like a lie. Worse than a lie. God, why don't I have the words to express . . .

"I wish you weren't the father," she whispers.

And that breaks something in me.

I turn away from the lights and head back toward where the Pig is parked outside the restaurant. I keep walking even when I hear her call my name. The word floats in the wind behind my back, hovering, then is cut off as if it has fallen and shattered on the ground.

TWENTY-SIX

THE LOG CABIN IS ON FIRE when I walk in fifteen minutes later. In a resort town like Jackson, during the tourist season, it's always Friday night. Music that is nothing more than a throbbing pulse almost batters me back out the door. Beneath the beat is a layer of shrieking chatter and drunken laughter. Bodies bump against me when I duck down my head and push into the noise. My eyes are assaulted by the multicolored strobes. The air inside is very hot and it reeks of cheap liquor, smoke, and sweat. I feel fuzzy, like I'm already drunk.

Using my right elbow as a wedge, I shoulder my way in what I think is the direction of the bar. Once I find it and manage to work through what must be the local rugby team—beefy men in striped shirts stained with dirt and blood—it takes almost five minutes to catch the attention of a bartender.

He shouts something at me. A question.

"What kind of tequila do you have?" I shout back.

He shouts again. I still can't hear him.

"Chinaco?" I yell at him. "Herradura?"

He raises his eyebrows and shouts back again.

"Tequila!" I try.

He nods. He begins to turn away but I lean over the bar and grab the back of his T-shirt. It stretches as if he doesn't feel the tug until I think it might rip. Then he spins back angrily, shouting again, and tries to knock my hand away. This time I can hear him. "What the fuck?" The rugby players on either side of me press in a little closer. A couple of them are standing up for the bartender, saying, "Let go of him, dude."

With my free hand I hold up two fingers. The bartender looks at my face for a second, giving me a hard look. But then he turns away quickly to pour the shots. I doubt he recognized me, but I'm feeling every inch the man who he might have seen if he did. An elbow from the left bumps my ribs and I meet the bumper's eyes for a minute—a meaty, florid face that mouths "Sorry" before it, too, turns away.

My two shots appear pathetically small when they are placed before me. Not nearly enough, even though they are filled to the rim and the sticky liquid has slopped down the sides. I throw both shots down, one after the other—a double-tap to the gut—and feel the heat blossom. My stomach tries to object violently but I hold down the mescal with a bite from a lime wedge the bartender lays down just in time.

"Eight dollars," he mouths. Other people are screaming at him but he stays with me, looking solicitous now through my watery eyes.

Pulling out my wallet, I yell at him, "Two more!" I open it without caring if anyone sees the badge and put a twenty on the bar.

My shoulder is gripped from behind. I pivot around, expecting the rugby player's florid face again. Instead a small dark face thrusts itself right at me. Special Agent Angela Hernandez. Her brown cheeks have been drunk pink. She's once again in her Hollywood attire, a T-shirt with a black lace bra visible beneath it and tight jeans below. No gun in evidence tonight.

"What are you doing here?" she shouts from an inch away, blowing more flammable fumes into my nose and mouth. "And just my luck—all alone!"

"Who are you here with?"

She jerks her head down along the bar. I lean over it to see, wondering if Alana Reese would be foolish enough to enter a crush like this and allow her pet federal agent to get drunk. But it's not Alana who meets my eye from down the packed bar. Again, it's Danny Gorgon and some others from Alana's entourage. They must have left the Granary right when Rebecca and I began our walk.

He's staring back at me, not smiling anymore, from between a bracket of admiring young women.

"Where's Alana?"

"At home. It's my night off." She says some more but I can't hear her until I lean my ear against her mouth. "I said, until midnight, anyway. That's when I turn into a pumpkin."

I put my mouth to her thick hair, trying to find her ear. "I thought he was her lover. He's your date now?"

She laughs and turns my chin with her fingers so she can talk into my ear. "No. He's looking for some new chippy to take hiking to this hot spring he knows about. It's his big come-on. After that, it's a big letdown. Believe me. I've seen it—Alana sent me up to spy on him this morning. Guy's got a tiny dick and he doesn't know what to do with it." Her fingers stay on my chin even when I turn my head back to look at her. She's grinning. Then she turns my face away again and her lips touch my ear. "I'm glad to see you. You can't leave me with these people."

"He's still mad at me?"

"Now he wants to—again, I'm quoting here—gouge out your eyes and skull-fuck you. Only he knows who you are now, so he's too chickenshit to come at you directly. That means you'd better watch your back. Or maybe I'll watch it for you!"

Angela yells something over the bar, apparently having caught the bartender's eye far more quickly than I had. He puts two more shots of tequila on the bar.

"You find your stalker?" she shouts at me as she puts money on the bar.

"Hooked and booked."

She puts one of the tiny glasses in my hand. "Then we've got something to celebrate!"

TUESDAY

TWENTY-SEVEN

THE ODOR OF CHEAP TEQUILA goes deeper than just a stench in my nostrils or a reek in my mouth. It goes all the way to the marrow of my bones. To each tiny brain cell that lies in the bottom of my skull like so many dead, stinking fish. It's so bad it makes Mungo's breath smell like rose petals as she stands panting over me in the sun-heated loft.

I lift my hand to pat her head and the skin of my arm peels from my side with a tacky sensation. Dried sweat. I vaguely remember running all the way back to the cabin instead of driving. The reason Wokowski kneed the old man in the groin must have made an impression on me. At least I'd done one thing right last night, other than arresting Armalli. But I'd done a whole lot wrong, too. I refuse to allow myself any further contemplation.

Mungo, her head held low, shifts from paw to paw in discomfort as I thrash my way out of the bed. The sheet has been twisted into a fat, damp rope and has wound its way around my body. I keep my eyes scrunched into slits to defend against the onslaught of light pouring in through the overhead windows. The wolf follows me with scratching claws and lurching steps as I nearly fall down the steep stairs leading to the main room.

Feeling ten feet tall and as thin and fragile as a piece of paper, I sway into the bathroom. I kneel before the toilet and taste thick, salty bile. With my elbows propped on the toilet seat, I drool into the bowl but nothing else will come up. I don't think I've eaten in nearly twenty-four hours. *I'm getting too old for this,* I tell myself to keep from thinking more deprecating thoughts, but the truth is, I'd never been young enough for this.

The man is there behind the mirror. He's waving at me, trying to get my attention. I can't see him—I keep my eyes averted—but I can sense his smirk, his bloodred lips lifted to show his long, sharp canines. The dead black eyes are bright and laughing.

"Fuck you," I tell him, washing my mouth and spitting water. Still not looking at the reflection. "Really. *Fuck you.*"

Through the open bathroom door Mungo anxiously watches me talking to the sink. Her ears are pricked all the way forward. "Sorry, girl. I'm okay," I tell her, lying. "I'm not going crazy."

I pad barefoot across the main room, clicking my parched tongue at her to follow along, and jerk open the front door so she can go out. Mungo takes two quick steps onto the porch then freezes. Her tail snaps up between her hind legs as she smiles her anxious grin.

A man is sitting on the porch steps.

He turns his freckled cannonball of a head to look up at us. This simple motion is no easy feat for him because he has no neck. McGee looks like some wise, sad troll straight out of a Tolkien book. Smoke curls up from the bent cigar that droops dangerously close to his beard. His normally bright eyes are yellow, cloudy, and shot with red. Mine probably look the same. Maybe worse.

"We fucked up, QuickDraw," he tells me. His voice, always harsh, is even harsher. "We really screwed the fucking pooch this time."

Mungo slinks around him, staying as far away as possible, then bounds away into the pines to relieve herself.

I know I fucked up. God, I feel it all the way down to the depths of my soul. But how does he know about it already? I don't really hear the odd use of the word *we*—I assume he includes himself for ever having trusted me with his friend's daughter.

"You talked to Rebecca," I croak.

He glares up at me, as if he can't believe I have the balls to speak her name. A blossom of shame erupts in my chest and I'm sure it's as visible as a scarlet letter spreading over my skin. An S for stupid. Spineless. *Substandard.*

"Rebecca?" he barks. "Just to ask if she knew where the fuck you went last night. . . . She didn't, by the way. . . . I'm talking about Cali Morrow! . . . She's down at the hospital, getting glass shards picked out of her face."

I stumble out on the porch's warped boards, not even realizing I'm still naked. My legs are weak. I drop down next to him on the steps. "Cali? What happened?"

"Like I said, we fucked up." He shakes his massive head. "Goddamn, Burns, we fucked up. . . . Someone broke into her place last night. . . . Pushed his way right through the door. . . . He came after her—"

"Where's Armalli?"

The answer is the worst thing imaginable. "In the jail. Where the hell do you think?"

I put my elbows on my knees and my hands over my face.

Then he continues where he left off. "Don't know yet if she was raped or not. . . . Not for sure. She was hysterical when I tried . . . to talk to her a few hours ago. Wouldn't stop crying. Claimed he didn't, but you never know what a vic will say. . . . All I could get was that she said . . . she ran into a wall trying to get away from him . . . smacked into a picture frame. That's where she picked up the glass."

Into my hands I say, "What happened?"

My own flesh causes the words to sound muffled and distant. I'm picturing Cali leaping down the Teewinot couloir, hopping from ski to ski, laughing and spraying me with slush. I'm picturing her trying to comfort me in the bed upstairs. And I'm picturing her sad but proud and kind last night when she told me to hold on to Rebecca.

I can feel McGee's eyes on me. For all the weight of his stare he might as well be sitting on my shoulders.

"Good thing she had the silent alarm on. . . . Because *we* sure as hell weren't watching her last night. . . . Jackson PD showed up after the alarm company called. . . . They knew the score, and came up with their sirens on. . . . Saw a guy come running out and go around back. . . . Dressed in some sort of coveralls and wearing a hood. . . . They couldn't find him, though. Not even when they brought out the dogs."

I move my hands away from my face to look at him and wish I hadn't.

"No one could reach you," he goes on. I remember leaving my cell phone in the truck. And leaving the truck at the Log Cabin Saloon after Angela got out and I'd run/staggered the five miles to the cabin. "I even drove myself out here at three in the goddamn morning but you were out, your piece of shit truck wasn't here. And you weren't with my Rebecca either. . . . I know that, too. You are a major fuckup, Quick-Draw." He allows himself a bitter chuckle. "And now I'm fucked up, too. . . . I got a call from the Assistant AG. They want me back in Cheyenne, pronto. . . . To explain why we left Cali Morrow unprotected."

We sit in silence for a few minutes. I can see Mungo's

face staring out at us from behind a screen of low branches. Even her look is reproachful. I call softly to her but she doesn't move from her hiding place.

"How could we have known that more than one person was after her?" I hate myself for asking this question, for even thinking of excuses.

"Doesn't matter. Someone was. . . . And she got hurt on our watch. That's all that matters."

"There was no way we could have known," I say out loud to myself.

Feeling sicker than I can ever remember feeling, I think about arresting Armalli last night. How it felt so good to do it so cleanly, especially when the temptation had been strong to make him pay me back a little for what I had suffered. There had never been any doubt that he was the stalker—the pictures and drawings on his walls, Bill Laughlin had seen him lurking outside Cali's house, he had a rifle and mud on his boots. An alternative had never been imagined. And I'd been so sure when I saw that flashbulb pop of evil light burst from Armalli's eyes when I said Cali's name. I'd been so goddamn sure.

How could I have been so cocky? How could I—who's had ten lifetimes' worth of bad luck since that night two years ago in Cheyenne—have thought anything could be that easy?

"Who was it?" But there's only one name in my head. Wokowski.

He shrugs his massive shoulders. "Hell if I know. Wokowski was on duty . . . but no one was with him. He was doing a solo patrol. . . . He could've slipped into some coveralls, dropped by the house." He flips the still-burning stub of the cigar out into the dirt lane. I don't get up to crush it out— I let it smolder. "The governor's going to hear about it anytime now. . . . Alana Reese is already making noise about that. . . . Then you can bet your ass the AG is going to get another call."

I can picture the Attorney General's indignation that the

celebrity's daughter his office was supposed to protect had been assaulted, and the way it would be passed along the phone lines in greater and greater intensity. Like a snowball rolling downhill. And I'm standing at the bottom of the hill, with McGee's aging bulk just above me. I'm going to get smacked. We're both going to. And I, at least, believe I deserve it. It's my karma. My folly. My lack of imagination. But not Cali. She didn't ask for any of it. But the very worst of it—almost as bad as what's happened to Cali—is the satisfaction, the gloating I know will be going on in the plush administrative offices. They'd surely been hoping she'd get hurt on our watch.

McGee is thinking along the same lines. "We're going to be the whipping boys, no doubt. . . . This is just the sort of thing they've been looking for for years. . . . We're in the doghouse now, lad. . . . No—we're buried *under* the doghouse."

He leaves unsaid his pension, his much-needed medical benefits. I know better than to say again it's not our fault.

"What do you want me to do?"

McGee speaks without looking at me. "I suggest you get your ass down to the hospital . . . and see if you can do something to alleviate the damage there."

I stand up slowly and call to Mungo one more time before I start to walk in the door.

"And take a shower and put on some clothes," McGee adds. "Christ, you stink."

TWENTY-EIGHT

THE WALK FROM MY CABIN to my truck is long, but the walk down the hallway toward Cali's room is far longer. And that is partly due to the fact that I can see Angela Hernandez standing in the hallway, watching me come toward her. In one hand she holds a large bottle of Evian water. I start to take my sunglasses off but then decide to keep them on for a while.

Angela does not smile when I get close. "I guess you heard what happened," she says.

"Yeah."

"I thought you had the guy. Hooked and booked, you said."

I don't say anything. She looks almost as bad as I feel, with dark rings under her eyes and her normally russet skin the color of ash. Putting the bottle under one arm, she takes a bottle of aspirin from a pocket, opens it, and shakes four pills out. She swallows two of them then chases the pills with thirsty gulps of water. I appreciate that she shares the pills and bottle with me, but I don't appreciate what she says next.

"I thought you were supposed to be some kind of super-star, Antonio Burns."

"I'm not."

After a moment she decides to take pity on me. "Cali's okay. Her face was cut up a little and she's got some bruises. She wasn't raped, if you hadn't heard. She and the doctor agree about that. At least not physically. It appears like this time he didn't try to kidnap her. He just wanted to rough her up a little. Scare the hell out of her."

I let out a sigh. But my guilt and pain are undiminished. I reach for the doorknob but the FBI agent touches my arm.

"You don't want to go in there, Burns. Ms. Reese's with her daughter."

"*Ms.?* Not Alana?"

"She seems to feel I should have been doing something other than drinking with you last night. Gorgon told her about us leaving together—I think he followed us out and saw us talking in your car, the asshole. But I guess he forgot to report that you wouldn't even kiss me. So she's probably not going to be buying my screenplay anytime soon, and I'm being re-placed by another agent tomorrow." She finally smiles a little as she says this last part, as if we are fellow casualties.

We're not, though. Not even close. She may go back to anonymously chasing bank robbers at the L.A. field office but I'm probably going to be fired. Disgraced. And McGee is going to get the same kick in the ass.

I push my sunglasses up on my head and look at the door. No, I definitely don't want to go in there. But like all the hard things in life, it's best to jump right in without hesi-tation. I turn the knob and push the door open.

The room is blindingly bright. Brighter still is the glare Alana Reese gives me. "Here comes Wyoming's finest. Our so very *special* agent, Antonio Burns."

Each word bites at my flesh.

The movie star is standing just inside the door so I have

to almost brush by her to come into the room. I can feel the animosity coming off her like radiation.

Cali is sitting on the edge of the hospital bed, dressed in her pajama pants and a T-shirt. Some bruises are evident on her arms. Pink turning to blue. Her pretty face is half covered in white tape but the hurt in her eyes is what pains me the most.

"Mom," she says, "give him a break. He did what he could. He thought I was safe. Everyone thought I was safe, me included."

Alana whirls to her daughter. "He was supposed to be protecting you, Cali. It wasn't *your* job to tell him when his work was done." She turns back to me, smiling grimly. "I'm afraid even your governor agrees with me. I spoke to him an hour ago, Agent Burns. They're going to be meeting with your supervisor tomorrow morning. I'd pack my bags if I were you. Hang up that badge you're so proud of."

I stare back with a pretense of confidence. "There was no indication that anyone else was after Cali. I know without a doubt that Myron Armalli was following her around, writing her letters, and that he is obsessed with her. When I arrested him I believed—wrongly—that she was out of danger. I can't tell you how terrible I feel about it."

"So *you* decide to stop protecting her? The moment when she needed it most?"

There's no point in arguing. Just as there will be no point when McGee and I are called before the suits.

"Can I talk to your daughter for a minute, Ms. Reese? Alone?"

"No, you may not. I'm afraid that once again, just like at the party that you disrupted the other night, I must ask you to leave. You have proven yourself quite incompetent at your job and I can think of no reason for you to remain—"

Cali interrupts her. "Go, Mom. Give us a minute."

Alana looks like she might argue, or break into a rage, but

she gauges the tone in Cali's voice. Years of practice in never, ever, making an unglamorous scene take hold. She gives me a few more moments of her icy stare—shooting sharpened icicles into my head—then walks out, slamming the door.

I sit down on the bed next to Cali. She is looking at her hands where they're folded across her lap. She won't meet my eyes.

"I'm sorry, Cali."

She nods her head a couple of times, still looking down.

"Tell me what happened. I need to know just how bad I fucked up. Hurt me."

Her lips are swollen on the side of her face but I see them lift just a little in a faint, sad smile.

"I went home after the Granary. I was too tired to do anything else. I fed Lester then changed into some pajamas and got into bed. I don't know when, but sometime late the doorbell rang. I went downstairs." She glances at me then quickly back down at her hands. In an even quieter voice she says, "For some reason I thought it might be you."

My heart sinks even deeper into my gut.

With another small, sad grin she continues, "Lester was hissing and spitting in the entry hall, so I thought he must smell Mungo. I checked myself out in the mirror, then opened the door without even thinking. I didn't look out the little window. I didn't even think there was anything to worry— Sorry, I don't need to hurt you that much, do I?"

She inhales and exhales, her fingers quivering.

"I opened the door but was so . . . tired or something . . . that I forgot to turn off the alarm and undo the chain. A man with a brown suit covering all of him and a black hood over his head was outside, pushing against the door. The chain broke. I hit the mirror with my head."

I can see goose bumps now on her skin. And I can hear the blood pumping in my own ears, like I was there. She's stopped talking.

"Who was he?"

"I couldn't tell. It was like a blackout or something. More like the world just turned inside out. The only details I remember are about me, running, screaming, fighting. He seemed very tall, very big and strong, but maybe that's just because I was so scared."

"Did he say anything?"

After a moment she shakes her head, the short blonde hair drifting forward to cover her bandaged cheeks, and answers in a voice quiet but pitched high. "I was screaming too loud to hear if he did. I ran for the upstairs bathroom, the only door with a lock on it. But he pulled me down on the stairs. I somehow managed to kick him off me—good thing I've got skier's legs, right?—and made it up there. But the door is pretty flimsy and he could have broken it down if he wanted. Maybe he heard the sirens, but I couldn't hear them. All I know is that the next thing two city cops were coming in."

We sit in silence for a long, long time. Tears run down her cheeks and drip from her chin. She's still staring down at her hands.

When I finally manage to speak, my voice sounds far off. Deep, as if it were coming from the bottom of a well. "Was it Wook?"

She shakes her head. "No. I don't think so. He showed up after the town guys. He's the one who brought me here." Then, after another minute, she asks, "What are you going to do with Myron?"

"I'm going to make sure they hold him for some hunting violations and suspicion of harassment, at the very least. Even though he was in jail last night, that doesn't mean he didn't do some of the other stuff. He'll be in for a couple of weeks, I bet, until they can do a competency exam and all that."

I still have a hard time getting my mind around the fact that I may have arrested the wrong guy, a harmless, screwed-up kid. I have a hard time facing the fact that there actually *is* someone else out there who wants to do her harm. Who wants to at the very least keep scaring the hell out of her, beating her up and psychologically traumatizing her. It's the kind of coincidence that's hard to imagine. In books and movies they always mean something sinister—the detective will boldly state that he doesn't believe in them. But I know that's bullshit. They happen in real life all the time.

"When you get out of here, stay with your mom and Angela. Okay?"

"How about Uncle Bill's? He came by this morning and invited me. I know he has some guns—a rifle and some handguns—so he should be able to protect me, right?"

"How did he look?"

"Not good. Like he had a rough night. Should I stay with him?"

I wonder, with a new sad pang, if the old legend is starting to free-fall. "No. Go to your mom's. Stay with her and her bodyguards. With Angela Hernandez and the other FBI agent who's flying in. It doesn't sound like Bill's well enough to look after you."

She nods her head. "Okay."

It's like this guy's trying to scare the hell out of her and hurt her, but not kill her. Not yet. I don't know what he's thinking. It's escalating, but I don't know why he hasn't taken it all the way when he so obviously could have. And he doesn't seem particularly afraid of getting caught. He's playing a game, but this time I don't know the rules. Usually there's something motivating criminals, greed or a thrill or rage. But this guy—I don't know.

The silence in the room is more painful than her mother's words. I stand up then crouch in front of her, trying to get her to meet my eyes.

"I'm going to find who's been doing this, Cali," I tell her. "I'm going to take care of it. Even though I'm about to be taken off the case. I fucked up, but you didn't. I'm proud of you. You're a total badass, you know, fighting him off three times. He won't get a chance at a fourth. I promise."

She still doesn't look up at me. Her only response to my attempt at encouragement is to say in a little-girl's voice, "I thought you said I was safe, Anton." The tears start sliding off her chin again.

TWENTY-NINE

I FIND WOKOWSKI in the basement gym of the Sheriff's Office. He's gloved up and pounding away on a heavy bag, dressed in a T-shirt and workout shorts that are drenched with sweat. Big beads of it run down from his close-cropped blond hair. The three or four other men lifting rusted weights stop what they're doing the second I walk through the door. Wokowski appears oblivious—his face is clenched like a fist and his eyes are scowling at the leather he's pummeling.

I walk up to within a few feet of him but he still doesn't seem to notice me. The bag receives jarring jabs and huge, hooking body shots. His chin is tucked into his chest and beneath his eyes are the same dark smudges Angela Hernandez had on her face. A day's growth of beard further darkens his countenance. His forearms are glistening with sweat but I can't spot any obvious defensive wounds on them. That doesn't mean that it wasn't him—the heavy coveralls Cali described could easily have shielded his flesh.

But it has to be him. There's no one else. It also doesn't

make any sense—why would he attack her when he was on the verge of winning her back? Of having a decent shot at it, anyway. It doesn't make any sense, I tell myself again. I'm totally adrift, without facts or evidence or motive.

There's one fact that I can't get past. I have no other suspects.

Wokowski throws a savage hook that nearly folds the eighty-pound bag in half. Then he whirls to face me as the bag is still shuddering on its chain. His eyes are shot with red and his breath is coming in shallow pants.

"Fuck!" he says loud enough that the obscenity reverberates around the concrete walls.

I'd been sure he'd been so focused on destroying the bag that he hadn't noticed me. But I was wrong.

"I don't like the way you're looking at me, Burns," he breathes, glaring.

I give it right back. "You shouldn't. Where were you when it happened, Wook?"

The pumped-up muscles beneath his tight T-shirt swell even further. So do the massive corners of his jaw. His eyes narrow into crimson slits. The ceiling, which in this windowless room is not more than eighteen inches above my head, seems to press even lower.

"Fuck you," he says.

He pops me in the chest with one of the wet gloves. Not hard enough to hurt, but with enough force to cause me to stagger backward a single step. I almost bounce back swinging. Somehow, though, I manage to hold my feet still and keep my arms at my sides. Along with the throb of blood in my veins, I can feel the wide eyes of the weight lifters.

"C'mon. You want to go?" he asks, touching the gloves together.

I don't say anything.

He reaches out to push me again. This time I knock the glove away with a swipe of my palm. The temptation is almost overwhelming. But I haven't boxed in almost twenty years, not since my brother and I saw *Rocky* on a Manila air force base and made our father set up a ring in the hot Philippines sun. And Wokowski probably has inches of reach and more than fifty pounds on me.

"I asked you a question, Sergeant. Where were you when it happened?"

He stares at me for a long time through his bloodshot eyes. I can feel him willing me into the ring that's in one corner of the basement, where yellow tape reading "Police Line—Do Not Cross" is strung between four posts around a moldy gray mat. There's little doubt his superior size and strength would prevail there, but I want it as bad as he does. I'm willing to take the chance, willing to cheap-shot him with a sharp elbow or knee to even the odds a little. It's only the need to know that keeps me from walking over and ducking under the tape.

Wokowski rips the gloves off his hands and throws them down at my feet. He takes several deep breaths.

"Patrolling in the valley, okay? I heard the alarm call go out on the radio. I drove there as fast as I could. I got there ten minutes after the city guys. I'm the one who took her to St. John's. So either you believe me or you can get your skinny Mexican ass in the ring."

No one's this good an actor. Not even a professional like Alana Reese and especially not Danny Gorgon. Wokowski would have to be either completely innocent or totally insane to be able to pull off the look of righteous fury on his face.

"Then who was it?"

"I don't know," he says, punctuating the last word with a pivot and a bare-handed blast at the bag. When he spins back to me I notice that his knuckles are starting to bleed.

"I'm going to find him. Then I'm going to take him apart."

Wokowski nods. "You do that. I'll be right behind you."

We stand looking at each other for a minute longer. The fury seems to slowly drain out of him. His lips start quivering, almost like the big man might be about to cry. I turn away from him and walk over to a vacant bench press. I sit on it and rub my aching temples with the heels of my hands. I can tell by the smell of Wokowski's sweat that he follows me.

When I open my eyes and look up, he's standing over me.

"I know what everyone's saying, Burns. And they're full of shit. If they weren't, I'd be the first one coming after you. You know that. So listen: *There was nothing you could do.* We both thought she was safe, with Myron locked up."

What he says causes an even stronger reaction in me. Especially since it's coming from the man who'd been my enemy twenty-four hours ago. Sympathy and pity are hard enough to take from a friend. From him, it's almost too much to bear.

My cell phone starts playing that stupid song as I walk out of the Sheriff's Office. Rebecca, I think, feeling a tiny bit of hope and a lot of dread—*What will I say? What can I do?*

But the text on the flashing screen tells me that the caller is the Assistant Attorney General himself. A well-dressed, weasel-faced man, he's McGee's boss, the office's number two man, its designated executioner, and also, not surprisingly, a guy who happens to be a complete prick. Six months ago he'd stood motionless over McGee when Ross collapsed on a courthouse floor. A heart attack. I remember the slight smile I'd seen on the Assistant AG's face. An expectant smirk.

The song plays three times before the phone is once again quiet. Getting in the Pig and starting the engine and air conditioner, I wait for the single beep alerting me that I have a message before punching any buttons.

I have screwed up a *very* simple case, weasel-face tells

me in an attempt at a reprimanding tone that does little to disguise his delight. I have embarrassed the office yet again. A suspension is being contemplated. An internal investigation into my conduct—or lack of it—as well as that of Mr. McGee, is being commenced immediately. I am to have no further contact with Cali Morrow, Alana Reese, or Myron Armalli. And, as if the message isn't enough, I'm ordered to call him back for a person-to-person ass-reaming posthaste.

I don't call him back. I don't even call Rebecca.

Instead I eat a big plate of spaghetti at the cabin to try and fill the void in me. When that doesn't work, I pick up the book I've been reading and flop down on the porch with it. Maybe the story and the printed words themselves will clog my brain to the exclusion of all else. Keep the dogs at bay for a while.

Smoke Jump's ending is tragic, but right now it feels unreal. I can't get a grip on the depth of it, or feel much of the impact the author obviously intends. The dogs barking and yipping in my head are a constant interruption; they're impossible to ignore. But I try.

A fire had blown up in Lander, and by some unseasonable trick of the wind it began heading east toward Jackson Hole. Patrick Morrow, who had resigned from his smoke-jumping team upon impregnating and then marrying Alana Reese, had decided to finish out the summer anyway. For the fun of it. For friendship. He and his best friend, Bill, and five other men were deployed in the vicinity of Elation Peak. The freakish easterly winds increased and the fire threatened to overrun the friends. They elected to make for the summit of Elation Peak, where they hoped to find fuel-less ground—no trees grew on its tabletop apex—on which to escape the blaze. Laughlin led, rock climbing up the butte's back cliff. He made it to the top but Patrick didn't. Cali's father fell into the flames, where he burned to death.

I remember, but the author doesn't mention, Laughlin's

habit of dangerously underrating climbs. Maybe it wasn't intentional—maybe he just didn't know how good he was.

I put the book away with the others in the cabin and return to the porch to call for the wolf.

Mungo has taken up her usual position across the lane behind a screen of pine branches. Watching me, thinking I can't see her. She's pulled her lips up, exposing the tips of her big canines. I sit down on the steps to let her play it out. I'm surprised when after only a few minutes of this game she comes out and slinks back toward me, out from the trees. She approaches slowly with her head held very low and that same shy grin on her face. Not looking at me, but watching all the same. She comes right up onto the steps and stands by the cabin's door behind me. I suppose she's anxious to get in out of the heat.

Not turning around, I say, "You can wait just a minute, wolf."

Then she does the strangest thing, something she's never done before. I feel a soft weight on my shoulder. She is resting her head—the prickly, whiskered underside of her jaw— on me. It's such a dog thing to do, so devoted and touching, as if she's trying to soak up a part of my pain, that my throat constricts. Loyalty. That's what it is.

Intending to just close my eyes for a few minutes, I sleep on the couch for two hours. Heavy, thick, all-engulfing sleep. After I get up and eat some more—just to have something inside me—I sit again on the cabin's narrow porch. The afternoon sun, I hope, might somehow rouse me from what still feels like a bad dream. One of those dreams where you're furious, frightened, and totally incapable of any decisive action, but where it all, at the same time, feels suffocatingly calm.

I'm pregnant, Anton, I hear Rebecca saying. *I'm pregnant.* Then, *I wish you weren't the father.* I divide it up in my head, trying to make it into two separate pieces that maybe I can manage to chew up and swallow.

I'm pregnant. Does she intend to keep it or get an abortion? One option will make me a father, an immature, too-unprepared father; the other is . . . unthinkable to me now. Even though I'd never believed those long, uncomfortable Sunday mornings in the *estancia*'s tiny *iglesia* would have any effect but the inverse of what was intended. Roberto's preaching was much more persuasive, and he believed in one thing only: Freedom. But this, goddamn it, is mine. And Rebecca's.

What about the other thing, the part about wishing I weren't the father? Because she doesn't love me, or because she doesn't think I'm suitable or ready? Or maybe, just maybe, because she doesn't feel ready, and the fact that it's mine makes what would otherwise be an easy decision to abort that much harder. And if that's true, then I can still hope. I cup this tiny spark in my hands and blow on it, willing it into a flame.

I find the phone book the landlady had left for me in a kitchen drawer and look up the number for the Spring Creek Ranch. Dialing is harder than anything I've done in a long time. Harder than walking down the hospital hallway to face Cali and my professional failure. I have no idea what I'm going to say. Or what I'm going to do. *Just say what you feel,* I tell myself, even though I know I lack the language to make it coherent. *Say it anyway.*

The desk clerk tells me that the Hershes are out. Driving up past the Tetons to Yellowstone for the day, I'm told in a friendly, vacuous manner, as if I were just calling to chat. They're expected back for dinner at eight. Do I want to leave a message? She'll scribble something down and slip it under their door.

Hanging up the phone, I resist the urge to smash it on the porch railing. To throw it across the road and into the trees. Instead I take those deep belly breaths, vow to keep the spark alight, and reverently pack it away into a compartment in my head. The place where I keep my most treasured things. It'll keep there for a few hours.

Now what? Where the hell is Roberto? Shouldn't he have shown up by now? I wish he were here.

I need to move. I have to do something. *You've got to get up some momentum,* I hear my brother telling me. *Go fast. Go fast all the time. You slow down, and then all the shit you shouldn't have done will catch up to you.* It was the way he lived, the way he climbed. And look where it got him.

Inside the cabin, I take out the piece of lethal metal and plastic that is my .40 H&K. I eject the law-enforcement cartridge, which holds fifteen fat hollow-point rounds, then rack the slide to eject the lone remaining bullet. I fieldstrip the gun on an old T-shirt spread out on the dining-room table. Oil the parts. Wipe it clean. Reassemble. Then I load it again, even putting the sixteenth round back in the chamber. I slip an extra clip in my pocket. My mind is perfectly quiet while I do all this, and for some reason it feels very good.

THIRTY

IT'S THREE HOURS later when I park the truck in front of my dark cabin again and rest my forehead on the steering wheel. Sidestepping explicit orders, I'd spent the afternoon and evening hanging out in a far corner of the hospital parking lot. Charles Wokowski and Bill Laughlin had been the only visitors to come and go.

Wook had visited twice, wearing a grim expression on both occasions and once bearing flowers. His cop's eyes had picked out my truck in the lot. He'd glanced over at me without slowing his pace and given me a short, quick nod. Laughlin had come once, late in the afternoon. He moved slowly, carefully, as if he were, like me, nursing a brutal hangover. I had to resist the urge to get out of the Pig and offer him some more expressions of my respect for him. *Smoke Jump* had me picturing him standing above a cliff at night as three-hundred-foot flames roared around him and licked his partner right off the wall. The only thing that kept me from getting out of the car was the awful embarrassment that once again I'd utterly failed to protect his adopted niece.

I'd left then to drive by a flower shop to buy the biggest spray of bright red tulips they had. Then I'd attached a note. *Think of three words when you fall asleep tonight—Anton Loves You. We'll talk tomorrow.* At a secondhand store I found a pair of tiny baby sneakers for a dollar. I'd driven my gifts to the Spring Creek Ranch atop Gros Ventre Butte and laid them at the door of the condo where Rebecca and her father were staying. The act eased the blackness that was threatening to swallow me. I could at least hope for hope. I drove back to town and resumed my vigil outside the hospital.

At eight o'clock a black Suburban with tinted windows pulled up and Cali had been hustled into it along with Alana, Angela, and two of her mother's oversized bodyguards. I'd followed them at a distance back up the valley to the ranch. I'd watched unseen, parked on the shoulder of the highway, as the front gate was padlocked behind them.

How much longer can I wait, can I hang on? The cell phone chimes its mocking song. I thumb it off without looking at the screen. Three times it had rung while I was driving up the valley and once Rebecca's name and number had appeared on the flashing screen. The other two calls were from the Assistant Attorney General. Two messages had been left. I hadn't listened to either of them. I could guess what the weasel-faced suit would have to say, and I'm not sure I want to know yet what Rebecca is thinking. I'm not ready. *Fall asleep tonight thinking of me.*

I throw myself back in the seat and stare out at the night. Then my right hand unconsciously jerks toward the passenger's seat. My fingers close around the plastic grip of my gun.

Something is on the porch.

It's a black shape, far darker than the bleached pine boards that make up the steps. It's huddled on them—a void of light. After a moment it takes form and I realize it's a man sitting there in the darkness with his elbows on his knees. There's a tiny orange glow to one side. A burning ember—

the hot end of a pale, stiff joint—moves slowly to about where the head should be and then sucks bright enough to illuminate a face.

His features are half hidden by long black hair. But even in the faint orange light I recognize the high cheekbones and the lean features.

"Thought you'd fallen asleep, *che*," Roberto calls to me in his soft voice, exhaling sweet smoke that drifts into the truck. "What's going on? You drunk?"

I open the door and get out. "Just generally screwed up. Where have you been, 'Berto? I haven't seen you around in two days. I thought maybe you'd left for Salt Lake without saying good-bye."

He looks the opposite of what I feel: totally serene and in control. Like a king surveying his dark domain.

"Kicking back," he says, now lifting a squat bottle and putting it to his lips. "Came down off Moran today. The Sickle and Scythe, a route that your buddy Bill Laughlin put up in sixty-eight. God, it was good up there. You should've been with me, bro."

"I wish I had been."

I sit down next to him on the wooden porch steps. Mungo comes padding up out of the trees. We're both quiet as she trots across the road and climbs up the steps. She sniffs at me for a minute then lies down between us.

"That's some dog you got. You shouldn't keep her locked up like that." He grabs the ruff of her neck and shakes it affectionately. "Ain't that right, *mariquita*?" Mungo doesn't flinch away from his touch.

"I guess you made yourself at home."

He *tsks* his tongue against the roof of his mouth. "You left a window open. That's like an invitation to us criminals, *che*. You really should be more careful. So, you get your man? The stalker?"

"Last night I thought I did. This morning it turned out I hadn't."

He drops the joint into the dirt and crushes it under a boot heel so that the remaining paper and marijuana disintegrate into the dirt. Reaching to one side of the steps, he lifts what I now recognize as my special bottle of Chinaco Reposado, toasts me, then drains the last few swallows.

"What are you going to do now?"

"I don't know."

"What about your girlfriend? That Rebecca chick who thinks I'm such a bad influence?"

"I don't know."

"Shit then, Ant. You don't know much." He throws the squat, round bottle into the blackness across the road, where it swishes through branches before landing with a thunk. "Somebody'll find that a hundred years from now and think they got a really cool artifact."

"Good thing Mungo's already come back."

Roberto stands up in one swift motion that seems to contradict the odors of lazy sweat, tequila, and pot emanating from him. "So, you ready to go? I got my gear right here." He points into the shadows of the porch where there's a large lump shaped like a backpack.

I laugh for what seems the first time in forever. He has a knack for showing up when I need him. It's good to see him right now. And it's good to be touched by his impulsiveness. He wants to climb, he climbs. He wants to get high, he gets high.

I shake my head. "I can't, 'Berto. I really wish I could but I can't. I'm too tired and I've got too much work to do."

"Bullshit."

"No, I'm serious. Things have been really fucked up lately."

"That's what you get for being a cop, trying to make everyone else play by your rules. Now c'mon, *che*. Get your shit together. Let's go." He grabs one of my arms and hauls me to my feet. I don't resist, but I don't exactly leap. Mungo stands up with us. "You need to feed the Rat, bro. A little adrenaline will blow out all the shit that's clogging up your heart."

"What about your meeting with the Feds? It's in two days, right? Thursday night? You still going to do that?"

His face grows serious and he nods. "Yeah, I think so. If it's for real. That guy they want—my old friend Jesus—he's messing with the wrong people, you know? He's doing women and kids and shit. Yeah, I'd like to fuck with him a little. 'Specially if they're willing to give me a clean break. But like I told you, there's one thing I got to do before that, *che*," he adds, his smile a Cheshire grin in the darkness, "and that's climb with you."

I find myself smiling back, thinking, *My brother's like a virus. He infects you.*

"What do you want to do?"

"The North Face Direct."

I laugh again. "Yeah, right. There's no way in hell I have time for that. You, either. It took us three days when we did it with Dad. And we were speedy little guys back then."

"We can be up and down the Grand in a day. Twelve hours or less. No ropes, *che*. We'll solo the motherfucker. It'll be faster."

I shake my head without taking my eyes off his. He's still smiling at me, and I can't stop smiling back. "I can't do it, 'Berto. Too dangerous for me. And I haven't been climbing nearly as much as you—I'm in no kind of shape for that. No way."

But while I stand there looking at my brother, I remember that maybe I've lost the only woman I have ever loved. I've surely lost my professional reputation and my pride, anyway. I've screwed up the job of protecting a woman who trusted me. Who am I to refuse a trip into the sky with my beautiful, mad brother—even if the trip might not include a return ticket?

WEDNESDAY

THIRTY-ONE

ONE PART OF the night sky is alive with color, the planets and stars pulsating blues and reds and yellows against a black-velvet backdrop. The other part—the North Face of the Grand—looms up over me on three sides and it's as dark as a celestial black hole. It yawns farther and farther over my head with every high step on the scree. I'm ascending into another world. A harsher, purer world, where the things that seemed so important below lose their significance.

Roberto moves ahead of me like a phantom, leading me higher into the night. I've always liked watching him move. Every step, every swing of an arm or turn of his head, is utterly unself-conscious. Each motion is nothing more than a fluid contraction of the requisite web of muscles. There's no interference from his psyche, no second-guessing or worrying if he's being observed. He's not even breathing hard. If he's breathing at all I can't hear it. He makes no sound except for the occasional scuff of a Vibram sole on stone.

We're ascending into the tight confines of the Teton Glacier. The rock walls of the Grand and Mt. Owens loom over us, nearly three thousand feet high. Although it is just so much sucking blackness overhead, I know the North Face of the Grand is to our left. We'd climbed it once with Dad when I was fourteen and Roberto two years older. At the time it was the biggest, scariest thing we'd ever done. It was terrifying even with Dad there guiding us and with the three fat ropes we'd brought as lifelines against the forces of gravity. The ropes might catch a fall but they provide little psychological support when you're just a boy and you've got all that space beneath your heels. And then there are the things the ropes can't help—the twin dangers of rockfall and high-altitude lightning storms that can blow up out of nowhere and go off like an atomic bomb.

I can still remember the feel of the rock on that trip—the adrenaline causes everything to be imprinted deeper in your memory. It was sixteen years ago but it still tingles in my fingertips. Low on the face it was glacier-polished and smooth as glass, while higher it had a texture like sugar and the weather had formed pits and knobs. I recall the way the gray, pink, and white granite streaked my hands with damp soot.

We have not spoken a word since abandoning the Pig at Lupine Meadows. Roberto headed up the trail without a backward glance at me, the dark hole in the night sky pulling at him with an even stronger force than it pulls at me. A monstrous Pied Piper piping in a couple of hungry rats.

I caught up to him at one point. I found him standing a little way off the trail and pushing down the sleeve of his windshirt. In his hand I caught a thin flash of moonlight on a needle. I passed by without a word, pretending to not see him.

But now, as we step onto the glacier, Roberto says over his shoulder, "Check it out. On the right."

There is a wide crevasse running alongside us. I twist on my headlamp and point it into the chasm. It reflects back an eerie blue light as strange as that in my brother's eyes.

The glacier is not steep but the rigid soles of my mountain boots threaten to skate on the hard summer surface. It wouldn't take much of a fall to slip down into the crevasse. And God only knows where the bottom is. I was guiding once in Alaska when a glacier on Denali spit out two climbers who had disappeared more than three decades earlier. Their bodies were perfectly preserved, like they'd been in a time warp in the center of the earth. Although it's oddly warm, walking on this glacier in the predawn darkness, the thought of an icy entombment makes me shiver. But Roberto doesn't stop to put on his crampons so I don't either. Instead of walking slowly and cautiously, my brother is picking up speed as the altitude draws him into the sky.

A bergschrund—a wide gap between the rock wall and the ice—finally brings us to a halt at the base of the wall. I'm panting from the long approach, my polypro underclothes soaked with sweat. Like me, Roberto seems to remember everything about the long-ago climb here with our father. He moves left along the bergschrund's lip until he finds the bridge of snow leading across fifteen feet of bottomless space.

"Think it will hold?" I ask when he pauses before the bridge. I've turned on my headlamp again to study it.

"Only one way to find out, *che*."

I stand next to him before the bridge and study it with my light. It's about three feet wide at the narrowest point and looks from the side to be about ten feet in depth. The rock on the other side is sheer and smooth as glass, polished by thousands of years of grinding ice. I pull my long ax off my pack and gently probe the foot of the bridge. The upper crust of snow is hard, like burnt toast, but when I push a little harder the ax slides cleanly into lighter stuff. When the head presses flat against the surface I pull it back out.

"I don't know," I tell my brother.

"You've already said that a couple of times tonight. You're holding on too tight."

In the light of my headlamp he's giving me one of his

signature looks. A deep stare from his blue eyes framed by all
that sweat-soaked black hair. He has the stare of a messiah,
but it irritates me right now. Some messiah; a drug-addicted
killer, a possibly suicidal adrenaline junkie.

"To what, Roberto? Living?"

His eyes remain fixed on mine. "To everything, *che*.
Fucking everything. Can't have any fun unless you're willing
to let go every now and then, see what happens. Loosen your
grip, little bro."

He's probably talking without thinking, talking shit, but
because of his soft voice and his eyes I worry over his words
like Mungo gnawing on a rawhide chew stick.

While I'm standing there thinking in the dark, Roberto
brushes past me with a soft hiss from the rub of our nylon jackets. He steps right out onto the bridge without hesitation, then
moves lightly across it. His boots barely crunch on its surface.
At the far end he finds a few small edges in the rock for his fingers and the toes of his boots and pulls himself up onto a narrow ledge. He moves sideways toward where an alcove cuts up
through the face. I take a deep breath as if to fill myself with air
and make myself as light as possible then step with a quaking
boot onto the bridge. The bridge holds my weight.

The alcove is like a chimney or a three-sided elevator
shaft rising hundreds of feet up the wall. I remember this as
the start of the route from that August dawn sixteen years
ago. Only then it hadn't been choked with snow and ice.

"Let's haul ass," Roberto says. "Won't be long to sunup.
Don't want to be sitting on our thumbs when the rockfall
starts." He gives a short laugh when I touch my cheek, as he
knew I would, at the mention of rockfall. Then he sits to snap
his crampons onto his boots.

The snow is soft at the bottom of the chimney. I swim up
it after him holding my long ax in both hands and planting it
sideways in the snow. It's technically easy, and mentally no big
deal, but it's physically more exhausting than the harder moves

I know are lurking ahead. I'm panting and sweating by the time I scramble up onto the first large ledge on the face.

For the first time I pay attention to the wind. It had been steadily rising since we left the car and began hoofing it up Garnet Canyon. It flowed over the pass between the Middle and Grand Tetons and rushed down at us as if trying to push us back. Then, when we entered the deep cirque beneath the North Face, it had almost disappeared. Here now, high on the face, I can feel its strength. It rustles over our nylon shells and shoves us around with occasional gusts. Looking up, I can see a streak of spindrift tearing off the summit like a flag in the night.

We follow the ledge past a small cave. It's where we had bivied that August fifteen years ago, safe from the rockfall that whistled by in the late afternoon. I shine my light in the cave and can recall exactly where I had shivered in my sleeping bag all through the night. I can even remember Dad joking that my eyes looked ready to pop right out of my head.

At the west end of the ledge another chimney takes us higher. The back wall of this one is choked with vertical ice instead of snow. We climb it by swinging our picks directly into the ice or by torquing them into cracks and stemming with crampons on opposite walls. The crampons screech and spark until they find purchase on the rock.

We're getting high now. We're probably close to a thousand feet off the deck. All that space pulls at my back.

The Second Ledge angles steeply toward the abyss. We move across it cautiously for several hundred feet. One slip or a rolled ankle on a loose stone and I'll be sliding off the lip.

"How's the job? Doing justice. You still locking up them nasty addicts and jaywalkers?" Roberto shouts over the wind.

"It sucks," I yell back.

"Know what Richard Pryor said 'bout justice? JUSTICE is for JUST US. Dude may be a flaming crackhead, but he knows what he's talking about."

It's not until we're near the top of the three-thousand-foot face that I get truly gripped. And the Rat gets a high-altitude feast.

From the Third Ledge we climbed a sixty-foot corner using rock shoes now to smear on thin edges and pockets. At the top of this there is a narrow rail of rock leading to the left. It's about as wide as a bookshelf and it tapers down to nothing at a distant corner. There it actually inverts, a turning place where the whole world gets upside down.

Roberto crawls out onto this bookshelf in slow motion. He's on his hands and knees at first, then, as the shelf narrows, he's actually slithering along on his left shoulder and hip. Pulling on tiny edges with his hands and pushing on others with the toes of his boots, he creeps out an inch at a time. I watch with my heart in my throat. *He's doing what he wants,* I tell myself again and again. *That's as good a way to die as any.* But I can't help imagining him shifting slightly away from the rock and falling into space. I can already hear my own grieving screams.

He turns the corner as slowly as I've ever seen him move. His head disappears, then his sideways shoulders, then his hips and finally his boots. I think I take my first breath in several minutes.

Then it's my turn.

I'm shaking as I follow, being very careful to focus on nothing but the cold rock at my fingertips. I try to meld into the stone, to shrink down on the shelf and burrow into it. The wind claws at my jacket. *Rebecca,* I think. *My child. Let me live and I'll never solo up here again.* I've made that promise before but *this* time—just as I had before—I mean it.

When I stick my head around the corner I catch sight of my brother again. He's traversing up a seventy-five-degree slab that drops off into nowhere. Absolutely nowhere. I can't see the edges he's using. Watching, crouched sort of sideways on one hand and one knee, I start to breathe hard and fast.

I'm perfectly still except for the shaking, and it's as if I'm running a sprint. My blood thunders through my veins like a high-speed train through a tunnel.

Why didn't we bring a rope?

It takes me a few minutes, but I manage to screw up my courage. There's nothing else to do. I sure as hell can't back off this ledge. And I sure as hell can't stay here—the stone is already transferring a debilitating numbness into my wrist and kneecap.

I inch around, looking desperately for any good handhold. There's nothing but a few rotten edges. I grip first one and then another, praying they don't break off. Then with agonizing slowness I put my weight to them and pull myself around the corner.

The will to live, the idiocy of being up here without a rope, almost overwhelms me. I have a child. I have a woman I should make my wife. *Win her. Win back my job. Fight for all of it.*

I find tiny nubbins for the inside edge of my boot soles and stand there, feeling the dreadful weight of the void sucking at me. Staring at the rock just above my face, I try to find another hold. Someone has hammered a secure-looking piton into a tiny crack. It's not concern over whether the piton is still sound that keeps me from reaching for it, but ethics. You don't pull on gear. It's cheating.

I hesitate for a long moment, thinking about it, then I grab the fucking thing with a relieved groan and wiggle my index finger through the steel eyelet. Nothing's ever felt so good. I don't care if my brother sees me. Later, I know, I'll confess and my brother will mock me for my weakness but he won't attach any other importance to the crime.

He's waiting for me on another ledge—this one broad and flat and wonderfully safe—with his feet dangling out over the void. He's grinning at me but he says nothing when I pull myself up beside him and let the adrenaline crawl back into the little nodes in the small of my back. He punches my arm, but not hard enough to knock me off. Then he points out at the valley.

"What's the matter, bro? That little traverse freak you out?"

"Yeah. It freaked me."

The Snake River is very clear from this height, its water a flashing vein of mercury in the dawn light. Beside it the highway is already bustling with traffic. Just to the east, though, where the land humps up a little, smoke is billowing into the air. A great dark cloud that is tinted with orange at the bottom.

"It's burning," 'Berto says. "Check it out, *che*. The whole fucking valley's going up."

THIRTY-TWO

T HE REST OF the climb to the summit is technically
easy. There's another chimney or two that embrace me
within the comfort of three solid walls, a pitch up some steep,
loose blocks, and then it's just a scramble to the summit.

But my mind is burning just as brightly as the valley below. Fire. It was fire that took Cali's father. Fire that stole
from Alana Reese what was most loved by her. And now the
valley's ablaze once again.

We are beginning the final easy pitch when a man steps
up onto the summit block. He's leaning hard against the
wind. I rest for a minute, watching him turning his head and
staring out at the surrounding peaks and then out at the valley, and hoping he's not one of those assholes who likes to
throw rocks into the void. He glances down at the North
Face with what appears to be a quick shudder. Then he does
a double take, seeing Roberto crawling up the final yards
toward him without a rope. His mouth moves and I lip-read
an awestruck "Holy shit!"

Another man steps up onto the block. He's wearing a

jacket with the insignia of Exum Mountain Guides, a company I'd worked for a long time ago. When I move closer I recognize him—Jason something—a guy who was just starting out as a guide when I was quitting. He smiles knowingly as he watches us crawling up to the summit, understanding what we've been through and also surely noting the lack of ropes, harnesses, and gear.

He shades his eyes against the rising sun and squints first at my brother then at me. "Holy shit," he too mouths. Then he calls out over the sound of the wind, "The Burns brothers?"

Roberto doesn't answer even though he's closer. I hear him mutter a couple of curses in our mother's language. I yell, "Hey, Jason! You know what's going on down there?"

But he's staring at my brother, who is more famous for both his climbing and extralegal exploits, no doubt wondering what he's doing back in the States and whether he's still a wanted man.

When he finally answers my greeting it's not to greet me in return. "The park's radio guy called our hut last night, trying to figure out if anyone's seen you. Something's going on in the valley, man. We're to report if we spot you." He looks uneasily at Roberto, assuming the message has something to do with him.

"Have you heard what's going on in the valley?" I ask again.

"All I know is that there's been some kind of shooting and an assistant prosecutor is missing. And that some maniac's lit a fire in the valley."

A brand-new fear turns the sky a tick brighter.

I run awkwardly in my stiff mountain boots, leaping small ledges and over boulders, rushing down toward the rappel ledge below the summit spire. My vision stays fixed on the rough ground—on not falling—but I'm intensely aware of the space all around me. The impossible amounts of air above, to the sides, and below. Bright blue sky and distant ice-covered peaks and dirty white glaciers. It's perverse, but I feel a bit of pleasure along with the apprehension. A revival. I've soloed the North Face and lived. And now the waiting is over. I'm needed down there, in the real world, where there has to be something I can do.

I temper the emotion by reminding myself that Cali might be in trouble. In very, very bad trouble.

Four climbers clad in Gore-Tex and with sticker-covered helmets are gathered at the rappel station, tying knots and double-checking one another's rap devices. I push through them, acknowledging the startled faces by saying, "Sorry. There's an emergency below. Mind if I borrow your ride?"

I grab the twin ropes hanging over the edge without waiting for an answer. The ropes are looped through a Gordian knot of bright, multicolored slings looped over a spike of rock. I check to see that the ropes are bound together with a tight double fisherman's and that the slings aren't too worn or weather bleached.

"Hey, man . . ." one of them starts to protest.

But his complaint is cut off by the deadly earnest expression I feel on my face. Or maybe it's because I hear Roberto coming up behind me.

"I've seen you, dude," another says to him cautiously. Respectfully. "You're the guy who soloed the Nose in like three hours, right? That was so fucking sick. What'd you come up? The North Face or something?" His friend nervously nudges him to shut him up.

I don't wait to hear my brother's response. I'm already leaning over the edge, feeling the cold air rising up my jacket from below. Since I don't have a harness or a rappel device I've wrapped the rope around my shoulders, hips, and groin in the old-school method Dad had taught us. After lowering myself a few feet my boot soles lose contact with the vertical stone.

I'm hanging free, spinning as the rope squeezes me and hisses against my nylon shells like an enraged python, spiraling down toward another narrow ledge above the peak's Upper Saddle. Other than that and the cliff, there is nothing but space—thousands of feet of it—and Idaho and Montana and then Wyoming swimming before me with every rotation I make.

My boots thump down on the ledge just as my gloves start to burn through and my jacket begins to melt under the rope's pressure. I take off at a run down a steep ramp of broken rock and snow leading to the Upper Saddle. At one point the ramp narrows to nothing, but I half-leap and half-climb past the exposed section. I barely consider the potentially fatal air below.

In about two minutes' time I'm whipping an ax off my pack as I scramble into a narrow couloir and begin riding it down on the seat of my pants. Depressions and sun-spots in the steep snow threaten to launch me into the air. When my speed gets too great I use my ax's spike as a two-handed brake. I look back only once—I see Roberto sliding behind me, his long black hair streaming uphill.

At the broad, snow-covered expanse of the Lower Saddle, there are several bright tents fluttering in the wind that is sweeping between the Middle Teton and the Grand. Climbers are stomping around in their boots and racking gear and stuffing packs, not exactly getting an alpine start. Beyond them is the aluminum-and-canvas hut of the Exum Mountain Guides.

When I barge through the thin door, the hut-tender—a young woman—stares at me in alarm. She's sitting up in her sleeping bag reading a book.

"I'm Antonio Burns. I need to use your phone."

I look around the cluttered hut, taking in the bunks and dirty dishes sitting in a pan of half-melted snow. On a crooked counter is a small phone. It's nothing more than a combination of cell phone and radio. I expected something bigger, something meatier, would be necessary to connect this world to the one down below.

"You're the guy the ranger called looking for last night? Woke us all up—"

"Did he leave a number?"

"No. Hell, I didn't know what he was talking about. And none of us knew if you were up here."

So I dial 911. The emergency call is picked up by a dispatcher in Idaho who agrees to transfer me after I explain my location and law-enforcement credentials. I wait for a long, long time. The girl pulls on some fleece then wanders outside to either get away from the wild look in my eyes or to give me some privacy. Through the metal door I can hear her talking to my brother. It takes him about a minute before he has her laughing at something.

Finally Sheriff Buchanan comes on the line.

"I'm up-valley at Alana Reese's ranch. On my cell phone. You need to get out here as soon as possible." Even through the static and the wind that's rustling the canvas walls, the sheriff's voice sounds bewildered and panicked.

"What's going on? I'm no longer on her daughter's case. I'm supposed to stay away from them."

"I think you're back on now, or will soon be. Four hours ago Bill Laughlin shot an FBI agent and tried to kidnap Alana Reese. She escaped, but he took her daughter. He's gone crazy."

I take the phone away from my ear and stare at it like an idiot. What seems like minutes tick away as I stand stupefied, until evidence of a sort begins to assimilate in my mind.

Sights and sounds come back to me. Angela Hernandez saying that someone had broken into Alana's house and stolen her wedding dress. Cali telling me that Laughlin has always been in love with her mother—that she'd found a scrapbook hidden away. The words in *Smoke Jump*—that Laughlin had competed with Patrick for Alana and lost. Lester hissing at Laughlin when he'd come into the living room, the cat having been on the counter two days earlier when someone had tried to come through the window. Cali telling me that she could stay with him, that he has guns. The pawnshop owner telling me that he'd sold stun guns to a lot of "geezers." And Laughlin saying, "You look out for her, you hear? She's a lot like her mother. Gives off a scent of something. Makes guys go crazy. Do the damnedest things."

And Laughlin knows avalanches. He'd told us stories about all his close calls with them. Myron Armalli and his letters had been nothing but a lucky diversion for him.

I put the phone back against my ear in time to hear the sheriff saying, "Your boss has been calling for you from Cheyenne. He left a message for you. He said, and I'm quoting here: *'Unfuck it.'* "

"Tell me what the hell's going on."

"Like I said, Bill Laughlin's gone crazy. He lit a fire in the valley—"

"I saw it."

"It started about a mile west of Alana Reese's ranch. As dry as things are, it sparked right up with the help of what the Forest Service guys are saying was a couple of gallons of gasoline and a drip torch. The wind didn't help either. Within an hour several acres were burning and it was headed right toward here—the house. It was only because of the fast response of some Hot Shots on leave that they were able to dig a break and keep the house from going up. The barn and the stable didn't make it. Neither did some of the horses. God, it smells awful. Before that, though, while the people in the house were evacuating, Laughlin came in with a rifle. It was him, although we haven't gotten a formal identification yet. They say he was absolutely raving. He tried to get Alana in his car, but she ran off and hid. Then he hit Cali with the butt of the rifle and started dragging her toward an old beat-up station wagon. The FBI agent, Angela Hernandez, tried to stop him but he shot her."

"Is she all right?"

"She will be. She took a bullet in the chest but the doctors say it didn't hit anything vital. They've got her at the hospital now."

"He took Cali?"

"I'm afraid so. The witnesses, Alana Reese among them, saw him shove her into some sort of cage in the back of the station wagon. Then he took off. We have a BOLO out on it right now, here, and in Idaho and Montana, but so far no one's seen anything. How long will it take you to get here?"

"Give me three hours."

There's a pause on the other end of the line. Then she speaks fast, sounding more rattled than ever. "Three hours? That's too long. Do you understand what I'm telling you? A county attorney's been kidnapped. We've got a fire out of control. And your job's on the line, Burns."

"I know. I'll be there as fast as I can."

"In kidnapping cases like this, time is of the essence. We don't have time for you to breakfast, shower, and shave."

"I'm on the Grand, Sheriff. It's going to take me some time to get down."

Roberto comes into the hut alone after I switch off the radio phone. I quickly tell him what's happened. And what I'm going to do.

"I probably shouldn't go down there," he says. "Wouldn't be prudent, *che,* know what I mean?"

"You'll be arrested on sight," I agree. "And the place will be swarming with Feds since one of their own's been shot."

I dump out my pack on the floor of the hut, spilling axes, crampons, PowerBars, and a first-aid kit. The only thing I put back in is my remaining full water bottle. Then I squat and lace my boots tight for the downhill run out of the mountains. The whole time Roberto hovers over me, seeming oddly indecisive.

"You gonna be okay, Ant?"

"Yeah. I got to go." I kick the ground hard with the front

of each boot, testing to see whether my toes will bang against the leather. "What are you going to do?"

He looks up at the Middle Teton. "Beg some food off these guys, then head up there. I'll drop down the other side," he says, meaning Idaho, "and make my way to Salt Lake. You sure you don't need me right now?"

Something in his voice or in his eyes makes me look at him for a moment. He's studying me much the way McGee has been lately.

"Nah, bro. I'm gonna be fine. You do your thing. Get with the Feds tomorrow if that's what you want to do. If they don't jump all over your pal." I nod at the Grand's sharp spire and can't help but grin at him. "Thanks. I needed that." After a quick hug I push him away. "Take care, Roberto. Call me. Let me know what happens."

The winding trail leading down Garnet Canyon is crowded with more climbers hoping to make an early-season ascent. Their faces are both eager and nervous as they crane necks upward, staring at the Grand's pyramid, as they hump their heavy packs full of ropes and cams up the trail. I come pounding down at them like a big stone rolling down from the sky. They curse as they scatter before me and yell more curses at my back.

THIRTY-THREE

THE IRON PIG waits like a faithful hound in the crowded parking lot at the Garnet Canyon trailhead. As usual, the old truck starts right up on the first twist of the key. I ram it into gear and spin the tires, spraying dirt, as I tear out of the lot. Too late I notice the elderly Park Service volunteer who'd been walking behind me. Her dusty scowl chases me all the way to the highway.

I call Rebecca on my cell phone. A message comes on, telling me that there's no service where she is. I call the Spring Creek Ranch but no one answers in the condo. The operator tells me that she thinks she saw Ms. Hersh out walking with her father. Finally I'm forced to leave a three-word message with the annoyingly laconic desk clerk—*Wait for me.*

It isn't far to Alana Reese's ranch, which says something about the value of her property. I rumble only twenty or so miles up the valley on 191 toward Yellowstone before reaching the rail fence that marks its southern edge. Enormous clouds of gray-black smoke billow up to the east, but whatever flames are building them are concealed by low hills. Every hundred yards or so along the highway, groups of sightseers pull over, eye-balling the smoke through the lenses of their video cameras.

An unmarked iron gate stands at the entrance to the ranch. A Teton County Sheriff's car is parked there facing the highway. The deputy behind the wheel raises a hand to stop me as I turn in. He isn't anyone I recognize. But he tells me that they're waiting for me "up at the castle" before I even have the chance to tell him my name.

I drive for three or four more miles on a private gravel road. The land on either side changes from rolling prairie interspersed with stands of aspens and cottonwoods to a smoldering moonscape at a point so sharp and obvious it's like falling into a pit. One moment it's beautiful, pure alpine grasslands—the next it's a literal nightmare. The transformation occurs atop a small ridge. A line of green cottonwoods once ran along it. What's left of them looks like a conga line of twisted black demons. The wind is blowing wisps of smoke from the few remaining branches.

In the rearview mirror the Grand stands like a beacon, cold and white and clean and sharp. It's hard to believe that three hours ago I was standing on top of that mighty beast—in another world entirely.

Up ahead on the top of a second, bigger ridge is what the deputy described as the castle. I slow and stare at it. It's constructed out of the same lodgepole-pine logs that frame my small cabin. But this is no cabin—it's a mansion, a literal castle, with wooden turrets at the several complex corners within view. A shockingly green lawn surrounds the structure, blocking out the blackened earth and charred pines before and beyond. I realize that this lush lawn is what saved the house. That, the fast-acting Hot Shot crew, the relatively light wind of the early-morning hours, and a hell of a lot of luck. But the once-massive barn-and-stable complex a few hundred yards to the south was not so lucky. The hoses of a local fire engine are still spraying that smoking ruin.

I have an image of the predawn hours—roaring flames, searing heat, panicked shouts, screaming horses, the sound of a rifle shot. I close my eyes and open them, suck in a breath and let it out, then spit out the window. The air tastes of an infernal barbecue.

I park among the police and fire vehicles that line the circular driveway. A few people—civilians—wander on a porch to one side of the house, staring at the witches' cauldron of smoke and wearing shell-shocked expressions.

At the top of the main steps are two of the biggest oak doors I've ever seen—easily ten feet high and probably a foot thick. They look as solid as the cop who stands before them. But unlike the dark wood, Wokowski's face is pale when I get out and walk toward him. The mirrored sunglasses he wears seem to draw in all the devastation around us, focusing it into the deep sockets under his heavy brows. I'm glad to no longer be heading his shit-list.

"It was Bill Laughlin. The bastard's gone nuts," he says as I come up the steps. Then, "Where the hell have you been?"

"Climbing. I was taken off the case, remember?" It comes out harsher than I intend it to. Wokowski is clearly devastated. I soften it. "Tell me what happened, Wook."

He raises one hand and pushes his sunglasses tighter against the bridge of his noise. It's a small, touching gesture, like wiping away a tear. It contrasts with the big clenched jaw and the jutting brows. I can see the outline of the engagement ring under the taut material of his uniform shirt.

"Cali came here yesterday after checking out of the hospital. At about four this morning someone noticed that the ridge back there was on fire and set off the alarm. Cali, her mom, and all the guests ran to get in their cars and drive out. Laughlin was out here waiting. Yelling at everyone, demanding that Alana come with him. She ran back in the house and hid but Cali stayed and tried to calm him down. According to her guests, Laughlin started grabbing at Cali. Trying to force her into his car. When she fought him off, he hit her with the butt of his gun. Then he took her. And he shot the Fed when she tried to stop him."

He speaks with his hands clasped in front of his utility belt. The fingers swell and turn white as if he's fantasizing that Laughlin's heart is being crushed between them. Or maybe it's his own. He lets them drop to his sides when he notices me staring at them.

"You went to his place in town, right?" I ask.

"No one was there. I went in two hours ago with a couple of my SWAT guys. No warrant—I figured we'd be covered by the emergency exception. The place was a mess, but we found an empty box of bullets on a table. Also a charger for a Stun Master 625 from a pawn shop in town."

One of the giant doors swings open softly on well-greased hinges and Sheriff J. J. Buchanan joins us. Her gray-and-brown hair is lank and greasy looking, and her leathery face looks just as bad. It definitely has more wrinkles than when I'd last seen her two days ago. Behind her is an entry hall big enough to park all the cars in the drive. I can't see the ceiling.

"Sorry it took me so long," I tell her. I don't bother to add that I'd risked breaking my neck during my wild sprint down from the peak.

She looks at Wokowski. "You filled him in?"

"Yeah."

"What's being done now?" I ask.

The sheriff answers, "We're looking everywhere for the station wagon. But no one's seen a thing. And there are a thousand back roads around here in the forest. Every cop for a hundred miles is too busy to look seriously, trying to keep all the tourists from cooking themselves and evacuating the nearby homes. They say the fire's going to be picking up speed in a few hours, heading east toward Preacher Park."

"What else?"

"I've called in every available officer in my department. The police chief for the Town of Jackson has done the same. The problem is that most of them are getting stuck dealing with traffic and keeping the tourists from getting themselves hurt. The fire is taking up all our resources. We've also notified the FBI. Of course they're interested in the kidnapping, and the fact that one of their agents has been shot has them quite excited. If we can get a lead on where Cali is, they might be willing to send in the Hostage Rescue Team from Quantico. As it is right now, they're sending a team of four agents in from Salt Lake. Apparently they have a bunch of them doing something big in Salt Lake."

I manage not to look startled. And not look especially worried at this last bit of news. But I need to call Roberto and warn him before he gets to Salt Lake.

"Can you think of anything else we should be doing, Burns?"

They follow me when I walk back to the Pig and spread a topographical map on the hood. For want of anyplace else to look, I stare at the area called Preacher Park. Where the sheriff had said the fire is headed.

A tripod mark, like a crude oil derrick, on top of the butte catches my eye. In tiny print I see the word *Elation*.

"What's that?" I point at the drawing of the derrick.

Wokowski bends close and studies it through his sunglasses. "Elation Peak. There's a fire-lookout station up there—that's what that symbol means. It's unmanned this early in the year."

"You ever read *Smoke Jump*?" I ask them both, talking fast. They nod. "Elation Peak is where Cali's dad—Laughlin's best friend—burned to death. Laughlin was in love with Alana and still is. But Patrick Morrow took her away from him, and Alana's continued to reject him all these years. There were questions raised in the book about whether he'd done all he could to save his friend. And there's no doubt it was

Laughlin's decision to run for high ground that got Morrow killed twenty-five years ago. If you read it a certain way, it's like he killed him."

"What are you saying?" the sheriff demands. "That was a quarter century ago."

"He still didn't get the girl. Alana. And I think he's been pissed about it for all these years. Not just pissed—enraged. And obsessed. After all, he acted like an uncle to Cali so that he could be closer to Alana. Now that he's dying anyway, I think he wants to give his old pal Patrick the finger one last time. Alana, too. If he can't do it through Alana because of the bodyguards, and because she managed to get away last night, he's going to do it through Cali."

In the distance I can hear the helicopter working. I don't wait for them to digest what I've told them or argue. I point at the helicopter and ask, "Whose is that?"

Wokowski answers quickly, his voice stronger. "The Forest Service's. It's a Bell Jet Ranger with a rig for carrying water."

"Who's in contact with it?"

"A fire command center's being set up at the station in Moran Junction. They've got to be running it."

"Let's go."

THIRTY-FOUR

THE OFFICE FOR the Bridger-Teton National Forest is five miles off the highway and close to the shore of Jackson Lake. It's yet another log cabin, far smaller than Alana's and far bigger than my own. Out in the parking lot several uniformed rangers and volunteers are doing their best to shoo away the tourists in order to open up the parking places for the emergency vehicles. I give them a flash from the red-and-blue lights under my grille when they try to wave off my truck. Already fire-fighting crews are assembling. The young men and women wear green fire-retardant pants and yellow shirts. Some of their clothes and faces are streaked with dirt and ash, indicating they'd probably been out in the field already. A catering truck is dishing out hamburgers and sodas.

Wokowski is right behind me in his department Chevy Tahoe with his lights also spinning. Sheriff Buchanan, who had ducked back inside the log castle to say something to Alana before following us, shouldn't be far behind. The sergeant and I don't wait—we immediately head into the big cabin's central room.

It's crowded with people, and the floor is strewn with the cables of communications gear and laptop computers. I overhear people yelling into phones about tankers, helicopters, retardant, low relative humidity, unstable air, urban interface, and setting up "anchor points." No one pays me any heed when I walk over to the big topographical map that takes up most of a wall.

A bearded young man with Coke-bottle glasses and a radio headset stands before it. He's marking the map with pushpins connected by red thread. They seem to outline the border of the area already burnt. It starts small on the west, maybe an inch or so wide on the low hills before Alana's castle, then it spreads out from there in a broad, convex angle. The largest side takes up more than five inches of red thread. Two big blue arrows show how the wind is coming out of the northwest.

"Hey," I say to the guy with the earphones.

He nods distractedly, glancing up from my boots to my dirty nylon pants and my ragged polypro shirt, and looks away while pressing one side of the headset closer to his ear.

So I continue to study the map without his help. The lay of things is obvious enough. Within the ragged circle of thread is a toy Monopoly house where Alana Reese's castle should be. A hotel would have been more appropriate. A small "#1" is penciled in above it. There are two other houses in the rough triangle of thread, #'s 2 and 3, but there's no way to tell if these have remained untouched as Alana's had. There are more than ten others just beyond the red line.

Moving my eyes to the east, I find the broad area of high hills called Preacher Park and, within it, near the pass between Jackson Hole and Lander, a circle of thick contour lines marked Elation Peak.

I look back at the advancing red thread and then at the map's legend. The fire is less than thirty miles away. And the big blue arrows are pointing right toward it.

"Hey," I say again to the guy with the earphones.

He continues to ignore me. I tap his shoulder and put my finger on the butte. "Is the fire going to reach this?"

He turns quickly, frowning, looking affronted by my touch. "Who the hell are you?"

"I'm with the Wyoming Division of Criminal Investigation. This is Sergeant Wokowski from the Teton County Sheriff's Office."

The technician glares at us both—my scarred face and filthy climbing clothes, then Wokowski's Neanderthal countenance behind the mirrored shades and the way his uniform is stretched tight over all those thick muscles. He decides to answer the question.

"Yeah, it's going to go up for sure," he says. "That's a nasty little hollow just upwind of it. There was a blowdown there five years ago, turned the whole place into kindling, and ever since, we've been trying to figure out how to burn it off or clear it out without endangering the surrounding forests and homes. Didn't have the money to do it, though. Or the manpower. There are too many deadfalls and snags in there—no way to control it. When this fire reaches there, look out. It will go off like a bomb. The winds will swirl around down in there and probably generate a firestorm. That mountain will go up, too."

Wokowski the former smoke jumper gives a curt nod, but I have to ask, "What's a firestorm?"

"It's a feedback loop. A phenomenon where you've got a lot of fuel—dry timber and grass—in a deep valley like that so it will burn hot enough to create its own winds. Sometimes like tornadoes, almost. With a superhigh fuel load like you've got in that deep valley, it makes for a convection cell of smoke and gas. You can get area ignition, a sort of spontaneous combustion— an entire section of the forest detonating in an instant." He presses the earphone closer to his ear again then says, "Look, Officers, I'm kind of busy. . . ." He starts moving the pins again.

I don't understand half of what he's said but it sounds bad.

Very bad, judging by the look on Wokowski's face. The same image that's probably in his head comes into mine: Cali being thrown off a three-hundred-foot cliff into a "firestorm." Sort of like what happened to her dad.

"How long until the fire reaches it?" I ask him.

He tries to ignore me once again but Wokowski grabs his arm and turns him around. "You're going to talk to us."

I repeat my question.

"Okay, okay. Right now, it's slowing down some. Winds are dropping a little, so it's moving at about three miles an hour through heavy timber cut up and stalled by a lot of dry meadows. The winds are going to be picking up, though. Really picking up, like to thirty or forty knots. Later this afternoon or tonight. It's going to start moving a hell of a lot faster then. It'll blow about midnight, I guess. Could happen earlier, though."

I ask Wokowski how long it would take to drive out there. About an hour, he says, almost grunting the words. Then with a very determined look, he adds, "But we can make it in forty."

"No, you can't," the young man chimes in with surprising backbone in the face of Wokowski's expression. "Look here—the fire has passed over parts of 287 and is still burning other parts. There'll be timber all over the road. And we're getting reports about just how thick the fuel is up there. That makes for a lot of heat. It's likely some of the road has simply melted away."

Sheriff Buchanan comes into the room with Alana Reese in tow. Just what I don't need right now. Alana looks like a different woman—she almost looks her age. Her blonde hair is uncombed and dark flesh puffs out beneath her eyes. She no longer has an aura of complete control. I feel something like pity as I notice this. Despite the actress's diminished presence, the volume of noise in the room suddenly ebbs as people stop and stare. I wave them over to us and point at the map.

"I think I know where they are. Elation Peak."

But the actress snarls at me anyway, showing sharp little teeth, "Then why are you still here?" She closes her eyes hard and reopens them. "I'm sorry. Did you say . . . I don't—"

Wokowski doesn't let her finish. She's looking like she might faint instead of continuing to speak anyway. He says to the sheriff, "We need to reconvene the SWAT team. Right now. And we need a helicopter to take us in—the road's out."

"Do you know who's running this show?" she asks him.

Wokowski looks around quickly and points at a bald man with a goatee. "That's Fred Williams, Bridger-Teton's fire director."

The director is already coming toward us. He's in his sixties, tall and fit, and despite his age, he walks with an athlete's bounce. After nodding politely at the sheriff and Alana, he slaps Wokowski on a meaty shoulder. "How's your knee, Wook? You thinking about hanging up that badge and coming back to us? We could use you, you know. This is going to be a big one."

The rest of us are quickly introduced. Before my hand leaves his grasp, the sheriff is already explaining the situation to him. When she describes Cali as an assistant county attorney, Wokowski jumps in, adding that she also used to be on a Hot Shot crew. Williams nods, evidently remembering. "But I didn't know her," he says apologetically to Alana.

The sheriff tells him of our urgent need for a helicopter. "We need it now. We need to get up there right away."

But he shakes his head. "I'm very, very sorry to hear about this happening to your daughter, but I can't put more lives at risk by allowing one of my helicopters to drop anyone in there. Especially since you don't know for sure that she's on Elation. At this point in time it would be suicide for everyone—it would take too much time to get your SWAT team properly outfitted, picked up, and carried in."

All of us begin to protest, but he holds up a hand.

"And that valley could go up within a few hours. Even if it doesn't happen until midnight, the winds pushing ahead of the fire will make any flight in there too dangerous. It's already pushing fifteen knots and rising fast. We only have the one bird up right now, dropping water, and we're going to have to set her down in another half hour."

"She's a friend of mine, Fred. A very, very good friend," Wokowski tells him, his meaning clear.

The director looks away from the sergeant uncomfortably. He shakes his head. "I can't, Wook, I can't. You don't know for sure she's there. Even if you were sure, I can't risk my crew. I don't have the authority, not in this world or the next, to take on that kind of liability." Then he raises his hand again before Wokowski starts a new protest. "I can do something, though. If the winds there aren't too bad yet, we can do a fly-by to see if anybody's home."

It takes ten minutes for the director to set up the fly-by. Ten minutes where all any of us can do is think about Cali burning.

Finally we're waved over to a table with a radio on it the size of a large briefcase. The bearded technician from the map is plugged into it and he's talking into his microphone. Seeing us gathered around him, the technician turns a knob and the air fills with a hiss of static until a voice comes over.

"This is Ranger 204. Give me the coordinates again. Over."

The techie spins in his chair and studies the map on the wall, reading out grid coordinates to the pilot on the other end of the radio.

"Okay, got it. Give me a few. I'm lifting off Six Lakes, coming over Crystal Peak. Probably about twenty kilometers from the target." In a minute his voice grows more excited. "Jesus, I hope you guys are calling in reinforcements. This one's going to keep us in overtime for at least a month. A real monster! It's all over the whole western horizon. When I got a look at it up close earlier, I swear the flames out front were three hundred feet high. It looks like it's somewhere around twenty miles away now. Over."

The four of us stand in total silence around the techie, ignoring the whirl of activity all around us. Alana turns to the wall and begins crying quietly.

"It's coming into view. Looks kind of like a mesa, pretty flat on top and steep on all sides but the west. You guys can say good-bye to your lookout on top—that sucker's right in the monster's path. Don't see any people, but those big windows on the lookout are propped open. Hang on . . . I'm going in closer."

Wokowski soundlessly sags against the map. All the color bleeds from his skin. His eyes are shut. I take it to mean that if the windows are open, someone's there.

"Have him come pick us up right now. We need—" I start to say but a sound from the radio cuts me off.

"Holy shit! What was that?" A sharp crack carries into the room over the static. "Jesus, there's a hole in the windscreen! I think somebody's shooting at us! Hey! There's a guy with a rifle in the lookout!"

"Get them out of there!" Williams tells the radio operator, who is already doing exactly that. The pilot probably doesn't need to be told.

There are maybe twenty seconds of silence from the radio—it seems like twenty minutes—until the pilot comes back on, his voice calmer but not completely hiding his anxiety, and reports that he's heading for Jackson to have the helicopter checked out and the windscreen repaired.

"I would tell you to call the cops," the pilot adds, "but whoever was shooting at us is going to be toast soon enough. Sleep tight, asshole."

"Do you have another helicopter?" Wokowski asks the ranger.

He shakes his head. "We have two on the way from

Missoula, but they won't be here until later tonight. Maybe the morning."

The techie with the headset interrupts. "Excuse me, Dr. Williams. But in another half hour it's going to be blowing more than thirty knots. I'm hearing that it's already more than forty-five at Teton Pass. No helicopter's going up in a wind like that."

"How about a plane?" Wokowski asks.

All of us but Alana look at him. How will he land a plane where there's no runway?

"I can jump in," he explains.

"I've got a plane and a pilot," I say automatically, thinking of Jim.

No one says anything for a long moment. I think we're all trying to stretch our minds around the details of the sergeant's proposal.

"Call him," Wokowski says. "Tell him I'll be at the airport in an hour."

"That's ludicrous, Wook," Williams says. "I know you're a tough guy, but do you really think you can jump in without getting shot out of the air, come down on your bad knee, manage to land on the butte despite the high winds, take on a man with a rifle by yourself, and save the hostage? This isn't a movie. Excuse me," he adds with a glance to Alana. "Besides, how would you get out?"

"Fire shelter," Wokowski says, then explains to the sheriff and me. "They're like pup tents made of aluminum and fiberglass. They reflect heat and don't melt, even when it's more than a thousand degrees. Smoke Jumpers and Hot Shot crews all carry them for emergencies."

The ranger scoffs again but gently. "Wook, you know they're unreliable at best. We both know people who have died in those shelters. And with the fuel in there, this fire will be burning at far more than one thousand degrees. That's much hotter than the conditions the shelters are designed for."

"Not on top of the butte. It's mostly grass and rock up there. I've seen it. A shelter will work."

The ranger is still shaking his head. "Not in my district. I can't accept that kind of liability, either legally or morally," he repeats.

"I can," Alana says, turning her red, wet face to us. "I'll do anything, pay anything, if you'll—"

"Ms. Reese," the sheriff says sharply. "We aren't going to send a man in there. I'm going to call the FBI again," she adds, trying to sound hopeful despite the obvious. "I'll see if there's any way for them to get the HRT here sooner. Maybe they'll have some suggestions."

Saying, "I need some air," Wokowski turns and walks quickly for the door.

Outside in the parking lot the witches' cauldron to the east is in full brew, the setting sun casting its orange rays over us and coloring the smoke to even more hellish shades. He strides across the lot, jangling his car keys. It will be night in another hour, and I wonder what the sky will look like then.

"Hey, Wook," I call.

"Call your friend," he says without turning. "Tell him I'll be at the airport in an hour."

"I'm coming with you."

It sounds crazy, even to me. But really, what have I got to lose? And I can step out of a plane and huddle in an aluminum pup tent as well as anyone.

"You're a certified sky diver?" Wokowski asks, stopping by his black-and-white police SUV. "I thought you were a climber."

"I've done a lot of jumps," I exaggerate. Not certified, but maybe certifiable. I'd jumped with my father twice. It had been fun—a quick adrenaline rush—and it hadn't seemed all that difficult. You just arched your back until the static line released the chute and then you rode softly down to the ground. No harder than riding a roller coaster or jumping into a lake off a high cliff.

"Sorry, Burns. I've got to do this alone."

"No, you can't, because you're *not* a climber. You think you'll just float on down to the mesa top? Even in the dark, with the sky lit up the way it is, Laughlin will blow you away. The only way to do it is to come down behind the butte, and the only way up from there is to climb. You saw the lines on the map—every side but the westernmost, the direction the lookout faces and where the fire's coming from, is dead vertical. You need me to get you up that at the very least."

He sucks in his lower lip and chews on it. I see my face in duplicate in the lenses of his sunglasses. I look more determined than I feel.

Then he nods minutely and turns again toward his truck. I'm getting into the Pig when I hear him call, "Burns!"

"What?"

"Thanks."

THIRTY-FIVE

I DRIVE TOO fast down the highway, using my flashing lights and horn to cut my way through the slow-moving traffic. It seems that every tourist in the western United States is flooding into Jackson for the show. Cars and motor homes line the highway now. Drivers and passengers alike crane their necks to stare at the billowing smoke. I have to continually remind myself to ease my foot off the gas, that getting into an accident won't get me there any faster.

It's almost fully dark when I turn off Cache Creek Road and onto the dirt lane that leads to my cabin. I have just enough time to go by the cabin, relieve and feed Mungo, and collect some gear. In my head I'm composing a mental list of what we'll need. When the cabin comes into view, though, the list goes out the window. Rebecca's green Saab is parked snug against the porch. All the lights inside are on.

Mungo bounces out the cabin's open front door and greets me more effusively than she has since I left Denver a week ago. She plants her big paws on my shoulders and licks my face.

"You're a great guard dog," I tell her. "Is there anyone you haven't let break into the place?"

"Hi," Rebecca says from the doorway behind her.

She's barefoot, dressed in a pair of baggy khaki shorts and one of my T-shirts. Her hair is loose. It hangs in dark tangles down to her breasts. On her lips is a slender smile. Like the *Mona Lisa*'s. She owns me and she knows it, and the knowledge of that possession just might please her.

I say nothing. Two quick steps take me up the stairs and a third carries me across the narrow porch. Then she's in my arms.

The kiss is high voltage. Like a current is flowing through us, charging my exhausted shell of a body. When, too soon, she pulls her face back, she looks me in the eye and says with a gently reproving tone, "You didn't let me finish talking the other night. You walked away from me."

"I didn't know what to say."

A smile radiates from her eyes and mouth, showing the beautiful new creases on her cheeks. "Oh, you do all right. The shoes, the flowers, and the note said it all. I followed your instructions. When I woke up this morning I walked with Dad up on the hill and could barely wait to drive straight here. I even called the paper to tell them about the fire and that they would have to send up someone else to cover it."

The fire.

I walk past her into the cabin, trying as I hard as I can to focus on remembering the things I need to throw into my pack. The living room has been cleaned. The hardwood floor sparkles with fresh polish. Her laptop computer is open next to mine on the dining-room table. She's brought the tulips and the baby shoes and placed them like a centerpiece.

The gear room, too, has been cleaned. Coiled ropes are stacked neatly on the bed, and carabiners and cams I'd left piled in heaps on the floor have been organized and placed on hooks on the wall. I start tossing things into an open pack. Every movement requires careful, conscious thought.

"Where have you been, anyway? Mungo and I have been waiting for you all day."

"Climbing."

"Alone?" I can tell she's trying hard not to have the word come out as an accusation.

The answer, I know, is worse than yes. "No. With Roberto." I turn and look at her. God, she's beautiful. My breath leaves my lungs without me wanting it to. "It's what I love to do, 'Becca."

She studies me back. "Every time I look at your face, Ant, I see that scar. You almost died when you got that. It reminds me how close it's been for you. You've been touched by death; it put its brand on you. And that's okay. Really. But what's not, what I don't understand at all, is why you keep going back for more."

I put my fingers to my temples and massage them. "What if I told you that you couldn't write stories anymore? That I wanted you to go to work as a stockbroker. Or an accountant. Would you do it?"

"It's not the same and you know it."

"The passion's the same. Listen, 'Becca. There are two times when I feel totally alive, totally focused on *being* alive. One is when I'm making love to you. The other's when I've got a lot of air below me, when I'm holding on to the rock with all my strength." I force a smile into my eyes. "And as much as I'd like to, honey, I can't make love to you all the time."

The smallest of smiles raises the corners of her lips. "Maybe you could. You could try it."

For a moment I feel like I could. Make love to her for the rest of my life. All day, every day. The moment ends when I look at my watch. She speaks before I can tell her that I've got to go.

"What about your job? That's not a passion. Not anymore. I can tell."

"Yeah, I think you're right. But it's all I know how to do."

"You're young, Ant. Barely thirty. You can learn to be good at something else."

"I'll think about it. Just not law school, okay? Promise me you'll never ask me to go to law school." That makes her laugh. It's a small, light chuckle that shoots right through my chest. I put a rope on top of the pack and cinch down the straps. "Listen, I know it's a bad time, but I've got to go—"

When I sneak a look her way I see the spark that had so briefly returned to her eyes has been extinguished.

"You're going climbing? *Now?*"

"That woman you met the other night? Cali, the assistant county attorney? She's been kidnapped. I don't have time to explain, but this old man she calls her uncle is holding her on a peak near here. We think he's going to throw her off." I pull the pack up over one shoulder. For what it's worth, I'm careful not to mention jumping out of planes or the fire. "Will you be here when I get back?"

She stares at me and shakes her head in disbelief. I feel like a recalcitrant but loved child all the same, prone to breaking maternal hearts. "I'm going to go meet my dad for dinner. Then . . . we'll see."

When I look at her again she looks like a little girl now instead of a mother, standing there barefoot, so forlorn in her baggy shirt and shorts. "Go. Be careful, Anton. They say that fire's a big one. Stay away from it."

THIRTY-SIX

I PARK MY LAND CRUISER AT the empty curb just outside the airport's terminal. Wokowski's truck is nowhere in sight.

It's seven o'clock in the evening and this part of the valley sits in the great shadow of Rendezvous Peak's summit pyramid. Over the mountains the dying sunset is one of the most spectacular I've ever seen. The sky there is stained by the smoke to colors ranging from a dark orange to a vivid purple. The sun impales itself over the Tetons' sharp spikes with open-mouthed horror.

I watch it for a long moment before getting out.

From the back of the Pig I toss out a small tarp and spread it on the sidewalk. I open the pack, wondering what items I forgot to bring. On top of the tarp I pile a skinny 8.5-mm rope, a pair of lightweight harnesses, a dozen carabiners, and a half-rack of chocks and cams. Everything seems to be there. I carefully wrap all the metal parts I can with athletic tape so that they won't clink and rattle when we're climbing. When we scale the butte's back side I don't want to make a sound. I stuff everything back into the small pack. After a moment's thought I add in a pair of ascenders and etriers from a crate just in case Wokowski is less athletic on the rock than he'd appeared in the gym with the punching bag. I'm finishing tightening the straps when his Sheriff's Office Chevy Tahoe skids to a stop behind me.

He cuts the engine and headlights, jumps out, and calls me over. From the rear seat he drags out what looks like two backpacks, not much larger than mine but with even more nylon straps—a full-body harness, I realize—and a leather rifle case. After them he throws two big duffel bags down at my feet. The sheathed rifle brings a fat Jackson police officer hustling out from inside the terminal with a hand over his own holstered gun. He slows when he recognizes Wokowski and notices the official car behind my own.

"Going hunting, Wook? Little early in the season, ain't it?"

"Official business, Dave."

The man laughs. "Sure. Somebody probably spotted a twelve-point buck running from the fire."

"I'll tell you about it later. Can you get us out onto the runway in a hurry? We've got a plane to catch."

The officer, probably still believing we have an important elk to poach, is game. After providing a handcart, he leads us at a fast walk into the terminal and through an inner security door. We pass stacks of luggage and the back sides of the treaded machines that spin it out to the passengers. Another door, this one smeared with greasy fingerprints and covered with warning signs, takes us out onto the runway. There's an airport-security pickup truck here where we load our baggage. Wokowski and I sit on top of it as the cop drives us out to where the private planes are kept.

"Did the smoke jumpers lend you this stuff?" I ask, indicating the packs and duffels piled around us in the bed of the truck.

"You don't want to know."

"Why not?"

Wokowski smiles faintly. "Because when we get back, I'm going to be charged with a felony."

The plane is a red-and-white Cessna Caravan. It looks small and fragile in the runway lights, like it's made out of old Coke cans held together with library paste. The propeller on the front is already turning, giving off a choking, irregular roar. The pilot doesn't inspire much more confidence. Jim comes out of the door hatch and waves at us as we approach. Seeing his red ponytail bouncing and his earring glinting, this is starting to seem like a very reckless idea.

It's a strange feeling, getting into a plane you know you'll soon be jumping out of into that orange-glowing sky. I set down the duffel bags and take several deep breaths before picking them up again and trudging forward. Jim slaps my shoulder and says something meant to be encouraging as I haul the bags up the couple of metal steps that lead into the cabin. It's just as well that I can't hear his words over the throb of the engine.

The cabin holds only two seats in the forward area. The main part of the small fuselage is dirty steel, strewn clothes, and old mattresses. Several cases of the local nectar—Snake River Ale—are tethered to a part of the bulkhead for Jim to take back to Cheyenne.

The police officer shouts from behind us, "Whatever you boys are hunting, good luck!"

Then Wokowski trudges up the steps with the rifle and the parachutes. Jim comes up behind him and secures the door. Although the sound of it slamming is entirely different, I picture a cell door slamming shut. There's no turning back now, no admitting this is a very bad idea and hoping the winds will calm and the FBI's Hostage Rescue Team will make it in time.

"Uh, Ant, I got to tell you," Jim yells in my ear. "The suits say I'm not supposed to fly anyone on official business. They think they'll get sued if something happens. Tell me this isn't official, okay? Even if it is."

"Don't worry, Jim. Consider this a private charter. I'll pay you whatever you think's fair when we get back."

He nods, and I add, "By the way, thanks for doing this. I'm sorry about that thing with the gun the other day. I've been an asshole lately."

He grins. "Hey, QuickDraw, that was nothing. It's cool."

"Take us up to seventeen thousand feet," Wokowski yells at him. "Due east. I'll give you more directions as we go."

Jim nods and smiles again then makes his way to the front of the plane. Wondering what Wokowski thinks of our plane and pilot, I squat on a mattress and stare at the gear as the plane pulls out onto the runway. The engine knocks wildly as it accelerates.

"Put this on." Wokowski tugs an enormously heavy pair of coveralls out of a duffel bag. He also sets two football-like helmets with wire mesh face masks onto the mattress next to him. "Damn. Sorry, forgot to get us some cups. Watch for sharp branches. Cross your legs if you're going into one."

"What's it made of?" I ask about the dungarees as I step into them.

"Kevlar."

"Tell me—is it like a vest? Will it stop a bullet?"

He smiles grimly. "Not that thick. It might on the other side, after it goes through you."

He seems almost cheerful, finally able to be doing something for Cali, while I feel none of the excitement I normally do when gearing up for a climb.

"You've used a sport chute before, right?" Wokowski yells in my ear. "Rectangular canopy?"

I look at the pack he's holding up. It looks a lot smaller than the ones I'd jumped with when my father had taken Roberto and me. Those had been the size of a suitcase. But I was a smaller person back then. The plane is racing down the runway now, its nose starting to lift into the air.

"I think so."

Wokowski stares at me. "What do you mean, you think so? How many times have you jumped, Burns?"

We're in the air. There's no sense in lying about it now. "Twice. Fifteen years ago, when I was a kid."

He sits back on his haunches, still holding the chute in one hand and keeping his balance with the other. The cheerfulness is gone from his face. He says, "Fuck!"

"Just tell me what to do and I'll do it. Don't worry. It's on my head, not yours."

He stares at me, as if dumbfounded, for what must be half a minute before he speaks again. "I don't even know where to start."

"Start with what's most important."

He closes his eyes for a few more seconds, then stands up and motions me to do the same. He pushes me around so that my back is to him. I half expect him to kick me in the ass, and I probably deserve it. Instead he slips the straps over my shoulders, turns me back to face him, and connects more straps around my chest and up between my legs. While he does this he speaks in a low, urgent voice. "This is the rip cord." He points to a metal handle like a giant pull tab next to my right pectoral. "I'm not even going to bother trying to explain about the backup chute, 'cause the way we're doing this, if the main doesn't work, you're already dead."

I touch the metal cord three times for familiarity and luck.

"We're going to jump at fifteen thousand feet," he says. "The air's going to start getting thin as we get higher. Tell me if you start to feel light-headed."

"I was at fourteen thousand eight hours ago." I don't like being the ignorant one, being schooled by him. I also don't like the fact that he must think I'm a complete idiot for doing this.

He makes me feel even dumber by ignoring my comment. "That means we'll be about four thousand feet above the butte and the lookout, and about forty-five above the

surrounding forest. I wish we could land on something relatively flat like the butte, but like you said, he'll shoot us for
sure and probably Cali, too. So we'll try to land somewhere
southeast of it. Aim for any open spot you can find, and pray
you find one because the country is real ugly down there.

"You steer with toggles on the lines of the chute. I can't
show them to you—you'll just have to figure it out. Try to
land into the wind to slow you down. Run as you hit, or roll,
or do whatever you can to break your fall." He pauses to
shake his head while staring at me. "After that it's your show.
You get us up the cliff, then I'll take over with the rifle."

He begins pulling on his own Kevlar coveralls while I
look out the window.

We're almost directly above the fire now. The landscape
below is appallingly clear in the orange light. Staring down is
like getting a clear view of hell. Behind us is a flame-lit smoking moonscape of charred earth and ridges. Directly beneath
is perhaps a mile or more of burning forest. And it's burning
with a vengeance. As I watch, flames are shooting hundreds
of feet into the sky, trees are exploding in great showers of
sparks, and the earth is so hot it glows like lava. Farther back,
where the fire has already passed, embers glare up at the sky
with a thousand evil eyes. Ahead is our butte, surrounded by
mile upon mile upon mile of high-octane dry timber.

"Now here's the important thing," Wokowski yells in my
ear, drawing me away from the scene below. "We're going to
go out the door together and hang from the strut. When I
yell *Go,* you let go. I'm going to ride you down, arching on
your back. Then I'm going to push away. When I push away,
you count to three. Like this—one Mississippi, two Mississippi, three Mississippi, then you pull the cord! Got that?
Three and you pull the fucking cord."

I know that people have survived a chute not opening.
My dad had told Roberto and me stories about that. Two
guys he commanded once had failed chutes during a single

High Altitude Low Opening jump, and only one of them died. It's a hopeful thought for a moment, fifty-fifty odds according to that small sampling, until I remember what he'd said had happened to the survivor. I'm sure he would have rather been the one who died.

"How should I carry the climbing gear? And how are you going to carry the rifle?"

He clips the rifle's case on a short sling that dangles from the parachute's harness. Then he clips the backpack of climbing gear to mine.

"Make sure it stays below you. Don't let it foul the lines."

I expect us to circle around for a while, that there will be more time before I have to confront the horror of stepping out of the plane and dropping into the sky. I need time to digest what I'm about to do. But we're only in the air for a few more minutes before Wokowski tells me to put on my goggles and helmet. My hands are shaking with more than just the engine's vibration when I comply.

"There's the butte. Let's go, Burns. Remember to pull. Three seconds after I release you. And arch, okay? Arch like a motherfucker."

He slides open the door. The wind that tears into the plane is like Satan's breath—hot and stinking of sulfur. It blows over me in one continuous exhalation and whips loose papers and clothes around the inside of the plane. Wokowski grabs my arm and pulls me toward the open space.

I've looked down the seven-thousand-foot wall of the Washburn Face on Denali and felt nothing but the thrill that comes from conquering fear. At such times the Rat has screamed in exultation. Through skill and the strength in my muscles and mind I'd conquered that mile-plus of perpendicular stone and vanquished gravity and all the air below.

But now the Rat is as silent as the grave. And the air below doesn't look at all vanquished. Here there will be no strength or skill to protect me, no belay to act as a safety cord. All I can do is jump and arch and try to remember to *pull the fucking cord.*

Wokowski lets go of my arm and points at the wing. A rib of white aluminum diagonals from the wing to the fuse-lage. The strut. For a moment I'm shocked that he wants me to go out there and hang from the thing. But I do it. I do it with a numbness filling my brain like a dentist's Novocain needle pushed a little too far.

I grip it with all my strength, fighting to keep the wind from ripping me off. I turn my head back—a difficult move because of the bulky helmet—and see the tail looking as sharp as a razor blade behind me. It's going to cut me in half. I force myself to think of physics. The plane's going maybe 120 or so miles an hour and so am I. It's not like stepping out of a speed-ing car where the earth is still. But then, when you step out of a speeding car, the ground's not likely to be on fire.

Roberto wouldn't be this scared. He'd be grinning a big stupid grin and yahooing his head off.

It's too late anyway. Wokowski is beside me now, his great mass drooping in the wind and the rifle case swinging out behind him. "Hold on!" he screams into the gale.

What the fuck do you think I'm doing?

About two miles ahead and a mile or two to the south of the fire line the orange light illuminates a tabletop plateau. From this angle it looks like a giant doorstop, with the only low-angle side facing the flames.

My greatest fear is that I'll be mesmerized by the ground and forget to pull the cord. Dad had told me a story about that, too. About how a rookie just got hypnotized by the earth rising up to embrace him. Only it wasn't an embrace—it was the most vicious slap that can be swung. I tell myself again and again so it becomes a mantra: *When he releases me, count to three and pull. When he releases me, count to three and pull. When he releases me . . .*

"Go!" Wokowski screams.

I will my hands to let go from the strut but at first I don't think they obey. But then I'm falling, looking up and behind me in terror, half expecting the plane's tail to cut me in half. But the plane drifts by overhead, almost slowly, and suddenly I'm staring down as a new and far more realistic terror grips me.

I feel Wokowski's arms wrap around my shoulders and his legs around my legs like he's going to ride me into the ground. Before I have time to ponder this he shoves me from his grasp. The mantra takes over again. I count *one, two, three* with my left hand melding to the iron ring on my chest and the wind whistling through the helmet like a hurricane.

Three!

I rip at the ring. It comes loose in my hand. Nothing happens. *Oh God—Oh God.* I have a strange image of Wokowski's dirty laundry shooting up out of the pack. And I make a promise to myself. If I survive this, I'll live forever after a sedate, quiet life. I'll go to law school or anything. I'll hang up my ropes and axes for good. It's the same lie I've told myself again and again over a lifetime of adrenaline addiction. Like always, this time I swear I'm cured.

Then there's a noise like the tearing of paper and I'm jerked into the sky. It's as if God has answered my prayers, reaching down and plucking me from certain death.

A rectangle of white is rigid above me. The chute looks good. So impossibly fucking good. A voice calls from close to me, "You okay, QuickDraw?"

Over my shoulder, just a hundred feet away and a little higher than me, Wokowski is drifting along in the dark.

"I think so," I say through a dry mouth.

Below me, in the distant light of the fire, pine trees are silently flying by beneath my feet with alarming speed. One of the butte's walls is not far away to the south. Ahead a hillside is rising up to meet us like a catcher's mitt.

THIRTY-SEVEN

I FORGET TO CROSS MY LEGS like Wokowski had told me to and approach the ground in a full sprint, as if I'm running a one-hundred-meter dash. But my feet never touch the ground. The parachute hangs up between two trees and I discover that I'm madly churning air as I sway just three feet off the ground. I almost groan with relief—I no longer have to worry about being pancaked or impaled. Now, I remind myself, I only have to worry about falling off the cliff, getting shot, or being burnt to a crisp.

Nearby I hear several sharp cracks. For a moment I think Laughlin's down here somewhere, shooting his rifle. But then Wokowski's voice comes from somewhere not far away.

"Goddamn it!"

I assume he'd say something other than this if we were under fire.

By exploring the parachute's complicated harness with my hands and squirming, I manage to get myself unbuckled. I hit the rocky ground surprisingly hard for just a three-foot drop, with my feet tangled in the climbing pack. Reaching up, I tug at the chute's steering lines and realize that it's not going to come free. There's no time to deal with it, and besides, I'm not going to lug it up the cliff. I listen again for the direction of Wokowski's curses then shoulder my small climbing pack and head in that direction.

The hillside is choked with dry, crackling wood. Felled trees lie at angles everywhere, their intermeshed branches creating deadfalls as tall as I am between the still-standing trees. This entire forest will go up like the flare of some giant match head when the fire reaches it. Pushed by the strong wind, ghostly eddies of smoke are already swirling through the trees. My boots crunch on the wood as I clamber over the tangles. The only other sound now is a distant roar, like a jet aircraft at full throttle, a few miles to the west. From the same direction comes an evil orange glow that penetrates through the smoke and the night.

I use Wokowski's curses to guide me through the forest. It takes me ten minutes to come to where he is draped over a snarl of downed and splintered wood. He's curled in a large ball, holding his right knee tight against his chest.

"Hey, Wook. You okay?"

He turns his face my way and curses some more, softer now. "I hit my goddamn knee against something."

"The knee that ended your smoke-jumping career?"

"No, damn it! This is my good knee!"

We're both silent as he rubs his leg. He manages to let go of it for a moment in order to tear off his helmet and goggles. His parachute rustles in the branches of a tall pine.

"Can you walk?"

"Shit. I don't know."

With my feet on solid ground—even ground that I can only look at now as fuel—I can feel my confidence beginning to return.

"We've got to move, Wook. We've got to get going."

He curses some more and tries to wriggle off the snag. I

hold out my hand to him. He grabs my wrist and allows me to lean back and haul him to his feet. Then he hops about for a minute on one leg—his good one, or at least his less-bad one—making grunting sounds as he tentatively weights the other.

"It hurts like hell, but I think it just got knocked. I'll make it, QuickDraw."

"Good. Because I can't shoot worth a damn despite that fucking name."

"Oh yeah. Sorry, Burns." He looks up at where his parachute is fluttering in the wind, wrapping itself around the top of the pine. "Where's your chute?"

"Back there. It wasn't going to come down."

I expect him to say something about my abandoning the smoke jumpers' property but instead all he says is "Good." He unhooks himself from his own harness and doesn't even bother trying to free his. "Evidence," he mutters. "Better off burned."

You can't just step over the line, Roberto would say. *You've got to jump!*

Despite the streaming clouds of black smoke that blot out the stars and the moon, Elation Peak is visible—a silhouette outlined by the orange radiance—across a mile or so of a deeply timbered valley. From this rear angle the butte looks like the stump of a giant tree that had once reached all the way to heaven. I lead off and Wokowski limps along behind me.

After a couple of hundred yards we stumble onto the small meadow we'd aimed for from the plane. The going here becomes a lot easier. Wokowski's gait is already steadying and we're picking up speed.

Coming closer to the base of the butte, I get my first good look at what we'll need to climb. It's not a near-vertical wall like the North Face of the Grand, but a broken cliff only five hundred feet high. Wooded ledges and abundant chimneys and cracks will make the climbing easy.

But apparently Wokowski doesn't see it that way. "You sure about this?" he asks. "We can try the slope."

"He'd see us coming. Besides, this is what I do."

I throw off my pack and then peel off the heavy Kevlar suit. Wokowski does the same. Climbing in them would be near impossible. Running had been hard enough.

"More evidence," he mutters. I realize he's making jokes—the first I've ever heard from him.

We both wriggle into the lightweight alpine harnesses I've brought and I tie us together with doubled figure eights. I begin a quick lesson on belaying but he cuts me off, telling me that smoke jumpers learn the basics in order to get in and out of the trees they frequently land in.

"I'll tug twice when I'm off belay. Two times again when you're on, okay?" It's time to start being quiet even though I doubt Laughlin will be able to hear us over the distant fire's jet-engine roar. He's five hundred feet above, across the summit plateau, and no doubt hypnotized by the approaching flames and his plan for his captive, whatever that is. "Then start climbing, okay? Just follow the rope. I'll try to find the easiest way."

Wokowski takes a handheld radio off his hip. I hadn't noticed it earlier. He depresses the transmit button and asks, "How are we doing?"

"Who are you calling?"

"A friend of mine. A spy who's hanging out by the map in the situation room."

The hissed reply is barely audible. ". . . fire's six miles from . . . Peak. Winds at fifteen knots . . . rising. Estimate . . . two hours."

"Say again?"

Nothing but static.

"We're going up the east wall," Wokowski says into the radio. "You hear? We're going up the east wall."

The static continues unbroken.

"Was that two hours before the fire reaches the butte's

west slope?" I whisper from where I'm already stemming my way up a wide gash in the rock.

"I think so. We'd better hurry up. We don't want the fire to come around and get under us." He doesn't mention that Cali will surely be cooked or shot by then.

Two hours is not much time. Not for me to drag a big man with two questionable knees up five hundred feet of stone. And then he'll have to somehow get into a position to take out Laughlin. I hope he doesn't try any good-cop bullshit, like trying to take him alive, and hope that the theft of the gear and leaving it for destruction means he's hopped all the way over the line. I don't ask, though. There are some things like murder—even when it's not exactly cold-blooded—that you just don't talk about.

THIRTY-EIGHT

M Y GOD." THE WORDS SLIP OUT of my mouth in a tone of awe and reverence.

The flames are gigantic. They claw and writhe hundreds of feet into the night sky. They fill the entire western horizon. And even though the fire is still a couple of miles away, across the summit and beyond a small valley, I can feel its hot, stinking breath on my face. It sucks then blows at me, respirating deeply like a bellows in its need for fuel. Suddenly this idea of Wokowski's that we'll ride it out in a paper-thin aluminum shelter is more than ludicrous—it's suicidal. We are going to die.

I pull myself over the final edge and run to a jumble of large boulders. The smoke, wind, and stinging ash curl around them, but at least the tall rocks protect my eyes from the unholy sight.

I can't resist another peek, though. *You've got to look the bony fucker in the eye,* Roberto would say, and I shiver despite the superheated air.

The plateau before me is a broad, downsloping tabletop of brush and stone. Thick smoke drifts across it, forming snakelike shapes that slither between the boulders. I'm thankful there are few trees up here to provide the hottest kind of fuel. The lookout tower, lit up by the oncoming flames, stands a hundred yards away at the summit's southwestern corner. It looks like a delicate spaceship on its four spindly legs. Like it might lift off into space, its booster ignited by the monstrous blaze.

"My God," I whisper again. Through smoke-stung eyes I spot a human shape curled between the pilings.

It's little more than a silhouette outlined by the fire, but the slumped shape of a body is unmistakable. I will my eyes to focus against the smoke and almost wish I hadn't. I think I can see the white-and-yellow pattern of the pajamas Cali had worn the second night in my cabin.

Some self-awareness returns and I huddle again behind the boulders. Putting my back to the big rock behind me and leveraging a foot on another rock, I tug hard on the rope twice, wait a few seconds, then jerk it twice again. The slack comes quickly as Wokowski scrambles up that last, easy pitch. He has followed me up the cliff faster than I'd expected. Either he's a natural or he's very eager to climb to his death.

I watch him pull over the edge. I guess I want to see his reaction, to share this horror. I'm glad I do. Even though I know he's seen hundreds of fires before in his previous career, his eyes still go wide and his muscular jaw falls slack. His mouth moves and I read the same words that I could only whisper. Then he crawls over the cliff's upper lip and limps forward to crouch at my side in the shelter of the jumbled boulders.

"You see anything?" he asks.

"Someone's tied up underneath the pilings."

"Cali," he says softly. I hadn't wanted to say her name.

Wokowski unslings the rifle from where he'd been carrying it over one shoulder and unzips the case. The bolt snicks back and forth as he checks its load. The rifle's long oiled barrel reflects the orange in the night sky.

I lean out a second time to peer from behind the rocks, then quickly sit back down again. The moment my head had broken cover I had felt a cold spot on my forehead the size of a silver dollar. It was the same sensation I'd felt that day in the meadow—of being watched through a rifle's sights—and somehow I'm certain that Laughlin knows we're here.

Wokowski's radio makes a series of farting noises. He lays the rifle across his knees and unhooks the radio from his belt.

"There's a radio in the lookout, isn't there?" I ask him.

Wokowski nods, coming to the same realization. "Yeah. They leave it up there in the winters, along with some canned food, in case a lost hunter or snowmobiler needs help."

So Laughlin could have been listening to Wokowski's spy telling us about the fire's progress. And he could have heard Wokowski reply that we were coming at the summit from the butte's rear wall instead of the forward slope.

"Say again," Wokowski says into the radio. "We're on top now."

This time the voice from the other end is fairly clear. "The weather op just told me that there's a high-wind warning in the valley now. Gusts up to forty knots. It's going to be picking up speed. You need to hole up ASAP, Wook."

"Okay. We're backing off. We're going to head for the highway and get out of here. Out." He turns off the radio.

I peek out again at the small plain before us, studying the tower's windows. As the helicopter pilot had said, the large glass panes appear to be propped open. There is no light from inside and the interior is dark.

Wokowski rips open the Velcro cargo pockets on his uniform pants, pulling out the three small packages that are inside. Each is about fist-sized and looks like an emergency blanket wrapped in clear plastic with a red pull tab. They are the fire shelters. Christ, they're small. The fact that he's only brought three is significant. Good.

Wokowski hands me one, saying, "It's like a big sandwich bag with a slit down the center. Peel it open and get in. Pull it around you. Find a clear place like on rock or dirt. Stay away from grass and brush. Try to find a depression, too, far away from cliff edges because they'll funnel up heat. Keep your nose in the ground even if you think you're burning. You lift your head and you die."

"These things work?" I take it and stuff it into my pocket. It doesn't weigh more than a few ounces.

He nods. "I've never had to use one, but I know people who have. Just stay in it and don't move no matter how hot it gets. It may not seem like much, but it'll reflect ninety-five percent of the heat."

A second jumble of boulders are piled between us and the lookout tower. I point to them, unholster my pistol—which seems as ridiculous here as the shelters—and run toward the rocks. The cold spot my imagination tells me is real slides back and forth over my chest and stomach. I dive for the shelter of the rocks.

This new pile of rocks is lower than the previous one. Lying in the dirt behind them and panting, I peer around a low corner and point my gun at the tower in an attempt to provide covering fire as Wokowski runs after me. I glance back at him and see he's limping fast more than running. But no shot or flash of light comes from the tower. Wokowski must have felt the same thing I did, though, because he almost throws himself on top of me.

"How the fuck are we going to do this?" I ask, not being able to put off the question any longer. "He's got to be up there, and we know he's got a rifle."

Wokowski tries to push his long gun into my arms. "You can cover me."

"You didn't hear me earlier. I can't shoot for shit,

Wook." My voice sounds high over the fire's deep roar. "And with your knee, you can't run for shit."

The answer is obvious. It will have to be me.

Wokowski is kind enough not to state the obvious for a few seconds. During the pause he looks at the ground behind our boulders. He twitches in surprise. "Look at this."

There's a small hole in the boulders, not much bigger than a badger hole. I roll over to look at it—anything to prolong the inevitable for another moment. It's a shallow cave. I work my headlamp out of my pocket and shine it in the opening, which is barely big enough for one man. Two gallon jugs of water and a pile of blankets are secreted inside.

"We can use it when the fire comes," I tell him, then mention the water and blanket.

"We should keep it in mind. It might be better than the shelters. Quicker than deploying them, at least."

Anything would be better than those flimsy bits of tinfoil. But I tell him, "There's no way the three of us would fit."

He looks into it. "We might fit if we had to."

Looking around the corner of rock again, I can see the fire is on the verge of dropping down the steep hogback ridge and into the valley. I remember the technician telling us that once the fire hit the hollow it would go off like a bomb. There's no putting it off any longer. The figure stretched between the pilings is no longer still—it's jerking and rolling on the ground. At least she's conscious. Then she starts to scream.

The sound of her screams is more terrifying than the flames across the valley. They are so raw and animal-like that I have to look away from the tower. She sounds nothing like the woman who had shouted in delight as she leapt down the chute on Teewinot, who just yesterday had looked up from the hospital bed with wet eyes and told me, "I thought you said I was safe, Anton."

"Cover me."

Wokowski nods, his jaw flaring at the sound of each new scream. "Watch out for the trapdoor, Burns. Once you're under the tower you're safe unless he hears you or decides to pop out and head over here."

I slip the gun into my right pocket and take a folding knife out of my left. I open the four-inch blade and hold the handle in my fist. Then, against all instinct, I run toward the screaming woman, the dark tower, and the coming flames.

THIRTY-NINE

I PUMP MY ARMS AND LEGS and suck in great gulps of the smoke and ash as I run. He sees me. I know it. He's up there behind the dark windows of the lookout, aiming his rifle. Maybe he's laughing at the way I juke and jive, vainly trying to present a tougher target. But the shot never comes to blow me backward onto my ass. I leap for the relative safety beneath the shelter's high platform, rolling, nearly taking an eye out with the open knife in my hand. I stare up at the ladder and the trapdoor before turning to Cali.

She's bound at the ankles and wrists with thick strips of duct tape. Another coarsely twisted piece of tape connects the two bonds behind her back, effectively hog-tying her. What looks like a yellowed wedding dress is wrapped around her throat. Her short hair, wet with sweat, splashes from side to side as she fights against the adhesive tape. I can hear her grunting with exertion. Beyond her the fire is swelling up on the far ridge, readying to make the hop down into the valley. *It'll go off like a bomb. Area ignition.*

I kneel in the streaming smoke and touch her hip, saying quietly, "Cali, don't move."

The feel of my hand on her skin causes her to jump as if I'd zapped her with a cattle prod. She whips her head around and stares at me, her eyes wide and red. But I don't waste time trying to calm her. All I do is whisper, "Hold still."

I flick the blade at the tape connecting her ankles to her wrists. It parts cleanly. As if it were spring-loaded, her body snaps straight. She rolls three hundred and sixty degrees, away from me, and manages to get to her knees before she falls over. I lunge after her, stabbing the knife down between her ankles.

"Cali!" I say louder. "Hold still! Let me cut it!"

Just then I hear a banging noise above my head. I look up—the trapdoor is open and Bill Laughlin's leathery face is visible, peering down at me. We stare at each other for what feels like several slow seconds from twenty feet apart. His skin is orange in the hellish light where it's not covered by the same kind of fireproof coveralls Wokowski and I had left at the bottom of the cliff. The hardman who had once been a hero of mine opens his mouth and shows me his teeth.

"Get out of here!" he shrieks at me, as if in pain. "Go away!"

Fuck you, I think, trying to reach around Cali in order to get at the remaining bonds without slashing her wrists. By grabbing a handful of her hair and yanking her toward me, I manage it. But she falls into me, and we both go down in the dirt. The long, straight barrel of a rifle slides into view from the trapdoor. I see Laughlin's hands working the bolt.

For the second time in my life I live up to the hated nickname. I pull the pistol out of my pants and feel it kick in my palm a half-dozen times. I fire up blindly, without aiming, in a technique that had worked once before. At the same time I hear the windows shattering and then, even when I stop firing, the thunderclaps of Wook's big hunting rifle as he punches bullets through the shelter's flimsy plywood walls. Laughlin's rifle falls to the ground but he either rolls or falls out of my line of fire. The trapdoor bangs shut.

"Anton?" Cali half screams in my ear. She's crawling over me, getting to her feet. "Did you kill him?"

"I don't know. We've got to get out—"

"No shit," she interrupts, grabbing me by my free wrist and pulling me up while I keep the pistol pointed at the trapdoor. "But where to? Who else was shooting?"

I answer both questions by pointing at the rocks. Wokowski is standing up now and walking toward us with the rifle still aimed over our heads at the tower. "C'mon!" he's yelling. "Run!"

Cali is barefoot and the ground is all broken stone, so we run in a kind of three-legged race with my arm around her back. Wokowski decides we're not moving fast enough. He puts down the rifle and limps toward us, now yelling for us to run faster, goddamn it.

We're almost to the rocks when I turn around to see if the fire's dropped into the valley yet. It has. The flames are spilling down from the ridge like a great wave of water, like a hellish dam somewhere upstream has broken. Worse than that sight is that I see something half fall and half leap out of the tower, not bothering with the ladder. Laughlin lands on his feet then goes down hard on the uneven ground. When he gets up I can see the shape of the rifle in his hands. Fuck. I should have thrown it off the cliff.

He's coming after us.

I want to stop and shoot at him but what seems like a lightning strike behind him goes on and on and on. The valley has detonated. A hot lash of superheated air whips across the back of my head.

Wokowski pitches forward at the same time I hear a sharp crack over the inferno's blast. It's followed by a tidal wave of heat and noise. Cali spills onto the ground just past him, pulling me down on top of her. The rocks and Wokowski's rifle are just ten feet away. I get up first and literally throw Cali toward the rocks, yelling about the small cave. I turn and try to help Wokowski to his feet. A second crack sounds and the bullet whizzes by my head, almost skinning my cheek.

Wokowski is like a slippery sack of cement. He flails and churns, struggling to pull himself up on me, as the rifle cracks a third time. Wokowski's flesh shudders in my hands with the impact of another bullet. I look and see Laughlin only a hundred feet away, limping heavily through the smoke toward us and chambering another round. The wall of flame is breathing on his back.

There's no way I can get Wokowski behind the rocks in time. We're both going to get shot *and* burnt if I don't leave him. But I can't. Then Cali is beside me, helping to drag the big cop.

When I look for Laughlin again he's been enveloped by the fire. The entire slope leading up to the summit goes up in a solid sheet of flame. The tower is gone, too. I remember again the term the techie at the ranger station had used. *Area ignition.* That's a mild way of putting it. The whole valley has gone up in seconds and now the summit is going, too. When he described it as going off like a bomb he was far more accurate. It even sounds like a bomb, and the rush of burning wind—sucking toward it to further fuel the beast—nearly knocks me off my feet.

With adrenaline spurting through my veins and terror seizing my brain, I somehow manage to heave us all up the final steps into the rocks. My elbow slams against stone and so does my head. I'd probably be seeing stars if they all hadn't just exploded.

Wokowski is suddenly stronger. I watch, and try to help, as he shoves Cali into the hole. I start pushing at him. But with the same amazing strength I'd witnessed at the gym when he was chopping the heavy bag in half, he peels me off and begins stuffing me in the hole after her. The air is burning. It feels like I'm drowning in a washing machine full of boiling water. Below me Cali is kicking and pulling, yelling, "Get in, Wook, get in!" and above me Wokowski is thrusting me deeper with his big hands.

The light disappears altogether as Wokowski fills the opening with his own body. Despite the pummeling I'm receiving from both sides and the narrow confines of dirt and stone, I get the aluminum shelter out of my pocket and am pretty sure I even manage to correctly pull the tab. My hands are suddenly full of diaphanous foil. I try to worm my way up, around Wokowski, but his big fists begin hammering at me, hitting me for real.

I fight back as best I can while clutching the foil, but my legs are folded so tightly against Cali's back and the sides of the hole that I can't get any purchase to shove my way past him. There's a roar like a train is thundering past overhead. And Wokowski's cries of "Stay the fuck down!" turn to the roars of a wounded bear. His fists keep hammering at me, harder and faster as he bellows, his body bucking like it's lightning-struck, even when I've stopped trying to force my way up past him. I have a horrible image of Laughlin dancing on his back in the flames. Clawing at his flesh.

Beneath me Cali starts screaming again. She's weeping and yelling Wook's name. The noise from above is truly hellish—it's something I know is being imprinted on my soul, something I'll never forget. Snot runs into my mouth and tears stream down my own cheeks. And over all the noise and pain and fear I smell the stench of burning flesh.

THURSDAY

FORTY

AFTER A WHILE there are only three sounds: a kind of low hiss from the ground above, Cali's weeping below, and the sound of my own ragged breath. Wokowski has long since stopped roaring, although I can't say how long ago he went silent.

I push against him, tentatively at first, then harder. His body lifts up from my palms far too easily, as if he weighs nothing at all. It's strange and extremely disconcerting. When I push again—harder still—he rolls to one side of the hole and flops on his back. Orange light from the still-burning embers littering the ground shows that his face is relaxed.

"Don't move," I say to Cali as I stand upright. The fire has passed. Flames light up the sky to the east now, racing to do battle with the soon-to-be-rising sun. The summit looks like the deepest pit of hell.

I look closer at Wokowski's face. Contrary to the raging he'd been doing earlier—his face surely contorted with pain and fear—now he looks almost serene. The mighty jaw muscles are slack. I touch my fingers to his neck to check for a pulse and feel nothing but dry, papery skin. I press harder, hoping and praying, but there's nothing there. When I lift my fingers away their impressions remain on his skin—two deep dimples. And then I realize why he'd felt so light. The fire sucked all the moisture from his body. He's just a shell, a dried-up husk.

My eyes start to fill up all over again, and it's not from the smoke. I reach behind one of his shoulders. Although I expect it, it still causes me to shudder. My fingers touch dry, warm bone.

Cali's still curled in a ball at the bottom of the hole. Her hands cover her face and her back trembles with sobs. She says through her fingers, more moaning than speaking, "Is he okay? Is Wook okay?"

I reach beneath her and manage to pull out the two blankets I'd noticed there earlier. The first I drape over Wokowski's face and chest. The second I spread on Cali's back before lifting her out.

"No, Cali. He's not. He didn't make it."

I carry her to a flat-topped rock where she huddles in her blanket and cries. I do the same as I sit next to her, holding her to me. Stop it, I tell myself. Wook's gone, that's all. There's no reason to mourn. And that's not him over there with his back burned away. It's just a carcass.

The thing that dries my eyes is the fervent hope that Laughlin hadn't been blown off the cliff by the explosion. I can't find his body, and I can't accept that he could have died that easy. I want him to have burned like Wokowski but slower, with a million times the pain.

Although I've lost a lot of friends over the years, mostly to gravity, for the first time I find myself really wishing for a heaven and a hell. Not so much so Wokowski can be immortal among clouds and harp-strumming angels, but so that Laughlin will roast for all eternity. Burn, baby, burn.

But even that thought is not entirely satisfying. No, I want to be the one to make him suffer. I want to be there in the pit, skewering him with my pitchfork and turning him over the coals. I want to be able to talk to him as I make him scream loud enough to silence the voices in his bleeding brain. Make him understand why he's being punished and, hopefully, make him feel a little regret. Or a lot of it.

These thoughts are interrupted by the rising *thump-thump-thump* of a helicopter's blades digging into the murky air. The noise comes out of the west, where stars are now becoming apparent as bright stains in the dark sky. Three of them become more distinct as the sound comes closer. From among them a big spotlight starts slashing through the smoke. I raise an arm and wave at it, almost reluctantly, because for some reason it seems too soon, like an intrusion rather than a rescue.

The helicopter circles a few times, cutting at us with the light, before it scatters ash and reignites embers as it sets down gingerly on the still-smoking ground.

A man in green fireproof pants and a yellow shirt jumps out. He runs toward us awkwardly, bent over at the waist.

"Are you all right?" he yells.

"The two of us are."

"Is there anyone else?"

"Yeah, two more. But they're dead."

"Come on," he says to Cali as he takes her wrist. "Let's get you inside first." Then to me, "Please wait until I come back."

He walks her through the churning ash to the helicopter, keeping her head down with one hand. Once he has her seatbelted inside, he comes back for me. I've been wrapping Wokowski's corpse with the extra blanket. I pick him up—it sickens me again, how light he is—and wait with the big cop cradled in my arms. The wetness on my cheeks and the taste of salt in my mouth tells me I'm crying again.

"We need to leave the body for the accident investigators."

"No. He was a cop."

The ranger tries to stop me but I pull away from him and walk toward the helicopter. He tugs on my shirt a second time, causing me to shrug off his hand roughly. After that he allows me to walk on my own, warning me to lower my head and not walk to the uphill side of the machine. I carefully slide Wook onto the vibrating metal floor. Then I climb in next to Cali and snap shut my own seat belt.

"What about the other one?"

I look around the moonscape one last time. "Fuck him."

We lift into the sun's first rays as they curve over the earth and knife into the haze. Below us the forest is gone. Square miles of land look like something you'd sweep out of the bottom of a fireplace. My eyes are drawn to the south where a high band of cliffs undercut by a sparkling river has protected a part of the forest. Dusty pines still grow atop the cliffs along with cottonwoods and shiny aspens. I'm glad that something has survived intact. I know I haven't.

Cali is staring at her knees, where her pajama bottoms are streaked black with ash and dirt. I put an arm around her shoulders but can think of nothing to say. Beyond the pilot and crew chief I can see the Teton spires pushing up into the sky. There's Mt. Moran and the Skillet Glacier that Cali had wanted to ski, then the Grand's steep snowcapped ridges and the great North Face, and then Teewinot with its thin ribbon of snow trailing all the way down from the summit. It's hard to believe that less than a week ago we'd been leaping down that and laughing. It's even harder to believe that I had regarded it as a glorious release from my problems.

FORTY-ONE

WHEN WE STEP onto the parking-lot asphalt at the Moran Junction ranger station, the helicopter's crew chief palms my head to keep it down as he guides me toward a crowd of people. An ambulance with flashing lights waits nearby, and I'm forced to lie back on a gurney even as I protest that I'm not hurt. Cali is more compliant when she's laid down on another next to me. Beyond a temporary chain-link fence is a horde of tourists who stare through the mesh with curious eyes. A hundred or more cameras are aimed our way. Their owners are shouting questions, wondering what all the commotion is about. I peer through the fence at the crowd and try to spot Rebecca. If she's there, I can't see her.

It's not a heroic homecoming. And it shouldn't be. Only if Wokowski were still alive, as the audacious instigator of the harebrained rescue, would it be appropriate to celebrate.

Someone is pushing through the EMTs, rangers, and police officers around us. A woman's voice sounds close to choking as she shouts, "Let me through!" It's Alana Reese, and she's even less composed than she'd been at the fire headquarters. Her blonde hair is wild and her mouth is twisted in an ugly grimace. Her movements as she breaks free from the people around us are jerky and frantic. She runs to kneel beside Cali's stretcher. She takes her daughter's hand and covers it with her lips and tears.

"I'm okay, Mom," Cali insists. But it doesn't stop her mother from weeping over her.

People turn their backs, embarrassed for the actress. But they also spontaneously gather closer so as to shield the mother and daughter from the camera lenses. After a few minutes Alana raises her head from where it's been buried in her daughter's neck and looks at me with red, running eyes. She doesn't say anything, but I think I can read an apology in the way she nods at me and makes a brave attempt at a smile.

I manage to get out of there, although it seems like everyone is trying to stop me. The paramedics want to take me to the hospital, talking about needing to test for smoke inhalation. The Forest Service people want to talk to me about the blaze. The sheriff and two angry-looking guys with FBI badges want to know what the hell happened up there. And all I want is to be alone. Well, not exactly alone.

A young fire crew member gives me a ride to the airport, where the Pig still waits at its illegal parking place by the curb. From there it's just fifteen minutes to my cabin. *Be there, Rebecca. Be there.*

When I turn into the lane I see that a car is parked tight against my porch. But it's not Rebecca's shiny green Saab. It's a small pickup of indeterminate make and vintage, even rustier than my Land Cruiser. Actual holes have been chewed through the fenders, panels, and doors. The windows are dark with cracked purple tinting. It has Idaho plates from a small county on the state's northeast border with Montana.

The bumper stickers belie the truck's ominous appearance. One is a Jesus-fish symbol that has sprouted legs. Another reads, "I'm a Gay New Yorker Here to Take Your

Guns!" And then there are numerous stickers from environ-
mental and pro-choice groups, as well as a Jamaican flag and
a marijuana leaf.

I pull in behind the pickup and get out. The front door
opens and Mungo slinks toward me, dancing shyly across the
porch. My brother steps out after her.

"Nice wheels," I tell him as Mungo wags her tail and
pushes her nose over my clothes. I push her away, not wanting her to smell the odors on my clothes.

"Was all I could borrow, *che.* Didn't want to draw any attention by stealing one."

"I thought you were going to lay low until meeting up
with the Feds this afternoon in Salt Lake. You don't get going, you're going to be late."

"I was worried about you, little bro. You looked a little
wigged up there. Thought I ought to check up on you before
I leave."

He goes on to explain that he'd slept a few hours in a
borrowed bag at the Exum hut before climbing the Middle
Teton. Then he slipped down into Idaho from the mountain's west face. He'd called a friend in Driggs who'd lent
him the pickup, then driven over Teton Pass into Jackson.

"Couldn't you have found something less conspicuous?"

He just grins and shakes his head at me. "You look like
you've been dragged through a cesspool."

I walk past him through the door and collapse onto
the couch. "It was worse than any cesspool. A thousand times
worse."

Roberto follows me in and helps himself to a Snake River
Ale from the refrigerator. He sits down at the table. "*Now*
did you get the guy?" He's staring, sensing that something's
very wrong with me but not understanding what.

"I didn't. But the fire did." I tell him what had happened, everything up until the end—that part, Wokowski's
death, I'm not ready to talk about. My words dry up when I

reach the point where the flames are all around us and we're diving for the supposed safety of the hole.

Roberto tries to fill the silence that follows by shaking his head some more and saying, "I wish I'd been there for you, bro." Then he tries in a lighter tone, "Besides, I would've liked to have seen it."

"I'm glad you weren't. I almost got cooked. Two men did, and one of them was a friend of mine." My throat constricts so tight when I think of Wokowski that it threatens to pitch my voice high. I try to shrug it off. "Right now you ought to be worried about missing your hookup with the Feds. And getting me arrested and fired for harboring a fugitive."

"Thought you'd already gotten yourself fired, *che*."

"Just warned off the Morrow case. Now that Laughlin's burned up, I guess I'm in the clear. Everything's going to be cool with the office." But it's not the office I'm worried about. "Listen, 'Berto, I can't talk about this anymore. Not right now. Tell me, have you seen Rebecca?"

He takes a long pull from the beer, half draining it. Then he lets his grin come back onto his face even though his eyes are still probing me. "If she saw me, she wouldn't stick around very long."

"You scare her, 'Berto. It's nothing personal. It's got more to do with me than with you."

I walk out on the porch and dial Rebecca's cell phone but she doesn't answer. No service, an automated voice tells me.

Mungo, who's followed me outside, cocks her head at me. The sly, shit-eating grin displays the tips of her teeth before she looks away.

Information gives me the number for the Spring Creek Ranch. The front desk there tells me that no, Mr. Hersh and his daughter have not checked out yet—they've asked for a late departure at noon. I realize it's been more than twelve hours since I shouldered my pack and walked out on Rebecca.

When I'm connected to the room, it's Rebecca's father who answers. "Anton," he says stiffly. "What do you want?"

"Please put Rebecca on, David."

He doesn't say anything for a moment, and then his voice is angry. "Why do you think my daughter would be interested in talking to you after you left her again last night, when she came to you?"

"Please. Get her." I want to explain about the fire and the kidnapped prosecutor but none of it will come out.

There's another long silence on the other end. Mr. Hersh sighs. "None of this was my idea, you know. She wanted to go about it her own way. Feel you out, I guess, before putting it to you directly. And from what I understand, the feeling-out process didn't go too well."

"I know. I fucked it up. Please, just put her on."

"I can't. Her paper called early this morning. They wanted her to cover the fire until they could get another reporter and a photographer up here. Then, at breakfast, one of those movie people she recognized but I didn't was introduced to her. In the ensuing conversation, an interview was agreed to. She thought it might make for an interesting story, to view the fire with a movie star. That's where she is this morning."

"Was it Alana Reese?" I'd just seen her at the ranger station. Why hadn't Rebecca been there, too?

"No. Even I know who she is. It was a young man. Gordon, or something like that."

Danny Gorgon. What had Angela said, about how he was too chickenshit to come at me directly, but watch out, that he'd try to do something nasty behind my back? My legs feel weak. I feel as if I've been socked in the stomach. I have to brace myself against the porch railing.

"Where are they?"

"They must have taken a hike together. Rebecca came back to the room to change and get her hiking boots. She said something about how they were going to go and view the fire from a place this Gordon knew about. A place that hadn't burned. A thermal spring, I believe."

I hit the END button without saying good-bye then sag even farther against the rail. Roberto comes out and sits on the steps. Even before he went to prison he was like that, hardly being able to stand a few minutes indoors. He strokes Mungo's head with one hand, cooing in Spanish to her. When I pull the car keys from my pocket, Mungo's ears catapult forward.

"You look seriously freaked, *che*. Where you going?"

"To get Rebecca."

"She in some kind of trouble?"

I shake my head. "Don't worry about me. You leaving for Salt Lake?"

His blue eyes burn right through me. "Yeah. I guess," he answers slowly. "Trap or not, I'm gonna walk into it. That's what you think I ought to do, right?"

I'm finally learning not to worry about him. If it is a trap, he'll go to prison for a long, long time. And if he runs, he'll keep soloing and using until one or the other finally kills him. He lives how he wants.

"Shit, 'Berto. It's your choice. Either roll the dice or get out of here, go back home."

His strange blue eyes never leave my face. He doesn't even blink. "How about I come with you for now? You're looking seriously wigged, *che*. Like you might need your big bro around."

I walk down the steps into the lane and open the truck's door. "No. This isn't anything dangerous. Not physically. Not for me, anyway. Besides, if I'm seen with you we're both going down. I'll see you around, 'Berto. Good luck."

Only later do I realize that I forgot to hug him good-bye.

FORTY-TWO

THE TRAILHEAD LEADING to the spring is not far from both my cabin and the hospital. It's on the Elk Refuge, up an unmarked offshoot of the dirt road that cuts through it. I guess it will take me no more than twenty minutes to be on the trail. But when I pull onto the refuge road from Broadway, I find that it's clogged with traffic.

A long line of cars stand idling on the prairie. Brake lights are lit up all the way to where the road rises up into some low hills. They've come to view the fire's devastation, like it's some gruesome accident that just demands active rubbernecking. There are some breaks in the traffic where a few humped buffalo have set up an unofficial roadblock. Tourists are getting out to snap pictures of the surly beasts and further stalling traffic. Making things worse, other cars are returning from the hills and the road is too narrow in many places for passing.

I beat both fists on the steering wheel. Mungo pulls her head back inside the window and stares at me in concern.

"Hang on, girl."

Pressing down on the gas pedal, I nose up onto the grass on one side of the road and start bouncing over the prairie. When thin groups of trees block my path I swerve back down onto the road, cut through the line of cars, and climb back up on the other side. I can't drive as fast as I'd like because of all the buffalo. But I still leave a big cloud of dust and a symphony of blaring horns. I hope they all get gored. I'm too busy steering to look back at the chaos I'm leaving behind me. I don't bother checking the rearview mirror to see all the middle fingers that are surely upraised in my wake.

I almost blow by the turnoff for the trailhead. It's barely visible around one bend in the road, nothing more than a pair of faint tracks half covered by grass and brush. The Pig's big tires spit dirt against the undercarriage as I accelerate onto it.

For two miles it climbs east into the Gros Ventre Range. The woods grow thicker on both sides as I gain elevation. At some turns I have a view of the raw, blackened landscape to the north. I shiver, unable to forget hours earlier having been in the middle of what had caused that. I've never known nature to show her power so nakedly.

The double-track dead-ends in a small turnout surrounded by a buck fence. A break in the fence and a Forest Service backboard mark where the hiking trail begins. Two cars are parked here. One is a red Range Rover with a rental sticker on the back bumper. The other is Rebecca's green Saab. Barely taking the time to shut off the engine, I'm out of the Pig and running with Mungo loping behind me.

The trail is well maintained and obvious. It zigzags up a well-maintained forested hillside to where it then follows a rocky ridge even higher.

The ridge itself starts out broad and tree covered but soon narrows to only twenty or thirty feet across. At times it narrows even further, becoming little more than a knife edge of vertical stone. There is a steel cable bolted to the rock to form a handrail at one such place. I scurry across it without needing to touch the metal, but behind me Mungo lets out a small cry of concern. I turn around and see her hesitating.

I could probably coax her across but I can't spare the time. Instead I yell for her to stay there—that I'll be back soon. Then I turn and keep running.

The fire hadn't reached the top of the ridge because of two hundred feet of blank, unvegetated stone below. The cliff served as a firebreak, containing the fire to the north and funneling it beyond the low hills toward Elation Peak. A fast-flowing river tumbles at the cliff's base, undercutting it and further protecting it. Beyond the river the earth is still smoking. Only five miles to the north is the box-shaped outline of Elation Peak. It causes me to shiver again.

In the distance, farther up the ridge, I can see where it bisects a hanging valley that droops between two large peaks. The dale on the left has what looks like a small lake in it. It glistens in the sunlight where it's not surrounded by trees. A waterfall spills down toward the river far below. It looks like some kind of magical Shangri-la, especially with all the devastation around it.

With worry and rage pounding in my blood, I race over the ridge, careless of the drop on both sides. It doglegs at one broad spot and the trail switches to the other side. As I clamber over some boulders, reaching a flat area the size of a small room, I notice that a man is sitting on top of some rocks on the other side. Looking as if he's meditating, he faces to the north and Elation Peak. The sun is in my face so I can't get a good look at him but I'm sure it's not Gorgon. His posture isn't right for the arrogant prick, and he doesn't have the same muscular outline.

One of my boots kicks loose some rocks. The man's form jumps at the sound and he turns to face me. My skin crawls on my bones as I make him out.

FORTY-THREE

I STOP DEAD IN MY TRACKS. Only my right hand moves to snatch the gun from where it's clipped to one side of my hip. I jerk it out and point it at his chest as my thumb automatically flicks off the safety.

"Hey, Bill."

Bill Laughlin is naked from the waist up except for blood and ash and huge raw blisters. A pair of what might have been jeans covering his legs are in charred tatters. The fireproof suit he'd had on last night is nowhere to be seen. It appears that it hadn't done him all that much good anyway—nearly every inch of his body has been terribly burned, from his scorched scalp to the soles of his bare feet. His face is lumpy and swollen. The wrinkles around his eyes and mouth have stretched out beneath the bloating skin to resemble old knife cuts. Both his pupils have ballooned to fill the irises, and the whites of his eyes are crimson with blood. He looks like something that has crawled out of hell.

The pain he's feeling must be truly incredible—there's not supposed to be anything as agonizing as a third-degree burn. Especially a full-body burn. He would have been far better off if he'd died up on the butte. But rather than pain, I see only a chilling animosity in his gaze. A coiled, violent madness as evident here in the sunlight as it had been last night.

My hand tightens around the pistol's beveled grip as I consider my choices. I can take him in. Where? To the hospital? He'll probably die there from the burns within a few hours. If not soon, then soon enough from the inoperable aneurysm that's leaking in his head. But a soft bed and painkilling drugs are better than he deserves. For all the trouble he's caused, twenty-five years ago and then again within the past two weeks, he deserves a far less pleasant death.

"Thinking about jumping?" I ask him.

"It crossed my mind," he says. "But you've given me a better idea, Burns."

His voice is little more than a rasp. I have no doubt that his lungs have been seared. There's a wet rumble behind the words, indicating that they're filling with fluid. He shakes his head, as if trying to clear his thoughts, then winces from the movement.

"You're not going to shoot," he tells me. "Put the gun down. I'm no threat to you now."

He limps down from his rock and onto the broad, flat shelf where I'm standing. Behind him he leaves a wet footprint of blood, skin, and pus. His face is twitching slightly beneath the swelling and the sores.

"How'd you get off the butte?" I keep the H&K fixed on his breastbone.

He chuckles wetly, clears his throat with effort, and says, "Guys like you and me, we're resourceful. I fought forest fires for twenty summers and fought gravity the rest of the year. There were plenty of little hidey-holes up there. Not as good as the one you took, but I found one."

"By the looks of you, it wasn't good enough."

He chuckles again and coughs. This time he spits out

phlegm. Or maybe it's lung tissue. "I figured that while I'm still breathing, I might as well take a last look at that spring where the three of us used to swim naked. My God, even then, that woman was a goddamn tease. Thought it might be a good place to croak. Send her a last message. But I don't think I can make it on my own. So the hospital will be even better. They're there, aren't they? Cali and the bitch? Maybe she'll want to spit in my face. I can still spit right back."

I stand immobile, frozen by the vehemence of his words, with my gun aimed steadily at his chest. *What am I going to do?* I ask myself. Laughlin must sense my ambivalence, and also must be aware of my desire to put a bullet through him, because he asks in an even quieter voice, "Is Cali okay?"

"She survived."

He shakes his head, slower this time, while keeping his gaze on me. "I didn't want to hurt her, you know. But in the end, it was the only way."

"To get back at Alana? For rejecting you?"

"It was never my plan to hurt Cali. Just to use her. Scare her to scare the bitch. Make her think someone was going to take away the thing she loved the most. Make her suffer a little, you know? Feel fear and loss. But I wasn't going to hurt Cali if I didn't have to. It was supposed to be the bitch up there last night for the finale. When she got away, I had to improvise. I'm resourceful, like I said."

"Cali loved you like an uncle."

He shrugs. "I loved her mom like a woman. You know what that's like?"

"Your brain is leaking, Bill."

He laughs. And as soon as he does he begins coughing even harder—wet hacking that shakes through his body. When he finishes retching and sputtering, he stands up straight and looks at me again.

"Thought I'd buried you." His Adam's apple bobs in his throat, as if he's holding back another laugh. "Under the snow. I figured that would be another good way to scare the shit out of that woman, the way she was always surrounded by bodyguards. Kill her daughter's bodyguard. Show her she's not as safe as she thinks. That she's not immune."

The feeling of being under that mountain of snow comes over me again. The silence and the pressure and the panic. The gun is starting to shake a little in my hand.

He lurches a step closer and leaves another footprint on the rock. We're about six feet apart now. I can smell the barbecue-like scent of charred flesh rising off him. The sky behind him seems to become a sharper, brighter shade of blue. A breeze rushes up from beneath the cliff and is cold on my sweat-soaked skin.

His voice goes very soft again, becomes almost pleading. "All I wanted was a little affection, you know? My best friend gets fried after stealing the bitch from me and what does she do? She treats me like *I'm* the one who died. Avoids the sight of me. Like *I* was the corpse, not *him*." Then his tone grows harsher. "For twenty-five years the only way I could get close to the cunt was by hanging around with her daughter. Then I get this thing in my head, and I've run out of time. I'd wasted my life for nothing. All that was left to do was make her pay for those goddamn wasted years."

"Did you kill Patrick?"

" 'Course I did," he snaps, his tone growing harder still. It's almost a growl. "What do you think? He takes my woman and acts like we're still pals. So I pushed his ass into the fire. Right off that butte. The dumb fuck went down screaming. Cali would have gone the same way. I can almost hear Alana screaming, too. Music to my ears."

My arms are starting to ache—both with the weight of the gun and the need to put a bullet through what remains of this man. A man I'd once admired.

His blood-filled eyes jerk to one side of me. "What's this? A wolf? Am I seeing things now?"

Mungo has finally caught up. She's walking slowly toward us with tentative steps. Her black lips are pulled high and her fangs are bared—looking nothing close to a nervous smile now. The fur around her neck and shoulders stands straight up, causing her to look huge and fierce. A low rumble vibrates from her chest.

"That's right," I tell him. "She's a hellhound. Come to guide you to your new home." This is a new Mungo—I've never seen her snarl before and the sight of it is almost as alarming as what I'm thinking of doing. She's watching Laughlin intently, as if frightened by the menace in our postures but intrigued by the smell of roasted flesh.

Shoot him, I tell myself. *Just shoot the asshole and get on with it.*

"Arrest me, Officer," Laughlin says, looking at me again with what might be a swollen leer. He holds his hands out to me, the insides of his wrists touching. "Cuff me and take me in. Let's go see the bitch at the hospital."

"Under other circumstances it would be my pleasure, old man. But now, why don't you just jump?" I gesture with my free hand toward the cliff edge behind him.

"Because there's opportunity in terminal illness, Burns. Doesn't a dying man get a last request? Her bill is still outstanding. She hasn't paid enough."

I step forward—one long step across the line—and raise my right arm higher so that the pistol is pressing against the blistered flesh of the bridge of his nose. He doesn't even blink. I hear myself say, "You remember Charlie Wokowski?"

"Who?" Laughlin asks with his eyes—all pupil like a shark's—fixed on me over the short barrel of my gun. They're narrowed in puzzlement. I can feel the rumble from Mungo's chest building in my own.

"Charles Wokowski. The other man who was with me last night? The one who's in love with Cali? The one who was going to ask her to marry him?"

Laughlin doesn't say anything. He doesn't know what I'm talking about, and a part of me wonders if I've been infected by his hatred and madness.

"He's dead," I tell him. "He burned to death because of you, just like your friend Patrick. I want you to know because he was a friend of mine. He burned for me."

Laughlin finally closes his eyes, realizing now that I'm not going to take him anywhere. He yells very loud, "Go to hell!" Then he hugs himself, wrapping his blistered arms around his equally burnt chest.

I feel a wolfish smile pulling back my lips. I'm thinking of Wokowski and how my fingers had permanently dimpled his dry skin when I tried to take his pulse. Of how when I'd reached around behind his neck I'd touched charred bone. With these same fingers that now hold the plastic grip and the steel trigger.

"Go to hell!" Laughlin yells again, spraying me with spittle. Those monstrous pupils open again and bore into me.

"Okay. But you first."

A smile bends his lips and they start to bleed. The rictus of pain seizing his facial muscles causes the smile to widen and narrow as if it were hooked up to a strobe. His red eyes begin spasming from side to side—from me to somewhere behind me. I almost laugh, thinking he's sane enough to try that old trick. My finger takes up the slack on the trigger.

A soft voice says from behind me, "I knew you were up to something, *che*. Shit, just when I'm about to step into the light, here you are, jumping off into the darkness."

"What the hell are you doing here? You're supposed to be heading south."

"I thought you looked a little freaked out. So I followed you."

Roberto walks up beside me. He leans around me and looks closely at Laughlin's face and where the gun is touching his scalded skin. What he sees there doesn't even make him flinch.

"Who's this scabby motherfucker anyway?"

"Believe it or not, this is Bill Laughlin. The legendary hardman. He somehow lived through the fire and showed up here. I remember you saying you wanted him dead after we repeated that sandbag of a route in the Bugaboos. Your wish is about to come true."

Roberto looks at me and cocks his head to the side. "You gonna arrest him or shoot him?"

"Shoot him."

"Even though he's unarmed?"

"Yeah."

Roberto laughs. "You wouldn't be standing around talking if you were going to do it. You aren't cut out for this, *che*. You're a lawman, not a killer. And now you're even forgetting the cop stuff. Remember anything 'bout powder burns?" He points at where the short black barrel still presses against the bridge of Laughlin's nose.

"That's right," Laughlin blurts. "An execution and everyone will know it! You've got to take me to the hospital!"

For the first time I think of the consequences. The real world consequences, not just those to my soul. It's almost funny—I haven't been thinking of them at all, but my *destraillado* brother is. I slowly pull the gun away from Laughlin's face—his eyes twitching from my brother to me—and shuffle back three feet. I keep it aimed at the same spot.

Roberto moves back with me, *tsk*ing his tongue against the roof of his mouth. "Give me the gun, bro. This is my kind of thing, not yours. You aren't cut out for shooting an unarmed asshole. I am."

He reaches out and grabs the short barrel.

"I'm not going to let you—" I start to say. Roberto tugs at the gun but I won't let go.

Then Bill Laughlin moves. He takes a single, staggering

step toward us, his arms flying wide as if begging to be shot. Or to fall prostrate at our feet. Mungo moves, too, faster than a rattlesnake's strike. In the lower periphery of my vision I see a flash of white teeth before they clamp down on the scorched flesh of Laughlin's ankle. Through his scream I think I can hear the sound of bone on bone.

Roberto and I watch, both of us still holding my gun, as Laughlin stumbles backward. Howling. Mungo's head jerks from side to side with lightning-fast tugs, pulling his leg out from under him. Laughlin is falling backward now, and not stopping. His arms are windmilling wildly in the air. He's going over the edge, I realize.

Mungo releases her jaw from his ankle just as her big front paws start to skid over the edge after him. I let Roberto have the gun and snatch at the tail that's flailing in the air. Grabbing a fistful of hair, I hang on. Then I pull her back.

"There you go," my brother says happily, his eyes crinkling with mirth. "Your soul's intact, lawman. You, *mariquita,* are one *bad* dog."

I lean over the edge in time to watch Laughlin cartwheel in the air. He only bounces once, and for a moment I'm filled with the horror that his madness will somehow allow him to survive yet another of nature's deadliest forces, one that he's escaped from so often. That he'll land in the river and again escape. But he doesn't. He doesn't reach the river and he doesn't escape. He splatters onto the rocks at the river's edge and bursts like a paper bag full of ketchup and white china.

Roberto leans over next to me and chuckles. "Fucker's taking a dirt nap now."

FORTY-FOUR

I LOOK AT my watch. "You're going to be late, 'Berto. You've only got five hours to make the drive. Are you going to Salt Lake or not?"

Roberto's still looking over the edge, transfixed by the sight of the same death he's been toying with for all these years. The end he's been taunting, allowing it to pad just behind him as close as a shadow. I've done it, too, but far less recklessly. With the exception of that single mad night on the Grand, anyway.

Laughlin had also allowed it to pursue him for years—for decades—and now it had finally caught up with him. The end looks bad, very bad, but it's still a better one than he deserved. After what he'd done to Cali's father, after what he tried to do to Cali and her mom, after what he'd done to me on Mt. Wister, and after what he managed to inflict on Wook, I wish he'd hit the rocks in slow motion. I wish it had taken him minutes of super-slow-mo to burst open.

At least now all that envy and spite has been squeezed out of him. Exposed to the light and the mountain air. Like with Wook, I know there's nothing left down there but a carcass. But I still have the urge to spit over the edge.

My brother doesn't answer my question right away. The sun is hot on my head and neck, and cold sweat is running down my flanks. The hanging valley that cups the little lake in its palm is only a quarter-mile farther up the ridge. I need to get up there. Fast.

I repeat my question.

My brother turns to me, handing me back my gun. "If I square things with the Feds," he says, "I can spend more time hanging out with you, little bro. In a while, at least. Someone's got to watch your ass, you know, 'cause you don't know what the hell you're doing. Or even who the fuck you are." A slight smile comes and goes as he talks. "And this guy they want, my old *compadre* Jesus? He's gotten crazy. Not in that way"—he jerks a thumb down at Laughlin's corpse—"but even worse. I won't mind fucking with him some. Looking forward to it, actually."

It's my turn to smile. "So you're going to become a lawman. My big brother. Who'd of thunk it?"

He chuckles and holds up his hands. "Whoa! Now don't start talking shit."

"Good luck, 'Berto. Call me. Let me know how it goes."

He steps forward and puts his arms around me. He thumps my back twice with the heels of both fists. I feel all that wild energy throbbing like a nuclear reactor beneath his skin. My gun is in my hand as I grasp his back. I don't know which feels harder or more dangerous—the gun or him.

He pushes away from me. "C'mon, *che*. Let's get out of here."

"You've got to head down on your own. There's something I've got to do up here. The reason I came in the first place."

"You didn't come just to snuff this guy?"

I point up at the hanging valley, unconsciously using my

gun hand. "Nope. I think Rebecca's up there, farther along the ridge at a hot spring. I think she's with a guy who doesn't like me too much."

Stepping back, Roberto looks at the gun and his blue eyes narrow to slits. My blood is starting to rush in my veins again and he senses it.

"Let's go find her, then."

I hold up a hand—the empty one—with the palm out in a restraining gesture. "No, this is just me. Don't follow. Don't interfere again. Go to Salt Lake. This is very, very personal, 'Berto. Something between me, Rebecca, and this guy."

His eyes keep roving up and down from my face to the gun. "That's exactly what I was talking about. I got to keep you from getting down to your baser self, see. There can only be one sociopath in the family, and that's me. It's what big brothers are for. Riding herd. Kicking ass. I'm coming with you."

It takes more time than either of us has to spare for me to convince him that I'm not intending to kill anyone. I'm impatient as I do it—we've already said good-bye and in my mind he's already gone. Roberto doesn't look convinced. But I finally manage to get him to leave, and my brother begins to disappear down the trail. He looks back a couple of times before he fully fades from view. I call Mungo to my side and we head away from the sun toward the hanging valley.

The valley itself descends in a broad scoop from a saddle between two minor peaks. Ash-covered snow still lingers high up in the pass. Farther down is a slope of talus, and below that is a field of grass and alpine flowers. The little pool is at the very bottom of the valley, just before it drops off a cliff. It's surrounded by a thick stand of aspens. Except for the occasional shimmer of water, my view of the pool is blocked by all the new green leaves. Overflow water spills down the cliff beneath the lake and drowns out any other sound.

Mungo slinks along at my side. Her lips are lifted only a little now, exposing her usual shifty grin, but the blood matting her muzzle makes her look very different.

I don't know what I expect to find. But two images play prominently in my thoughts no matter how hard I try to shut them off. One is of Danny Gorgon attacking Rebecca. Forcing her. The other is of him and Rebecca embracing in the warm water of the thermal lake. I refuse to contemplate my response to either scenario, but I know that if it turns out to be the former, then Danny Gorgon will die no matter what I told my brother or whether or not he believes I'm capable. If it turns out to be the latter, I think I might die.

I feel like an angry, vengeful phantom when I enter the trees. Mungo, too, seems to be in a stalking mode. The bone-white trunks rise from dark, rocky earth that slopes down to the pool. The sound of falling water covers whatever noise we make, masking even the rattling of the leaves. But it doesn't cover the roar rising up my spine and buzzing in my skull like a swarm of wasps. Then, before I'm anywhere near ready, the trees fall away behind me. Mungo and I step out onto a rock shelf a few feet above a small beach and the water.

The pool is no more than fifty feet across. It's shaped like a frying pan, the handle being a stream of mingled hot thermal water and snowmelt flowing down into the shallow basin. Visitors have piled rocks against the cliff edge to form a sort of protective wall there, through the cracks of which leak the waterfall. The water is the color of pennies and it smells of sulfur.

Danny Gorgon is alone in the water.

He stands thigh deep with the sun shining in his golden hair and darkening his tan. One hand is rubbing his erect penis while he leers at someone below me and to my left. Somewhere close to where the waterfall spills off the cliff edge. A vibration at my hip tells me that Mungo is growling again.

Rebecca is sitting on a boulder. She is fully clothed, in

hiking boots, baggy shorts, and one of my T-shirts from a guiding service in Alaska. She's not looking at Danny but out over Jackson Hole and beyond it to where the Tetons pierce the sky. The aspens block out all sight of the blackened moonscape in the valley directly below. Her profile is to me. Her thick hair is loose in the breeze and it veils her face.

"C'mon in, girl," Danny calls to her, stroking himself. "I *know* you want some of this."

I watch Rebecca, waiting for her response. But she still doesn't look his way.

"C'mon," Danny says again. "Get your sweet ass in here!"

It looks as if Rebecca is shaking slightly. I stare at her, trying to read what's going on. Is she shaking from excitement, the way she sometimes did with me? Is she crying?

With both hands she pushes her hair behind her ears and holds it there. She looks at Danny before quickly looking away again. For that single second of time, her face is clear to me. She's laughing.

"You're the most pathetic man . . . I've ever seen!" she calls back to him over the falling water's noise. "Do you really think I'm just going to jump in there . . . because you show me your thing. . . . I'd like to write about it . . . but no one would believe me." She's laughing so hard she has to support herself with her elbows on her knees. "God, I wish I'd brought a camera! I can't wait to tell my boyfriend." Her hair comes loose again and falls over her face as she turns back to look toward the Tetons. "And you know my boyfriend, don't you? He's a cop. His name's Antonio Burns."

The wasps fly out my ears and disperse into the air. I feel a huge grin creasing my face at the same time the leer sinks from Gorgon's. His skin darkens but his hand doesn't stop moving. It keeps stroking, but it's now a mechanical motion rather than a passionate one. I have to hold back a snort.

"Bitch," he says. "Your boyfriend's—"

I flip a pebble into the water directly in front of him. It

splashes a small spout of water against his side. His head jerks toward me. I'm pointing the gun at his chest, a bloody-mouthed wolf at my side. With my free hand I touch a finger to my lips.

His square jaw drops and his mouth opens in a wide O. The hand finally stops its back-and-forth motion but remains gripped to the fast-fading erection. Then he begins to involuntarily urinate into the copper-colored water.

Keeping the gun aimed in his general direction, I step down to the beach. By walking carefully on the larger stones so as not to make a sound, I come up behind Rebecca. Mungo isn't so stealthy now—she rushes toward her while making crying sounds. I have to hurry to keep up. Gorgon takes the opportunity to run. He splashes through the water like a startled deer pursued by a bear. I stop paying attention to him altogether when he scrambles up a bank on the opposite side and crouches among some rocks and baby aspens. I put the gun back in the clip holster on my hip.

"Rebecca," I say at the same time Mungo clatters up to her, dancing, and shoves her pointed face under one of her arms.

She stands and whirls around in alarm, mid-laugh. The laugh is frozen in her throat for a moment, uncertainly, until she sees my grin. Then it spills the rest of the way out, harder now but without a sound. She meets me halfway when I put my arms around her. Her eyes look wet before they disappear from view against my shoulder. Her silent laughter caresses my neck and her body quivers in my arms.

It's a good minute before either of us speaks. Then she asks, "What happened to Danny?" as she loosens her grip on me and glances around.

I point to where he's peeking out at us.

"What's he doing over there in the bushes?"

"Search me."

She shakes her head and laughs again. "What are you

doing here, Anton? How did you get so dirty? And what happened with Cali Morrow? I couldn't just sit around waiting, so I thought I'd do some work. Maybe take a look at the fire and get an interview from that creep."

"I'll tell you about it some other time. But I need to know something now. Can we work things out?"

She rises up on her toes and tilts her head forward until her forehead is touching mine. Our eyes are two inches apart and staring. Creating their own little world against everything out there in this one. I study the flecks of gold, green, and black in her brown irises.

"I did a lot of thinking last night," she says slowly, picking her words as carefully as if she were writing. "It was so unexpected. I know it can happen, but still, I didn't expect it. It made me a little crazy. And I didn't know what you'd do, what you'd say. You'd been having such a hard time with that trial in Cheyenne. You seemed to have enough stress in your life." I remember how I'd come home every day with clenched fists and almost dizzy with pure anger and outrage that was undissipated even after the hours on the road. I remember how much I'd needed her—and how I'd used her.

"My first impulse was to schedule an abortion for the day you were leaving town. And that's what I did, too. But then I couldn't go through with it. I ended up out at my dad's, and I told him everything."

"You should have told *me.*"

She nods slightly. "But you weren't acting very approachable. And it was *my* choice. I was afraid you'd try to insist I get an abortion, and that I'd hate you for it. I know you don't like things tying you down, Anton." Her eyes cant up in a smile here. "For the past decade you've been pretty much living out of your ugly truck. . . . And then there's your recklessness. What kind of father will you make?"

I want to close my eyes here, with guilt and shame, but I don't allow myself to.

"And how will I stand it? Well, I've figured out how. I just will. That's all. The problem is with me, not you. I'm just so scared of losing you. You have to convince me that I'm not going to lose you. That's your job."

"It could happen a million ways, 'Becca. A car accident. A plane crash. A brain tumor. I can't convince you—"

"But the soloing. That's pushing it, Ant. Don't try to tell me otherwise."

I close my eyes and open them. The spectacular slivers of color are still there, only two inches away and even brighter now.

"No more soloing. I swear. And I'm reconsidering my retirement. Believe me, I want us to have a lot of years together. Are we cool?"

She kisses my mouth. "Okay. We're cool."

I pull away. Beyond her the Teton spires are huge in the periphery of my vision. The snow and ice on the summits reflect sunlight all the way across the valley to where we stand. With Danny Gorgon cowering across the water as my only witness, I slide down out from her embrace and sink onto a knee in the damp earth.

FORTY-FIVE

REBECCA AGREES TO FOLLOW ME back to the cabin. I watch her in the rearview mirror for the entire drive. Even though it nearly causes me to wreck on several occasions, and to almost run through a surly buffalo roadblock, I never take my eyes off that small rectangle of glass for more than a few seconds. I'm terrified she'll change her mind; that she'll suddenly turn away and burn rubber back to Denver.

She's still behind me, but I curse out loud when I turn into my dirt lane from Cache Creek Road. There's yet another car parked against the porch. It's a cream-colored Cadillac with sparkling chrome. Have the FBI agents learned about Roberto being in town? About him being around the cabin? But as I study the car I realize it's too flamboyant for FBI agents. They tend to drive cars far less conspicuous, like enormous SUVs with black-tinted windows and antennae sprouting from every surface. This car has a Hertz sticker on the bumper and Wyoming plates.

Whoever it is, the timing couldn't be worse. I pull in so close behind the Cadillac that my brush guard looms over the sedan's rear bumper. I'm tempted to put it through the trunk. The last thing I need right now is more interference. More trouble. I check my rearview mirror one last time and, with a rush of relief mingling with trepidation, watch Rebecca park behind me.

Then I notice that the cabin's front door is standing wide open. Someone else has broken in.

I let Mungo out of the truck. Making that crying sound again, she immediately races back to where Rebecca is turning off her engine and unfastening her seat belt. The wolf's nails tap on the Saab's side window and door as her tail sweeps the dirt.

"It's about time you showed up," Ross McGee bellows at me from the porch. He's rolled out the cabin's open door on his walker.

At the sound of his voice, Mungo stops her frantic assault on the side of Rebecca's car and rushes back to stand by my side. A low growl is coming from her chest. I realize I like this new Mungo. I should let her taste blood more often. Exposed by raised black lips, her white teeth look easily two inches long and as sharp as knives. I almost wish I hadn't washed Bill Laughlin's blood off her muzzle.

My boss is dressed in a navy pinstriped suit I've never seen before. It looks crisp and clean and it doesn't have the usual food stains running down the front or the snowy flakes of dandruff on the shoulders. His beard is clean, too, white and freshly shampooed.

Although I'm glad it's not the FBI waiting on my porch, right now McGee isn't much of an improvement. "What are you doing here, Ross? I thought you were in Cheyenne."

"I was. I just flew back. You and me . . . we need to have a talk, lad. Now tell that creature to ease up."

I stroke my wolf's head and tell her, "It's okay, Mungo. He can live . . . for now, anyway. But if he stays more than ten minutes, you have permission to bite his ass."

Mungo lowers her lips and the harsh rumbling noise that's coming from her chest fades away.

"What's wrong with that dog? She got rabies or something?"

"I think she's gotten in touch with her inner wolf."

Rebecca drags her fingertips across my arm as she walks past me. She climbs the steps and bends to kiss one side of McGee's beard. "I'm glad you're here," she tells him. He wraps a thick arm around her waist and pats the rear pocket of her shorts fondly while giving me a wink. Rebecca laughs but I don't.

"What are you still doing with this cad?" he asks her. "I'd like to think a goddaughter of mine would have more sense . . . than to date a fool who spends his free time dangling from cliffs . . . and is mad enough to parachute into a forest fire."

Rebecca looks sharply at me. "What? Parachute . . . never mind—I don't want to know." Then back at McGee, "Love is blind," she says simply.

McGee raises both his thick arms and clutches them to his chest while making a gagging noise.

"Do you mind taking Mungo for a walk?" I ask Rebecca. "I'll try to get this dirty old man out of here before you get back."

McGee leads the way into my cabin while Rebecca coaxes the wolf down the lane. Both Mungo and Rebecca look over their shoulders at me as they walk away. Rebecca smiles again, and even Mungo seems to grin.

I stand impatiently in the spartan main room, watching as my boss takes a long time in getting himself a glass from the cupboard then finding ice to fill it with. I know better than to offer any help. After accomplishing that, he pours in a large amount of dark rum from his flask. Finally he rolls back toward me then sinks down onto the leather couch with a loud groan.

"I don't know how *you* do it . . . a smart, beautiful girl like that, a stone-headed cretin like you—" he starts to say.

"This is a really bad time, Ross. What are you doing here? What happened in Cheyenne?"

His frown at being interrupted is affected—I can see he's eager to talk. To tell me something. But first he says, "What the hell were you thinking . . . jumping out of that plane?"

It's intended to be a rebuke, but I know McGee well enough to discern the hidden approval in his voice. He is a man who knows a lot more than me about taking chances. In a prior life his wartime adventures in Southeast Asia had proven that. As had the slew of medals he was decorated with.

"Hell of a goddamn risk," he continues when I don't say anything. "Fucking miracle you pulled it off." He drinks from his glass and looks away from me. "But at a price—I heard about the sergeant. . . . Now they're sending a crew up to that mountain to look for the other body."

I don't make any comment, although I'm tempted to tell him that they won't find it there. "What happened in Cheyenne?" I ask again.

After another sip from his glass, a longer, deeper one, he begins telling me what had occurred at the governor's office.

McGee's boss, the Assistant Attorney General, and the AG himself—our *über*-boss—were present. The two of them and the governor took turns reaming him for having been so reckless as to have put me in charge of such a sensitive case. And for having utterly screwed it up by allowing Cali Morrow to come to harm. It was a black eye that the state's law enforcement might never recover from. They were giving the Feds total command and latitude. And they were laying total blame where it belonged—squarely on McGee's shoulders. Shaking their heads with mock sorrow, their lips tight with pretended anger, they delightfully told him that it was an inglorious end to his twenty years of service.

"A regular gangbang," McGee calls it.

They didn't care that we believed she was safe once we had Armalli in custody. All the evidence—physical and otherwise—pointed to him. There was no reason to go on protecting her when we had every reason to believe her stalker was locked securely in a cage at the Teton County Jail.

A new criminal investigation into my involvement in the triple homicide two years ago would be commenced immediately. And there would also be a parallel investigation looking into whether McGee had inappropriately used his authority to quash the initial investigation in order to protect one of his agents from multiple charges of murder. McGee's cooperation in both investigations would be required, and his immediate resignation was demanded.

A secretary had then interrupted the meeting, saying the governor had an emergency call. It turned out to be Alana Reese. The governor took it on his speakerphone, expecting it to be yet another nail in McGee's coffin. He even introduced the men present in the room and told her the purpose of their meeting. But the actress, instead of demanding that McGee and Burns be lynched from the nearest lamppost, did an amazing thing. She *ordered* the governor to undo whatever he was doing with regard to McGee and me. The governor—picking up the phone now—refused, telling her it was justified based on a long history of improper and possibly criminal behavior, and that it could not be undone.

McGee starts to chuckle, and for once it doesn't turn into a cough.

"The lady made him put her back on the speaker. . . . Then she told him again that he would undo it . . . threatened to give millions of dollars, if necessary, to whoever opposed him in the next election. . . . To even campaign for him or her. . . . She wouldn't give an explanation—she just demanded it be done. And it was, lad. It was."

No doubt the animosity the administration bears toward McGee and me has now increased tenfold. This victory will cost us in the end, but I can't help feeling a little of my boss's elation. Even though I'm not sure how much longer I'll be doing this job. That depends on Rebecca.

"So you flew up here just to tell me this? All clean and fresh and in that fancy suit? You could have called and left a message, Ross."

He grins even wider, showing all of his crooked yellow teeth. "That's not the end of it, QuickDraw. . . . I'm finally going to meet the little fox. . . . She invited me to dinner tonight . . . out at her ranch."

The thought of McGee dining with the actress is more than unlikely—it's simply impossible to imagine. "You've got to be kidding me." I shake my head at him, wishing I had a drink of my own to salute him with.

"Lady even sent her private jet to pick me up. . . . She invited you, too, by the way . . . but she said her daughter told her that you'd be busy." He leers at me now, cocking an eyebrow, then glances toward the open front door.

I turn to look, too, and see Rebecca throwing a stick down the lane for Mungo to retrieve. Mungo stands beside her, watching the stick turning in the air then skittering in the dust, before turning back to Rebecca and lolling out her tongue.

"Now you tell me—what the hell happened up on that mountain?"

Sitting down myself now, still looking out the open door to where Rebecca and Mungo play in the road, I tell him about jumping from Jim's Cessna with Wokowski. And, in a brief, terse way, about what had happened to Charles Wokowski. I tell him everything, about the engagement ring Wook had showed me and the way he shoved Cali and me into the hole ahead of him. My throat is tight by the time I finish. It takes an effort to keep my voice from breaking.

McGee, despite his well-practiced callousness, appears to feel it, too. He looks older. Sadder, and not nearly so full of wicked energy. The wrinkles around his eyes are as deep as I've ever seen them and he slumps back in the chair.

He shakes his head sadly. "He was a good man . . . a good man. . . . Didn't like you much—he _had_ to be a good man."

We sit in silence for several minutes. Rebecca throws a stick again and this time Mungo brings it back to her. Then Mungo stands in front of her, the stick clenched between her fangs, and snarls at Rebecca. Rebecca puts her hands over her heart and pretends to swoon in terror. The wolf drops the stick, wagging her tail now and appearing—as much as a wolf can—to laugh. I want to be out there with them.

At last McGee growls, "So Laughlin got cooked in his own fire, eh? . . . That's justice, at least. No trial, no muss, no fuss."

I rub my hands over my face and feel the dirt embedded there. I push them through my hair and they come away greasy and smelling of smoke and sweat.

"No, he somehow lived through it. I told you he was what climbers call a hardman. He managed to cross the burnt-out zone and make it to a ridge just a couple of miles from here. But then he fell off a cliff about two hours ago." I don't mention the wolf bite that will be discovered on his ankle. It would be too hard to explain. And it might be interesting to see what the federal investigators make of it.

In giving him a sanitized version of the afternoon's events, I also don't mention anything about Roberto's presence or about me putting my gun to Laughlin's head.

When I finish, McGee is staring at me. He's leaning forward with his hands on the walker. It's as if he's trying once again to judge what's in my heart and in my head. As if all the faith he's built up in me is now in jeopardy. I feel my face get hot.

"Tell me you didn't push him," McGee says quietly, his small eyes as dead serious as his voice.

"I didn't push him, Ross. He jumped at me, tripped on Mungo, and fell."

"Look at me, lad. Look me in the eye."

"I did not push him."

The staring goes on. It takes great effort for me not to look away, knowing that it might be construed as guilt. I meet his gaze evenly and hold it.

After a few long seconds of this he lets out a phlegmy sigh. "Don't get all pissy on me, QuickDraw. But you give me a bad feeling sometimes."

"I did not push him, Ross."

He nods and finally looks down at his drink. "All right."

The big glass of rum, which is still one third full, goes down his throat in one long swallow. The ice knocks against his teeth and he sucks the last drops of rum through them. Slumping back on the couch, he wipes his mouth with his sleeve and closes his eyes.

Outside Rebecca is calling to Mungo now. For a minute I think the wolf has run off somewhere, maybe chasing the stick or distracted by a squirrel, but then I catch the shape of her head poking out of the branches on the other side of the road. She's doing her you-can't-see-me-because-I'm-a-wolf thing. And Rebecca's playing her part, looking off in another direction with her hands on her hips. I hear her calling, "Where's Mungo? Where could she have gone?"

I walk into the bathroom and turn on the cold tap. Cupping the water, I splash it on my face and try to rub away the streaks of soot and dirt. They don't come away easily. I scrub at my skin with a rough towel until the only marks left on my face are the thin white scar running from left eye to lip and the creases of exhaustion and grief. More cold Teton water seems to help the latter, but has no effect on the scar. I scrub some more and look at myself for a long, long time. Longer than I have in many years. Then I walk back out into the main room.

"Hey, McGee. Do you want to know something about me? Something that will really piss you off?"

He appears to have been close to nodding off, or sinking

into some personal reverie. But now his eyes snap open as he raises his head. The blue irises seem to be almost blazing with curiosity from beneath the bristling white brows. And, I imagine, a little bit of dread.

"What is it, Burns?"

"I'm going to marry your goddaughter."

ABOUT THE AUTHOR

CLINTON MCKINZIE is the acclaimed author of *The Edge of Justice* and *Point of Law*. He was raised in Santa Monica, California, and he now lives in Colorado with his wife and son. Prior to becoming a writer, he worked as a peace officer and deputy district attorney in Denver. His passion is climbing alpine walls.

Don't miss the next thrilling
Antonio Burns novel

CROSSING
THE
LINE

by

Clinton McKinzie

Available May 2004
from Delacorte Press

Please read on for a preview.

CROSSING THE LINE

on Sale May 2004

My rust-shot Land Cruiser, the Iron Pig, swayed within its lane on Highway 191. It was rocked side to side by gusts of wind barreling down off the high plateau of the Red Desert. Out of respect for the wind and the tumbleweeds and the writhing grit, I held the needle at just below the seventy-five-miles-per-hour speed limit. But even though the highway was clear of all other traffic, the massive grille of a Chevy Suburban rode hard on my old truck's bumper. Its windows were darkly tinted and antennae bristled from its roof.

I glanced in the rearview mirror and my knuckles whitened where they gripped the wheel. Another gust hit and for the hundredth time I considered stomping on the brake.

No, Ant. You've got to play nice. For Roberto's sake. But I needed to vent.

"You guys are real sly, real inconspicuous, using a truck like that. Nobody would ever suspect it belongs to the FBI."

I said it loud enough to be heard over the howl blasting through the wide-open windows.

"You sound jealous, Burns. You need to understand that the taxpayers wouldn't approve of us spending too much time waiting for tow trucks, which is something I expect you do quite often in this piece of shit."

Her voice was clipped and sharp, and the curse word she uttered had come out strange. I'd only met her five hours earlier, in a hotel suite in Salt Lake City, but I suspected that Mary Chang didn't use even the mildest profanity lightly. She'd seemed nice enough then, but a little rigid. The long, mostly mute drive hadn't loosened her up much. It hadn't exactly relaxed me either.

I looked at her in the rearview mirror. She was huddled against the side door directly behind me. Her small hands clasped her ears, trying to either cut the noise of the wind and the tires or hold back her jet-black hair.

Hearing our voices, my wolf-dog jerked her head back into the truck. She twisted around to stare curiously at the woman seated beside her. One of Mungo's lips had been curled inward by the wind, exposing a row of long teeth. The effect was goofy rather than menacing. She canted her head as if trying to understand our exchange. A ribbon of drool fluttered out of her mouth and pasted itself across the FBI agent's white silk blouse. In the mirror I watched Mary grimace, wrinkling her nose as she looked down at her shirt. I had to hold back a smile. Good dog.

After a moment the beast turned again, dusted the agent with her tail, and swung her head back out the window.

I didn't like federal agents. Not even young, pretty ones. They tended to treat local cops with either condescension or disdain. Mary's silence and aloof, serious expression for most of the ride reinforced this belief. They also stole our best cases and never shared the credit. Bigfooting, it was called. I knew generalizations were smallminded, but it was a prejudice that right then—after five hours of being tailgated by her jerk of a partner in that black behemoth—I was having trouble conquering.

I couldn't see him through the tinted windshield just yards off my bumper, but I carried a vivid image of him from that morning. Tom Cochran was a red-faced man with red hair that was carefully styled into a sort of pompadour. When we'd been introduced in Salt Lake, he'd let my hand hang empty in the air between us for a threecount before shaking it.

"You're the guy they call QuickDraw, right?" he'd asked, using the nickname the way it was intended—as an insult. The scowl he gave me was one I suspected he practiced each morning in the mirror while he moussed his hair. But I knew he'd come around once I got myself into a better mood. Being likable is a part of my job, even though it takes more and more effort as the years go by.

"Can we turn on the A.C.?"

"Nope. Roberto hates air-conditioning." I nodded my head at the man riding shotgun next to me as I said this. Roberto was slumped in the reclined passenger seat, apparently asleep. Flaps of dark hair whipped across his face and obscured his features. His arms were folded loosely on his chest.

"He *is* in custody," Mary pointed out.

Which was technically true, even though she'd taken off his handcuffs in Salt Lake as a kind of good-faith gesture. But I didn't care.

"He's also my brother. And he's doing you guys one hell of a favor."

A movement at the periphery of my vision caused me to look his way again. Roberto wasn't asleep after all; his thumb twitched erect for a second before lying back onto his fist.

"Don't forget we're doing him one, too," the FBI agent said.

Outside was a desert landscape of red earth and sagebrush, corduroyed with dry gullies. The sun was baking the ground. I reached for the CD player—the only obvious modification to the old truck other than the oversized tires and the front-mounted electric winch—and cranked up the disk Roberto had given me.

It wasn't at all what I'd expected. The music was weird and disturbing. As a kid he'd liked hard rock and punk. The Dead Kennedys. Suicidal Tendencies. Even, in milder moods, the Clash, and, later, the Red Hot Chili Peppers. But this was some sort of opera. The plastic case said, *José Cura. The Puccini Arias.* A man sang in a tenor that sounded dark and thick, his voice carrying what seemed to me like an undercurrent of suppressed rage. It made me wonder what my brother was on these days.

The music began to match the landscape as the miles passed. It concentrated the intensity of the heat and the sun and the wind, and gave it an almost liquid sensation.

What *is* he on these days?

At first it was only adrenaline, an addiction we both inherited from a father who spent every moment of his generous military leave dragging his sons up mountains. Then, as a young teenager, Roberto began to experiment with pot and hash and soloing—rock climbing without a rope. Psychedelics and ever higher ropeless ascents followed. And then it was cocaine, at about the time the climbing magazines made his big-wall solos famous. He dabbled with everything, and perfected what he claimed was the ultimate way to take the amp of adrenaline and push it through the roof: speedballs, an injected combination of cocaine and heroin. Judging from the music, I guessed that these days he'd backed down to just the horse.

Roberto suddenly lunged forward in his seat.

"Ant! Check it out! That Sentinel Rocks over there?" He pointed out the window to where some jumbled granite boulders wavered on a distant ridge.

"Yeah, 'Berto. I'm pretty sure. Dad took us there a couple of times when we were kids."

"Pull over, *che*. I need to get some air under my feet."

Roberto twisted around to look at the federal agent. "You mind?"

In the mirror I saw her jump, alarmed at the speed with which he moved. Maybe that was why she seemed so nervous. She was scared of him. I was a little bit, too.

"Sorry. No stopping. We're on a tight schedule."

Roberto pushed his sunglasses up onto his forehead and showed her his strange blue eyes. They were totally out of place against his brown skin and black hair.

"C'mon, now. I'd be a much happier rat if you'd cut me a little slack." He smiled at her.

She wasn't able to hold his gaze. Looking away, out the window, she said, "Mr. Burns, we have a job to do. This isn't a rock-climbing vacation."

"Listen. Your job's to nail Jesús Hidalgo, and it requires me risking my neck, not you guys. I'm the one he's going to come after when he finds out someone's been talking about him. And you people have kept me in a box for like two weeks. So c'mon, I need a break. Just one hour. A little climb. Please? Pretty, pretty please?"

Mary Chang shook her head again with her hands still clasped around it. Not in negation this time, but slower, as if in pain. Then she dropped one hand to look at her watch. Letting out a sigh, and maybe another curse, she dropped the other hand and reached for the purse at her feet. She came up with a cell phone.

"We're going to turn off and stop for a bit," she shouted into the phone. She listened for a minute, then said, "No. We're stopping for one hour. No, Tom, you listen. I'm in charge here. We're stopping."

She didn't look at Roberto when he grinned even broader and said, *"Gracias, guapa."*

"Thanks," I added, feeling guilty for having vented on her earlier.

The Suburban flashed its lights and honked its horn when I wheeled the Pig off the highway even though it was obvious I wasn't going to stop. The Suburban fell back. We bounced and switchbacked for a mile and a half up a dirt double-track toward the base of a leaning sandstone tower, which stood on the ridge like a drunken sentry guarding a mighty herd of chaparral.

Cheyenne had probably once huddled here in the fall, waiting for the buffalo to come south. Basque sheepherders would have taken advantage of this sheltered spot once the buffalo and Indians had all been conveniently slaughtered. Now, judging from the litter of green glass, beer cans modified into crank pipes, condom wrappers, and cigarette butts, it was only used by teenagers from the ranches north of Rock Springs who came here to party. I knew a lot about such parties—I'd often joined them, undercover, as a special agent with Wyoming's Division of Criminal Investigation.

Roberto hopped out of the truck and began rooting through the crates of climbing gear I kept in the back. He dragged out harnesses, carabiners, and a rope while I let the wolf-dog out of the backseat. Mungo gratefully crouched and watered the dry earth, then danced over to my brother's side. She was fascinated by him. She pranced around him like he was a strange, handsome dog or a wolf himself.

"That's the ugliest dog I've ever seen," Roberto said, not unkindly, as the now very dusty Suburban skidded to a halt behind us. When Mungo leapt away from it, he added, "Skittish too, not like that monster Oso. *That* fucker would have charged then torn off the bumper."

Mungo wasn't pretty. She was bony-spined and her heavy gray coat hung from her frame like secondhand clothes. Her usual attitude was cringing; tail tucked between her legs and head held low whenever anyone paid any attention to her. Lately, though, she'd been showing a little more backbone. It was something that had started after she nipped a man she thought was threatening me, and tasted blood for the first time. But she still wasn't anything like Oso. He'd been a hulking brute with a surprisingly soft, squishy heart until a suspect in a murder investigation blew apart his muzzle with a hollow-point bullet. My fiancée rescued Mungo from a wildlife refuge that was about to be shut down and have its animals destroyed. Rebecca had thought this craven creature could replace the beast I'd lost last fall.

"What do you think you're doing?" Tom Cochran yelled at us through a rapidly descending window.

I decided that I definitely wasn't in the mood to start being nice. But I was pleased to see that, even backing away, Mungo had squinted her yellow eyes and raised her lips. It wasn't much of a snarl, though—it was more like a nervous grin.

"Taking a break, asshole," Roberto answered us all. Then to Mungo, in a lower voice and while bending to stroke her bristling fur, "Hey, it's okay, girl. Ignore him. Dry air up here's messing with his hairdo."

"What did you call me?"

Tom threw the door open and leapt out of the Suburban. He was wearing new jeans and pointy boots with riding heels. Going cowboy, like so many did when they visited my state. He'd taken off the dress shirt and sport coat he had been wearing in Salt Lake and was now clad in a white

T-shirt that was a couple of sizes too small. He held his arms out from his sides a little farther than he needed to, even though he was wearing one of the Bureau's new 10 mms and a pair of handcuffs on his hip.

Mungo's eyes twitched toward me. Her clenched teeth were exposed now. I was tempted to nod, just to see what she'd do, but shook my head and showed her my palm. Then I flicked my fingers at her. Quick as a rabbit, she spun and leapt into the brush.

Roberto straightened up and looked right at Tom.

"A-S-S-H-O-L-E, if you can spell better than you listen. I called you an asshole, asshole."

Tom stared back, his face growing redder beneath his mirrored aviator's shades. The color of blood in his face merged with all the freckles. Mary got out of the Pig and came between them. She held up a hand in each direction.

"Cut it out, both of you."

"I've had enough of this," Tom said, looking at my brother but talking to her. "Two weeks of this guy bullshitting and giving us nothing but lip. Let's haul his junkie ass over to Colorado and see how he likes those escape charges they have waiting for him."

I wondered if they were playing good cop/bad cop. With me, a cop, and Roberto, who had been dealing with cops all his life, it would be a silly game. Roberto apparently decided to bring this fact to their attention.

"Guess that means you don't want to catch the guy who sliced and diced your buddy down in Mexicali."

And that jacked up the tension, as my brother knew it would. He'd told me earlier that both the Feds in our little caravan had worked with the narcotics agent whose death in Baja California two months ago had been in all the papers.

The blood drained out of Tom's face as fast as it rose in Mary's. "You scumbag," Tom said in lower, harsher voice. His fists were balled and beginning to rise. "Don't you ever mention that again."

Roberto was smiling. Mocking. "What, Mexicali? Or your dumb buddy who got himself cut up?"

"Stop it, 'Berto. Shut up," I said.

I'd been taking a perverse delight in the confrontation, but I didn't want to hear a dead narcotics agent derided. Not even a federal agent. Nor did I want my brother to blow his one chance at amnesty.

Mary seemed to be thinking, as if considering just how much they really needed Roberto and his information to do whatever they were intending to do. I took one of my brother's arms and pulled him back before he could do anything to hurt Mary's decision or further squeeze Tom's trigger.

Belatedly, Mary made her decision. She faced my brother and pointed a finger at him.

"That's enough, Mr. Burns. We need you, but not enough to put up with any abuse or provocation. If you don't want to cooperate, then you'll be turned over to authorities in Colorado tonight."

She waited for my brother to say something. He didn't. She glanced at her watch.

"All right, then. You have one hour."

They must need him very badly, I thought.

Roberto maybe sensed it too, because he jerked his arm out of my hand. Oh shit. He stepped forward, back up into Tom's face. My brother wasn't as big as the FBI agent—the top of his head came even with Tom's freckled nose—but there was an obvious menace in Roberto that dwarfed the other man.

Things were on the verge of really getting out of control. Roberto, when he fought, fought like one of our father's Celtic ancestors, whom the Romans had justifiably called berserkers.

"You're right," my brother said quietly. "I shouldn't have mentioned that. Sorry, man." Then he turned away and went back to sorting through the crates of gear.

I stared at my brother's back. *What's going on with him?* I'd never seen him back down. Not from anything. He'd never cared about the consequences. *Destraillado,* Mom called it. Unleashed. Tom's fists were still clenched.

"He should be in handcuffs," he told his partner. "Hell, they both should be in handcuffs. A lunatic and a renegade cop. I can't fucking believe we have to deal with these people."

Noticing me watching him, he spat in the dirt.

"Bite me, Tom," I said.

"Cool it, all of you. That's enough."

Mary swatted at herself, attempting to dust Mungo's hair from her skirt and blouse, and plucked at where the clothes were pasted by sweat to her skin. Tom couldn't help but watch her, and I saw that my brother, smiling again with his eyebrows raised slightly behind his sunglasses, was doing the same. The disheveled hair and clothes were undeniably sexy on her. They were such a contrast to her rigid personality. Especially in this testosterone-charged environment.

She must have felt the eyes, because she stopped touching herself and walked stiffly in her heels to the rear of the Suburban. From a cooler there she took out three bottles of water and passed them around. It was a peacemaking gesture.

I joined my brother in examining the rock that was leaning over us. There was a single crack splitting the overhanging wall of the eighty-foot tower. It started out three inches wide at the bottom then contracted to just an inch or so before it reached a cavelike alcove near the top. Above that, the final few moves to the summit were invisible as the sun was right behind it and the indirect radiance made close scrutiny impossible.

"Which end you want?" Roberto asked, swinging the coiled rope in one hand.

"The sharp end."

"Okay, little bro. You lead."

The rope hit my chest. I unwrapped it from where it was tied around itself and began carefully flaking it out on the ground, working out the kinks. Roberto shimmied a harness over his brown canvas pants and dragged off his shirt. The two federal agents watched us as if we were performing some voodoo ritual.

I was pleased to notice that there weren't any scabby pinprick tracks on the insides of Roberto's arms. It didn't mean much—I had known junkies who injected their thighs, scrotums, and even between their toes to escape being marked—but it was a positive sign because my brother had never cared about detection.

He looked good, too. Fit and almost ridiculously strong, although his normally dark skin seemed a little translucent from two weeks confined indoors. He'd even cut his hair, which used to reach halfway down his back.

After shimmying into my own harness then tying into one end of the rope, I clipped a handful of cams and hexes onto a sling and put it over my head and one shoulder. My climbing slippers were tight enough to curl my toes but familiar as I squeezed my feet into them and laced up.

Reaching up, I placed my right hand high into the cool crack and made a fist. I placed my left hand just below it in the same way. By clenching my fists and flexing the muscles in my hands, I was able to lock them in. A jam, it's called. Weird, but it works. I pulled up on the clenched fists and got a foot wedged in a couple of feet farther down by turning it sideways then twisting it in with my knee raised high.

I wriggled up this way, replacing fists and feet always higher, as sweat ran over my skin and my breath grew ragged. The crack narrowed until I was able to hang securely off a single jammed fist. Then a cupped hand, and finally just my torqued fingertips and toes.

"Wow," I heard Mary say from below me. "Look at that."

It was the first real sign of life I'd heard from her. And I took an embarrassed pleasure in bringing it out.

"It's not that hard," Tom said dismissively. "Takes practice, is all. There's a trick to it."

"Then maybe you ought to go next, Tom."

Blood began to stain the yellowish stone because I hadn't bothered to tape up. I was setting my jams far too quickly, showing off a little for my brother and the Feds. Every ten feet or so I slotted a mechanical camming device into the crack and clipped to it the rope trailing from my harness. I could feel the slight weight on the rope from Roberto's belay.

After ten minutes of grunting and panting I hauled myself over a small ledge and into the hole eighty feet off the ground. In this small alcove were two old bolts someone had long ago drilled into the rock. They felt secure when I tried to shake them, so I clipped a bight from my end of the rope into them.

"I'm off," I yelled down.

Roberto started climbing before I even had him on belay. I reeled in the rope as fast as I could, my bloodied hands shoving the rope through the belay tube and getting warm from the friction. I couldn't see him when I craned my neck out over the edge, but I could see the two federal agents in the shade below. They were gaping upward with open mouths. Even Tom wasn't able to look away.

I couldn't see Roberto, but I was long familiar with the way he climbed. Fast and smooth. He sort of graced his way up the rock without any of my less elegant grunting and gasping and bleeding.

When he planted a palm on the ledge and mantled up on it, I saw that he hadn't bothered to lace up his rock shoes. I clipped a bight from his end of the rope into the bolts and said, "You're off."

"You're looking strong," he told me, punching my chest. "Still a wiry little guy, but strong."

I felt the flush of a little brother's pride at the words.

"You're getting slow, 'Berto. Thought you would have been up here a long time ago."

I don't think he heard me. He stood on the edge—toes in space—and stared out at the desert landscape without expression. You can see a long way in this state. A lot farther than you can from a prison cell. I hoped he was realizing that.

We don't look that much alike. His face shows more of our mother's mestizo heritage than mine. His cheekbones are higher, his nose slightly hooked. But like me, he has our father's square Scots jaw. Our eyes are the greatest difference between us. Mine are coffee brown; his are a brilliant blue. I also carry a long white scar on my left cheek from rockfall—a reminder of my own mortality. Roberto has no such scar.

His chest, shoulders, and back still held the taut slabs of prison muscle from the time before his escape ten months earlier. Since then he'd been on high peaks in South America, and the exertion and deprivation had carved distinct lines through the bulk. Honed was the word that best described him. He looked like he'd been carved out of stone.

"How is it that you know this narco Hidalgo?" I asked him when he slumped down beside me. It was the first time all day that we'd been alone.

"Dude used to think he was a mountaineer. I saved his shit on Aconcagua 'bout ten years back." Then he shrugs. "After that, I did some muling for him and his buddies. They call themselves the Mexicali Mafia."

I remembered the story, but I hadn't realized that the man Roberto rescued was the notorious drug lord. Roberto had come across three men dressed in designer mountain wear—the kind of clothes made for anything but mountain climbing. Puffy jackets by Ralph Lauren and leather boots that had never been treated to repel snow and water because it might ruin the finish. The three were in bad shape, weak and suffering from cold, altitude, and hunger, near the summit of the twenty-three-thousand-foot peak. Roberto tied them all into a rope and more or less dragged them down. When I'd first heard about it, he only described them as a trio of rich guys from Mexico City.

"You've met him too," he added now, turning and grinning at me. "Well, almost. Remember that time we were down in Baja. . ."

He reminded me of a trip we'd taken eight years ago, when I was in grad school at Boulder. Dad and Mom were in Saudi Arabia, leaving the two of us on our own for Christmas break. It had been a cold early winter, so we headed south when I picked him up from where he was living in Durango. We drove the Pig all the way down to the Sea of

Cortez. For one week we kayaked and dove, sleeping on deserted beaches, spearing fish to cook on yucca fires, mellowing at night on Tecate and lime (me) and tequila and hashish (him). The next week we climbed pristine desert walls in the Sierra Juárez.

Roberto had heard about a particular one—supposedly virgin, unclimbed—but never seen it. He knew how to get there, though, and we cut through then retied a barbed-wire fence on the way. On this particular wall—a twelve-hundred footer—we'd been caught by a freak rainstorm then darkness when we were high up on it. The water sluicing down the wall made it impossible to finish the climb and hike off, and we hadn't brought enough gear to rig all the rappels necessary to bail. So we spent a long, wet night on an edge not much wider than a bookshelf.

Waking up hadn't been pleasant—it was a bullet striking the rock near my head that brought me out of my shivering stupor. Splinters of quartz had cut into one of my ears.

Two men and a battered Jeep were parked near my truck at the base of the wall. One of the men was aiming up through a rifle's sight for a second shot while the other was bent over like he might be laughing.

Roberto shouted down at them in Spanish—words I didn't think at the time would help our situation: "Motherfuckers! You shoot again and I'll cut your throats!"

The one with the gun yelled, "You're trespassing. Our boss doesn't like trespassers. 'Put them back on the ground,' he told us."

"I'm invited, you dumb animals. Go tell him it's Roberto Burns. Before I come down there and stick that rifle up your ass."

The men laughed some more and the one with the gun pointed it. But there was an uncertainty in both their gestures. The rifle didn't fire a second time.

"You really know the guy who owns this place?" I'd asked him as I frantically readied the soggy ropes for a fast sprint to the summit.

The men got into the Jeep and drove away to check with their boss.

"Sort of. You wouldn't like him." He laughed. "Trust me. We need to get out of here, *che*. Fast."

And we did. Driving out a different way and over another barbed-wire fence before the men returned.

"That was Hidalgo's land," Roberto now says. "His inland *estancia*. He told me about that wall after I pulled him off Aconcagua. Said I ought to come down sometime and give it a shot."

"If you really knew him, then why were we in such a hurry to get out of there? Why'd we drive over all those fences instead of just going by the house?"

"I didn't want you to meet him, bro." He wouldn't explain why.

Now it gave me a small thrill, learning that eight years earlier I'd come close to meeting one of the continent's most brutal drug lords. A man believed responsible for hundreds of torture killings—his way of silencing those whom he suspected of disloyalty. His method was not only to kill the suspected individual, but to also kill every member of his family. Even close friends sometimes. It was a method that assured no one would ever testify against him. Simple and very effective. No one would sentence their entire family to death no matter what kind of protection or reward they were offered. And I felt a different sort of thrill, too, because my brother had been protecting me from him even way back then.

"I'm surprised they let us do this," I told him.

"Didn't have no choice, *che*. Those two want Hidalgo bad. They'll do whatever I want."

If they were dealing with my brother in the first place, it had to be true. What I didn't understand was why he was dealing with them. Putting himself in danger of more time in prison if things didn't work out, and risking a bad, bad death if they did. And maybe for not just him, although I didn't want to think about that. Not yet.

"I still don't get why you're doing this, 'Berto."

He shrugged. "Things are changing. I can't explain it right now." He glanced over his shoulder at me and then down again. "Now watch this. I'm gonna freak 'em out."

He stood and reeled about thirty feet of slack from his harness. Next he made an overhand knot. I didn't realize right away what he was doing because I was thinking about what he'd said, and trying to guess the reason or reasons he was here.

What was going on with him? Why didn't he just stay in South America where Grandpa's compadres from the bad old days during Argentina's Dirty War could protect him from extradition? Why hadn't he knocked Tom Cochran's teeth down his throat? And why had he apologized? I didn't think I'd ever heard him apologize before. Not in thirty-two years of knowing him.

The click of a carabiner's gate snapping shut startled me out of my thoughts. He had clipped the knot to the bolts. He'd also unclipped his own anchoring knot. He dropped the coil of slack rope next to me on the ledge.

Finally I realized what he was about to do.

"Don't do it, 'Berto. You'll ruin my rope."

"You don't need a rope, Ant. You've got to learn to let go."

Then, with a scream of utter terror, he spread his bare arms and jumped off the ledge.

Long seconds later the carabiners and knots slammed together with a sound like a whipcrack as his weight hit the end of the rope. I rechecked the bolts then leaned over to see the mouths below gaping even wider. It was as if a flash-bang grenade had exploded over their heads. Mary Chang was frozen in place and seemed to be gasping for air. Tom was swearing loudly.

Swinging free above them, laughing silently, was my brother.

And he was just getting warmed up for really scaring the hell out of all of us.